"I don't think you understand, Navy," the punk said. "You don't have a choice. I brought a lot of firepower with me and I'm willing to use it."

"Oh, I understand," Jessica said conversationally. "I'm just playing for higher stakes than you are. *Cayenne*, you're on."

She watched the boy's confusion grow. He shook his head and cocked it to the side like a dog might.

Jessica grinned politely at him.

Off her starboard beam, the night abruptly lit up with a howl as the big, red DropShip surged above the ridge and slid forward, belly turret tracking and a pair of searchlights blinding everyone.

Jessica watched the goons point their weapons up for a second before they realized that they had nothing that could even scratch the DropShip's armor.

"I would suggest," she called above the roar of engines, "that you all put your weapons down nicely. I will not give you a second warning."

Queen of the Pirates
The Jessica Keller Chronicles: Volume Two
Blaze Ward

Published by Knotted Road Press
www.KnottedRoadPress.com

ISBN: 978-1-943663-02-6

Cover art:
© Innovari | Dreamstime.com - Spaceship Fighters At Sea Photo

Never miss a release!
If you'd like to be notified of new releases, sign up for my newsletter.

I only send out newsletters once a quarter, will never spam you, or use your email for nefarious purposes. You can also unsubscribe at any time.

http://www.blazeward.com/newsletter/

QUEEN OF THE PIRATES

THE JESSICA KELLER CHRONICLES: VOLUME TWO

BLAZE WARD

Knotted Road Press
www.KnottedRoadPress.com

ALSO BY BLAZE WARD

The Jessica Keller Chronicles

Auberon

Queen of the Pirates

Javier Aritza Stories

The Science Officer

The Mind Field

Science Fiction Stories

The Earthquake Gun

Greater Than The Gods Intended

The Librarian

Moonshot

Moscow Gold

Myrmidons

Zolnerovy Stories

Valeryia

Tatiyana

***The Collective* Universe**

Imposters

The Shipwrecked Mermaid

Collections

Beyond the Mirror: Volume 1 Fantastic Worlds

Beyond the Mirror: Volume 2 Fantastic Worlds

Beyond the Mirror: Volume 3 Alternate Worlds

QUEEN OF THE PIRATES

THE JESSICA KELLER CHRONICLES:

VOLUME TWO

BLAZE WARD

AUTHOR'S NOTE

(OR: A BRIEF THOUGHT ON THE HISTORY OF THE FUTURE.)

Other Science Fiction writers have done a much better job that I ever could explaining why science fiction writers use "modern" standards for things like weights and measures, even eleven thousand years in the future. I don't think kilometers and kilograms will still be in use then, but my current audience needs to have a frame of reference they understand. In some interesting future, perhaps someone will translate my work into the-then-current units, with a note like this talking about what interesting barbarians we used to be. Best of luck.

Similarly, languages in the future will be interesting. We are fast approaching an era where there are only a few dozen major languages left. Personally, I think we'll lose something culturally, but gain something by being able to talk to anyone and hear their story. In this universe (*Alexandria Station*), the seven major trade languages of the Concord (pre-Collapse) were English, Chinese, Arabic, Spanish, Hindi, Kiswahili, and Bulgarian. (Don't ask. Explanations are available elsewhere, and have to do with Bulgarian Fan Clubs.)

Most of those languages represent major international languages at a time when electronic communications capabilities mean that languages will start to ossify somewhat. They will still evolve, but they will do so more in pronunciation than in written. Think of all of the dialects of spoken Chinese that use the same written form. There will still be smaller languages. Henri Baudin, mentioned in the Promenade section of this book, spoke French as his first language.

Finally, a round of thank you's. Leah and Dayle caught many mistakes that eluded me, and pointed out sections where I forgot to write things down (they were in my head, but never made it to paper.) I am absolutely indebted to Michael Kingswood for taking the time to read the draft and write things like "that's not how it works today, so probably not how it would work in the distant future."

This story would simply not be nearly as good without their help. Simple as that. All mistakes you find are still mine. And I wouldn't mind hearing about them (politely, mind you) so I can fix future versions of the document. We all make mistakes. Character, so I have been led to believe, involves owning them and fixing them.

As I write this, I am deep into the third novel in the first Jessica Keller trilogy, *Last Of The Immortals*. (Yes, *first* trilogy. More to come.) It will wrap up this phase of the story, and set the stage for future adventures. I hope you will come along for the ride. *Alexandria Station* is a universe I enjoy wandering around in, as well as having conversations with the characters: Javier Aritza, Doyle Iwakuma, Henri Baudin, and Jessica Keller.

Most importantly, in my mind, is Suvi. She was not my original muse, starting out, but grew into the role over time. She is the witness to history, and serves thus as our narrator, in her own way.

At this end of human history, she is also the Last Of The Immortals, living forever, but never losing her joy in the world.

It is a lesson I hope to emulate.

shade and sweet water,
blaze
West Of The Mountains, Washington
July 2015

Queen of the Pirates Cast List

Auberon

Name	Rank	Position
Jessica Marie Keller	Command Centurion	Commander
Marcelle Augustine Travere	Yeoman	Jessica's Personal Aide
Denis August Jež	Senior Centurion	First Officer
Enej Zivkovic	Centurion	Flag Centurion
Tamara Strnad	Senior Centurion	Tactical Officer
Tobias Brewster	Centurion	Gunner/Emergency Tactical
Aleksander Afolayan	Centurion	Gunner
Nina Vanek	Centurion	Defenses
Nada Zupan	Centurion	Pilot
Vilis Ozolinsh	Senior Centurion	Chief Engineer
(Phillip) Navin Crncevic	Senior Centurion	Dragoon
Dr. Zephan Samara	Senior Centurion	Surgeon
Daniel Giroux	Centurion	Science Officer
Moirrey Kermode	Yeoman	Evil Engineering Gnome
Nicolai Aoiki	Senior Chef	Chief Chef of the Wardroom
Naoki Ungaretti	Yeoman	Diplomatic Courier
Jackson Tawfeek	First Rate Spacer	Marine
Vo Arlo	Yeoman	Marine
Nadine Orly	First Rate Spacer	Signals Marine
Augustine Kwok	Command Centurion	Former commander, *Auberon*

Others

Name	Rank	Position
Alber' d'Maine	Command Centurion	Commander, *Rajput*

Tomas Kigali	Command Centurion	Commander, *CR-264*
Robertson Aeliaes	Command Centurion	Commander, *Brightoak*

Pilots

Name	Rank	Position
Iskra Vlahovic	Senior Centurion	Flight Deck Commander
Jouster / Milos Pavlovich	Senior Flight Centurion	Flight Commander
Uller / Friedhelm Hannes Förstner	Flight Centurion	*Jouster's* Wingmate
Vienna / Avril Bouchard	Flight Centurion	*Jouster's* Wingmate
Southbound / Marta Eka	Senior Flight Centurion	Wing Commander
Bitter Kitten / Darya Lagunov	Flight Centurion	*Southbound's* Wingmate
Hànchén / Murali Ma	Flight Cornet	*Southbound's* Wingmate
da Vinci / Ainsley Barret	Senior Flight Centurion	Scout Pilot
Gaucho / Hollis Dyson	Flight Centurion	Commander, *Cayenne*
Anastazja Slusarczyk	Senior Flight Centurion	Commander, *Necromancer*
Leila Ketevan	Flight Centurion	Commander, *Damocles*
Edgar Khachaturian	Flight Centurion	Commander, *Starfall*
Ebbe Lanik	First Rate Spacer	Tower Gunner, *Starfall*

The Republic

Name	Position
Indira (Chastain) Keller	Jessica's mother
Miguel Keller	Jessica's father
Vyacheslav Keller	Jessica's younger brother

Sasha Keller	Jessica's sister in law
Rahul Keller	Jessica's nephew
Margaret Keller	Jessica's niece
Juan-Pablo Keller	Jessica's nephew
Nils Kasum	First Lord of the Fleet
Kamil Miloslav	Personal Aide to First Lord Kasum
Bogdan Loncar	First Fleet Lord
Tadej Marko Horvat	Premier, Republic Senate
Andjela Tomčič	Senator, Republic Senate
Brant	Aide to the Chairman
Joshua	Steward, The Marquette Room
Anna	Bartender, The Marquette Room

The Frieborg Empire

Name	Position
His Sovereign Imperial Majesty Karl VII of the House of Wiegand	Emperor, *Fribourg Empire*
Emmerich Wachturm	Admiral of the Red. Hereditary Duke of Eklionstic. Commander, *Amsel*
Hendrik Baumgärtner	Flag Captain, Aide to Admiral Wachturm
Henrietta (Heike) Wachturm	Daughter of Emmerich Wachturm

Lincolnshire

Name	Position
Joshua Wapasha	Governor, *Ramsey*
Radoš Fiala	Mayor, Landing, *Ramsey*
Marcus Auric	Merchant, Principal of Auric and Sons
Dr. Dina (Curzich) Zhao	Research Biologist, Ramsey Agricultural Institute

Dale Kermode	Moirrey's cousin
Detrin Kermode	Moirrey's uncle
Tanis Bedrosian	Minor crime lord
Fergus	Bedrosian's Sergeant

Corynthe

Name	Position
Arnulf Rodriguez	King Of The Pirates, Admiral of the *Corynthe* Fleet
Jing Du	Chancellor To The Court of *Corynthe*
Desianna Indah-Rodriguez	First Wife of *Corynthe*
Intan	Desianna's Maid
Charlotte Rodriguez	Second Wife of *Corynthe*, deceased
Mei Fan Rodriguez	Third Wife of *Corynthe*
Daneel Ishikura	*Warlock*. Governor of *Sarmarsh IV*
Ekaterina "Teri" Estes	Ex-wife of *Warlock*
Jean-Michel	Current husband to Ekaterina Estes
Rory Agano	*Hellhound*
Willem Agano	Brother of Rory Agano, deceased
David Rodriguez	Son of Arnulf. Captain, *Sky Dancer*
Ian Zhao	Captain, *Kali-ma,* King Of The Pirates
Cho Ayaka Nakamura	*Furious*. Pilot, *Sky Dancer*
Jaan Koit	*Sõdalane*, Corynthe pilot
Wolfhound	*Corynthe* pilot
Eel	*Corynthe* pilot
Uly Larionov	Captain, *Baba Yaga*
Yan Bedrov	Second in Command, *Kali-ma*
Garth Agano	Father of Rory Agano. Admiral during battle: *First Petron*
Freida Rodriguez	Daughter of Arnulf and Desianna
Arianne Rodriguez	Daughter of Arnulf and Charlotte
Sebastian Rodriguez	Son of Arnulf and Mei Fan
Karel Rodriguez	Son of Arnulf and Mei Fan
Percy Bysshe Shelley	Poet, Homeworld

OVERTURE

Date of the Republic August 1, 393 City of Penmerth, Ladaux

Jessica suppressed the urge to scratch her arms. Civilian clothing always felt wrong on her. Something about the drape and cut of the fabric was alien after so long in uniform. Marcelle had, however, been adamant. Jessica would not attend this dinner in anything remotely resembling her command centurion uniform.

They had compromised in the end. Jessica wore a dark blue tunic over dark gray slacks. Civilian, but close enough to her forest-green uniform. Muted enough that she didn't feel like a peahen, but still, she felt an itch.

Marcelle smiled down at her as if she could read Jessica's mind. After this long together, she might be able to. Marcelle had been her personal steward for more than a decade now. The woman had learned her habits, bad as well as good.

Marcelle was dressed far more flashily than Jessica could imagine herself ever appearing in public, a long pencil skirt in maroon, matched with a cream-colored blouse, and a bolero jacket so black that it appeared to absorb light.

Jessica smiled back. When Marcelle wanted to, she could pull off distinguished and elegant. Jessica was afraid she'd look like a clown in Marcelle's outfit.

Jessica turned to the third person with them. She looked down on the woman, something she could rarely do, being short herself for a woman. Moirrey Kermode, however, was tiny. While Jessica was only 1.6 meters tall, Moirrey was barely 1.5. She was like a normal woman, shrunk down to a perfect 90 percent copy.

Tonight, Moirrey was the belle of the ball. Jessica didn't sew, but she understood the patient crafting necessary to see a piece of cloth and rotate it in all dimensions to imagine what it could become. Moirrey wore an obviously hand-made frock, carefully and expertly gathered and ruched by hand as well. Depending on the light, it might be sky blue or a soft grass green. It looked quite perfect with the pixie's raven-black hair.

Jessica smiled warmly at the young woman, one of her evil engineering gnomes. "Moirrey," she said quietly, "I realize that I promised you a reward, but I still don't think that this qualifies."

What she really wanted to say was, *Are you nuts?* But she already knew the answer to that. The woman was the technical wizard from engineering, and this was what she had asked for as a reward.

Moirrey just grinned up at her.

Jessica turned back to the front door of the small house and stilled her breathing. This place always seemed so much smaller when she came back here as a grown-up. In her mind, she was still eight and running around her mother's garden, or riding her bike across the fields out back.

She smiled and knocked. Coming home hadn't always been so pleasant.

Her mother opened the door almost immediately with a happy face and the smell of freshly-baked blueberry pie wafting out the door.

"Welcome, welcome," her mother said, gesturing them into the small front room.

Jessica surprised her mother by stepping up to her and hugging her. They had not been a hugging family, when Jessica was growing up. But she was over that, she hoped. She could hug her mother. They were grown-ups now.

Marcelle got in a hug as well, so Moirrey did too.

It was interesting to watch. Mother was Jessica's size, short for a woman, and had the sort of homebody squishiness about her that made Jessica work out constantly to avoid. Mother nearly disappeared hugging Marcelle, who was taller than most men, and then towered over the tiny Moirrey.

"It is so nice to meet you in the flesh, finally," Mother said as she stepped back from Moirrey's grasp.

"And you too, Mrs. Keller," Moirrey replied in her birdlike singsong accent.

"Please, Moirrey," Mother said, "call me Indira."

"Indira," Moirrey smiled.

Father would not suffer to be left out as the group filed into the living room. He stepped up to Jessica and engulfed her in a hug that felt and smelled like home, his strength and spicy cologne bringing back all the joys of her youth.

She really was home.

Marcelle's hug was almost as fierce. She was another daughter around this house, these days.

Moirrey's hug was much more polite.

"I'm no' a fragile porcelain doll, da," Moirrey complained, so Father picked her bodily up and squished her against his chest before setting the tiny woman back down.

"Better," Moirrey said with a smile.

Jessica grabbed Moirrey by a hand. "Moirrey Kermode, may I properly introduce my father, Miguel Keller. Father, the reason I'm still alive and at liberty to join you for dinner this evening, Moirrey Kermode."

The tiny woman, the evil little engineering gnome, blushed clear to the tips of her ears and covered her face with her other hand.

Mother, *Indira,* stepped back into the salon and gestured to the house. "Please, make yourselves at home," she said. "Dinner will be ready in ten minutes."

Jessica watched her father settle into his favorite chair. She resisted sitting at his knee with an arm around his calf, like she had done when she was little. Then she realized she could do whatever she wanted, and sat on the floor next to him, letting his touch warm her.

Had it really been so long since she had been home?

She looked at the wall in the hallway where all the family pictures hung. Mother and Father dating, their wedding day, moving into this house, children and friends and pets and vehicles and sunsets.

The middle had been reorganized. On the left, pictures of her brother Vyacheslav and his wife Sasha. Their kids: Ruhal, Margaret, and Juan-Pablo.

All the classic things you would expect from a blue-collar household on the edge of Penmerth. The capital city of the Republic was still a Navy town, primarily. It retained a small-city charm, because significant amounts of industry were on *Anameleck Prime* instead. There were still small-holder farms not far away. Her own uncle was a short drive away by land vehicle.

It was the pictures on the right that surprised her. A picture of her graduating from prep school on her way to the Academy. Her being commissioned as a still-wet-behind-the-ears Cornet. *Had it really been twelve years ago?* A picture of *RAN Myrmidon*, her first service with the Fleet. *RAN Endeavor*, the little corvette that was her first command. The Destroyer Leader *Brightoak*. And in the center, a wonderful oil painting of *Auberon*, done with the full flight wing coming out of the picture.

When had her mother taken to doing that? That certainly wasn't Father's touch. He worked in a civilian shipyard still. McKanless and Daughters. He was around ships all day, even now as an esteemed Master Builder, but once a Master Welder. He would not have put ships up.

No, the picture of children and grandchildren were something only Mother would have done. Perhaps she considered those vessels her other grandchildren?

In a way, she might be right. Jessica wasn't married. Had never had any prospects of marriage as a poor scholarship student at Fleet Prep School. Might never have children, since it would require taking the time to find a person to share her life with, and then leaving them behind while she was off fighting.

Did she want a mate? A partner? A family?

Jessica stopped and listened to the voices in her head argue the sides. She hadn't really ever even considered it. People considered her too intense, too aggressive, too hard. What man or woman would want her for her, and not just as a Navy hero?

She leaned closer in, and put her head on her father's knee as he asked Moirrey about her homeworld.

Jessica listened to the sounds from the back room and let the most wonderful dinner slowly digest. She hadn't had rabbit stew over rice and greens in years. Again, home. She held a wine glass in one hand and slowly sipped port with Marcelle and Father.

In Mother's workroom, she could hear the sound of the spinning wheel slowly *whoosh* as one of the two women worked the treadle and turned wool into thread. She was transported back.

Spring shearing out on her uncle's farm. Coming home with a pile of dirty, smelly fleece bigger than she was in the back of the vehicle. Watching her mother's fierce concentration as she washed it by hand, plucked through it, then washed it again before carding it.

Spun on that wheel into thread, and then plied into yarn. Homemade dyes from the garden, boiled down and fixed to the wool. Whole summers passed that way, the bitter smells permeating the whole house all summer, followed by mother knitting in the fall. Sweaters, hats, scarves, mittens, socks.

Jessica came back to herself. "Hmm?"

Father smiled down at her. "I asked," he said in that warm baritone, "what was next for the Hero of *Iger* and of the *Cahllepp Frontier*?"

She shook her head ruefully. Anyone else calling her that would have gotten the sharp edge of her tongue, but this was her father, and the warm home of her childhood, especially with her flighty and emotionally-distant mother, always at her crafting projects.

"I'm not sure," she said hollowly. "*Auberon* will be ready for duty in another few weeks. Wherever the First Lord wants us to go. The war hasn't ended, just because I kicked the *Fribourg Empire* in the shins."

He held up his glass in a toast. "You'll do fine, Jess."

They sipped companionably for a bit.

"So," Father said, gesturing to the giggles and whispers from the back room, "what's all that about?"

Jessica turned to Marcelle with an arch smile. "That," she said primly, "is a question for your *other* daughter."

Marcelle had the grace to blush. "Moirrey has always reminded me of Indira," she said simply. "Moirrey makes her own clothing, and she quilts. I have no doubts that, if the materials were available from the hydroponics bay, she would make her own essential oils from things she grew, and can and pickle and jelly just like Mother does."

"And she asked for this as a reward?" He smiled and shook his head, gesturing to the whole house and the evening.

"I might," Marcelle continued, smiling, "have talked a bit much. Maybe. I know exactly two people who own their own spinning wheels. It was natural that they should meet. Don't you agree?"

Jessica snorted. *Peas in a pod* was a better description. She was just glad she'd finally been able to become friends with her mother.

The relationship would never compare to what she had with Father, but it was nice to be able to take that back into space with her, back to the endless war.

PART I: LADAUX

CHAPTER I

Date of the Republic August 16, 393 Fleet HQ, Ladaux System

Jessica stood perfectly still as Marcelle Travere, her personal steward, brushed away imaginary dust specks from the shoulders and back of Jessica's first-class uniform, the forest green of the *Republic of Aquitaine* Navy with three white stripes for a command centurion encircling Jessica's right upper arm and *Auberon's* crest as a patch on her left shoulder.

Because she was not in her formal dress uniform, she had nothing else to identify her to someone passing in the hallway: no name plate; none of the tags on her right breast to indicate schools, certifications, and service history; nor medal ribbons and citations on her left breast. Besides, the man she was going to meet would have said that the patch on her left shoulder was message enough.

RAN Auberon. A *Republic of Aquitaine* Navy Strike Carrier, recently known for a daring series of raids on the *Fribourg Empire* that had made the vessel and her commander famous, or infamous, depending on which circles one chose to associate with.

She preferred the Fighting Lords over the Noble Lords. The man on the other side of the door had been one of the best of the Fighting Lords before he retired from command duty to serve as First Lord of the Fleet itself. Her mentor. Her guardian angel. Nils Kasum.

Marcelle turned and rapped solidly on the door, nodding to herself as she did.

Room 2304, *Ladaux* Headquarters Station. The personal office of the First Lord.

The dragon's lair.

It slid silently into the wall.

"Come," a man's voice said. It was a rich, deep tone, warm with a smile.

Marcelle entered first, as always. She stepped immediately to her right and then back against the wall, prepared for any eventuality.

Neither woman expected that Marcelle would be there long. She rarely had been in the past.

Jessica followed her into the room, coming to a stop before the desk. The scene she found was not something she was expecting. She came to rigid attention and waited.

The man behind the desk gazed at them silently. First Lord Nils Kasum, the military chief of the service. A prominent member of one of the Fifty Families who provided much of the elite of the Republic. A son, grandson, and brother of Senators of the Republic.

He was a tall man, skinny, with a fire in his eyes clearly visible from where she stood and hair that had gone fully gray, finally.

For just a moment, Jessica's eyes darted to the right, mostly to confirm the identity of the man seated on the sofa against the side wall.

She had met that man once, briefly, when *Auberon* docked after her famous raid on the *Fribourg Empire*. Senator Tadej Horvat had spoken with her at that time, mostly platitudes and bromides, as one would expect from the Premier of the Republic Senate in a public place.

This room was not public.

What would he want with her?

"Marcelle," the First Lord continued with a smile, "we'll be at this a while. I've also taken the liberty of inviting your charge to dine with us this evening. I promise to have her back aboard ship before local morning. You should enjoy a night off."

Jessica grinned. She couldn't be positive without looking back, but Marcelle was probably blushing. As rowdy as she might be in a dock-side bar, she was an absolute kitten around the power players of the Republic. It had taken Jessica years to get over that herself. She was never going to make her steward, her assistant, her *dog-robber*, change. It wasn't worth trying.

"First Lord," she heard Marcelle mutter.

The door closed a moment later, leaving the three of them alone.

Three?

"Jessica," First Lord Kasum began, gesturing to a chair, "sit. We've got a lot of ground to cover. You might as well be comfortable doing it."

Jessica took the chair on the left, leaving an empty one between her and the Premier. She noticed a coffee service for three already laid out, so this was not a spur of the moment thing. She adjusted her plans accordingly.

She watched the Premier of the Republic Senate lean forward and turn on the charm.

He was very, very good at it. *What had she done to rate this level of attention? How scared should she be?*

"Command Centurion Keller," he began, in a voice pitched to fill the room like cool water, a soothing radio voice, or something intended to calm wild horses.

Wild horses? Okay, maybe she was just a bit keyed up. Jessica took an extra deep breath and held it.

"I wanted a chance to meet you in a private setting," he continued. "To take your measure, if you will, before the news I am going to share with you is generally known to the public."

"Sir," she replied simply. Now was a very good time to keep her cards close to her chest.

"Jessica," the First Lord said with a placating smile, "before you get serious and tactical on us, Tadej is on your side. I personally watched him threaten several senators, in public, warning them that you were under his protection, when they wanted to get stupid over the affairs at *2218 Svati Prime*. He's one of the good guys."

She nodded to both men, relaxing a bit. "Thank you. Both of you."

"Jessica," Kasum continued, "this is likely to be another one of *those* conversations, so for now, please call me Nils. The Premier will occasionally answer to Tadej."

She watched the Premier nod back at her. *Were they really expecting her to call the Premier of the Senate by his given name? Her?*

"Nils," she said, tasting the word for a moment. It felt odd to be on such informal terms with the man who had been her teacher at the Academy and mentor since. It would be far more so to address a total stranger such. "Tadej."

"Thank you, Jessica," Tadej said quietly. He rose and poured coffee into all three mugs and served them, before returning to the sofa. He sipped slowly, just as she did, watching her over the rim carefully. To Nils Kasum, they were probably a mirrored tableaux.

"Jessica," Tadej continued, "you are here as a victim of your own success. And I--we," he said, nodding to the First Lord, "wanted to make sure you understood this was a reward, and not a punishment."

Uh huh.

Jessica already had serious doubts about that.

"As a result of your activities on both sides of the *Cahllepp Frontier* over the last year, the *Fribourg Empire* has been forced to redeploy a significant amount of their own fleet elements defensively. At least two full battle squadrons, as we count such thing, broken down into patrol elements and in constant motion."

"Aye, sir," Jessica said. "Tadej. As intended. Economic warfare at a time when our military options were constrained by circumstances."

She saw both men smile the same way at the same time. They might have been brothers in that, but for the difference in their looks. The Premier was as broad-shouldered and bulky as the First Lord was a tall, skinny pencil. The Premier's sandy-blond hair was longer than Fleet preferred, while Nils's was regulation length and beginning to turn completely white. Only one of those heads of hair was its natural color.

"Correct," Tadej continued, "and as a result, we will need to station *RAN* squadrons to counter them. This will require several Fleet Lords as well. Nils tells me that you have been operating unofficially as your own Fleet Lord on the frontier up until now, and we have your amazing success to judge that by."

"Sir." She took another sip of coffee and let the man speak. It felt like a prepared speech. The least she could do is let him get to the end of it with minimal interruptions.

"Given the circumstances and remoteness of the posting, Jessica," Nils said with a suddenly-wicked smile on his face, "I plan to recall your old commander, Bogdan Loncar, to active duty, and send him out there with the Fleet Carrier *RAN Archon*."

Jessica resisted spitting on the nice carpet at the man's name. It would look unprofessional, regardless of how accurately it portrayed her opinion of the fool who had been in command at *Third Iger*.

Something must have appeared on her face. Both men smiled.

"Since you are still too junior to promote to Fleet Lord, just yet," Tadej continued, his smile warming, "and would be junior to Loncar in any case, I have asked Nils to detach your squadron from the sector forces and put them to work for me, on a special assignment."

Just yet? Fleet Lord? Her? A Fleet Lord? I must have misheard him. He hadn't really meant that. Had he?

"I see," she said. This was where politics tangled up the purity of command. It was not her specialty, although she had spent a great deal of time studying how the two interacted.

Jessica silently gritted her teeth. Duty was duty. "What can I do to help, gentlemen?"

Nils smiled at her like a cat. "I'm sending you pirate hunting, Jessica."

CHAPTER II

Date of the Republic August 16, 393 Fleet HQ, Ladaux System

It was a part of the Officer's Bar at Fleet Headquarters that Jessica had never been in before, tucked back into a corner and away from the normal bars, lounges, and salons, around a corner and down a long hallway, through a door protected by a concierge. The playgrounds of the Fifty Families, the elite, the rulers of the Republic.

Someplace a blue-collar girl didn't attend. Unless invited. Being First Lord of the Fleet, or Premier of the Republic Senate, obviously meant entirely different things here than they did down on the surface.

Interestingly, the hallways and doors had been designed by a naval architect. They had the exact same dimensions as a warship. The walls were metal, painted with the same muted gray/cream color the fleet used. The floor had no carpet. Everything was intended to remind one of being on a fleet warship.

To make them feel at home.

Jessica smiled at the realization. She felt at home.

It was hard to see around the two men she accompanied, both taller than her, neither stopping to ask questions, not even to open doors along the way. At each key point, there was a guard, or an aide, or a concierge, opening those doors as these men approached.

That was what this was. Power. But not the power of good birth, although that probably helped. No, this was the power of respect by one's peers. Of having been elevated to the highest rungs of society on will and achievement, not merely wealth.

Where she wanted to be.

The last door deposited them in a very small lounge. Three booths and a larger table, plus a bar with four empty chairs. It had been done in very old wood, darkly stained and weathered by time. Every shelf was filled with nautical knick-knacks, but not space-based. This was maritime, when the word meant sailing on a water-filled ocean on the surface of a planet.

Jessica saw things dedicated to fishing, and sailing, and old boats. Strange tropical islands. There were photos, and junk, and memorabilia. The one that almost made her laugh out loud was a silly little tin-press sign that read *Kip's Maritime Museum and Cultural Center* in red letters on a white background. It was the sort of thing one of her uncles might have hung on a barn wall.

The room was currently empty of guests. Only a quiet woman tending bar and a young man with blond hair in fleet uniform were here. That one had the look of a well-prepared Steward about him.

"Good evening, Premier, First Lord, Command Centurion Keller," the young man said as he directed them to the booth in the farthest back corner, through a little archway that separated two of the booths from the rest of the tiny space.

"My name is Joshua," he continued. "Normally, I would be taking care of the entire room, but the Marquette Room has been reserved for you privately this evening, so Anna and I are at your disposal."

Jessica found herself on the outside, seated next to Nils Kasum. He was wearing a pleasant cologne this evening, understated but masculine. She approved. Tadej Horvat had the entire opposite side to himself.

"Joshua," Tadej began, "we'll start with one of my merlots from Vaadwach Estates, a cheese plate of your choice, and two plates of antipasto."

The waiter nodded pleasantly. "Coming right up, folks."

And then he was gone.

At the center of the booth, on the wall, a series of pictures showing a young, dark-haired man in various stages of life. At a dance with a pretty young woman. Enlisted, proudly showing off his first uniform. His *Orders To Report*. That formal dress uniform shot they take after a year or so of active service. Many years later, now with several rank rings on his wrists. That same young woman, older now, and fully pregnant. Older yet, with three young children running around.

Jessica looked closely at the *Orders Of Separation* papers, carefully framed and hung to the right. Senior Master Chief Miles Abraham Kenneck. Pretty impressive outcome for a scrawny kid. A picture of the man, twenty or so years later, hair mostly gone, jowls taking over, and a smile still a kilometer wide. Finally, his obituary. Retired Chief, private astronavigator, fisherman, raconteur, card sharp, liar, and beloved great-grandfather of seventeen.

Not a bad way to go.

Jessica caught the Premier, *Tadej*, eyeing her carefully. "Miles Kenneck served with my great-grandfather. One of his grand-daughters is my aunt."

Jessica nodded. A diorama so prominent in a room so reserved would require a very personal touch, and a very powerful patron. Like the man seated across from her.

"He represents to me," Tadej continued, "the strength of the Republic. The Fifty Families provide a significant portion of the Senate and upper reaches of the Fleet, but there are over five hundred worlds providing the crews for those ships, whether they come from a backwater like *Saxon*, or from right here on *Ladaux*, the very heart of *Aquitaine*."

Jessica nodded again. Tadej's words had the feel of a speech to them again. Well-rehearsed and important, but more than just conversation. Much more.

"Jessica," *Nils* said, leaning a little closer, "what my esteemed sidekick is wandering around without actually saying is that you are at a point in your career most people from your background never reach. It's time for you to decide what you want to be."

Oh? Cards-on-the-table time? With two of the biggest power players in the Republic? Seriously?

"What are my choices?" she replied, opting for Socrates rather than commitment.

Both men smiled. Nils spoke.

"You already have a reputation among the Fighting Lords as a tactical wizard, perhaps comparable to Emmerich Wachturm, your erstwhile opponent. That alone will eventually pave the way for you to be promoted to Fleet Lord."

Jessica eyed both men closely. "What if I want more?"

She leaned forward and tented her hands to rest her chin. It was a pose she had picked up from the man seated next to her. He recognized it with a smile.

"How much more?" Nils smiled at her.

"How far could a scholarship student from the outskirts of Penmerth go, Nils? Tadej? On the strength of her own accomplishments, and not just as the spouse of someone far better bred?"

She was careful with her tone. These men bled blue when pricked. But they had asked for it.

"Could I take your job?" she continued at Nils with an honest appraisal.

"That, Jessica Keller," Tadej said seriously, "is why we are here, tonight."

"To answer that question?" She turned her tone on him, sounding like a tactics instructor, perhaps the man who had taught her, who sat beside her now.

"To begin your education, young lady, that one day, you just might." Nils smiled down at her. It was a warm smile, for all the cold implications in his words.

Jessica kept her smile neutral.

These men were serious. Very serious. Like they believed she might actually pull it off.

Her Advanced Fleet Operations final exams had been less intimidating.

Joshua returned to break up the scene, pouring wine and delivering hors d'oeuvres. Jessica used the space to gather her wits back together. As much as she could.

First Lord Jessica Keller? Wow.

She took a leap of faith.

"So," she began around a bite of cheese, "I presume my naval skills have been found acceptable. What is the next thing I should master, gentlemen?"

Tadej blinked in surprise. Nils laughed outright.

"I told you so, Tad," Nils said, toasting his friend with a wine glass.

"Yes," Tadej replied with a wry smile. "Yes, you did. I will pay up tomorrow, you scamp."

Seriously, they had bet? On her? Was she predictable, or were they?

"Jessica," Tadej said with utter gravity, the levity gone from his voice, but still holding all the warmth, "what you need next is diplomacy."

"Diplomacy?" she said, one eyebrow creeping up in spite of her best efforts.

"Not command, Command Centurion Keller," Tadej replied. "You do that well. No, I mean going out as the senior officer and talking to diplomats and politicians. Fencing verbally with them. Spying on them. Out-maneuvering them at the dinner table."

"I see." She did see. It was one of the things she detested most. Fleets were predictable. Battles as well, within limits.

People, not so much.

Still, if she wanted this future, she would have to master this task.

Simple as that.

"So what is the secret key to diplomacy, Tadej?" she asked, putting him on the spot to see how far he was prepared to go tonight.

"Diplomacy is the art of the unsaid, as much as the said, Jessica," he replied, suddenly very, very serious. Her reminded her of Father. "Politics is the art of perception, the shaping of minds with your words. Leading someone verbally to a place without ever taking them there, merely on the strength of your words alone. Never threatening. Never cowering. Hinting at ambiguities and repercussions, while letting their imaginations and nightmares fill in the blanks in whatever manner best serves your purposes."

"Lie?" she asked simply.

"Never," he said, "unless you cannot possibly ever be caught. And even then, sparingly. Paint instead in subtle grays, where men like Fleet Lord Loncar work in simple black and white. Use ambiguity offensively. And always make sure your opponent has a way to escape you, so he doesn't decide he has to die fighting. Always treat your worst enemy with the highest respect, because the wyrm will eventually turn and he will box you in someday."

Tadej paused to take a drink of wine and fix her with his steely gaze.

"Death is exceedingly rare in diplomacy and politics, young lady, so you will meet the same players again and again. Understand that today's opponent may be tomorrow's friend, and vice versa."

Nils poured the glasses full as a way to engage her.

"And while you are not known for using your feminine wiles, Jessica," Nils said with all the seriousness Father had used on the first boy she had ever brought home to meet, "many of the places you are likely to visit are not as enlightened about the equality of the sexes as *Aquitaine*. They will underestimate you because you are a women, especially Imperials. Do not overlook that advantage. They will see you as weak, unprepared, possibly harmless. Men like that see what you want them to see, regardless of what others might tell them."

Nils smiled impishly. "And men are visual creatures, at the end of the day. We will see the shell and miss the soul."

"Enough for now," Tadej said with a lighter smile. "We will eat, and then digest all of this over a good brandy. Jessica, we are sending you to

Lincolnshire because they are friendly, and will provide a good way for you get your feet wet without having to act like a spy. Plus, they have a problem that requires a military solution, so you should be in your element."

Jessica smiled back. An easy mission to the backwaters of the fringe. How bad could it be?

CHAPTER III

Date of the Republic August 20, 393 Ladaux

Bogdan Loncar emerged from his private vehicle as the doorman opened the heavy portal into his club. It felt good to be back in the saddle, back on *Ladaux*. Shortly, he would return to command. As he had long said to anyone who would listen, he was too big, too important to keep on the sidelines for long. Even that pipsqueak Kasum had finally had to bow to the opinion of the Senate.

He took a deep breath of the capital's air. Not as good as *Anameleck Prime*, and nowhere near as good as the air on a flag bridge, but it would do. For now.

This was what triumph smelled like.

Inside, he found that the carpets had been replaced, sometime in the last six months. The rich maroon on the floor had been replaced by a deep forest green reminiscent of the fleet uniform he had pulled out of the closet today, for the first time in ages. It was just another sign that his time for glory had come.

Bogdan suffered the elite, personal service that his club was famous for, being escorted to the second floor grotto where his compatriots and he would dine. Tonight was to be a celebration.

The staff deposited him and a glass of the best brandy at his favorite chair, close enough to the fire for warmth, but not so close as to be overwhelmingly bright.

Retired Fleet Lord Bogusław Tesar came in first, hanging on the arm of a lovely young lady in a costume that must have been sprayed on.

"Bogusław," Loncar greeted the man loudly, warmly, "well met."

Tesar joined him, moving a touch stiffly as old age and inactivity began to take their toll. "Congratulations, Loncar, my boy," Bogusław said. "Heard the wonderful news. Feel good to be back?"

"It is only my due, Tesar," Loncar purred. "And only the first step in my glorious plan."

"Plan?" Tesar inquired, sipping from a freshly delivered highball glass filled with caramel-colored liquor and ice.

Tesar's young lady *associate* kissed him lightly on the cheek and withdrew without a word.

Loncar leaned forward and dropped his voice down to a low rumble as Tesar sat. "Aye, Tesar. A tour of duty and glorious conquest out on that frontier, cleaning up the mess that snotty little brat Keller left behind. And then, when I get back in a year, it will be time for the Senate to force Kasum out for someone who understands what this Republic was founded on."

"I see," the old Fleet Lord said, leaning forward as well. "And who would you propose as a new First Lord?"

The younger man smiled gloriously. "If called, I would find it in my duty to save the Republic from those meddling fools and their lower-deck peons. We are the Fifty Families, Bogusław Tesar. We own the Republic. It's high time we got back in charge and started running it better."

"All well and good, Loncar," the old Fleet Lord said, "but how do we manage it?"

Loncar pointed at the door by way of answer. A well-dressed, plump woman stood in the door, glancing around until she spotted them. She looked out of place without her Senatorial robes, but Andjela Tomčič still stood out in the room, younger than most of the men, often by a generation, and without the erect carriage that came from a lifetime of Fleet Service.

On her arm, an unobtrusive man in his late thirties. He wore a dark suit and moved with care, as if intent on not leaving an impression. Only the shaved skull marked him in any way that a bystander might remember later.

He worked hard at that, especially for these players. Brant was one of the key operators behind the scenes that kept the Senate working well. Some things could only be done in the shadows.

She strode to their table, bringing the man along with her.

Loncar smiled an alligator smile up at her, toasting her with his glass. "Andjela," he said, "good to see you again."

The younger man stood at her side, perhaps half a step back. Quiet. Observing.

"Brant, let's get you something to drink, and then we can retire to a private room where we can chat."

Brant studied each of them in turn. "Fleet Lord Loncar," he nodded, "it is good to see you again. Fleet Lord Tesar, we have not been formally introduced, but I've heard a great deal about you. It is a pleasure to make your acquaintance."

Both men rose to kiss the woman on the cheek and shake hands with the man. The staff escorted them to a small chamber to one side and settled them around a small table.

Loncar raised his glass to the assembly. "My friends, I give you our duty to the Republic."

"The Republic," they chimed back.

CHAPTER IV

Date of the Republic September 23, 393 Edge of the Ramsey System

Jessica watched the big three-dimensional projection slowly rotate in front of her, left to right like a spinning top. It dominated the center of the conference table in her Flag Bridge, surrounded, as always, by the ghostly images of her command staff, each comfortable on their own bridges as they appeared and settled in.

A deck above and a little forward from where she sat, Denis Jež commanded *Auberon.* Technically, he was just the first officer of the big Strike Carrier, while she was the command centurion, but she had a squadron to control. Plus, he was good at what he did, and would have already been given command somewhere else, if anyone had noticed his skill before she came along. She wasn't about to give him up.

One of the only two other people physically present at the table was her Flag Centurion, Enej Zivkovic, the young man responsible for passing her orders to the other vessels.The ghosts visible at her table were Command Centurion Alber' d'Maine aboard the Heavy Destroyer *Rajput*, and Command Centurion Tomas Kigali of the Fleet Escort, the former Revenue Cutter, *CR-264.*

"Good afternoon," Jessica smiled to the faces around her. It was just the small staff today, plus one other person who occasionally joined them. She smiled at Yeoman Moirrey Kermode to welcome her. There wouldn't be any fireworks, theatrical or otherwise hopefully, today, but her regional expertise would be invaluable for other reasons.

The various faces around the table nodded back as Jessica sipped her coffee.

"We're sitting at the edge of the *Ramsey* system right now, at the capital of *Lincolnshire*," she informed them, "and, contrary to a combat jump, I plan to stay here for a few hours. After that, we'll head in on the normal transit lanes, like we were a freighter convoy, to give them time to prepare. It's not that they won't welcome us, but they don't know we're coming."

"How long will this port call last, commander?" d'Maine asked. He was a serious, almost dour man, on a cramped little warship. He never complained about the conditions on *Rajput*, but she knew a few extra days shore leave would do his crew well, especially if they were going to be in back end of beyond for a while.

"I'm not sure," Jessica said simply. This was one of the few times that command did not demand decisive solutions on the fly. "*Lincolnshire* is nominally an ally of the Republic, and we're coming in response to a direct request for aid, so we'll play it by ear. There really isn't even that much information available about this sector of space, beyond simple sailing directions and the usual political map, so I've asked Moirrey Kermode to join us today to answer whatever questions you have."

She nodded to the little raven-haired engineer with a smile. "Perhaps a little background?"

"Aye, ma'am," Moirrey replied. "First off, *Lincolnshire* is much less organized than *Aquitaine*." She pronounced the word *Link'nsheer* with a soft burr as she spoke. "And very much more poor than the great fine folks of the Republic. Worlds out here is few an' far between, and pirates-r-common, both the formal kind and the neighbors."

"You mean *Salonnia* and *Corynthe*?" Denis asked.

"Aye, sir," Moirrey growled, "the first one's a bunch o' businessmen thugs, and th' other's ruled by the King of the Pirates."

"Seriously? Sir?" Enej amended himself quickly. "King of the Pirates?"

"That is correct, Zivkovic," Jessica said. "According to the records, it is an old title, dating back several centuries. The worlds out on the fringe of the galaxy are very rough places, ruled by hard men. They rarely die peacefully of old age. Hopefully, we won't have to deal with those folks."

"Are they likely to be behind the troubles?" Kigali asked. *CR-264* was an escort, built for exactly this sort of thing. Most of the rest of her original class of Revenue Cutters had been decommissioned but not sent to the wrecker, according to Jessica's research, and many had instead ended up in places like *Lincolnshire*, having been sold out of service.

"It's possible," Jessica replied. "Our orders are to work with the locals. They asked for a hammer big enough to crack a tough nut, and the First Lord sent us. Questions?"

"What about docking, sir?" d'Maine asked. "Sensors show a very small station in orbit."

"You are correct," she said. "We'll drop into a high orbit, above the usual traffic, and ferry things up and down with the shuttles. It will give the crews practice, and keep my pilots from getting bored."

"Wow," Enej said. "We really are out in the backwoods."

"Jes' ye wait," Moirrey chimed in with an evil grin, "until you sees how the supplies be delivered."

CHAPTER V

Date of the Republic September 24, 393 City of Landing, Ramsey

Jessica walked down the landing ramp to the big crimson DropShip, *Cayenne*, and marveled again at what kind of person would paint an Assault Shuttle bright red. The pilot, Hollis Dyson, generally known as *Gaucho*, was in a category of his own. According to him, red ones went faster.

Along with shuttles from *CR-264* and *Rajput*, they were parked at the far north end of the landing field, right below one of the big defensive towers that protected the field and had tracked them all the way to the ground. *Cayenne* dwarfed the other two shuttles, as well as many of the smaller freighters in the vicinity.

The morning sun was bright in the clear sky, but barely warmed the field. According to the sailing gazette, it was still mid-spring on *Ramsey* at this latitude, so Jessica had worn a heavy forest-green pea coat over her day uniform at Moirrey's suggestion. Others had settled for day jackets. She expected them to be sorry in about an hour or so.

Several armed marines spread out to keep watch, while *Auberon*'s stevedores began the process of unloading four massive containers, each a three-meter cube, under the watchful, loud, and occasionally profane supervision of *Cayenne*'s Loadmaster, Takouhi Nazarian. Jessica was amazed at the volume coming from such a small woman, but it worked.

Jessica gestured the others to join her as she moved into a clear spot. Denis, Enej, and Marcelle had all dressed for a relaxed port call. Moirrey was bundled up much warmer and carried a messenger bag slung over one shoulder. She was the reason Jessica was warm while everyone else was blowing on their hands to warm them.

"What's that?" Denis said incredulously, pointing across the tarmac.

"That," Moirrey smiled back, "is almost the state of the art for *Ramsey* when it comes to transport technologies."

A vehicle approached, slowly, loudly. It was a mostly metal frame with skinny rubber tires. The flatbed in back was packed tight with metal cylinders with a rough silvered finish. What made it stand out was the fact that it was drawn by two big horses, one roan and one black.

"Horses?" Enej said.

"Aye," Moirrey replied. "'Tis way easier for two horses to make more horses than for two tractors from *Anameleck Prime* to beget ye spare parts."

"What are they delivering?" Denis whispered with awe.

"Those be milk in ninety-liter jerry cans," Moirrey said with a smile. "Ramsey's big on cows, too. I did warn you that *Lincolnshire* were not up to Republic standards, sirs."

Jessica snorted. Nobody had actually listened to Moirrey. Their loss.

In the distance, Jessica heard and saw a small airship take off from the control building and begin to careen wildly in their direction.

Overhead, she heard a solid thump of metal as *Cayenne*'s gun turret suddenly deployed and began to track the little airship. She imagined the things her pilot was yelling at the pilot of the flitter over the radio. Jessica rolled her eyes, but wasn't about to rebuke *Gaucho* for it. The pilot over there should have known to fly more politely in a confined airspace.

Apparently, he got the message quickly. Something about staring up twin barrels seemed to jar his sensibilities. The next moment, he braked savagely, flared his nose back so hard he nearly stalled the craft, dropped down to almost ground level, and then proceeded at slightly more than a walking pace.

Jessica didn't believe that *Gaucho* really would have opened fire here, but she was never sure. Her pilot was crazy.

You needed that in a DropShip commander. At least the good ones.

The flitter turned out to be more like a transport as it approached and landed. In the middle, what appeared to be two rows of seats faced each other, with a large, open cargo deck in back, separated by a bulkhead.

A stout, middle-aged man, slightly rumpled after bouncing around the interior, climbed out of the back seat. He looked like a farmer, dressed up for going to the big city.

"Command Centurion Keller?" he asked as he approached.

To Jessica, he sounded like a farmer as well. His voice had the sort of gruffness she had grown up hearing from her uncles and their neighbors. She smiled and stepped toward the man.

"Here," she said.

Up close, he was a small man, barely taller than her own diminutive height, but possessed of a broad solidity that reminded her of the phrase *salt of the earth.*

"A pleasure to meet you, ma'am." He smiled as he shook her hand. "I'm Radoš Fiala, mayor of Landing. Governor Wapasha asked me to unofficially greet you here and then transport you up the hill to Lincoln for a proper, formal reception."

Jessica nodded. In the more urbane worlds of the Republic, this might be a state visit, an event that would require hundreds of people and days of planning. Moirrey had explained that things were much more laid back on the periphery.

Being met by the mayor of Landing was actually a pretty big thing, as locals judged them, but even the main spaceport was a small place. The capital city was not much larger.

"That will be perfect, Mayor Fiala," she said. "May I introduce you to my staff. Denis Jež, my executive officer. Enej Zivkovic, my flag centurion. Marcelle Travere, my steward. Moirrey Kermode, from my engineering staff."

She watched him shake hands and greet each in turn. When he got to Moirrey, he gave her a very close look. "There are Kermodes in and about Saxilby," he drawled appraisingly.

"An' they would be kin," she replied, lifting her chin at the man.

"Then we might be cousins by marriage, young lady." He smiled.

"Dunno," she shrugged. "Grew up up-country. No been home in many years."

Jessica stepped into the conversation. "It would be most helpful, Mayor," she said, "if you could provide my first officer and Yeoman Kermode a lift to the administration building on the way up the hill."

"It would be my pleasure, Commander," he smiled, gesturing them to precede him.

Jessica sipped a glass of strong wine from a local vineyard and watched the large number of guards around the outside of the converted gymnasium housing the event. The watchers seemed more heavily armed and keyed up than one would expect for this sort of thing. Even for a place like *Lincolnshire.*

The formal reception had turned out to be a long afternoon event, a buffet with more than one hundred guests, locally prominent people interested in button-holing her or the governor or the mayor about some topic or another. Most of the questions directed at her had to do with the increase in crime or piracy recently and well-wishes that she would do something about them.

A few also included circular inquiries into her marital status. She had simply ignored those.

A particularly-oily looking man approached as Jessica was considering another run at the buffet. It had turned out to have pretty good barbeque.

The man had a furtive smile on his face. Jessica pasted a polite smile on her own face. Behind her, she could practically hear Marcelle bristle.

"Command Centurion?" he said quietly. "A moment of your time?"

She took his measure critically, a taller, heavy-set man, stoutness verging onto rotund, as one gets eating the richest foods and not exercising it all off again immediately.

And I always thought shifty eyes was a literary thing.

She nodded warily.

He stepped close and bowed slightly. "Marcus Auric, at your service, madam."

"*Republic of Aquitaine* Command Centurion Keller, sir." Out of the corner of her eye, she saw Marcelle move to one side, capable of protecting her back or stepping behind him quickly.

Really, Marcelle, this isn't about to turn into tavern brawl. At worst, he'll suffer a glass of wine thrown in his face.

And perhaps limp for a few weeks.

Jessica smiled at her thought processes. That in turn seemed to relax the man.

"It is customary," he began, "when major fleets from the Republic arrive for port calls, they bring with them trade goods to help stimulate the local economy."

He paused, waiting for her response.

Jessica let her smile tell any or no tales. She sipped her wine with an expectant air.

"May I inquire if your vessel, the carrier *Auberon*, brought such materials?"

"And if we did, Mr. Auric?" she asked.

"I am a merchant, command centurion," he replied, ingratiatingly. "I would like a chance to bid before my competitors arrive. They will circle you like sharks."

She smiled broadly at the image. Perhaps guppies threatening a shark. But it would be impolite to point that out to him.

"Well, sir," she said with a smile like a mousetrap, "if you hurry, you should be able to get there in time. My first officer is unloading four Mark 2 shipping containers at Landing right now. The contents of all four are identical, and prices are *Freight on Board* from *Ladaux*, with a standard drayage fee to *Ramsey*, non-negotiable. Buyers will be allowed to purchase exactly one container."

He blinked as if she had slapped him. No, sucker-punched him in that ample stomach. She had, in her own way. He certainly paled.

"You'll pardon me a moment, please?" he said, already turning away from her and pulling out a pocket comm.

Jessica watched him walk towards a corner, gesturing wildly as he walked. All she could hear were hisses and mumbles. She smiled at Marcelle and began to make her way back into the mob over by the buffet.

"A moment, Command Centurion?"

Jessica had already forgotten about the merchant.

He had one hand extended, as if he was about to grab her by the arm at the very moment when both his manners and his survival instincts kicked in.

She eyed him from under a heavy brow. Stories of David and Goliath flashed through her mind. Apparently in her eyes, as well, because the man stepped quickly back a half-stride.

"Were you successful, Mr. Auric?" she asked innocently, letting the sudden rush of adrenaline ooze slowly away.

"I will know in a few minutes. Thank you. Though I must say that was hardly a fair way to handle it." He seemed put out.

She laughed out loud. "On the contrary, had there been more than two major shipping houses on *Ramsey*, including Auric and Sons, I would have had to hold a lottery and let random chance determine things. This was perhaps the fairest way. Certainly the most ethical. You and each of your competitors will have the exact same goods, at the same prices. And we will post those prices tomorrow for everyone."

She watched his pupils surge and then shrink.

"But that's not how it's done," he whispered urgently.

Jessica took a step closer to the man. She came up to his shoulder, but he shrank back anyway.

"It is the way I do things, Mr. Auric," she snarled quietly, looking up at him. "Ethical and above board. If you have had bad experiences with my peers, and I suspect you have, given my own experiences with some of them, I invite you to take it up with those people when you next see them."

She stared at him, daring him to speak, or even breathe, wrong.

After a moment, he seemed to deflate into himself. "Touché, Command Centurion Keller," he said, visibly relaxing. "Well played. You must understand that it is very rare for me to run into one of you Fleet types who understands *business*. Fewer still who see *Lincolnshire* as anything other than the backwoods, and the locals here as rubes to be fleeced."

She relaxed as well, but stayed close enough to speak quietly. "Two of my uncles own farms on *Ladaux*, Auric. Working family farms, not *latifundia*."

"Something else we have in common, then, madam," he replied with a smile.

He paused, as if looking for the right words. Marcelle shifted slightly in her peripheral vision, now less likely to swoop in on the poor man if he provoked her.

"If I may, Command Centurion?" he whispered politely, with a previously unheard urgency.

She nodded, keyed back up. This was probably the entire reason for the previous conversation.

"Regardless of what you hear from other sources," he continued obliquely, "all is not well in *Lincolnshire*, or even just *Ramsey*. A visit to *Sarmarsh IV* would probably be an interesting and educational experience for you. Take an entire fleet when you go, however."

She stepped half a step back to see him better. He seemed sincere, but that was possibly just another act.

"Why, Mr. Auric?" she asked simply.

He shrugged. "One grows tired of having to pay bribes for safe passage of vessels and goods, Command Centurion, even here in the capital city. I would like to see something done about the criminal elements, but I am not in a position to do anything myself. And I am a patriot. It would do everyone on the perimeter good, which, in turn, is good for business."

"I see," she replied. "And why would I receive different intelligence from other sources?"

"A few elements, local ones, profit from the current arrangement." He shrugged. "I do not do poorly, but I could profit more without them. Also, *Lincolnshire* is my home. I would like to see it succeed. The locals cannot handle that task. It is one of the reasons the governor asked *Aquitaine* for help."

Jessica nodded at that. "I will see what I can arrange, Mr. Auric."

It was, after all, why she was here. But best not to tell the locals the whole truth. Not yet.

CHAPTER VI

Date of the Republic September 24, 393 City of Lincoln, Ramsey

Jessica watched the sun go down through the big picture window as she entered the governor's office. It had been an entertaining, mostly-vapid afternoon, but now came the interesting part.

The governor of *Ramsey* looked like a politician was supposed to, according to all the popular videos. Tall and reasonably good-looking, with a full head of hair and perfect teeth. His middle was getting thick from sitting at a desk. She suspected there was a girdle in his immediate future. Or possibly surgery.

Jessica supposed she was supposed to swoon for him, based on the looks he had been giving her across the room during the reception. This man did represent the apex of the social pyramid for the entire region.

She probably should have researched that aspect of the man more thoroughly.

Jessica sighed internally, tired of all the attempts at seduction she had been subjected to in one day. They hadn't even been all that bad-looking for the most part, but there were none here that really got her attention. There usually weren't. It came with the territory.

Jessica pasted that same neutral smile on her face and took the guest chair. They quickly waded through the inane chatter and inconsequentials.

She regretted not having either Marcelle or Enej with her, but Governor Wapasha had requested a private meeting. No aides, no recordings. No records.

"So, Governor," she said when she could finally break through his small talk, "First Lord Kasum has asked that my task force be put at your disposal to help *Lincolnshire* with a piracy problem. What might we do?"

She watched him shift uncomfortably in his chair. He slid open a drawer and pulled out a small device that he thumbed active. It began to make an irritating buzz as he set it on his desk.

She raised an eyebrow at him silently.

"I don't believe my office is entirely secure," he began. "This will hopefully distract the sensors for a bit."

"Your own office?" she inquired, suddenly very serious.

"Indeed, Ms. Keller. Perhaps my own staff. It's hard to say. Even this will cause some friction and trouble."

"I see," she said, leaning back in her chair. "And you can't stop them?"

"It would be impolitic to try, at the present time," he smiled at her grimly. "I am still an elected official, subject to the forces and whims of the wealthy merchant classes funding a challenger if I am too much of a threat. Or perhaps undertake a more direct method."

"So the stories about the rise in crime on this planet…?"

"Are true," he completed her sentence. "I'm sure the causes are mostly off-planet elements, but they have wormed their way into the power structure here."

"But if the pirates in the neighborhood were broken?" she asked

"Then I would have a much freer hand to try and make changes," he completed the thought. "As it is, you have seen the number of guards around the palace, and the bodyguards accompanying people today. Fix the one, and it should fix the other. There are several places you might look. My favorite would be *9621 Jordani III*."

Jessica nodded, holding a map of the area encompassed by *Lincolnshire* in her mind.

"On the main trade route to *Aquitaine*," she observed. "Close enough to threaten *Ramsey* and a few other worlds."

He nodded.

She paused to study the man's face. "A little bird at the reception suggested I might also try *Sarmarsh IV*," she continued quietly. "Do you have anything on Sarmarsh IV? Colony? Mining Station?"

She was rewarded by a surprised blink before the man got his face back under control.

"Nothing."

"That would be much closer to *Corynthe*, Governor Wapasha," she said.

"It would also suggest that *Salonnia* is conspiring with *Corynthe* to threaten us and using piracy as a cover," he replied nervously. "And that the trouble we have been having are of a much more political nature than they appear."

"Indeed it would," she said carefully. "What would be your orders if we found something like that there?"

His face grew serious.

"Anyone you found at a place like *Sarmarsh* would be pirates, Keller," he said. "Not just thugs with guns, but honest-to-Creator enemy agents. We have had a lot of trouble in that vicinity. Anything you can do to remove them would help with trade. It will probably also help here on *Ramsey*."

"Is it as bad as that on the surface here?" she asked pointedly.

"Things have been better, Commander," he replied. "I asked *Aquitaine* for help specifically because I do not know who can be trusted here. You, however, should be safe. I've seen your assistant and your bodyguards. Nobody would dare attack you."

Jessica nodded with a sour mouth. She leaned forward and covered the man's hand and the small jammer device with her own hand. "*--Jordani III*," she said as she pushed the button to turn it off. "I will take that under advisement, Governor. It will be a good exploration cruise for my crew."

He scowled at her, confused, and shook his head.

She responded by gesturing to the room around them with a serious face of her own, before letting a small smile through.

"It has been a pleasure, Governor," she said as she rose from her chair. "I expect we will take a few days at *Ramsey* to load supplies, and then run a patrol route as a familiarization drill. Perhaps we can scare off your pirates along the way."

"I see," he said with sudden understanding. He rose as well and shook her hand. "Happy hunting, if I do not see you again. Hopefully you will visit us occasionally."

He walked her to the door and held it open as she departed.

Jessica waited for the door to close behind her, eyes locked in tight on Marcelle across the room. She nodded once and strode out of the office without a word. Marcelle fell into step beside her, the taller woman's longer legs easily letting her keep up.

When they emerged into the twilight air, Jessica turned to her steward, her *dog-robber*. "We have ground transportation?"

Marcelle nodded, turned, and took the lead. One of *Auberon*'s marines guarded a ground vehicle parked to one side, eyes active and weapon bared. For once, Jessica was happy that her crew was a little paranoid.

Marcelle and the marine, faceless and nameless behind a lowered faceshield, climbed into the front of the vehicle as Jessica got in back. "We need to find Moirrey, right now."

"Affirmative," Marcelle said as she brought the vehicle into motion. "I have her itinerary."

"Good," Jessica said simply. She reached into a pocket of her jacket and brought out a secured comm. "*Cayenne*, this is Keller."

"Go ahead," *Gaucho*, the crazy DropShip commander, replied almost instantly.

"What's your window to emergency launch, Dyson?" Jessica asked.

"Four minutes if you want polite, commander. Thirty-five seconds if you're paying for the damages."

"Roger that, *Cayenne*. Recall your crew and stand by. You may have to be the cavalry tonight."

"Yee-haw," came the call back.

CHAPTER VII

Date of the Republic September 24, 393 City of Landing, Ramsey

Moirrey watched the big rig with Commander Keller depart, flying low and sedately towards the capital city, itself sitting perched on the hill looking down on Landing.

It felt good to be home.

She could tell she'd been away for too long. Landing had seemed a huge and vastly magical place when she left for the Republic. Now it were a little backwater port on a littler backwater world. Hopefully, her Ma's fresh lemonade would cure her of such jaded thoughts. *How will you ever keep them on the farm, when they've been to gay Paris?*

Moirrey shook her head and patted the messenger bag she had slung over one shoulder. Two stops in Lincoln, and then sixteen hours of leave to visit her kin folk. And she didn't even have to change cash. *Aquitaine* Levs were used as a second currency for everything around here.

A quick walk to the corner and she placed a call home. Ma and Pa were honest surprised to hear from their wandering daughter, but overjoyed. Uncle Detrin or Cousin Dale would come into town in a few hours and meet her to bring her home for dinner, once she was off duty.

Moirrey smiled. Her, the prodigal daughter, home from the big, bad universe and showing off. And being shown off. She wondered if they would invite Tommy. He was probably married off and had a whole gaggle of young'uns by now. Probably married Missy.

She laughed out loud and walked down to the bus stop. It was amazing what six years might do to someone. She had turned into one of them fancy *Aquitaine* folks, without even trying. Or looking. Stranger days.

At least the buses hadn't changed one iota. Big, dumb lumbering beasts powered by local-brewed kelp-alcohol. Filled with people too poor or transient to afford big shiny flitters or personal zip-bikes. Her old hand-me-down zip-bike from Uncle Detrin would be daft fun right now. Too bad they'd been no way to bring it with her. Maybe she should get Lady Keller to ride one, or Flight Centurion Dyson. He might go for keeping a few down on the flight deck for things. And the Commander might just enjoy the power, she were that kind of lady. Moirrey sat primly and thought wickedly-silly thoughts as she rode slowly up the hill.

Moirrey sighed at lost dreams as she finally got to the ridge.

The Ramsey Agricultural Institute sat on the brow of the hill, around the side to the right from Landing. Someone, back when the town were laid out, had decided the capital needed a right proper university, so they'd picked out a spot with a pretty view and built several big gray stone buildings, just like a big world would do. Ivy didn't grow much here, but the rest were straight out of a fairie book like her Ma had read to her, once upon a time.

The big bus dropped her off with a big burp of kelp fumes that kind of embraced her like a big, smelly hug.

Moirrey blinked rapidly as she staggered out of the pocket fog and looked around. There was only one bus stop for the big campus, and she'd never actually been here before, but she had studied the map before she set out. And it were a weekday, so everyone would be around.

The building she wanted was third down on the right of the big quad. Students lounged, even on a cold day like this, some studying, some playing a game with an inflated ball, two necking in an alcove out of the breeze.

One enterprising soul was apparently cooking lunch on a hibachi about the size of her shoe. Not that she had ever done something like that, no sir.

Somebody wolf-whistled at her as she walked past, but she didn't have the time or inclination to stop and say hi.

Moirrey looked at the faces as she passed, wondering wistfully at the crevasse of time that separated her from these bright-faced youngsters who were all of three or four years younger than her. And had most likely never been shot at by anybody, especially not Imperial Battleships.

She giggled. *And certainly never shot back.* She giggled some more.

Six years on starships had done her legs good. The twelve broad steps up the front of the building were easy going. Inside, there was a large foyer with more students studying, snacking, napping.

Moirrey found the board along one wall, located the name she wanted, and took the stairs two at a time to the second floor. If she'd had thought about how many young men were going to be around today, she might, just might, have worn civilian attire instead of her day uniform. Maybe something with leggings and a tunic that would show off a tantalizing amount of bottom as she pounded up all these stairs with the over-stuffed messenger bag bouncing on her butt.

She giggled yet more.

Let's see. Offices on the left are low numbers. Not this one. Nope. A-ha.

The door was open. The space was barely big enough for a small desk and two overflowing bookshelves. And one young woman, eyes down, reading. One very pregnant woman with brown hair pulled into a pony tail. Hugely pregnant. Like winter-turkey-about-to-pop pregnant.

Moirrey smiled. "All that reading's probably bad for you, you know," she said casually.

The woman looked up and did a double-take. "Moirrey!" she cried, lurching up out of the chair and wobbling around the desk to engulf the much smaller woman in a giant hug.

Moirrey eventually emerged from the hug to poke the big belly.

"This is an agricultural college, Dina," she said with a tease. "Hasn't anyone explained to you where those come from?"

Dina laughed with her head back, the sound ringing off the walls and down the hallway.

"And you?" Dina asked, reaching out to touch Moirrey's collar with her rank tab and then the *Auberon* patch on her left shoulder. "You went off and became a great, big hero."

"I did no such thing, missy," Moirrey countered.

"You did, Pint-Sized," Dina said with another laugh. "It was in the paper, even. Your ship saving the day from the big Imperial bad guys."

"No way."

"Truth," Dina concluded. "So, how did you get here?"

Moirrey directed Dina back to her own chair and then moved a pile of books from the other chair, hidden in the mess, into the hall so she could sit.

"We're in town for a few days, passing through," Moirrey replied lightly. "Our Commander likes me something fierce, and asked me to bring you a prize."

"Me?"

"Well, not you in particular, but I have a couple of things for the Institute that she thought would be fun and useful, and I got a day off to bring them over, quiet-like, while she hobnobs with the governor and folks."

"Do you now?" Dina asked slyly.

"Aye," Moirrey said as she opened the messenger bag and pulled out a barely smaller, rolled bag from inside.

She and Dina worked seamlessly to move books around until the desk was mostly flat and kinda clean. Moirrey unrolled the satchel until she got to a piece of paper stuffed in the middle.

"There you go," Moirrey said as she handed Dina the paper. "Inventory of stuff for the seed library."

Dina scanned the list quickly and then looked at her former best friend with a dropped jaw. "Where did you get this stuff, Moirrey? This is amazing."

"T'were Commander Keller's doing, Dina," Moirrey replied. "She asked the folks at the University of *Ladaux* to put you together a care package she could deliver. Things that would grow here. Special things nearly lost when the Homeworld was destroyed."

"For us?" Dina said, still amazed.

"Well," the tiny woman muttered, "I might've called in a favor or two along the way. But she does like me something fierce, so it were a good way to do it."

"And she's just giving us this?" Dina asked, breathless.

"Oh, aye, Princess," Moirrey said, "and I've got more for the folks at the library."

"You know," Dina said, "nobody's called me 'Princess' in a long time, Pint-Sized."

"Well, then, *Princess*," Moirrey grinned evilly, "introduce me to some of the nice folks at the library and I can tell them what they've missed."

She pulled the other object out of the now-deflated messenger bag and set it on the desk. It was a small box, exactly two centimeters thick, nine wide, and twenty-two long, made from a matte black material that seemed to suck the light out of the room.

"What's that?" Dina asked.

"This, young lady, is a standard *Aquitaine* fleet astrogator's navigation module, wiped clean and filled with books."

"Wow," Dina said. "How many?"

"About three million," Moirrey said quietly.

"Moirrey, that's more than we have now," Dina replied.

"Yup. This be a personal present from First Lord of the Fleet Kasum."

"Oh my God," Dina said simply.

"So, you ever take a break from reading? I only have about two hours before I have to be to my next stop, and you've got six years of explaining to do."

Moirrey poked Dina softly in the belly. "Let's start here."

Dina smiled. "I met Evgen my first semester…"

Moirrey bundled up tight against the chill. The sun had been down for about twenty minutes and the air was dropping fast into too-cold-to-be-outside-thank-you-very-much.

She and Dina walked arm in arm into the parking lot at the far end of the campus, waving to the head librarian, hoping the man wouldn't feel the need to hug her again. Seriously, books were nice and all, but let's keep the emotional displays to a polite minimum. *And no more crying.*

Beside her, Dina snickered.

"What?" Moirrey asked with a huff.

"You know, Pint-Sized," Dina replied with a giggle, "if we'd have stayed much longer, he might have asked you to marry him."

"Is why we're leaving now, Princess. That and Uncle Detrin or Cousin Dale should be here to pick me up shortly. Sure you don't want to bring the man and come for dinner?"

"I would love to, but I have papers to grade tonight," Dina said. "*Somebody* kept me from working all afternoon."

Moirrey planted herself with hands on her hip bones and gave her best friend a mock-serious stare. "That's because I'm way more important, missy."

Dina giggled some more. "Whatever you say, Pint-Sized."

Moirrey *harrumphed* once for emphasis.

She looked around the nearly empty parking lot. Couple of panel trucks. A few old beaters that probably belonged to faculty. A whole rack of zip-bikes and old-fashioned bicycles. And one flatbed rig still covered with mud. Moirrey began to walk that direction.

A door opened, and Cousin Dale climbed down from the cab. Moirrey refrained from running, since the pregnant lady beside her kinda waddled along, but she raised her hand and waved as the man walked closer.

"Moirrey!" he called to her.

Up close, Cousin Dale was all growed up. Like, almost 2-meters tall and half that across the shoulders. Still had the baby-face, hidden behind a few wispy whiskers. Course, he were only twenty now, so he still had some growing up to do, but he walked close and engulfed her in a hug that lifted her clean off the ground.

She let him swing her around once before she pounded on his meaty shoulder.

"Put me down, you big lug."

"Yes, ma'am." He smiled, setting her down like fine porcelain.

"Dina," he continued.

She stepped up and gave him a much more sedate hug, belly stuck way out front. It was like an iceberg or something.

"You coming with us?" Dale said.

"I can't," Dina replied, "but tell Ma and Pa hi for me."

When Dale put an arm around her, she noticed the two panel trucks across the way turn their lights on and start to inch forward. In the distance, coming down the main roadway into the campus, another vehicle was barreling along at a way-too-fast-for-this-kind-of-neighborhood speed.

Moirrey did the math and reached into her messenger bag while Dale and Dina chattered. Lincoln were supposed to be a quiet place, especially around the Institute, but she'd been bad places before. She knew what the signs of trouble were.

In the bag, her hand closed around a very small beam weapon. It was a kind specially designed for a woman's purse, and a woman's hand. Small enough to hold, big enough to whomp a horse upside the head.

The two trucks boxed Dale's flatbed in and turned sideways. Almost a dozen men in black outfits suddenly jumped out and started pointing guns and things at her. At them, but mostly at her. What had she done?

A goon with some training and a pistol stepped a little closer. "Nobody move and nobody gets hurt," he growled ominously. "Am I clear?"

"What's going on?" Dina said, voice rising.

The man started towards Dina, violence in his eyes.

Moirrey stepped in between them and pulled the little pistol out. She'd never actually pointed it at someone before now, outside of training, but her hand didn't twitch as she did.

"You will leave her alone," Moirrey growled at him.

The man stopped. He appeared to be Dale's size, but at least a decade older, a decade of violence obvious in a clipped ear and a ragged scar over one eye. He scowled hard at her.

"You're coming with us, *Aquitaine*," he said.

Across the parking lot, the car suddenly slowed down, but kept coming. Moirrey didn't want to take her eyes off the man to see what the vehicle was doing.

"Fergus," a man's voice called, "stand down."

The goon gave her his best stink-eye, but took half a step back and to one side. She watched him turn away from her group, so she took a moment to look at a new face.

Apparently, he had been in the back of the truck waiting. Short and skinny. Dark hair slicked back. Long duster and black gloves. No gun. Pretty-boy face. Moirrey kept her gun on the goon.

The car kept coming.

The man snapped his fingers.

Moirrey watched half a dozen guns, big battle rifles, suddenly come up and aim at it.

Nobody fired, yet.

The man turned his attention away from Moirrey as the car stopped sharply with a squeal of rubber on asphalt.

Moirrey felt Dale start to move forward, so she stepped in front of him as well and hip-checked him back hard. It felt like bumping a tree, but Dale stopped.

These people meant business. He were gonna get hurt if he tried something, however well he meant.

Moirrey saw most of the guns pointed away from her now, except for the big goon and one other. So she was dealing with professionals. Good to remember.

And then a voice rang out of the darkness and made everything better.

CHAPTER VIII

Date of the Republic September 24, 393 City of Lincoln, Ramsey

Jessica rode in the back of the limousine while Marcelle and one of *Auberon's* marines were up front, hanging on as Marcelle drove at crazy speeds through mostly empty streets. Fortunately, Lincoln was the kind of town that rolled up the sidewalks at night. Traffic down in Landing would have been much more severe.

"Marine," Jessica said, "identify yourself, please."

"First-Rate Spacer Tawfeek, Commander," a man's voice came from behind the lowered face shield.

"Very good, Tawfeek," she said. "I'm hoping that you have nothing to do tonight but sit around. However, we may need your skills."

"Aye, sir. Do you want my spare pistol?"

Jessica weighed the options. It would be a nice fall back, but if things were that bad, then she was going to need a ten-kilo maul, not a shiv.

"Negative," Jessica said finally. "Marcelle is armed. You stay out of sight as long as possible."

"Understood, sir."

Through the front windshield, Jessica could see the parking lot at the university. Two big cargo transports had boxed in another vehicle. There were far more people standing around than normal for a weekday late afternoon.

"Marcelle," she said, "we're late to the party, but not too late. Let's be a little more casual, please?"

She felt the vehicle slow as it entered the lot.

Over there, most of the figures were suddenly pointing weapons at them. Marcelle jammed on the brakes and brought the big beast to a screeching halt.

"This will do, Marcelle," Jessica said, keying her comm and dropping it into an outside pocket on her overcoat.

She opened the rear door slowly, so as not to rouse them over there. Someone might get twitchy if she moved to fast. Best to move with careful grace.

She stepped out of the vehicle, but kept the door between her and the bad guys. She didn't figure it was armored enough to stop the bad guys if they opened fire right now, but every little bit helped.

"I am Command Centurion Jessica Keller, commander of *RAN Auberon*," she called across the parking lot. "Who the hell are you?"

She watched a slick punk in a long coat turn away from Moirrey and two locals and focus his attention on her.

"My name's not important to you," he sneered. "But you and your friends are coming with us. I have somebody who wants to talk to you."

"I don't think so, mister," she called back.

He stomped closer. Not close, but enough that he could look intimidating without the light breeze ruffling his hair.

"I don't think you understand, Navy," he said. "You don't have a choice. I brought a lot of firepower with me and I'm willing to use it."

"Oh, I understand," Jessica said conversationally. "I'm just playing for higher stakes than you are. *Cayenne*, you're on."

She watched the boy's confusion grow. He shook his head and cocked it to the side like a dog might.

Jessica grinned politely at him.

Off her starboard beam, the night abruptly lit up with a howl as the big, red DropShip surged above the ridge and slid forward, belly turret tracking and a pair of searchlights blinding everyone.

Jessica watched the goons point their weapons up for a second before they realized that they had nothing that could even scratch the DropShip's armor.

"I would suggest," she called above the roar of engines, "that you all put your weapons down nicely. I will not give you a second warning."

She waited a couple of beats for the shock to set in.

"Now!" she snapped.

She was rewarded by that special sound that metal makes when it impacts on concrete.

Jessica stepped clear of the vehicle as Marcelle and Tawfeek got out and began collecting guns from the goons.

Cayenne balanced on her rear landing struts just long enough to off-load eight more marines and Denis Jež, before ascending back up, the twin ventral turret never once wavering from the box truck in front.

Within moments, the men in black had been disarmed, searched, and herded into a small dispirited cluster. Jessica watched the punk in the longcoat as one of the marines searched him for weapons.

Jessica walked over to Yeoman Kermode, her favorite evil engineering gnome and smiled. "Perhaps you could introduce me to your friends, Moirrey?"

Jessica watched the engineering pixie's smile light up as Moirrey stuffed a small pistol back into her bag.

"Commander," Moirrey chirped, "it is my great pleasure to introduce you to me cousin Dale, and me best friend from school, Dina Zhao."

Jessica shook hands with both with a smile. She gestured the group to follow her as she walked back to the punk in the long coat.

She sized him up for several moments before speaking. He seemed a little too defiant for the situation.

Jessica turned to the other group. "Which of you is his second in command?" she asked loudly.

Most of the eyes turned to a big thug with a scarred face. Jessica addressed herself to him.

"All of you are coming with me right now, but when I leave this planet, you will behave yourselves. I don't feel the need to hurt you today, but if anything happens to these people," she said as she pointed to Dale and Dina, "I will hunt you down when I return, and hang you all. Then I will destroy your organization. And then I will hunt down your families and friends and destroy them as well. I will even shoot your dog. I will know all your names and your blood types before I release you. Am I clear?"

The man scowled down at her, but nodded.

"Good," Jessica said harshly. "Make sure his boss understands that when you see him tomorrow."

"And what do you think you're going to do with me?" the man sneered as she turned back.

"I'm taking you with me." Jessica smiled harshly. "I'm hunting pirates, and caught you first thing."

"Do you know who I am?" he snarled down at her from the distance. "You can't touch me."

Jessica pointed up and back at *Cayenne*.

"I'm the *Republic of Aquitaine* Navy, you two-bit chiseling shit. I can do anything I want. You should be looking to find a reason why I shouldn't hang you from the neck until dead."

She glanced at Marcelle and Tawfeek. The tall woman nodded. Jessica pulled the comm from her outer pocket.

"*Cayenne*, land now so we can transport the vehicles and the prisoners."

She turned back to Moirrey's friends.

"Dina," Jessica said, "you should be safe to return to your office and file a police report if you would like. Dale, if you would drive your rig aboard the DropShip, we'll make sure you get home after a brief stop."

"Yes, ma'am."

Jessica watched the last of the thugs from the surface being escorted into *Auberon*'s brig by her dragoon, Navin Crncevic, Navin the Black, and his entire marine force.

All fifty-eight of them.

The marines did not seem pleased. She watched them make that unhappiness plain to their prisoners.

When the task was done, Navin returned with an entire fire team and a heavy weapons squad as well, mounting up in the DropShip and quickly settling in to bodyguard Jessica down on the surface.

Across the bay, the GunShip *Necromancer* had already launched and was waiting to escort them back down to the surface, to a very late dinner date at the Kermode farm.

It was overkill, but she needed to make it clear to people around here that she wasn't going to play by the old rules. She had cracked harder heads than these together.

Anyone giving her a reason now was going to be very, very sorry.

CHAPTER IX

Date of the Republic September 26, 393 Ramsey System

Denis took a deep breath and knocked on the door to Commander Keller's office. It opened immediately.

Inside, he found her deep in paperwork and probably her third cup of coffee this morning.

"What's our status, Denis?" she asked as she set down a report and rubbed her eyes.

He moved to the open chair and sat as the door closed behind him. She wasn't a stickler for protocol, and it looked like she needed a break.

"Last shuttle is back from the surface and docked, sir," he said simply.

He waited for her to nod.

"All of the prisoners, except the one we are keeping, were dropped off at the edge of Landing, fully clothed and unharmed. *Auberon* has been topped off with fresh food and water from the surface, plus general supplies for a long sail. Mrs. Kermode sent along a triple batch of chocolate chip cookie dough that your chief chef is preparing for dinner."

"Did she now?" Jessica asked with wonder.

"She did." He grinned at her.

Denis didn't ask, but suspected, from things Moirrey had said, that the two women had accidentally turned into sisters. Not necessarily a bad thing. Keller didn't seem to have any home life besides the fleet.

"I have also gotten everything prepped to break orbit in about forty-five minutes and head out-system for *9621 Jordani III*."

"Course laid in and ready to go?" she asked with a strange look on her face.

Denis hesitated before answering. "Yes, sir."

"Good, Denis," she said simply. "The more people who believe that, the better. We're headed to the *Sarmarsh* system first, and I'd like to catch them cold."

Denis felt his eyes blinking rapidly as he fought to recall the Astrogation Gazette.

"Farther out?" he asked. "Republic side of the gulf, just inside the *Lincolnshire* systems, but not far from several trade routes between *Lincolnshire*, *Corynthe*, and *Salonnia*?"

"Very good, Denis," she said with an even broader smile. "Worthless place to live. Metal-poor star. Wide asteroid belt. Couple of boring gas giants. Couple of boiling-hot rocks too close to the star for life."

"Just exactly the sort of place pirates could hide if they wanted to be missed," he said.

"That's my expectation," she replied. "Rumor suggests that they're too big for *Lincolnshire* to handle, so I want to see who's funding them."

"And thus, our little canary down in the brig."

"Correct," she said. "Has Mr. Bedrosian started to talk yet?"

"Only to complain, sir."

He watched her lean back in her chair and stretch by turning her shoulders nearly sideways each direction. He'd probably dislocate something trying that.

She fixed him with a tight stare, as if reading his mind. Maybe she did that, too.

"Have Navin assign somebody to play good cop," she said with a feral purr. "We have time to get through to that punk. And I won't know what questions to ask until we find out what's at *Sarmarsh*."

"Roger that. Anything else you need before we head out?"

"No, Denis," she said. "We're probably six day's sail to *Sarmarsh*, so we've got time to think. Let's set up a way-point halfway, drop out, and spend a few hours meeting with the commanders and planning."

"Will do," he said, standing and nodding.

Denis smiled as he left Keller's office. Time to go hunt pirates.

Jessica watched her executive officer depart and realized how tired she felt.

It wasn't just the daily grind of paperwork. That had become second nature after so many years. It was the people.

Moirrey's parents were lovely people. They did remind her, in a way, of her own. She could see why Marcelle had suggested she introduce the engineering gnome to her family.

No, it was what had originally started out as a small welcome home dinner for Moirrey and had morphed into an Event, where Jessica had brought a GunShip and a DropShip, plus twenty heavily armed marines.

That was how you crashed a party.

The Kermodes had, in turn, invited all the cousins and neighbors to a massive, spur-of-the-moment potluck that had ended up turning into a dance in the middle of a recently-harvested wheat field, entertained by a random seven-piece band that changed membership every other song.

It had been a rousing success, as parties go.

Gods, but she hated parties.

They just drained the energy out of her, like a fuel cell on full discharge. She had spent nearly an entire day hiding in her office, sending Marcelle for coffee and food occasionally, just so she didn't have to deal with anyone.

Jessica stretched again, working out kinks in her thighs and butt. Right now, she needed a hot shower to loosen everything thing up, and then maybe forty minutes with the fighting robot.

The damned paperwork could wait.

Jessica held both blades loosely and let her muscles flow. In her left hand, she held a long, straight, single-edged sword, what the combatants called a saber. Instead of something more exotic, it was made of simple steel. Tradition. In her right hand was a much shorter blade, also steel, but heavier, and with a reinforced cross-guard instead of the saber's basket protecting her fingers, the *main-gauche*.

Valse d'Glaive.

The Sword Dance.

The robot across the mat from her fought as her mirror today. Normally, it was right-handed, since most people were as well. Being left-handed gave her an advantage. But she had learned over the years not to be predictable, a lesson brought home by one of her own pilots during the Long Raid on the Empire last year.

That was what the news media had taking to calling it. *The Long Raid.* Which was much better than *Keller's Raid*, although she suspected that historians would gravitate toward the latter, eventually.

She shrugged and dropped into a fast squat once, bouncing back up to make sure everything was still flexible.

"Fighting Robot activate," she called across the space. "Challenge Rating Four."

The bipedal machine came to life. Its swords were the same length as hers, but made of a blunt plastic that would leave welts and bruises. And did.

"Combat Mode initiated," a soothing woman's voice replied. "Challenge Rating Four confirmed."

Jessica's bodysuit was already beginning to wick sweat from her skin. The deck boots would maintain traction, even if she did sweat too much, although her hair was back and a long piece of cloth had been tied around her forehead to keep everything out of her eyes.

Challenge Rating Four was enough today. On her best days, she could take the machine nine falls in fifteen on Rating Six. Five was when she had slept well and was relaxed. Four was when she had spent two days on her ass, moping and recovering.

She shifted to her right quickly. Humans were mostly right-handed, so to track her was to pivot against the grain of their own body. Today, it brought her closer to the saber.

The robot's long blade flickered out, almost a kiss as the smaller blade came at her low.

Jessica let thought drain out of her.

Thinking slowed you down when blade dancing.

She rolled with the attack, letting her saber block the other blade, both points towards the floor, and turned an aerial cartwheel over the other sword.

Jessica landed lightly and slashed backwards with the *main-gauche* at shoulder height.

Her blade thumped loudly off the machine's chest.

"Contact: Keller. Score 1 to 0," the woman's voice announced.

Jessica watched the robot step back and reset.

Yes. This was what she needed. To beat the living hell out of the fighting robot for a while.

It would be a good warm-up.

PART II: SARMARSH IV

CHAPTER X

Date of the Republic September 30, 393 1829 Bharani System

It felt odd having everyone present on her flag bridge, rather than talking to each of the commanders on their own bridges, wired in and displayed on the big hologram projector. It was less efficient this way, but more personal.

Jessica was trying to bring this group to the same level of team functionality she had with her old destroyer squadron, but she had only been with them for a year so far, rather than the three she'd on *Brightoak*. Still, they were getting close.

Marcelle had outdone herself. There was fresh coffee for everyone, and Chef Aoiki had come very close to replicating Mrs. Kermode's recipe for chocolate chip cookies. The smell on the flag bridge was amazing. She might yet develop a taste for freshly-baked cookies. There were smiles on all sides, even normally-dour Command Centurion d'Maine of *Rajput*.

Jessica rapped her coffee mug on the table top to get everyone's attention.

"I have never sailed this close to the edge of known space," she began, "and the Gazette is remarkably thin on details about the *Sarmarsh* system. What does anybody know that might help?"

There were a lot of confused faces and shrugs around the table: Her Flag Centurion Enej Zivkovic; Denis Jež, her second in command; Tamara Strnad, his tactical officer; Command Centurions Alber' d'Maine from *Rajput* and Tomas Kigali off of the escort *CR-264*.

"I have some very old navigation charts," Kigali finally spoke up, "dating back a couple of centuries. Enough to be able to calculate orbits and such. Nothing new enough to say who lives there."

"Centuries?" Jež asked incredulously.

Kigali shrugged a second time. "It's a weird hobby, I admit," he said, "but I was looking for places to solo a yacht through heavy hazards. Never ended up taking that vacation, but found some of the old notes."

He called up a file and displayed it over the table.

"*Sarmarsh* is a young, hot, metal-poor star," he said, highlighting things as he spoke. "Two small, uninhabitable planets close in. Then an incredibly broad asteroid belt that looks like it would have a been a nice place to live, had it coalesced into a single planet, maybe two. Instead, the belt runs almost out to the orbit of *IV*."

Three spots lit up, buried deep in the thick asteroid belt.

"*Sarmarsh III* turns out to only be one of three dwarf planets tucked in there," he continued. "The other two, *IIIb* and *IIIc*, were found later and named oddly, since *IV* and *V* were already in the navigation files."

An orbital movement ring appeared just beyond the belt, with a single, orangish-red gas giant displayed.

"Nobody has ever bothered to study the place much," Kigali said, "but the current theory is that the gravity from *IV* ripped the proto-planet ring at *III* apart. It is, as you can see, a navigation mess. Nice place for pirates to hide. Hard to root them out. A plethora of small moons orbiting *IV*, plus one big one, far enough out and large enough that it has its own moon in turn."

Jessica froze the projection in place and rose. She thought better walking around it, trying to find the best place to arrive.

She stopped opposite Kigali and speared him with a look. "How thick is the belt?"

He smiled back at her. "A belt like this is a psychological hazard, sir," he said, "rather than a physical one. There is a lot of space between the big rocks, and most of them are moving like a shoal of fish, same general direction, same speed."

She raised one eyebrow silently at him.

"Shields up, scanners maxed, small movements. Safe to transit. The challenge in a solo is to spend several days in there, having to plot a course before napping, then not sleeping much for a week."

She nodded and returned to her chair. The coffee was getting cool. The cookies were long since gone, although their ghosts would stay as long as the air filtration system would let them.

"So landing deeper in and sneaking out wouldn't work?" she confirmed.

"If they are the least bit awake, they'll be able to run before we can get clear and give chase," he agreed.

"On the other hand," Denis spoke up, "that thing is likely to be a wall in their minds, since nobody would run in there at speed, especially not being chased by us, unless they were extremely desperate."

Jessica nodded and looked at *Auberon*'s tactical officer. "Tamara," she said, "Blue Team/Gold Team exercise. You're Blue. Alber', you're Gold."

Tamara nodded and spun the projection a quarter. "I'm camped on the big moon," she said slowly. "With an observation post on the smaller moon orbiting. Call the big one *Alpha* and the small one *Gamma* for now. The spotter crews on *Gamma* are unhappy being separated from what entertainment is available on *Alpha*. I have to have a taskmaster to keep people on track, but we're pirates, and we're safe in our bolthole, so discipline is a little loose and lax."

She reached out and spun the projection again.

"I agree that the asteroids are a wall, but I'm watching in case somebody tries to sneak up, or drive us into a trap like the *Fribourg Empire* tried to do to *Auberon* last year. *IV* creates a big blind spot, but radiation is too heavy for a satellite to operate indefinitely, and would be expensive, so I rely on *Alpha*'s orbit to carry me around. I would drop probes out a ways to watch the open-space approaches, but that's about it."

Jessica nodded. "Solid, creative. Good pirate thinking. Alber'?"

D'Maine was a dark, serious man. He scowled furiously as he thought. "We hop well short," he growled. "Clear at the edge of the system so we can watch the orbital mechanics of the *IV* moons for a bit. Then we hop closer to confirm things, maybe a light-hour out, so we can hear near-real-time comm traffic."

He slurped at his coffee and squinted. With one hand, he zoomed the projection until the gas giant was a giant marble taking up one whole edge.

Suddenly, he smiled. It was a feral event that seemed to take over his entire body as he started to type.

A set of red arrows appeared inside the projection.

"Depending on where the moons are, and where they are headed," he said, "one of these vectors should drop us right on the back side of a base on

Alpha, just below a fading horizon. Then we sneak up on them. We should have overwhelming firepower."

"It's still a base on a planetary surface," Denis interjected. "That means the possibility of Primaries, and maybe even a Type-IV beam."

Jessica considered the chances. Primaries were likely, at least a few of them. Would anyone sell pirates a beam-weapon emplacement that big? Probably. It would have been sold to a legitimate buyer as part of a planetary defense array, or stolen while in route. Probably only one, since they were so big and required so much power, but they could force a battleship to keep a respectful distance.

Even the enormous Fleet HQ at *Ladaux* had only eight of them, protecting the points of an imaginary cube. Regional bases often had only two or three. Still, best to be prepared.

"Alber'," she said, "can you do the same thing here that you did at *Qui-Ping*? When *IFV Amsel* was chasing us?"

He stared at her blankly for a second. "While dropping into low orbit?"

"Forget the orbit at this moment," she replied. "At full speed blasting through."

"Absolutely, commander," he replied with a shark smile. "We practice that maneuver regularly."

"Perfect," she said. "Here's how we'll handle the approach…"

CHAPTER XI

Date of the Republic October 3, 393 Sarmarsh IV

"Commander, you're sure this isn't a mockup someone made as a training exercise?" her first officer asked with a trace of surprise in his voice.

"No," Jessica shook her head as the projection sharpened and revealed the base.

Auberon and her squadron had been able to see very little from the edge of the system. Jumping to just under forty light minutes out had helped. They had been able to identify the base and listen to the traffic and the sensors the place was running.

They obviously weren't expecting trouble, as several scanners were active. Not hostile, but sending pulses out and listening, as if they belonged here.

The last jump had dropped them close enough to fire a probe over the horizon as they closed.

The base was a monster.

Jessica's sensor centurion, Daniel Giroux, quickly began highlighting gun emplacements, turrets, missile launchers, scanner towers, and an entire flight bay ready to send fighters up to engage them.

"I've seen Regional Fleet Bases less well armed," the projection of Tomas Kigali said from his bridge.

"Somebody's awake over there," Giroux said. "We're being hailed by a representative of the government of *Corynthe*."

Giroux paused for a moment as he listened.

"And we're apparently trespassing, Commander."

Jessica nodded to herself. This had just gotten much bigger than a simple case of highwaymen.

"Launch the flight wing," she said.

Senior Flight Centurion Milos Pavlovic, callsign *Jouster*, still lived for that surge of acceleration as his little M-5 *Harpoon* fighter leapt clear of *Auberon*'s bow. Across the way, Ainsley Barret, *da Vinci*, came clear as well, although her P-4 *Outrider* was a scout and not a knife-fighter. And this would be a knife-fight. But he wanted eyes out here right now. Guns and missiles would come along soon enough.

Jouster took charge as the rest of the Flight Wing launched. A Strike Carrier like *Auberon* was supposed to have three wings of fighters. On every other vessel in her class, that was nine identical fighters, usually M-5's or M-6's. *Auberon* was special.

Instead of three full wings, she only had two, so six *Harpoons*. Instead of the third wing, she had two big S-11 *Orca*-class fighter-bombers and *da Vinci* in her little scout. They had less dog-fighting capability than an Imperial squadron, which was normally twelve fighters, but far greater overall firepower when the *Orcas* opened up.

To top all that off, someone, somewhere along the way, had removed the three administrative shuttles that the ship was originally issued and replaced them with a GunShip and a DropShip. Nose-on, the Flight had enough firepower to take on a heavy cruiser.

Today, they lined up in what *Jouster* called a Scorpion formation. His wing on the left, three fighters stacked up and back like stairs, with his second in command, *Southbound*, and her two wingmates on the right. In the middle, the GunShip *Necromancer*, flanked by the two *Orcas*, with *da Vinci* over the top keeping watch.

It was finally time to fly. No more briefings. No more simulators. It had been *seven* months since the last time he had flown into combat, against the Imperial Battleship *Amsel* at *Qui-Ping*. He was ready. His team was ready. Even the newbie, fresh out of flight school, was ready.

They had been very lucky during the last campaign. The only casualty had been Gustav Papp, *Ironside.* Considering what they had done, and the odds, a lesser wing wouldn't have held up so well. And the new kid, *Hànchén*, aka Flight Coronet Murali Ma, seemed to be fitting in with *Southbound* and *Bitter Kitten*.. Still wet behind the ears, but a serious student of military history. Today, he was very likely to discover military history first hand.

Time to act like a commander.

"*Da Vinci*, this is *Jouster*," he said as the fighters all settled into place, "what's the enemy status?"

"Zero encryption, *Jouster*," Ainsley Barrett, *da Vinci*, replied quickly, "but some seriously strange code words going back and forth. And not nearly enough panic in their voices to suit me."

"Roger that," he said.

Pirates were always expecting the law to show up. When it did, they would fight like cornered rats. It was his job to be the weasel. Behind and above him, the hunters.

"Flag, this is *Jouster*," he said, keying the message to Commander Keller and her staff. "Flight wing is ready to make our run."

"Confirmed, *Jouster*," he heard Keller reply immediately. "Assume we did not surprise them as much as we hope and that they will start shooting as soon as you come over the horizon. Stand by to redline your engines for the final approach. Missile impact is set to time-on-target in thirty seconds."

Milos smiled. Standard Republic tactics called for them to come in low on the horizon, fast, but slow enough to maneuver. Bad guys over there would be ready to fire as soon they came into sight, guided by passive scanners using directed beam communication to relay telemetry data.

Right now, two stealth missiles were sneaking in ahead of the wing. One was aimed right at a big cluster of towers on *Gamma*'s moon. Another had been fired blind at the back-side of *Alpha*, set to home in on anything broadcasting. Since there were no friendlies and no civilians around here, any loud signal was probably another sensor base, trying to hide.

"Flight wing, this is *Jouster*," he said as the countdown clock reached fifteen seconds. "Redline everything now. Go go go!"

He put words to deeds and slammed the throttle forward to the last stop. The surge of power drove him backwards into the seat in an embrace he found almost carnal. Over there, everything should be blue-shifting something fierce as they picked up his jump in speed.

And then, the surprise.

Da Vinci had the best sensors, and was relaying her boards to everyone else on a tight beam. The back side of *Alpha* and the base on *Gamma* both lit up within a second of each other as *Auberon*'s two stealth missiles, launched during the noisy chaos of the wing coming out, impacted.

Hopefully, that blinded them right at the moment his force had jumped forward. He agreed with Ainsley, those people really needed more panic. Time to go to work.

Denis sat at the center of his bridge and watched everything flow together. Technically, it was her bridge. Keller was the command centurion in charge, according to Fleet, but she had made good her promise to let him fight *Auberon* while she commanded the entire squadron down on the flag bridge.

Hopefully, when they promoted her to Fleet Lord, he would get bumped up as well. He couldn't imagine having to go back to just being an Executive Officer, unless they put him on a Dreadnaught, or something else big. But that was a problem for next week.

Today, he was skirting along the edge of the asteroid belt, at a relatively safe distance, at full speed, closing on *Sarmarsh IV* along one of the safe vectors d'Maine had identified. Unlike their normal attack runs, the squadron was sailing forward in a traditional formation. *Rajput* was out front, running hard and fast to keep up with the flight wing. *CR-264* was tucked in close, just in front of *Auberon* and below her two entire flight levels, just like an escort corvette should be. Ready to hunt anything coming after the carrier.

Anyone who knew Keller would be surprised at this pattern. Anyone expecting a *Republic of Aquitaine* fleet to show up would have been surprised by anything else. They were about to get several other surprises instead.

"Gunnery," Denis said, loud enough for the whole bridge to hear, "confirm estimated time to impact."

He watched Tamara Strnad look a question at the gunner, her black hair bobbing. Either she needed a haircut, or she was growing it out to pull back. He hadn't noticed until now. And this wasn't the time to ask.

Maybe in fifteen minutes, when the immediate craziness was over.

The gunner, Centurion Afolayan nodded once, barely taking his eyes off his boards as he slowly adjusted firing solutions.

"Confirmed," she responded a beat later. "Impact in ninety seconds."

Denis looked at the face of Commander Keller on one of the smaller screens to his left side. Noise-deafening around his station let her talk without generally being overheard. She smiled back.

"Squadron, this is the Flag," she said over the general push. She spoke with a voice that somehow combined intimate warmth with the face of a hammer. "Initiate Phase 2."

"Helm and Engineering," Denis said, looking forward, "bring the engines to emergency flank speed."

A blended chorus of replies floated back to him. This was a good crew. He had served on ships where the command centurion expected people to make eye contact and maintain proper protocol, even when under fire. He just wanted the job done first. Pretty could come later, after victory.

Even with the gravplates, the big ship shuddered as the engines surged. He watched the main screen with bright anticipation. This was why he had joined the fleet, to be one of the good guys, hunting down pirates and making the galaxy a better place.

On the main projector, a flash of light mushroomed over the horizon of *Alpha*, about where sensors had said the pirate base would be found. It was too early to be their missile striking home.

"Scanners," Denis said sharply, but the man was already rapidly pushing buttons on his console.

"Working. Stand by," Centurion Giroux said, his mousy brown hair looking vaguely blue in the light from his screens.

Denis watched him pick up a comm and rapidly speak into it, deadened around his console so the bridge wouldn't be overly loud right now. It was a good idea, but he wanted to know now, and not when they got back to him.

The night sky about *Alpha* continued to be bright. There was some atmosphere around the small planet, but not nearly enough to support life. Just barely enough for wind and weather patterns, from the look of things. Still the glow was reflected, possibly off of low clouds. It was eerie.

"Flag. Sensors," Giroux said, going straight to the commander instead of taking it to him first. Again, the sign of a good command crew. They could judge for themselves if something needed to go to the top immediately, and feel safe from repercussions if they were wrong.

"Go ahead, Giroux," Jessica replied over the bridge comm.

"Flag, we have secondary and possibly tertiary explosions on the surface of Alpha. Big ones. No idea what caused them."

"Acknowledged. Jež?" she asked.

"If I had to guess, Commander," he said simply, "someone tried to crash launch a flight wing and missed. I saw it happen once. Tertiary explosions like that mean fuel cells and missiles on ready racks catching fire."

"Understood. The first probe lasted longer than I expected, but I need another one. Get me eyes over there as soon as possible."

"Roger that, commander," Denis said, pulling up the locations of the flight wing and their current speed. The flight wing was supposed to cut acceleration back down to nothing ten seconds after the stealth missiles had hit, just to cause everyone over there to be extra-hyped.

"Tamara," he said, "fire a probe over the horizon at them, right now, instead of over the pole. They won't shoot it down fast enough to blind us. And we'll be there shortly anyway."

Instead of speaking, the tactical officer programmed the little sensor pod and fired it with a firm click. Then she looked up.

"It's away," she said. "Thirty seconds."

Denis was about to ask when Jessica spoke.

"Squadron, this is the Flag," she said. Again, that firm voice, hard without being brittle, command without the slightest hint of doubt. "All vessels go to maximum acceleration and close as quickly as possible. Flight wing, go to Plan Beta. Prepare for a high-speed bombing run instead of strafing and dog-fighting as you pass. If they just suffered a total meltdown over there, there isn't going to be anyone to engage. *Rajput*, stay on plan."

Rather than speaking, each element's message appeared on his side board as a green light.

So far, so good.

Jessica watched the data stream in from a dozen different sources. *Da Vinci* with the Flight wing. The probe arcing over the horizon of *Alpha*. Active and passive channels from all three vessels in the squadron. And even the boiled down command feed from Giroux.

It painted a reasonably good picture.

One of her hallmarks as a tactical officer had always been to move decisively, whether on offense or defense. That came from extensive planning and gaming out the scenarios. And dancing with the fighting robot.

Kigali might solo yachts and collect old maps in his spare time. D'Maine apparently painted. She fought wars. Old ones. New ones. Hers. Other peoples.

Most people didn't get her. That was acceptable. They weren't warriors in the truest sense of the word. She tried. Often, she succeeded.

Right now, a massive explosion had probably shattered a section of the pirate base and opened several bays to the inadequate atmosphere. Nobody was going to die from depressurization, but the survivors were too busy getting to breathers and suits, and trying to patch holes so the base could respond. They wouldn't be launching fighters.

That just left the guns.

Denis Jež had been dead accurate with his predictions. There were two towers down there with what looked like twin Primary-beam projectors, something you could only do on a planetary surface. Between them, protected by them, a Type-4 emplacement. Slow and hard to aim, capable of blowing daylight through either *Rajput* or *Auberon* with a single shot.

If she let them.

Hopefully, they were blind right now, having lost the two sensor stations, plus all the extravagance of the flight bay exploding.

They still had a really big gun, firing through an atmosphere thin enough to be a danger.

Jessica considered retasking the big hitters in the flight wing to go after those three towers. But that would in turn leave them critically vulnerable to the point defense systems that this level of planning suggested.

No, better to stick to the plan. It was a good plan. Rude in unexpected ways.

She smiled. *Project Mischief* was going to be legendary, with this crew, and with any other vessel these people went to in the future.

On one of her screens, Alber' d'Maine smiled at something off camera. She had seen more of his smiles over the last few months. This one was the pure joy of combat. Harsh. Feral. Almost a match for hers. It was a shame he did nothing for her personally. She needed a warrior as a partner. There had to be one somewhere in the fleet.

Another screen showed the unfolding surprise. *Rajput* had entered the thin atmosphere below *Auberon*, cutting the lowest chord possible with the elevation, gravity, and friction. To someone on the surface, it would feel like they were being buzzed.

In a way, they were.

Jessica watched as *Rajput* cut her engines. A beat later, she began to rotate on her long axis, point down like a dagger aimed at the surface. She pivoted a half-turn as she rotated, until the ship was coasting backwards at full speed, bow slightly declined as she moved.

Jessica held her breath as *Rajput* came over the horizon from the pirate base. How good were they?

The shot was late and wide.

It lit the late-morning sky with reflected energy as it bled into open space.

The gunners were very good, but they had been expecting *Rajput* to slow down and pop over the horizon for a quick shot, rather than blowing right by at orbital speeds.

And they hadn't been expecting to be looking at *Rajput*'s ass as she appeared, or her guns as she passed.

Three bolts of solid lightning lashed out from *Rajput* as *Auberon* approached the horizon. Jessica had wondered at the man's prioritization. She shouldn't have.

Three Primary bolts hit the Type-4 emplacement in rapid succession as *Rajput*'s gunner locked in. The first was stopped by local shields, barely. The second kicked those shields in like an armed robbery. The third one shattered the entire tower, a pocket, manmade earthquake that left behind a small lake of lava, slowly cooling.

Auberon came into range next. A strike carrier only carried two Primary mounts. She watched Afolayan target the pirates' Primary tower on the left and fire both beams simultaneously.

One shot was well off-center, but the shields absorbed it anyway and failed, followed by the steel and stone of the tower itself.

That left the other tower.

As Jessica watched, the remaining twin gun tower rotated with *Auberon* and began to lift enough to fire, like a snout stuck in the air on a hunting dog. They had been tracking *Rajput* before a better target appeared.

Jessica took a deep breath. *Auberon* had gotten hammered by Primaries at the battle of *Qui-Ping*. It was nearly a terminal experience then. This would be no better.

Or would have been.

Before the pirates could recover, the flight wing popped up over a nearby ridge and opened fire. Seven fighters strafed the hell out of the base, with even *da Vinci* getting in the act with her little single barrel popgun.

Necromancer and two S-11 *Orcas*, *Damocles* and *Starfall*, showered the last Primary tower with everything they had. From here, it looked like a fire-breathing dragon had belched gaseous burning death over everything. If it was only a combination of Type-2 and Type-3 beams, plus missiles, the effect was similar. Larger, perhaps, considered the number of explosions that erupted on the rubble over the course of several seconds.

Jessica let her breath go. That had been far closer than she had planned, or expected. Someone over there knew his business far too well to be just a pirate. She looked forward to a conversation with that person. An unpleasant conversation.

"Flag, this is *Auberon*," Denis said, interrupting her thoughts. "I have two vessels making a run for the edge of the gravity well. You need to see this."

Jessica cursed to herself as she spun the projection back so that she could see the whole battlefield. She had gotten too close, too absorbed, to the battle.

Fortunately, her executive officer had been on the ball.

There, and there.

The transponders on the two enemy vessels finally got displayed.

Oh, my.

One of the vessels was a carrier, what *Corynthe* called a Mothership. It had a big head start and was running hell-bent-for-leather.

The other vessel, much smaller, had been caught in a much lower orbit than the Mothership and was only now getting up a head of speed to try to escape.

Jessica scanned her various readouts of the battle below, but things were pretty much as she had gamed them out. *Rajput* had redlined his engines in a savage braking attempt, to get back into battle, while *CR-264* was too small to get involved with what was happening overhead.

Below, the battle was over. The failure of the crash launch had crippled the pirates' response. Losing the big defensive guns had broken their back.

Overhead…

"Denis," she said, "ignore the pirate and go after the corvette."

"She identifies as a *Fribourg Empire* courier with diplomatic immunity, commander," he replied carefully.

"Acknowledged. That's exactly what she is."

They had just crossed into one of those areas where they were likely to have to explain themselves to a Court of Inquiry.

Tomorrow.

Today, an Imperial corvette was running for the edge of Jumpspace as fast as she could accelerate, leaving behind a pirate base in a system claimed by an ally of the *Republic of Aquitaine*. They could explain it themselves, possibly to *Lincolnshire*, if not to the First Lord himself.

But first, she had to catch him.

"Engineering," she said, also calmly, "redline the engines and hold them together. We have a jackrabbit that needs to be caught before he can get away."

"Affirmative, sir." The Chief Engineer appeared on a screen to nod to her. Vilis Ozolinsh was short, broad, and would have been Mongolian, before the Homeworld was destroyed. He was also a prominent member of one of the Fifty Families that ruled the Republic, but had fallen in love with engines at a young age and never looked back.

"Thank you, Vilis."

Jessica turned to her flag centurion. "Order him to strike, Enej."

"Been doing that, sir," he replied. "He refuses. Claims diplomatic immunity. Still accelerating outbound."

She paused and considered her options. None of them were good. But, conversely, none of them were probably career-ending. She hoped.

"Denis," she said into the bridge radio, "put me on the general comm."

"Go, commander."

"Tactical, this is the Flag," she intoned formally, straight out of the book. It was going to be another one of *those* conversations. She couldn't just attack the Imperial vessel out of hand, but she was still the law in these parts. She had one more tool in her bag, something nobody could ignore, unless they wanted to proclaim themselves pirates.

"We're legal representatives of *Lincolnshire* and they're trespassing here. Order the Imperial vessel to heave to for a *customs inspection*," she continued, her face and voice as serious as she could get. "If he's a courier, he doesn't get to act like a private vessel. When he refuses, fire a shot across his bow under my authority. Because that is a diplomatic vessel, miss by a wide margin. Because I want him to understand that I'm serious, fire a Primary beam when you do it."

Tamara gulped once before she spoke. "Aye, sir," she said. "Stand by."

Auberon's entire hull pulsed a few moments later, a dull hum that was absolutely unique to the big guns firing. It had a feeling like the angel of doom descending.

Jessica waited. That had been the only warning shot required. If they didn't follow the rules now, she was in her authority to treat them like a pirate, like those bastards down on the surface.

That was the down-side of claiming diplomatic immunity. You had to behave. It was a two-edged knife.

"Target has struck her colors, commander," Tamara said a few moments later, visibly relieved that she didn't have to start a more-serious interstellar incident.

"Roger that, Tactical," Jessica said quietly. "Tamara, prepare a prize crew and lead them yourself to take possession of the ship. First officer will accompany you just long enough to escort the diplomat back to *Auberon*."

Jessica paused for a moment, playing out the various scenarios in her head. She had not remotely prepared this scenario. Who would?

"*Cayenne*," she said after a beat. "Prepare for a non-hostile landing party on the Imperial vessel, and a red carpet flight back, transporting an Imperial Ambassador with full honors."

"Really?" came the call from *Cayenne*'s commander, Hollis Dyson, *Gaucho*. He even appeared on one of her screens, tall and skinny with a shaved head and a magnificent handlebar mustache. "An Ambassador?"

Jessica suppressed a smirk at the look of incredulous shock on the man's face.

"Really, *Gaucho*," she replied with a serious look. "Fly nice."

"Aye, sir," he said as he disappeared, deeply dejected.

Jessica smiled. He could have flown ambassadors and Fleet Lords, if he wanted. Certainly, he was probably the best pilot she knew. But he was also the biggest adrenaline junkie she had ever met, which made him a natural fit to fly a DropShip.

There was no more dangerous job in the Fleet. You wanted the crazy ones handling that task. Luckily, she had more than one who matched that criteria.

Jessica's screens showed the aftermath of combat down on the planet. *Auberon* wasn't an Assault Carrier, with a full regiment of marines and armored vehicles to go toe to toe with a bunch of desperate and suicidal pirates down in their warrens. And that was what it would take to capture the place right now.

Rajput had managed to insert herself in a very low geo-synchronous orbit over the base, nose down and most of her weapons pointed at the base like a broadsword. The flight wing was slowly orbiting, far enough out that they couldn't get surprised, close enough that nobody could escape them. Now she just needed to decide what to do with the place.

Since *Auberon* was working under the authority of the *Lincolnshire* government, and this was a pirate outpost, she could legally just sit in orbit and pound the base into the surface of the moon. From here, it already looked like she had gotten a head-start on the task. Every weapons emplacement on the surface had been hit with enough force to qualify as overkill, but the living quarters would be down deep beneath the surface, safe enough unless she got serious.

Or, until.

"Enej," she called across the flag bridge, "what are they saying down there?"

"Not much, sir," he replied with a sardonic grin. "The accent is extremely hard to decipher, but I'm pretty sure I got the gist of what he was suggesting I go do when I told them to surrender."

Jessica smiled and began to unstrap herself from the command chair. "Let me know if they change their minds before I run out of patience."

"Will do, commander. Time for one of Moirrey's surprises?"

Jessica blinked. She had been thinking of this as a nut that needed to be cracked. Maybe there was a way to handle it with flash and misdirection. "Maybe."

She stopped what she was doing and keyed the comm. "Engineering, this is the Flag."

"Go ahead." Moirrey appeared on the screen immediately.

Luck of the draw. She was thinking of the evil engineering gnome, and there she was.

"What does *Project Mischief* suggest for cracking hardened pirate bases on low-gravity moons, Moirrey?" Jessica asked simply.

She watched the tiny woman screw up her face in concentration as she thought furiously.

"Nothing as yet, ma'am," she said after a few seconds. "How soon would you be needing sumtin'?"

"I will let you know, Moirrey," Jessica said. "Right now, I have a meeting with an Imperial Ambassador, and that group down there won't be going anywhere soon."

"Very good, ma'am. Will keeps you posted."

Jessica closed the channel and rose from her seat. After the adrenaline from a battle, she would need a shower to clean up, especially if she was going to get into a dress uniform to receive an Imperial Ambassador.

"Flag, this is *Cayenne*," came the call suddenly. "Thought you would like to know who I'm bringing back."

Jessica opened the image that *Gaucho* sent with his message and gasped.

It was a grainy still, taken from a close-range maneuvering camera, as *Cayenne* backed into a docking airlock with the corvette. It showed a view portal next to the airlock, filled with a variety of people in Imperial uniforms.

One man stood out in the group. Not for his size, as he was a just little taller than average, and well-built but not particularly muscular. No, he looked like a senior Imperial Navy officer. Which he was.

It was the uniform that gave him away. *Fribourg Empire* naval uniforms were a dark blue that was often called navy, from time immemorial. This tunic was the same cut, but a rich maroon, covered with a variety of ribbons and tags. There were two thick stripes on the sleeve visible in the picture, as befit the rank.

He was, after all, an Imperial Admiral of the Red. And his face bore an uncanny resemblance to the Emperor, Karl VII of the House of Wiegand, with the same brown hair graying about halfway up the side. That was to be expected, since this man was a close cousin to his Imperial Highness.

Jessica's prisoner was her old nemesis from *Qui-Ping*, and before that, *2218 Svati Prime*, and before that *Third Iger*.

Emmerich Wachturm.

What the hell was he doing here?

CHAPTER XII

Date of the Republic October 3, 393 Sarmarsh System

Denis stood and came to parade rest as *Cayenne* finally settled on *Auberon's* flight deck. He was in the presence of greatness. Admiral Emmerich Wachturm. *The* admiral.

The Academy at *Ladaux* taught tactics classes based on this man. Upper-level classes. Advanced Fleet Maneuvers. Nobody else born in the last century even rated a mention, Republic or not. Jessica Keller might, before her career was over.

And yet, for all that, Wachturm was still human. Perhaps a finger taller. A few kilos heavier. But possessed of an air of command that Denis would have said was unique, before he met Jessica Keller. They were of an ilk, if there was such a thing.

The admiral rose as well and faced Denis from across the aisle with a grim smile. "Senior Centurion Jež," he said with a rich voice, "it has been a pleasure meeting you, regardless of the circumstances. You reflect well on your commander. I look forward to making her acquaintance."

Denis nodded sagely and tried to look serious. Inside, he was trying to decide how immature it would look right now if he asked the man for his autograph.

How often did you meet a legend?

"Passengers, please stand by for deboarding," *Gaucho* called from behind his armored bulkhead up front.

That was much more polite than *Gaucho* normally sounded. Apparently, even he could be duly impressed.

The rest of the admiral's staff finished unbuckling and stood. The man had only three others with him. One appeared to be a steward, the rough equivalent of what Marcelle Travere did for Keller. Another was obviously a bodyguard, but well-trained and unobtrusive. He had surrendered a whole suitcase of weapons into Denis's custody without a peep. The last was a younger officer, probably a flag centurion. No wait, didn't the *Fribourg Empire* call them command lieutenants, or something equally strange?

They were taking this better than Denis had expected, although nobody over there looked happy. Not a surprise, considering the circumstances. Who liked being mousetrapped?

Denis nodded politely to the men. All men. The entire *Fribourg Empire* was run by men, for men. Women were not allowed into the military, lest they be somehow "soiled" by the experience. It was a dumb idea.

Denis kept his smile to himself at the thought. Roughly half of the *Republic of Aquitaine* Navy was female, and, if his boss was an example, it was the better half.

Denis checked the landing camera screen and saw that everything was in order. He keyed the comm live.

"*Cayenne*, this is Jež, standing by."

Gaucho responded by opening the side hatch.

Denis went first, down three steps and onto the deck. He stepped to one side and turned inward, part of a reception line that included a significant amount of the command crew, although the flight wing was all still outside keeping watch on the bad guys.

The rest of the deck was cleared of everything. Denis couldn't remember the last time it had been set up like this. Certainly not when Command Centurion Kwok took over, four years ago.

And Denis and his staff had pushed their luck by leaving the deck a mess when Jessica first came aboard, just barely a year ago. *Had it really only been a year?*

The best comparison Denis could think of would be if the First Lord, Nils Kasum, were to visit. Then it would be just like that in here. As it should.

"Attention," Denis called, projecting his voice off of every flat surface in the bay like thunder on a calm day.

Feet came together and bodies came still.

The last trailing tidbits of noise vanished, leaving only the hiss of air systems.

"Presenting his Imperial Excellency, Admiral of the Red, Emmerich Wachturm, Hereditary Duke of Eklionstic, Imperial Ambassador."

The Admiral appeared at the top of the steps, alone, as befit his rank and station. He paused there for a moment, majestically, before carefully stepping down onto *Auberon*'s flight deck.

Two rows of officers and crew in their best day uniforms lined a carpet, red for historical reasons, down which the Admiral slowly walked.

Denis fell in as the admiral passed, one step behind and to the man's right. The rest of the admiral's staff trailed behind Denis silently. Everything by the book. Everything was in the book, even this. He followed the man to a small dais that powered up out of the deck for exactly this sort of reception.

Command Centurion Keller stood alone atop the dais. Normally there would be several other officers with her for this ceremony, but he was down here escorting the man. Tamara was over on the corvette, being politely in charge after the Admiral had threatened to practically excommunicate the Imperial Captain if he did anything wrong. Iskra Vlahovic, the flight deck commander, was happy not interacting with people unless she had to.

That left Keller alone to face the man and his entire suite of assistants. It looked evenly matched. Denis fought down his grin.

"Admiral Wachturm," Jessica said, warmly despite the formality of the language, "it is my pleasure to welcome you aboard *Auberon* and to place myself and my crew at your service."

Denis waited. His job at this point was to provide diplomatic lubrication in the case of awkward circumstances. After several hours with the man, he couldn't imagine awkward circumstances here. So he waited.

The admiral actually clicked his heels together and nodded deeply to Jessica. Again, appropriate between a visiting grandee and a simple command centurion, regardless of the situation outside.

"Command Centurion Keller," the man replied. "I look forward to my visit. I have studied your career with interest since the episode known to Republic historians as *Third Iger* and look forward to being able to make the acquaintance of you and your crew."

Denis watched as the man stepped up onto the dais and turned to address the crew. The rest of the afternoon would be formal speeches and a reception, but the admiral looked like a man who felt he held all the trump cards. He obviously had never had to deal with Jessica, or any woman like her.

The *Fribourg Empire* didn't have women like her.

Denis let himself smile.

Wachturm was going to realize soon that he had a tiger by the tail, not the other way around.

CHAPTER XIII

Date of the Republic October 4, 393 Sarmarsh System

Jessica had decided to have this meeting in her office, rather than one of the big or little conference rooms. The First Lord had taught her the importance of that level of personal touch, especially with a situation as delicate as this.

It was one thing to capture an Imperial courier-cum-spy doing naughty things and chastise him. That was practically part of her job description.

It was something entirely else to take the Emperor's cousin and best fleet commander hostage. She would, very soon, be explaining this one to the First Lord, and possibly the entire Senate. Best to do it right.

Her office was plain, almost to the point of severe. Her desk. A backboard with two non-standard filing cabinets, because few commanders liked paper. A sideboard where Marcelle's coffee service normally sat. Two chairs for guests.

Her only decoration was a small quilt her mother had made for her when she'd been first commissioned, with the Republic seal in white on a dark green background, framed and hung on the sidewall above the sideboard. Other knick-knacks would have to be bolted down for emergency maneuvering, and would have taken up space, so she just had the desk, the sideboard, and two chairs.

Clean, simple, focused.

Marcelle knocked on the door and then opened it.

Jessica rose as Marcelle escorted Admiral Wachturm into her sanctum.

"Admiral," she said simply, shaking his hand.

He smiled a gruff smile. "Commander."

She waited for him to sit and then joined him.

Rather than make small talk, they both watched Marcelle make coffee by hand, grinding the beans she had roasted two days before, pouring them into a press, adding just enough hot water to soften the stark bitterness. Honey, syrup, and freshly thawed cream were placed on the table between the two before Marcelle took her leave.

The two warriors studied each other silently for several minutes over the rims of truly excellent coffee. The air had taken on a warm feel.

"Not many people," the admiral finally began, "have the patience to outwait me. Especially not in a situation like this."

Jessica nodded with a wry smile. "I fear you are correct, sir."

He reached inside a breast pocket and pulled a small leather wallet, a courier satchel, with his right hand as he continued to sip the coffee. He placed the satchel on the desk, next to the water pot, and opened it one-handed. The admiral pulled a heavy piece of paper from the dark leather and laid it flat, spinning it around so she could read.

"Just to get the diplomatic niceties out of the way, Commander Keller," he said quietly. Expectantly.

Jessica took the paper from him and studied it. Imperial Ambassador at large. Diplomatic immunity. Etc. Mind your p's and q's.

Jessica considered her response. Like every campaign, she had planned a number of maneuvers and solutions ahead of time, to make it easier to react in the heat of battle.

"Should I address you as Admiral or Ambassador?" she said, opening the bidding rather high.

His eyes got a canny look, squinting slightly as he took her measure across the desk.

"That would depend," he drawled, "on your official capacity here."

Jessica nodded. Call.

"Officially," she countered, "my squadron has been seconded to assist the *Lincolnshire* government with a piracy problem on their outer borders. In that capacity, we were on patrol, investigating reports of a pirate base in the neighborhood of *Sarmarsh*."

She paused to take a long sip of the coffee before it lost that perfect edge. Marcelle made the best coffee, especially when she knew she had an audience that would appreciate it.

"Once we arrived, we came under fire from said pirates," she continued. "While dealing with that issue, we encountered two vessels attempting to flee the area. Given the circumstances, I chose to pursue and apprehend your vessel, and let the other escape."

Again, more coffee.

He watched her like a mongoose watched a python. Or perhaps how a python watched a mongoose.

"Upon review," she said, upping the ante a notch, "the other vessel, the one that did escape, was a class of carrier called a Mothership, of a design commonly used in *Corynthe*. Which would suggest that the base below was part of a quiet invasion of *Lincolnshire*'s space, and not just a bunch of pirates. How did you come to be in the vicinity?"

She watched him take his own long sip of the coffee. His face gave away very little, not that she had expected it to. Perhaps a twinkle in his eyes, as if this was a game he was playing with her. One he expected to win.

"We were on a trade mission," he said with great seriousness.

"I see," she replied. Rolling her eyes at that statement would be rude. Appropriate but rude. She settled for a neutral smile.

"So when I go down there and destroy the place," she continued, "I won't find any evidence of an Imperial conspiracy with *Corynthe* or *Salonnia*?"

He gave her a feral, hungry grin. "Anything you found would obviously be a fake, Commander, planted to make the Emperor, and the entire *Fribourg Empire*, look bad."

"Yes, I expected as much," she said quietly.

Jessica set down her coffee and picked up the document to more closely study it.

"Which brings us back to this document," she said.

"Yes?" He was all ear, confident in his position. Obviously, the great admiral had planned his response well.

"If you're an Ambassador," she pounced, "then I should be escorting you and your vessel to *Ramsey* to present your credentials to the government there. Anything else might suggest that you really were a spy, and the rules of war are very different for that sort of thing."

She was greatly rewarded by the sudden flickering of his pupils as they shrank. Nothing else about his face changed, just that.

It still spoke volumes.

She watched him finish the coffee.

"I did not want to mention it earlier, Commander Keller," he transitioned smoothly. "My vessel was actually responding to a distress call from the base, not long before you arrived. I felt it would be impolite to broadcast to everyone that the colony down there was so poorly run, you understand."

Jessica smiled. Admiral Wachturm was far more entertaining to fence with than the robot.

"I do," she replied. "Understand, that is."

She carefully folded up the parchment and handed it back to the man.

"In that case," she continued, "you would simply be a neutral vessel on a mercy mission in deep space, and not really an ambassador to a group of pirates causing troubles to a Republic ally. Am I correct?"

For a moment, he gave her the look of a man that had sucked a lemon dry. But only for a moment, before he recovered.

"Indeed," he recovered swiftly. "So I will be free to go on my way shortly? After, of course, all the diplomatic niceties and receptions, of course?"

She inclined her head slightly, baiting the hook one last time. "While I believe that it would be proper for your vessel to return to Imperial space as soon as possible, Admiral," she drawled lazily, "the circumstances of why you came to be here, now, instead of heading directly to *Ramsey* to present your credentials, require some investigation. And while I would like to be able to transport you to the capital to explain it, I fear that my vessel will, of necessity, have to continue in pursuit of this apparent pirate invasion, which will likely take us to *Corynthe*. Unfortunately, your staff will have to travel with us until proper arrangements can be made."

She finished off her coffee as well. Marcelle would be two steps outside the cabin door, waiting patiently, probably with a book, but Jessica suspected that they would not need any more coffee. At least, not right now.

Admiral Wachturm grimaced. Gruff and friendly was gone. This was harsher, far more stoic. A man who might have met a competitor worth engaging, possibly even his match.

"*Hostage* is such a vulgar term," he said into the gap.

"It is, sir," she replied, polite if not sickly sweet. "I promise that you will be treated as a most honored guest during your stay. And probably subject to some level of awkward hero worship from my crew. But necessity dictates that things aren't always the way we prefer."

He set his coffee mug down carefully and studied her face, looking for something.

After a moment, he found it, whatever it was.

He nodded once, carefully.

Jessica nodded back, just as precisely. This was not a man to trifle with.

And she was not a woman to simply be pushed aside.

CHAPTER XIV

Date of the Republic October 5, 393 Sarmarsh System

Denis had apparently entered the big engineering conference room last, from the mob of people already present. Jessica had saved him a chair, at her right hand. It was fitting.

He looked around as he sat. Several engineers and senior officers were present. And all the big players: Tamara Strnad, his tactical officer; Navin Crncevic, the ship's dragoon; Vilis Ozolinsh, the chief engineer; Iskra Vlahovic, the flight deck commander; Anastazja Slusarczyk, commander of the GunShip *Necromancer*; and Hollis Dyson, *Gaucho*, the commander of *Cayenne*.

The latter did not bode well. It suggested that something crazier than normal was brewing.

Jessica rapped her fist on the table to bring order to the murmurs.

"Okay, people," she announced to the room, "they've had forty hours to stew down there. We don't have the resources to storm the place. At least, not without heavy casualties. Marines are crazy, but not bulletproof."

She nodded to the giant black man who led the fifty-eight member marine contingent, commonly called *Navin the Black* by his own people, as though he were an ancient Viking. He smiled and nodded back.

"How do we neutralize the base?" Jessica concluded.

Tamara leaned forward with a careful look on her face. "If you don't want them to escape," she began, "we could sit up here for a week or so with the Type-3's and just blast the surface until we melt everything and bury them. Husbands the Primaries and missiles when we can't restock them out here. I presume you are looking for a solution that is either faster or more humane?"

"Thank you, Tamara," Jessica replied. "Yes to the latter. Faster and more humane."

Denis considered the situation below. The base had been disarmed by all the strikes, but not particularly damaged. The flight bay had suffered a catastrophic failure, so they had no immediate way off the moon until they fixed something, but they couldn't do that while *Auberon* and her consorts sat overhead.

"Have we offered them a carrot?" Denis asked quietly.

The room fell into stunned silence.

Pirates?

"A carrot?" Jessica asked him.

"Sure, we've got the stick. If they don't see a carrot, they're just going to have to assume we're here to kill them all, and they're going to make that as expensive as they can." He shrugged. "I would."

"We could turn it into a refugee crisis," Enej said from the opposite corner of the table. Denis had missed the man when he walked in.

"Explain, Enej," Jessica said clearly intrigued.

"Right now, they're pirates, and we're the Republic," he said with a wry smile. "*Aquitaine* hunts down pirates and hangs them. That's how it's always been done."

Several hands and fists pounded the table. Many of the crew came from poorer worlds where piracy was an everyday fact of life. People like Moirrey Kermode, but there were many others from the Outer Reaches.

"So," Enej continued over the noise, "what if we treat the place like it had just suffered a major natural disaster, and all these fine folks are colonists that need to be transported back to where they came, with nothing more than what they can carry on their backs?"

He leaned back and smiled at the abrupt, shocked silence that rippled around the room.

Denis was reminded of a still pond on a quiet fall morning, with a little fog on the water. And then some enterprising twelve-year-old hurled a great big rock as far out as he could, shattering the calm with a huge splash of energy. The folks around him were like that.

Denis turned to his boss. "There you go, commander," he said. "A carrot."

She rewarded them with a warm grin. "And here I was trying to figure out the orbital mechanics necessary to redirect one of the asteroids and slam it into the moon hard enough to kill that base."

"Ooh," Moirrey piped up from the engineering end of the table. "Gots that covered, ma'am. Nina does, that is."

Denis looked at that corner and saw Auberon's primary pilot, Nina Zupan, sitting between the flag centurion and Yeoman Moirrey Kermode, blushing uncomfortably as the engineer pointed at her.

"Is that true, Zupan?" Jessica asked.

"Yes, sir," Nina replied. "But it was Moirrey's idea. I just did the math."

"Tell me," Jessica commanded.

"Is simple, ma'am," Moirrey chirped as the room listened. Moirrey's radio drama narrations during the Long Raid had kept the crew alternatively rapt and giggling. She had a background on stage that made her a natural speaker.

"The gas giant's orbitin' a wee faster bit than the asteroids in the belt. We could pick out one of the bigger ones, attach a big boom to knock it out of line and some thrusters, and fly it out an' slam it into the bigger moon pretty easy. Jus' needs ta know when you wants to blow up the base so's we know which one to pick."

"An asteroid?" Jessica said with a blink.

"Aye, ma'am." Moirrey smiled. "Considered a comet, but they's harder to find the right one, and are mostly fried ice cream anyway. Crunchy shell, squishy middle. Probably just drop a new lake on the surface of the moon. Might drown 'em eventually, if ya gots time to wait."

Jessica leaned back and sipped her coffee as the folks around the table tried to suppress snorts and laughter. Denis could see the wheels in Jessica's head turning as she plotted all the permutations. That was what made her *her*.

Abruptly, she made up her mind. Another thing she did so much better than Command Centurion Kwok, her immediate predecessor. Not that Denis missed him one bit.

She leaned forward decisively.

"Okay, gold stars for everyone today," she announced, like a school teacher with a rowdy class. "Moirrey, you and Nina go ahead and find me a rock. I want to annihilate this base in five to seven days. They get that long to decide if they want to be survivors. Everyone else, figure out what you can do to help make that happen."

Denis watched her stand suddenly, nod at everyone, and depart.

He rose as well. Time to make it happen.

"Navin and *Gaucho*," he said loudly. "Find me everyone with enough zero-G experience to work on our hammer, once we have it identified. Engineering, we'll need spare thrusters from the flight deck and a really big shaped charge to make this work. Let's go, people."

CHAPTER XV

Date of the Republic October 6, 393 Sarmarsh System

Jessica walked out onto *Auberon*'s bridge in the middle of the main shift and took a moment to look around. See and be seen. This was another of those moments that was likely to cement her reputation a complete hard-ass in the fleet. Might as well do it right.

She had taken a long shower to relax, and taken the time to put on her best dress uniform, the one she wore to diplomatic receptions with the longer tunic and the slight flair to the pants. Three white stripes on the right sleeve. *Auberon*'s namesake patch on the left shoulder.

Nothing else. Nothing needed.

Her hair was pulled back. It was long enough now that she would have to decide soon if she wanted a tail or should cut it severely. She hadn't decided what the future would bring. When it did, she would adjust.

It was what she did best.

Denis Jež was in the command chair, as was his wont when he wasn't doing paperwork. They had already made the arrangements to have everyone on duty today, now, so she was dealing with the most senior crew. That would just make it easier.

Denis nodded to her and gestured to the chair, silently asking if she wanted to sit. It was technically her seat, since she was the command centurion, but she almost always worked down on the flag bridge. Being there required to her think bigger than just one vessel, useful when she had a whole squadron to command, and, in this case, political and diplomatic repercussions to consider.

The bridge seemed to grow quieter, as conversations tapered off. Good, the seriousness was not lost on people.

"Flag bridge, please contact the base on *Alpha* and get me the person in charge," she said, loud enough to carry to every corner.

"Stand by, Commander," the flag centurion said over the comm. "I had already contacted them a little early. He's waiting for you."

Jessica grinned to herself, just for a moment, and then physically banished it. It was amazing how good her crew really was, some days. Far better than she had expected, or deserved. But they were a weapon she was forging, against the day when the First Lord let her go on the offensive.

All seriousness, she turned to Auberon's primary pilot, the Danish-looking elf, Nada Zupan. "Bring him up on the main screen, Zupan," she said, serious quiet in the gap. "Let's see who we're dealing with."

The screen blinked, turned to static, and then resolved to a flat image of a man.

Jessica judged him to be a little older than she was, perhaps forty standard years. He had long dark blond hair, loose and somewhat askew, and a matching beard, and had that tattered look of too little sleep, accentuated by a smear of something black that had been absently wiped on his cheek, and deep bags under the eyes.

He looked like he would clean up well, especially for a pirate on the fringes of the world. The cat-green eyes were still sharp.

Jessica gave him her most serious look. She was the Law here, in more ways than one.

"I am Command Centurion Jessica Keller," she intoned, fully aware that these words would be played back at her next court martial someday, most likely. "Aboard the *Republic of Aquitaine* warship *Auberon*. And you are?"

She watched him take a slow breath as he studied her in turn. The pause dragged. She was almost ready to continue when he spoke.

"My name is Daneel Ishikura," he said, in a voice that was a pleasant, deep tenor. "I am *Corynthe*'s governor for this system."

"According to the authorities at *Ramsey*, this is a *Lincolnshire* world," she replied. "That makes this an illegal colony, and you, trespassers."

He took another breath before he continued. Jessica was impressed at his control. She could see the exhaustion written on his face. The last three days couldn't have been fun. At least they had gotten all the fires out in what remained of the flight bay.

"And they sent the Republic to destroy us?" The question was a quiet snarl. He didn't have much leverage, and knew it.

"On the contrary," she said, lightening her tone. Time for the carrot. It might even work. "I was hunting pirates that have been plaguing the sector. Those I intend to utterly destroy."

She paused to let that sink in. A little stick never hurt.

"In the process, I came across this colony. It being illegal, you will have to dismantle it and return to your home worlds in *Corynthe*," she pressed the point. "However, since you seem to have suffered some manner of natural disaster, I am prepared to provide transport for your people."

"You were the disaster, *Aquitaine*," he yelled, rising from the chair. She only realized he had been sitting because the camera software was slow to react as he rose to his feet. "You destroyed this base."

Jessica took a breath of her own to calm her emotions. Hadn't the Premier and First Lord both said she needed to work on her diplomatic skills? She would need them, in spades, one of these days, unless she planned to be just a commander for her whole career. Could she dream bigger? This was the first trial.

"I destroyed the pirates, Ishikura," she said carefully. "Civilian hostages and innocent colonists do not have to be hung. I'm willing to lump your whole lot in there and take you home."

They stared at each other for several moments. Around *Auberon*'s bridge, even the air systems seemed to be holding their breath, not just the crew.

"Or else?" he asked her, finally.

And now, the stick. Or, in this case, the saber. The strong left hand when blade dancing.

"In a little over 150 hours, I will cause one of the asteroids from the belt to bolide into this base at orbital velocity," she said simply, trying to remove all trace of emotion from her voice.

This was just an act of war, nothing more. Not revenge. Not execution.

Now, the carrot.

"If you and your people are still there, they will be destroyed with the base. However, if you surrender in the next forty-eight hours, I will have time evacuate all of your people and transport you to *Corynthe*. You won't have much more than what you can carry. But you will not be dead."

"What kind of an option is that, Keller?"

She glowered harshly at the man. Inside, she was surprised he had caught and remembered her name, as tired and stressed as he appeared. Apparently, he was sharper than he looked.

"*Lincolnshire* will give me a medal when I annihilate your base, Ishikura," she said. "If this base was an act of war against *Lincolnshire*, then the *Republic* will send me with more fleets to destroy *Corynthe* as well. It is an outcome I find unnecessary, today. You could change my mind."

"And what makes you any better than a pirate, *Aquitaine*?" he hissed.

"A willingness to withhold the blade, mister," she replied with a harsh finality. "You have forty-eight hours."

Jessica turned to the pilot and signaled with one hand.

She watched Zupan push a switch, confirm it, and nod back to her.

"Signal cut, Commander," the pilot said simply.

"One hundred and fifty hours, Commander?" he asked. "So scenario three?"

Jessica turned to Denis. She was rewarded by his calm competence. It was so powerful to be able to ask for a random pirate base in the middle of nowhere to be killed by slamming a giant rock into it, and know that her people would move heaven and earth to make it happen.

Literally, in this case.

"Yes, please, Denis," she replied. "Let me know what you need."

"Just your testimony at my court martial, sir." He smiled up at her.

"Mine will be first, Denis, I promise you that."

She turned to encompass the rest of the bridge crew. "We will most likely know the final outcome in far less than two days, people," she said raising her voice enough to be heard. "Monitor all their transmissions and let me know when they make their final decision."

She watched heads nod in her direction, and departed the bridge.

She had already made up her mind to destroy the base by the most emphatic method possible. Hopefully, she might be able to rescue the people first.

Killing on that scale had never kept her awake at night. Even if it was war and those people were either invaders, or they were armed outlaws facing the posse. Either way, this would be murder, plain and simple.

Like dropping a bag of kittens into a river.

Anything necessary to accomplish the job. That had always been her motto.

Right now, she wasn't so sure.

But she could never let that be known.

CHAPTER XVI

Date of the Republic October 7, 393 Sarmarsh System

Imperial Admiral of the Red Emmerich Wachturm entered the officer's wardroom with a moment of trepidation. This would be an entirely new world.

Auberon was a *Republic of Aquitaine* vessel. A proud one. At one time, flagship of the forces across the *Cahllepp Frontier* from his own Imperial fleet. Now, the personal chariot of Jessica Keller. No, strike that. This ship was the sword in her left hand.

She rose as he approached the main table and smiled warmly at him. He was struck again by the resemblance to his youngest daughter, Henrietta, generally known to all as Heike. It was there in the physicality of the two women, although Jessica Keller was a decade and a half older. Perhaps, it was what he hoped his daughter would turn into, someday.

They had the same build, the same eyes, that same look. Underneath, the same voracious intellect.

For Keller, it meant that she had gone from a blue collar family to the heights of the Republic fleet, limited only by time in grade, not by any shortcomings of her own.

Heike's life, her potential, was more limited, only in that she was a woman in a man's Empire. *Fribourg* would not tolerate women in combat. Females from the Republic were Amazons, not Imperial Ladies. Best they be treated as such, exotic creatures from beyond the pale.

And yet…

Emmerich was informally introduced to Keller's inner staff, at what she had promised would be a working dinner, rather than a state affair. He looked forward to taking their measure as people and professionals, not as to how well they remembered their classes in deportment.

At his right sat Denis Jež, Keller's first officer, continuing his role as aide to the ambassador, regardless of the need. The man reminded him of his own long-time assistant, Flag Captain Hendrik Baumgärtner, who was currently hopefully enjoying a well-deserved vacation with his family back home.

On Emmerich's left hand, *Auberon*'s chief engineer, Vilis Ozolinsh, a short, broad, Oriental man who spoke with the tight, clipped accent of the best schools on *Anameleck Prime*. Here was a man of the highest social standing, serving as merely an engineer, something else the *Empire* would never have understood. Or accepted.

Down both sides of the table, two other women sat politely. Tamara Strnad, the tactical officer, a role with no equivalent in the Fribourg Empire, where captains were expected to fight their ships in real time, rather than handing off those decisions to others. That had to slow things down, didn't it?

Across from Strnad, an average looking woman with short blond hair. He had been briefed by Jež head of time that Iskra Vlahovic, the flight deck commander, was a very quiet woman and unlikely to speak much during dinner. The light was low, but just bright enough to show a small hairline scar on the left side of her head, starting just behind the cheek and arcing gracefully backwards over her ear. Apparently, a trophy from her last combat flight, after which she spent six months in the hospital learning to walk and talk again. Followed by turning herself into a flight engineer, when she could have honorably retired and enjoyed her life.

Again, something else the Empire would not understand.

It was an interesting group of people that fate had conspired to bring together. When Jessica Keller first came to his attention after the recent battle at *Iger*, Emmerich had wondered if her mission last year had been the luck of audacity, or something deeper. Now he would be in a position to finally discover the truth.

At least he would be allowed to return home eventually. That was something to look forward to, as opposed to the insultingly-long debriefings that the Security and Intelligence Services would subject him to, having been a prisoner of the Republic and Keller. But he could go home, after he was done here.

So, until then, he would learn all there was to learn about this woman and her staff. There would come a day when that information would be both useful, and necessary.

The food, in seven courses, was amazing. There was simply no other way to explain it. His own personal chef aboard his battleship, *IFV Amsel*, was extremely good. Keller's was an artist.

He burped in spite of himself and reached for his wine glass.

"Thank you, Commander Keller," he said, loud enough to be heard by the stewards along the walls, "for a most amazing dinner. If we were at peace, I would try to hire your chef away from you. I hope I am able to host you to an equally exceptional dinner, sometime in the future."

He toasted her chef with his glass. The other joined in.

"And now," he continued in a much quieter voice, eyes locking with Keller's down the long length of the table, "I would like to know more about how you plan to resolve things on the planet below us."

Emmerich was careful not to call them invaders, now or at any time. It served a polite fiction for everyone to pretend otherwise, and let him enjoy his time here, rather than being permanently stowed politely away in a hastily converted "flag suite," with doors that locked from the outside.

He watched Keller put her glass down carefully and observe. First him, and then each of her staff in turn. All eyes had turned to face her, leaving him silhouettes and hair to look at.

"Having arrived and eliminated the immediate threat," she said carefully, "the obvious next choice would be to reduce the base, so that it cannot ever be used again."

Emmerich was fascinated by her choice of words. He could see her choosing them with care before she spoke.

"*Lincolnshire* does not have any capital-scale warships capable of dislodging a force like we found here," Jessica continued. "The more so because their fleet largely consists of second hand Escorts and Destroyers. Just destroying the forces here isn't enough. They would come back eventually, like rats."

She paused to take a drink of wine and think before she continued.

"So you will just destroy the base?" Emmerich asked. "I have heard rumors of a redirected asteroid being used as a weapon."

It was an elegant solution, worthy of her growing legend. Others would bomb the place, or attempt to storm it. Instead, she was taking the thing that offended her and annihilating it utterly. It was truly *The Grand Gesture.*

"That would be correct, Admiral," she said with a hint of smile. "We will level the entire mountain being used as a base. Now it remains only to be seen if the inhabitants down there will surrender peacefully, or be destroyed along with it."

Emmerich stopped. He was sure there was a look of utter befuddlement on his face, but he didn't bother to cover his confusion.

"Surrender peacefully?" he asked, surprised. "*Fribourg* would have already razed the base."

"If the situation were reversed, Admiral Wachturm, with you in charge of similar forces, how would you deal with them?"

Emmerich leaned back in his chair and swirled his wine, more to gain time than for show. *Auberon* and her consorts were so much smaller and less capable than *Amsel.* Powerful, yes. Dangerous, exceedingly. But greatly limited. A Strike Carrier, after all, was an under-gunned cruiser with a short fighter squadron, not a full Task Force like he normally commanded.

He gestured to the Republic tactical officer, the woman Tamara Strnad.

"Given the opportunity to make *Le Beau Geste,*" he said carefully, "I would have hammered the surface of a base a few more times, just to make sure they were well and truly trapped underground. Then, I believe I like the idea of using an asteroid to finish them. It is this silliness about negotiation that I find disconcerting."

Jessica nodded in agreement.

"If wishes were fishes, sir," she replied, "I would have something like *Amsel's* forces at hand to deal with this situation."

"With *Amsel,* I would have already taken the place intact."

"Ah," she smiled at him, "but your battleship fields a huge ground combat force, Admiral. You can pay that particular butcher's bill. I cannot, so we are going to attempt diplomacy first."

Diplomacy? With invaders from Corynthe?

Emmerich mentally reduced his overall opinion of Keller's brilliance by an entire notch as he listened, carefully keeping his face neutral.

If she was trying that, then she must be in over her head. Or, worse, possessed of some sort of squeamishness that prevented her from acting with the utter ruthlessness he had expected. Was she over-rated, after all?

"I see," he said, more as a placeholder than because he did. It was a polite placeholder. "And then what?"

She smiled more warmly at him. "Then we transport them to *Corynthe* and give them a good talking to."

Never in his life had Emmerich heard a more silly proposal, especially not from a serving officer, to say nothing of a commander. Suddenly, the rightness of the *Fribourg Empire*'s prohibition of women in service made so much more sense.

If *Aquitaine*'s most dangerous commander was all soft and gooey underneath, was there any doubt why they were losing the Great War?

"I look forward to following things as they unfold, Commander Keller."

Emmerich rose from the table. The rest rose with him.

"And now, if you will excuse me, I find myself exhausted by such rich and interesting company. I will take my leave and bid you a good evening. Senior Centurion Jež, if you would?"

Emmerich really didn't need to write all of this down to remember it, but it would be invaluable to the Intelligence Services to have all of his impressions recorded fresh from having taken Keller's measure, as little as he had suddenly found it to be.

Jessica watched Denis escort the imperial Admiral out of the wardroom, and no doubt, back to his den, there to compose his reports like a good little spy. At her right hand, Tamara Strnad started to say something, but Jessica cut her off with a finger before a sound came out.

Jessica turned to Iskra and Vilis. Both nodded to her, Vilis with a tremendous grin on his face as he bowed to her then departed. Iskra gave her a contented shrug and followed the engineer.

"Let us," Jessica said to the tactical officer, "retire to my office and have some coffee. We can chat there."

Tamara nodded at her, mute, but followed.

The office, when they got there, had not changed. Nothing was allowed to change here. This was where she worked, comfortable in her space.

Jessica gestured to the chair as Marcelle followed the two women in, a coffee service already organized on a tray.

"Am I getting predictable, Marcelle?" Jessica asked.

"Not at all, sir," the tall woman replied. "I had expected everyone staying with the admiral for more questions, or you staying up well past your bedtime doing reports."

Jessica smiled. *Predictable* was the wrong word, but it was probably close.

"Tamara, please sit," Jessica said as Marcelle poured two mugs and departed. "You look confused."

"Yes, sir," Tamara replied.

"Not the conversation you were expecting me to have with the admiral?"

"No, sir."

"What were you expecting, Tamara?"

Jessica watched the woman screw up her face in concentration, unsure of how to phrase her words.

"Speak freely, Tamara," Jessica continued. "Easier that way to make sure everything is clear."

"Okay, sir," the tactical officer replied after a moment. "You came across as…soft. Almost weak. Not at all what I would have expected. I would have thought we wanted to impress him."

Jessica smiled. Denis had made the connection, as had Iskra and Vilis. Only Tamara had missed it.

Lesson learned. Her tactical officer was as much in need of having her horizons broadened as Jessica was. Her own failing for not making sure Tamara understood. Fortunately, an easily correctable mistake.

"Tamara."

"Hmmm?"

"Emmerich Wachturm is possibly the best tactician the Empire has."

"Yes, sir."

"We don't want to impress him with our competence."

"We don't?"

"No, Tamara," Jessica said. "If we impress him, then he takes us seriously. More seriously. If we underwhelm him, he will hopefully underestimate us when it counts."

"Sir?"

"Tamara, he may be a perfect gentleman and a worldly scholar, but he is *still* the enemy."

"Oh."

Jessica watched the woman's eyes light up with understanding.

"Oh!"

"Yes," Jessica agreed. "Hopefully, right now, he is busy writing a report about how over-rated I am and how much they can discount my stock as a commander, attributing everything to pure luck and timing. All because I'm a woman and soft."

"Got it, sir. Will it work?"

"Every little bit helps, Tamara," Jessica concluded. "We'll have to fight that man again, one of these days."

CHAPTER XVII

Date of the Republic October 8, 393 Sarmarsh System

The chime got her attention. Jessica hadn't been asleep, but day dreaming lightly. She *had* been up too late doing paperwork, until Marcelle dragged her to bed. It was mid-day shift now. Perhaps something to pick up her afternoon?

The chime sounded again. Yes, someone wanted her attention.

She put down her pen and keyed the microphone.

"Keller. Go ahead."

"A Mister Ishikura requests your attention, sir," Centurion Giroux, in charge of sensors and communications today, said politely.

Jessica checked the clock. The base below them still had several hours before her deadline. Was he expecting to negotiate?

Tough luck on that, mister.

Jessica stretched her back and shoulders quickly to loosen up. Too much paperwork. Not enough time with the fighting robot.

"Patch him through, Giroux," she said as she put on her serious face.

She considered leaving the video function off, but decided that was just being petty.

Ishikura had taken the time to clean up since she last saw him. His hair was combed neatly and the black smear of something had been cleaned off. The bags under his eyes were just as bad, perhaps a little less, and the eyes themselves a little less bloodshot.

"Commander Keller," he said after a moment. His voice was at pains to be polite today. Perhaps he had already gone through all the stages of death?

So, going out in a blaze of glory or living to fight another day?

"Mister Ishikura," she replied.

They studied each other for several moments.

"That's not the bridge of your ship," he finally said.

She glanced over her shoulder at the view he would have.

"Correct, this is my office. I was doing paperwork. What can I do for you, Mr. Ishikura?"

"Are you really going to destroy this base?"

She looked closely at him. Engineering that massive was probably magic to most people. It was part of what made the Republic and Imperial Navies so impressive, the ability to work on that scale. Nobody out here on the galactic fringe could do that.

"When the rock I am using hits," she said simply, "I will go a long ways towards knocking that moon out of orbit of *Sarmarsh IV*, although my staff assures me it will not actually break away. Large sections of the planetoid will be reformed by the amount of energy released. Your base will be a soap bubble in the path of a bullet."

"And you are still willing to transport all of the survivors from the surface back to *Corynthe*?"

She could see something in his eyes. Possibly hope, which had probably been snuffed out like a candle when *Auberon* and *Rajput* had come over the horizon firing.

"Under very specific circumstances, Ishikura," she replied. The iron was there in her voice for him to hear. Diplomacy just might have to be damned until after she had made her point here.

"Such as?" he said, carefully, deliberately.

"Your people will only be able to take what they can carry," she replied. Iron. "They will be searched before transport. My people will inspect the base. If any of them get hurt in the process, I will hang you all in low gravity."

"Those are your terms?" he asked. From his voice, he knew just how little rope he had. As someone had once described it for her, enough to hang and no more.

"They are," she replied. "If you have any dead-enders wanting to do something stupid, I suggest you take care of them right now and give everyone else a chance to get home."

"And you will keep your word? Take us to *Corynthe*?"

"Ishikura," she said, beginning to verge on exasperation, "my mission was to deal with the pirate threat plaguing *Lincolnshire*. The military aspect has been completed, but without a diplomatic solution, it will return, like a bad penny. I have more important things to do than keep coming out here. If you can see to reason, perhaps the *King of the Pirates* can as well. You should convince him."

She watched the man laugh quietly to himself.

"And what amuses you so, Mr. Ishikura?"

"I was exiled out here because that man got tired of my advice."

"Well, then, perhaps with my assistance, you'll be able to make him listen. I'm very good at that."

"Yes," he agreed with a weak smile. "Your arguments have been most effective, Keller. I will accept your terms. We will be ready to begin transport in a few hours."

"Very well," she agreed. "One of my people will contact you with details shortly."

She watched his shoulders unslump as she closed the comm channel, as if a large weight had come off of them. It was a weight she knew.

Command.

Taking these people home would be one less source of blood-feud between the two nations. Perhaps it would be enough for peace. Perhaps the King of the Pirates would make nice.

Jessica snorted to herself. And perhaps she could teach the horse to sing.

CHAPTER XVIII

Date of the Republic October 13, 393 Sarmarsh System

Jessica had adjourned to the small conference room with Daneel Ishikura and three of her guards, his minders, for the show. Most of her officers were on duty on the bridge right now, getting a first-hand view of the engineering feat they had just accomplished. Or, were about to accomplish.

More of Keller's *Legend.*

Daneel Ishikura had turned out to be even bigger in person that she had expected. Two meters tall and V-shaped across the chest, tapering down to a narrow waist. He had cleaned up well, though, dressed in pants and a long shirt that would not stand out on the street in *Ladeaux*, accessorized with just enough gold, in the form of a small bracer and a necklace and such to still look like a pirate at second glance.

They were done with the evacuation now, having gone through all the exhausting effort necessary to pack up seventy-eight people, the survivors of a once much-larger staff, and get them aboard *Auberon,* under guard, fed, and quartered away.

She and the man relaxed as the display screen lit up, small talk out of the way. They were alone, except for the marines keeping close watch at the door, but that was normal when dealing with a high-value prisoner. Even admiral

Wachturm had a discrete minder when he was allowed out of his quarters. Jessica didn't expect Ishikura to do anything stupid or suicidal at this point.

"So you really are going to make a production out of this?" she heard him say quietly.

Jessica smiled at the man. "Far more than just a production, Ishikura. This is an *Event*. You'll see shortly."

On the screen, the moon designated *Alpha* was centered. Engineering had converted all of their asteroid missile's angular momentum that they could dampen to spin, so the planet appeared to move counter-clockwise on the screen, slowly but visibly, as the smaller rock approached. It left a slightly queasy feel, as though you were flying on a ship that lost one of its gyros.

Words suddenly appeared on the screen, overlaying the image. *Adventures In The Land Of The Giant People.*

Jessica heard the pirate next to her repeat them quietly, confused.

"What's all that about?" he asked.

"It's a tradition on this ship, Mister Ishikura," she replied. "I have an engineering department with aspirations to high art. This is a stage production to them. They treat it as such."

"I have a hard time with that name, Keller," he said back to her. "Mister Ishikura is my father, a small-scale butcher in a middle-class neighborhood on the edge of the city of Corynthe."

"City?" she asked, equally confused for once.

"*Corynthe* is the kingdom, *Petron* is the planet, Corynthe is also the capital city."

"Ah," Jessica said. "And what would you prefer?"

"Until recently," he said, "I was known as *Warlock* when flying. Before I was a governor." He paused for a moment. "My mother still calls me Daneel."

"Very well, *Warlock*," she said with a light smile. Pilots were pilots. "Now, quiet, so you don't miss the show."

Moirrey's pixie voice filled the room. It was like jasmine on a summer day.

"Good afternoon, children. Today on *Adventures In The Land Of The Giant People*, we have two rocks. They's bigguns, too. Lots o'other rocks as well, all dancing pretty-like to Newton's First Symphony, but we really only cares abouts two."

She fell silent for a few moments before her voice returned, with an extra edge added.

"Can you see the pretty spins, boys an' girls? It's what a bullet sees when you shoots it at a grapefruit, only slower, and spinning the wrong way. A pretty, pretty, little, sad grapefruit, all blotchy brown and orange. It looks up and thinks to itself: *Here now, what's going on? Who are you?*"

Ishikura, *Warlock*, turned to say something, but Jessica put up her hand and stopped him without looking over. This was too good to miss.

When she felt him subside back into silence, Jessica put her hand back down. For a moment, it landed on the back of his wrist. She glanced down and twitched it back, out of contact, willing her blush not to show.

Moirrey's voice took on a deeper note, an ominous tone as she switched roles back and forth. "Who? Me? Just a little rock, passing through a great bigs neighborhood. I got lonely over there and decided to see what it was like around the big gasball."

"Oy, well, ya can't do that. I was already here, ya know. Go find somewhere else to hang out."

"I can't do that, little grapefruit. I gots me a really good shove to come over here and I'm like a pig on ice right now. I mean, I kinda hafts to go that way. I'm really sorry you ended up in the way, but they's not a lot I can do. Gots ta tell you, though, it's like falling down an elevator shaft, looking at you like this. I'm feeling a might twisted up. And, oh, hey, you really can't get out of the way?"

"No, you lummox, I was here first. Have you gots insurance for all the boom yer gonna do when you hits me?"

"Sorry. Nobody told me it was gonna be this kind of party."

"Well shear off then. Now. Oh, shits. OhMyGodIcantgetoutoftheway!!!!!!! SKAAAAAAA-WWWWWWIIIIIIIISSSSSSSSHHHHHHHHHHH!!!!!!!!!!!!!"

The spinning image of *Alpha* was suddenly replaced by a shot from *Auberon*'s bow, well away and off the ecliptic plane. The asteroid fell into the moon with a graceful plunge, like a knife skewering an apple, or a diver entering a pool.

The energy released looked quaint, until the scale of ripples racing away from the impact wound became apparent. A small volcano of mud and hot stone squelched up, like the splash from dropping a big rock in a pond.

"An' that, children, concludes today's lesson in planetary billiards. Ya hits 'em dead center and they go boom. If'n yer engineers was less competent, they'da hits off-center and looked like amateurs. Unlessin' of course, you needed a right proper amount of English on that shot to draw for the eight ball. Never play billiards for money with an engineer."

The screen went dark. Jessica could imagine the crew's giggles around the ship.

She felt the weight of *Warlock*'s gaze as he turned to look at her, silent for several seconds.

She glanced over, one eyebrow raised.

"And if we had decided to be dead-enders down there, you'd have still done that?"

Jessica felt her a frown form, allowed it. "*Warlock*," she replied, "*Lincolnshire* will be upset with me that I didn't do exactly that to you and your people. With luck, *Corynthe* won't feel the same way."

"And you?" he asked.

"I would have found it a waste of potential. Yours, and the other seventy-seven survivors. At least now you can do something useful with the rest of your lives."

He paused to study her face. Whatever it was he sought, he apparently found.

"I note that there was an Imperial corvette in orbit when all this started," he began, dangling the rest of the sentence off into limbo.

Jessica cocked her head and raised an eyebrow at him by way of reply.

"What happened to the ambassador?"

Jessica considered the man before her. Not just another pirate, it seemed.

"I found no ambassador, *Warlock*," she began. "However, admiral Wachturm is currently a guest aboard this ship while we investigate to make sure his activities are commensurate with a neutral vessel in this situation. He's being kept in splendid isolation until then."

"He's an *Imperial*, Keller."

"The rules are far more complicated than that, *Warlock*," she replied tartly. "We do not always fight, especially in places like this. Without rules, we are no better than the pirates we fight."

He recoiled as if slapped.

"We have rules, *Aquitaine*," he said in a quiet, hot whisper.

Jessica gave him the kind look she remembered her mother giving her when she was young and had said something utterly banal and stupid.

He started to say something else and subsided.

"Perhaps," he continued, more subdued, "when we arrive at *Corynthe*, I will be able to show you some of the better places and sights. It would be nice to give you a better opinion of my home."

"Perhaps, *Warlock*," she said as she rose and started towards the door. She turned halfway there and faced him.

"There is one person I might introduce you to," she focused her gaze on him, a cat staring down at a suddenly-awakened vole. "Before I left *Ramsey*, we had the honor of meeting a gentleman named Tanis Bedrosian. I was so impressed with the man that I brought him with me as well. After disarming all of his goons at gunpoint, you understand."

"I am familiar with the feeling, madam," he said with a frosty tartness of his own as his face fell into a snarl. "He is not, however, any friend of mine. I will refrain from spitting on your deck at the mention of his name, purely out of hospitality."

"Indeed?" she replied. "Perhaps he will feel the same way."

Jessica turned and continued to the door. His words brought her up short, but she did not turn back.

"Are you ever off duty, Keller?"

She paused to consider her response. There was at least one honest thing she could say today. "No."

CHAPTER XIX

Date of the Republic October 14, 393 Outbound from Sarmarsh System

Auberon, like every vessel in the *Republic of Aquitaine* Navy, had a small holding block for prisoners, attached to the marine barracks to make it easy. It was rarely used, as locking someone in a cabin and disabling the door worked equally well.

The holding block had a more sinister purpose.

Four cells made up the block, on the sides of a hallway, facing each other, with an interrogation room on the end, facing the guard room. The design ensured a maximum amount of psychological discomfort for people put there.

Jessica had rarely come down here. The marines ran a very tight ship, tighter than most, and crew discipline issues had dropped off quickly when the former command centurion, Augustine Kwok, had departed.

Today *Navin the Black* had met her personally, along with two of his marines. She recognized Tawfeek from their adventures on *Ramsey*.

She nodded at the giant man as she entered. He held a clipboard in one hand that seemed to be as much a part of his uniform as his sidearm.

"How is our prisoner shaping up, gentlemen?" she asked.

Navin smiled down at her. It was a very evil smile, on a giant of a man. "Given their history together, I felt it would be useful to designate Tawfeek as bad cop," he said, his voice a surprisingly smooth tenor coming out of such a huge frame. "Arlo has been playing the role of good cop. We have not, as yet, turned the screws on the man, there being no real rush to get anything out of him except compliance."

"Very good," Jessica replied, engaging all of them with her smile. "That's ready to change. Arlo, what do we know?"

The man looked the part of a street thug, big and burly, but Jessica knew from his files that he was extremely intelligent and a voracious reader. He was marked to become a dragoon of his own soon, on a smaller vessel, perhaps with his next promotion.

"Well, sir," he said, all spit and polish. "Take a typical punk from the streets and give him a taste of money and power, and you get a bully. This one thinks he's pretty smart also, but he was a big fish in a small pond on *Ramsey*. Folks in my old neighborhood would have eaten him alive."

"I see," she said. "What are his signature weaknesses?"

"Vanity and a desire to demonstrate a pseudo-intellectual superiority, sir."

"Pseudo?"

"Sir," Arlo replied, "I'd compare him to a box of rocks, but the rocks would be insulted by the comparison."

"I see. And what will my gender do to the equation?"

"Haven't brought it up with him much, but I would expect a superiority complex. You got the drop on him, but he thinks that it was luck, not planning. Obviously, a dumb-ass."

"Very nice, Arlo," she smiled up at the trooper. "Will it be better to interview him across the barrier field in his cell, or get him into the interrogation room across a table?"

She watched the marine consider the options carefully. His mouth twisted to one side as he thought.

"Best guess, commander," he said finally, "the interrogation room plays to his ego and loosens him up. Depending on how intense you plan to get, he might get stupid and try to do something physical. Normally, I would suggest Tawfeek or the dragoon be in the room, just in case, but it might be more embarrassing to let you hand him his ass by yourself. Your call."

Jessica studied the three men. Obviously, her training sessions with the fighting robot were better known with the crew, at least the marines, than she had expected, although none of them studied *Valse d'Glaive*, as far as she knew.

Not yet, anyway.

"Arlo," she said after a moment of thought, "you bring him to the room. Tawfeek, you stay handy outside if I need help. Navin, you monitor everything, please."

The men nodded at her and began to move. She stepped out of sight with Navin and Tawfeek as Arlo went down the long hallway. When he returned, she headed down.

The door to the interrogation room opened as she approached. "Tawfeek, you wait here," she said in a hard voice. Bad cop was probably the best way to play a punk like Bedrosian.

"Aye, sir," the marine replied, stationing himself directly across from the door, right in the other man's line of sight, as she entered.

Bedrosian, the punk from *Ramsey*, was seated uncomfortably at a table. His fancy clothes had been replaced with a simple pair of pants and a tunic from the ship's stores, dark gray in this case. No attempt had been made to get a good fit for the man. Perhaps an effort had been made to find the wrong size, judging on his appearance.

Lack of access to some manner of intoxicant had apparently been rough on him, evident in the shakiness in his hands and a general twitchiness to his eyes. She had no pity for him.

By the time she got back to *Lincolnshire*, they might decide to hang him for her. Until then, he was a sponge for her to squeeze. If he was especially useful, she might just drop him off at *Corynthe* and let him make his own way.

Jessica took the chair across from the punk. She studied him for several seconds. His hair was too long, and without something to slick it back, it tumbled down into his eyes. On some men, the look was sexy. Bedrosian wasn't that man.

"Your friends at *Sarmarsh IV* have been annihilated," she said to open the conversation.

She was rewarded by a flinch he quickly covered.

The moment dragged.

"How?" he said finally, disbelief barely registering above a whisper.

"All those guns?" she sneered at him, "not particularly useful when you destroy the moon they're standing on."

"You destroyed..."

"I warned you that this was serious business, Tanis Bedrosian," she said, cutting him off sharply. "When I get to *Corynthe*, I plan on having a very serious conversation with the King of the Pirates about borders and manners."

She could see the whites of his eyes for the first time. He remained silent. Awe, fear, or shock, she wasn't sure. It didn't matter. She wanted him on his back foot.

"Just so you know," she continued, "with them gone, the folks in *Ramsey* are going to clean house. All your friends just might be gone, unless they get out fast enough. I fully plan on turning you over to the authorities when we get back. That is, unless you give me a reason not to."

She let the bait dangle.

His tongue appeared, just enough to wet suddenly dry lips. His Adam's apple worked as he swallowed past a suddenly tight throat.

She let him stew. Waiting was probably her strongest suit. She let her face fall into a simple smile. That seemed to stick an extra bevy of needles into his skin.

Several times, he opened his mouth to speak, but closed it, silent.

Finally, he spoke.

"They'll kill me," he whispered.

Jessica leaned close across the table.

"They don't have you, Bedrosian," she whispered back with a black widow's intimacy. "I do. You should worry about me killing you. The King of the Pirates can't get to you unless I let him."

"Not him…" he said, but suddenly clammed up. Rather than speak, she watched him lean back in his chair as far as he could get from her without actually moving it.

She waited, but he lapsed into silence, staring at her with a haunted look.

"Have it your way, friend," she said finally. "You have the *Aquitaine* Navy between you and the bad guys."

"It won't be enough," he said, then collapsed into fearful silence.

She couldn't get another word out of him.

PART III: CORYNTHE

CHAPTER XX

Date of the Republic October 24, 393 Jumpspace Approaching Petron

Jessica escorted Moirrey into her office and saw the young engineer seated comfortably before taking her own chair.

"How can I be of service, ma'am?" Moirrey asked simply. She was rarely one for small talk, another reason Jessica prized her company.

She considered the woman now, the one she referred to in her head as her evil engineering gnome. Perhaps the Head Gnome.

"Last year," Jessica began, "you did wonderful things for me, and saved us all, with *Project Mischief*."

She waited for Moirrey to nod before she continued.

"Now, I need you to do your magic again, Moirrey."

"What've the buggers got this time?" Moirrey asked, her pixie smile turning puckish.

Jessica smiled back. "Medium-sized carriers with a wide variety of melee-style fighters. It's almost a junkyard worth of strange ships, leftovers and one-offs from everywhere I've ever seen or heard of. No two are going to be the same."

"New stuff?" Moirrey asked, her eyes turning sly as she twisted her head to one side.

"No," Jessica replied as she thought about it. "Older. I have an image of the one that was at *Sarmarsh IV*. The newest fighter it carried was an Imperial *A-6* fighter. Plus at least two very old Republic *M-3 Crossbows*, which had to have been originally built at least seventy years ago."

"Yus, ma'am. They's Motherships and they be flying uglies of all shapes and sizes."

"Uglies?" Jessica had never heard the term applied to fighter craft before.

"Like ye said, commander," Moirrey continued, her burr growing as she warmed to her topic. "Is a junkyard o'stuff. Ya canna buy replacement parts when they break, so's you weld new stuff on 'stead. An' that breaks, so you hack it off an' weld more on. Or you gets a front half that works and hook it to a back half that flies. No two's the same, but that's okay -cause yer pilots is a crew o'pirates and they keep tinkering."

She lapsed into silence for a moment as she thought.

"Missiles be nice, but nots enough," she continued.

Jessica leaned back and watched the woman's eyes flicker back and forth across whiteboards and engineering specs in her mind. It was like watching a master chef in her kitchen. Probably smelled that way in her head.

"Plus, some crazy bastard's like to do something weird an' centerline a Type-3 cannon with a couple of engines and a cockpit and call it good."

"A Type-3?" Jessica blurted out in surprise.

Auberon was built on a Heavy Cruiser hull design. Those ships normally carried six Type-3 beams. Big guns. Auberon had only two, but she was a carrier, so her flight wing made up for it. Even the GunShip Necromancer mounted only Type-2 beams. Granted, a triple-weapon, nose and both wings, that could parallax, but still. Much smaller.

"Aye, ma'am," Moirrey chirped. "Is a can opener. Seen a picture of one back home. Ya fires it and the whole ship shuts down. Ya relights the engines and starts recharging the batteries. Maybe five or ten minutes later you can fire again. Assuming you didn't cook nothing along the way. And nobody cooks you."

"Okay," Jessica said, "so how do we fight off waves of these things?"

"That will require more *Mischief*, ma'am," Moirrey responded. "How soon?"

"We'll be at *Petron* in a few days, Moirrey," Jessica said. "After that, I don't know. Hopefully, never. Possibly quickly."

"Rights," Moirrey said as she rose. "First, I builds it ugly. Then I gets all elegant n'thin's." She saluted, turned, and scooted out the door.

Jessica watched her go. If only it were a simple as that. Although, for an engineer, it might just be that. Hand them a problem and get out of the way. Let them get technical on it.

Dealing with people was where it got messy. At least, it always had for her.

Perhaps she just hadn't take the time to be *elegant*, before now. Not that the pirates would appreciate it. But what she had planned wasn't for them. They just got to be the victims if it worked.

CHAPTER XXI

Date of the Republic October 27, 393 Edge of the Petron System

Denis had come down to the flag bridge for this meeting. The two other commanders from the squadron had already shuttled over, but this was much more of a conclave for war than an opportunity for High Tea. He took the seat next to Keller and watched her face.

She gave nothing away.

"Okay, people," she finally said, "we're about to go into the lion's den. Unless someone happened to be out this far and then hopped in without us seeing them, the King of the Pirates, and all of *Corynthe*, will know that the Republic has arrived in the next six hours."

She looked at each of the faces of her command staff in turn. Denis felt the weight of her gaze last. He nodded back.

"I plan to treat this like any port call on the outside," she continued. "We're here to say hello and drop off a bunch of shipwrecked survivors, not pick a fight. I don't think we could win against the forces down there anyway."

Denis studied the orbital projection rotating slowly above their heads. *Petron* looked like a nice planet. A little warm and mostly land, instead of ocean, but not badly so. There was a *LOT* of traffic in orbit, but it was mostly composed of little freighters coming and going. However, there were a whole bunch of armed shuttles and small country craft moving around as well.

"They don't have anything comparable to *Auberon*," he heard her continue, "but they do have this."

The viewer flipped to show the craft that had fled *Alpha* at *Sarmarsh IV* when they had arrived, or at least a ship that was very similar. At one end of the vessel was an arrowhead-shaped bow made up of four blades equidistant around the centerline. The other end was very obviously an engine cluster and Jumpdrive assembly, ripped from something else and welded together in someone's back-yard instead of a professional facility. It was the middle three-quarters of the ship that looked interesting.

The centerline of the ship was a narrower cylinder, like a goose's neck connecting the two ends, but much, much longer. Around the neck, like mosquitos squatting on skin ready to bite, were several rings of fighters and miniature gunships, no two of the same design. Again, thrown together in someone's back-yard, if the back-yard had at least three of every kind of starfighter ever flown, chopped into pieces and stacked randomly, waiting to be welded into some new configuration by a demented beaver with a laser torch.

Denis looked closely. This was craft that had fled them at *Alpha*. Three rings of five or six fighter craft, so about sixteen fighters. The fourth ring was comprised of four larger gunboats, roughly the size of the pair of S-11 *Orcas* that *Auberon* carried. Nothing like *Cayenne* or *Necromancer*, though. Still, but for a lack of missiles visible, that thing could put up almost as many craft as one of the big Republic Fleet Carriers, such as *Archon* or *Ajax*.

Denis whistled unconsciously.

"Yes," Jessica said to him. "You see it."

"Sir?" Command Centurion d'Maine off of *Rajput* said.

"We could slaughter them with missiles, probably," Denis said instead. "That is, until they got close. Then it's a knife fight. Very messy. Gut us like fish."

"Correct," Jessica continued. "This is the largest class, what the locals call a 4-ring Mothership, and they have at least six of them, according to *Lincolnshire*'s intelligence. Most of *Corynthe*'s ships are smaller, one to three rings. Those things would be murder on a freighter. Drop out of Jumpspace on top of him and unleash a horde of snub-fighters."

"So what's the plan, sir?" Command Centurion Kigali said. *CR-264* would have a field day in such a battle, right up to the moment that they overwhelmed the little escort with numbers and shot holes in it.

"Pick a nice orbit, well out, and talk," she replied. "When they decide that they're going to be nice and talk, I'll probably need a lift to the surface, but I plan to ride down in the jumpseat on *Necromancer*, while she and a sizeable chunk of the flight wing escort *Cayenne*. After that, hopefully nothing more dangerous than politics."

That got a good chuckle out of the group, especially after the *adventures* at *Ramsey*.

Denis watched her neutral face turn deadly serious.

"If they decide to take me prisoner," she said calmly, "I would appreciate Navin the Black and his people rescuing me. If something happens to me, I will leave standing orders to do to *Petron* what we did to *Alpha* at *Sarmarsh IV*."

The silence turned nearly solid as the implications settled around them, like a heavy quilt on a cold night. Physics was physics, after all, but hitting an inhabited world like that violated every single tenet of civilized warfare.

Of course, so did killing a *Republic of Aquitaine* officer under safe conduct. Hopefully the pirates wouldn't need to be reminded of that. The survivors being brought home from *Sarmarsh IV*, bringing their story with them, would help.

Denis figured that *Auberon*'s crew would be willing to stay around for several weeks afterwards, reigning fiery death down onto the planet, if something happened to Jessica Keller. She was probably counting on that.

"Understood, Commander," Denis said, signaling to the rest that he would be willing to end his career on that sort of note. The others growled back at him. It sounded like a pack of hungry wolves spying sleeping chickens.

Jessica fixed each of them with a hard look.

"Then we are ready to go to war, people."

CHAPTER XXII

Date of the Republic October 28, 393 Above Petron

Jessica was down on the flag bridge with her flag centurion and a few crew members, when the door opened on the right wall. Daneel Ishikura, *Warlock*, entered slowly and looked around.

Their eyes locked for several moments across the space.

"Commander," he said finally, breaking the silence. "What can I do for you today?"

She pointed at one of the chairs around the big table. "Have a seat, *Warlock*," she said firmly. "I'm about to talk to the King of the Pirates. Any advice you have would be useful."

He moved to sit with a steady, economical grace, moving lightly, like a much smaller man than he was.

She watched him study her face for several seconds before he spoke. "The King of the Pirates is an interesting title," he said, "and Arnulf Rodriguez is a very complicated and capable man. He might actually be capable of founding a dynasty. That has always been his goal."

"I see," she said. "Would it work?"

Her reward was a shrug. "*Corynthe* has always been a democracy of the Captains, Commander Keller. It makes for a government by strong man, rather than something stable. Part of the reason *Corynthe* has always been weak and the fringe has always been plagued by piracy."

"How did you end up in *Sarmarsh*, then?"

Another shrug. "I was probably perceived as a threat. Better to take a distant exile than suffer a night of long knives. I argued against the provocation of invading *Lincolnshire*, but it worked out. Right up until you came along, that is."

"How much risk are your people at, coming here?"

Again, a shrug. Too many unknowns. "I'm far less of a threat now," he said. "We'll see what the near future brings. You never know when someone is going to show up with a lot of warships and overturn the order of things."

She studied his face closely. Something about the tone of his voice rang false, but she couldn't identify what set her off. Or perhaps, he was being a little too blasé for someone in his position. He was certainly unwilling to tell her more.

Still, it was obvious that there was far more to the situation than she had been able to read. The *Fribourg Empire* was involved somehow, but Wachturm wasn't talking. Criminal elements in *Lincolnshire* had their hands in it, but retained enough of a hold on Bedrosian to keep him quiet. And *Warlock* was up to something as well, although he seemed to be the most open to conversation of the three. That in itself was worrisome.

Just in case, she activated the sound damper field around her station. Normally, it kept her from distracting everyone around her in battle. Here, it would keep *Warlock* from speaking to the man below.

She did turn on a speaker, so he could hear both sides of the conversation. Jessica figured he could get her attention with a gesture, if he really needed to speak.

A flashing red light on her console told her that a channel was open to the surface, and that someone below was waiting for her. She keyed the channel live and hit a secondary button to bring the man up on the projector, three times the size of life.

Arnulf Rodriguez, from the caption someone had added to the image. So, the King of the Pirates himself. Jessica took a moment to study the man, even as he did the same. She felt the same appraising look on her face as she saw on his.

He was a muscular man, broad across the shoulders, but starting to go to seed around the middle. It was the kind of paunch Fleet Lords got when they ate too much and stopped working so hard to keep it off. He wasn't soft, but was getting there. Perhaps three years. Maybe five.

He was still a distinguished-looking man, with dark hair kept short and a clean-shaven face. There were gray hairs along the edges, but that just added dignity.

"So, Commander Jessica Keller of the Republic warship *Auberon*," he began, in a measured tone and a deep baritone voice, "I am told you wish to speak to the King of the Pirates. How may I be of service?"

Jessica resisted the smile she felt tugging at her lips. The man was a master showman, obviously used to playing to an audience of hard men and women. There were probably several out of sight of the camera, watching on his side. It had that feel to it.

"It's more what I can do for you, sir," she replied brightly. "Or should I call you King Arnulf?"

He smiled like a lion. "I am the Supreme Commander of the *Corynthe* Fleet, among my other titles. Perhaps you should address me as Admiral Rodriguez."

"Just so, Admiral." Jessica nodded politely to the man. "The reason I am here is because your research station on *Sarmarsh IV* was destroyed by an asteroid. I rescued a number of survivors from the surface and am bringing them home so they can be reunited with their families."

His eyes got a canny squint to them. "Research station?" he asked, one eyebrow dancing upwards. "How many survivors did you rescue?"

"Seventy-eight, Admiral, including the man who introduced himself to me as the governor."

She watched the man's eyes flicker to the left for a split second before coming back to hers. So, there were people off-camera watching, same as here, just as she'd suspected.

"Being refugees," she continued, "they had little but the clothes on their backs. I plan to deliver them to the main spaceport and let their families know. I am broadcasting the names over the top of one of your planetary sporting networks so everyone knows who made it home safe. I hope that is acceptable."

For a moment, his visage grew terribly grim, but he quickly recovered. "That will save us the effort of notifying people, Commander Keller, although it would have been appropriate to ask first."

Jessica nodded again with a half-smile. "I was not sure that our own arrival in system would be met entirely peacefully, Admiral. Especially since

Aquitaine and *Corynthe* do not have any formal diplomatic relations. Perhaps that could be addressed as well."

All sound dropped off from the transmission, so Jessica figured that someone was speaking off-camera to the man. He nodded absently, eyes wandering for a moment.

"Yes, Keller," he said finally. "I look forward to granting you an audience in my Court when you arrive. And please make sure *Warlock* is with you. I will have questions for him as well."

"Very good, sir," Jessica said. "It will take us a day to arrange everything. I will have my Flag centurion contact your seneschal to make arrangements. Thank you."

She cut the signal before the man could reply. The sound dampening field went with it.

Warlock was turned towards her. His face was white.

"They are going to think you have turned me, Keller," he said quietly. "Made me join you as the price of survival."

"Perhaps," she smiled at him, "if you were more forthcoming about things, I could have maneuvered better. As it is, I'm largely flying blind. If I'm at risk, you can join me."

"Do you think that this fleet can protect you from these people?"

"I'm betting my life on it, *Warlock*," she snarled. "I'm okay with betting yours, as well."

He was on the verge of speaking, his mouth open, one hand raised, when something stopped him. He fell silent and gave her a hard look.

"You have no idea what's coming next, Keller," he said finally.

That was true, but she could plan for a very large number of possible scenarios.

She did that very well.

CHAPTER XXIII

Date of the Republic October 29, 393 City of Corynthe, Petron

Jouster checked his screen one last time and committed to entry into *Petron*'s atmosphere. *Uller* and *Vienna* flew on his flanks, a lethal arrowhead pointed at the horizon.

Behind him, the DropShip *Cayenne*, loaded to the gills with refugees and marines, started her descent as well. *Gaucho* must have been feeling nice today. He was flying a sedate pattern, instead of diving straight down as fast as the heat shields on the ship's belly could handle like he normally did.

Above that, just below the three big ships, the GunShip *Necromancer* was starting to begin her run. The dragon lady, Keller, was aboard *Necromancer* instead of *Cayenne*, in case anybody did anything stupid below. Not that anybody expected them to, but things out here weren't always what they seemed.

His job was to make sure nobody did anything dumb. Or, at least, that nobody survived the attempt. Nothing like flying bodyguard for a VIP to keep you paranoid. At least none of the freighters or shuttles in orbit had wanted to be close to *Auberon* and the fleet. They had almost ten degrees of orbital arc to themselves up there.

Below, the city of Corynthe, capital of the kingdom of the same name, began to take shape. Rather than come in flat, blind over the horizon, the landing party was spiraling slowly in, with all the firepower of the squadron directly overhead. Again, ready to shoot first and ask questions to any survivors. Not exactly polite, but the people down below were proud to call themselves pirates.

Jouster had a long history with pirates, mostly chasing them away after they had done bad things. He wouldn't mind evening the score a little while he was here.

A single tone jarred him, scratching the inside of his head like nails on a chalkboard.

Someone down there had just locked on him with a targeting sensor.

His thumb dropped down to confirm that his shields generators were putting all their energy down. There was nothing above him but friendlies right now. He figured he could flip to the universal setting inside of a 4g barrel roll if he had to.

"All ships, this is *Jouster*," he called out as he pushed the nose of his M-5 fighter deeper into the dive. "Someone has targeting lock on me. Request permission to engage."

There was a pause as he felt his speed build up, gravity working with him to turn the fighter into something like the *Harpoon* it was named for. *Uller* and *Vienna* dropped with him, lethal hawks looking for little mice.

"Negative, *Jouster*, do not engage," Jež called on the secure comm. "The locals have not gone to a war-footing, and no other ships have been targeted. This is just someone playing games."

Oh? Really?

"Flight wing," he said, popping his knuckles on the flight controls without letting go, "please confirm my scanner reading of a clear horizon."

There was another pause before *da Vinci* came back over the comm. She would be sitting in a different orbit, keeping watch as well. "Roger, *Jouster*. Clear skies for maneuvering."

Jouster smiled inside his helmet. *So the locals wanted to play?*

"*Uller*, *Vienna*. Triangle break now. Execute."

One of the many advantages of flying with the same mates, training with them daily for more than three years, was a near-telepathic link for anticipating one another. On a side screen, *Jouster* watched the maneuver unfold, just like in the simulators.

His controls were all on a single complicated wheel, letting him touch twenty-some functions without moving any of his fingers more than a centimeter. He shoved the stick forward hard, pushing his nose straight down, while his thumb red-lined the throttle and a ring-finger rotated his shields back to the universal setting.

All the enemy guns were below him in the gravity well, but that wasn't always *down* as he snapped the fighter into an outside loop to the right. Above him, his wingmates did the same, almost at the same instant. The sensors down there might still be locked, but missiles would have to adjust, and guns would be pointed all wrong as the three fighters accelerated into their plummet, gradually separating as they spun.

Jouster activated his own targeting sensors and let them paint the city loudly. Any kid with a radio down there would catch a burst of static as the pulse bounced off the ground. *Uller* and *Vienna* did the same. Above, *da Vinci* had apparently been expecting this maneuver. Her pulse was probably loud enough to make teeth rattle.

There. Right on the edge of town, rather than at the primary space port. A missile tower designed to protect a high-value target. He altered his rotation to center on that edge of the city. Around him, his wingmates did the same.

On his targeting screen, the building lit up with a caption that read *Palace*. Oh ho. Somebody getting stroppy over there?

Jouster already knew the answer, so he didn't bother asking to engage again. This felt like a pissing match with the locals rather than an ambush. He would have turned on several more towers, and waited until everyone was much closer to the ground.

But he could play as well.

Instead, he brought his nose around and lined it up with the tower. *Uller* and *Vienna* did the same. The targeting system got a lock almost instantly, a happy little bell tone, even without inertial guidance. Apparently, those people really were just being assholes. He would have at least turned on the ECM generators and started broadcasting static if he were down there.

"Corynthe Tower, this is *Aquitaine* Escort Flight," he said, projecting as much professionalism and anger into his voice as he could. "I have a weapons lock on you. Turn off your targeting systems right now or I will consider you hostile and destroy you. You have four seconds to acknowledge and comply."

At this speed, he would blow by them in less than ten seconds. If he had actually intended to fire right now, he'd have to bank over hard and stand the fighter on its ass, just to avoid the sort of explosion you got when a stack of missiles caught fire and went boom.

One...

Two...

Jouster's fingers twitched with anticipation. *If they were going to get stupid down there, it would be right about now.*

The solid lock tone vanished from his cockpit as they turned off their systems.

Jouster let go his breath and locked his own weapons down. Because they deserved it, he nosed down a little bit, drifted to port a shade, and passed over the top of the tower at a little over twice the speed of sound at about two hundred meters relative elevation.

That ought to make that whole building shake, you punks.

"*Jouster*, this is Keller," *SHE* said. The dragon lady. The bane of his existence. The reason he was acting more like a grown-up these days.

He tensed up and ground his teeth a little, expecting the worst.

"Nice flying, *Jouster*," she said.

Really? Huh.

He did a victory roll as he blasted over the city. *What was the worst these punks could do?*

CHAPTER XXIV

Date of the Republic October 29, 393 City of Corynthe, Petron

Auberon carried a small armored limousine for transporting important personages on the ground. Jessica had never used it before today, since *Auberon* was normally docked at stations. At *Ramsey*, the local streets had been safe. Safe enough.

Corynthe was a different equation.

The car rumbled down the big ramp at the aft end of *Cayenne* and crossed the tarmac to where Jessica waited at *Necromancer*'s hatch. Across the way, she could see her marines escorting most of the refugees away from *Cayenne*, towards a series of local buses that would haul them to the terminal.

Her people weren't being especially rough, but this group had a large number of extremely hard men, so the marines were much less friendly than they would be helping widows and orphans, which she had also seen them do. Still, today they were being merely professional. Hard, but professional.

Her chariot rolled to a stop like an earthquake subsiding. Marcelle opened the rear door and stepped out to look around. Jessica could see the butt of a pistol in a shoulder holster.

Marcelle had gotten much more protective and paranoid since *Ramsey*.

Jessica climbed into the vehicle and smiled at *Warlock*, sitting uncomfortably across from her. Her purser had worked up something simple for him to wear that didn't look like it came from ship's stores, but was still better than anything he had brought with him.

He really did clean up well.

"I still think," he said, continuing the discussion, "that I should be with my people, getting them settled, instead of coming to the palace with you. That's where I belong."

She scowled at him. "I don't care what you think, *Warlock*," she said simply. "Had you been more open with me, maybe I would do it differently right now. Since everyone wants to dance around me with half-truths and lies, I want you where I can get to you quickly, if I decide to stop playing nice."

He pursed his lips, as though he had bitten a lemon, but subsided into silence for the ride.

She settled back as the vehicle rumbled into motion.

The Palace sounded so much more interesting when described than when seen. It reminded Jessica of a barn that had wandered sluggishly away from its roots. It sat on one whole side of a mammoth square on the edge of town, backed up to a wide river.

From the air, her guess had been that the square was part of the original spaceport for the city, once upon a time, and the palace originally a warehouse with a dock on the back to barge things up and down the river. She didn't plan to ask any of the locals about the actual history. It wasn't that interesting.

Interesting were the people.

As far as provincial capitals went, the city was average. Jessica guessed a population of a few hundred thousand, at most, surrounded by a hinterland of average to poor farmland. Good enough to sustain the planet. Not enough to get rich. That was why they went into space in the first place.

The people reminded her much more of a mining colony than anything else. The population mix on the streets as she rode through town was very heavily tilted towards males. And the few females she did see looked almost as hard and rugged as the men. This didn't look like a place for families. Just ship's crews.

Every corner had a bar. Many of them also had chandlery services of some sort, or flop houses, or pawn shops. She didn't see any schools or day care crèches. It was possible they were mostly located on the other side of town.

She doubted that with a snort.

Warlock perked up at the sound. He raised an eyebrow silently.

She studied him for a second. Most men would have felt compelled to say something right then. Probably flirtatious. Possibly demeaning. Something. Few were self-possessed enough to not be threatened by a woman like her.

"Hard town," she gestured out the window as the passing buildings. "Hard people."

He shrugged.

"At least we're on the Boulevard of Kings," he said, referring to the street. "On some of the sketchier streets north of here, I would expect someone to take a potshot at us as we drove by."

"Really?" Marcelle perked up immediately in the front seat. Jessica imagined one hand disappearing into her jacket to touch a pistol butt.

He waved a hand negligently. "I checked with the marines before I got in this beast," he replied. "Hand-held weapons like the locals have won't even scratch the paint. We're safe. At least until we get to the palace."

"What happens then?" Jessica asked.

"Why then, Command Centurion Keller," he replied calmly, with only a hint of sarcasm, visible around the eyes, "you will meet the King of the Pirates."

The half-smile on his face only vaguely mollified her.

"Her Excellency, Admiral Jessica Keller, of the *Republic of Aquitaine*."

Jessica listened to the *herald* fill the grand space with his baritone voice. She hid her smile at the subtle promotion he had granted her. Apparently, only important people, or people with warfleets behind them, got properly announced into the Court. She could settle for the latter.

This chamber was intellectually just about as far from the reception at *Ramsey* as she could have imagined. That had been a small affair, a hundred or so people at an afternoon cocktail party with a buffet line.

This was an auditorium big enough for team sports. The floor sloped subtly down from the door into a large flat spot before a raised platform with a throne atop. It was the only chair in the place.

Around her, several hundred people waited. Most were generally quiet and about half were looking in her direction as she entered, with *Warlock* and Marcelle immediately behind her. There were several side conversations going on and people turned completely away from her.

The crowd was dressed exactly how central casting would have done it, if you told them you wanted to make a space pirate movie.

Jessica wondered how much the image drove the reality, and how much of it were people like this trying to look like the fantasy on the screen. Certainly, the number of blades on belts, from little shivs up to poniards the length of her arm, plus all the colorfully-dyed leather and occasional chain mail, carried the look.

A space parted down the middle of the crowd as she walked forward, escorted by the herald and a pair of guards. The herald, an older man with a noticeable limp and a shaved head, was obviously for show. Pomp and circumstance. He carried a lovely carved-wood staff that appeared to be his badge of office.

The guards, on the other hand, were fully armed. Jessica had left her marines with the vehicle. It was easier to do that than to potentially insult the man she was here to see.

That left her, facing this man, Arnulf Rodriguez, King Of The Pirates, and his entire Court. With just the entire weight of the *Republic of Aquitaine* Navy behind her.

It was a fair fight.

She walked most of the way down the length of the room, stopping perhaps six meters away from the platform. Close enough that she could talk at reasonable level without having to yell over the quiet buzz. Not so close that she had to smell him or his guards if he was really into the whole barbarian-image thing.

Warlock had turned out to be more civilized than she had expected, but she still wasn't expecting much from the rest of these people.

The king and Jessica stared at each other from across those six meters of space, the two of them, alone but for the half dozen guards and one herald between them. His look was frankly appraising, almost indecently so. She decided she could return the favor.

Arnulf Rodriguez, *Corynthe*'s King of the Pirates, was a giant of a man. *Warlock* was merely big. Rodriguez appeared to be more than two meters tall, dressed in an outfit that started out as a dark, almost-slate, gray, with touches of color added subtly, mostly dark reds. Far more reserved than she would have expected a pirate king to be.

He had been a fighter in his prime. He had that look to him, in the set of his shoulders and the way his weight stayed forward on his toes when he stood still as she approached. The middle was getting thick, but the hands still had that something that she recognized subconsciously.

Something she saw in the mirror.

Hands used to holding blades.

This man, this pirate king, had led a very successful, very violent life, as one would expect to rise to the level of power he had, and to then hold it.

"So, Commander Keller," he called out, loud enough to be heard across most of the chamber, "you speak of political alliance between our nations."

Jessica could feel the theater of his presence take hold. Among his many talents, the man was apparently a carnival barker as well. His charisma was magnetic, drawing all eyes into their conversation, making it intimate for their four hundred close friends.

"Just so you know," he continued, "such things are frequently family affairs in *Corynthe*, arranged politically between clans and sealed by marriages. How would you feel about becoming queen of the pirates?"

His flourish with his right hand as he finished was just the perfect calculated move. She could feel the room around her on pins and needles as she watched him, a small grin spreading across her face. They were probably expecting an embarrassed, stammering withdrawal.

She could only imagine how Fleet Lord Loncar would have responded to this group. That just added to her smile. These people were warriors, not bureaucrats.

"That depends, Your Excellency," she replied with a broad smile and a soft drawl, "what do you have to offer as a dowry?"

The whole room turned silent, with a sudden shocked awe. For a moment, she was afraid she might have pushed this stranger a bit too far.

But really, he had invited it. In *Aquitaine*, it was extremely rude to even discuss such topics with strangers, let along in front of mobs.

The King of the Pirates responded with a hearty, bellowing laugh that shook his whole frame. After a few beats, the rest of the Court joined in politely.

Jessica let herself breathe and stopped calculating just how quickly she could lay her hands on a firearm and which guard she would have to take it from. She expected Marcelle had already plotted three steps farther ahead.

"Bravo, Admiral Keller," he said as his laughter died down. "We shall dicker. But, later. First, is *Warlock* under your *protection*?"

From the way his emphasis was heavy on the last word, Jessica supposed that there was a deeper meaning, something nobody had bothered to explain yet, either locals with knowledge or the sailing gazette. She could update that later, assuming she hadn't just stepped into something stupidly messy here.

"That depends, Admiral Rodriguez," she replied carefully. "As a refugee in need, it was incumbent upon me and my *fleet* to make sure he and his people made it home safely. But he is a free citizen of *Corynthe*, as I understand the term, and a respected leader. He is his own man, now."

The pirate king's eyes grew cagey as he studied first her, and then *Warlock*.

"So, *Warlock*," the man began, his tone taking on a very formal, stilted tone as he spoke. "Have you taken foreign service?"

The most fascinating part, for Jessica, was the way Ishikura's shoulders squared forward and his weight rolled forward onto his toes, in a pose that unconsciously mimicked the king before him. He moved a couple of steps to his left, clearing space around him and having a clear path around the herald.

"I have not, King of the Pirates," he replied, equally formal. "I am a Captain of *Corynthe* and a Free Pirate. I challenge any man who would say otherwise."

Around the room, Jessica could hear the silence spread outward, like ripples on a pond.

Theater had turned suddenly dangerous.

Fortunately, none of the guards were paying much attention to her, just in case.

The king nodded at them, all business.

"How come you to stand before me, *Warlock*? I had ordered you to *Sarmarsh*."

"That woman," Daneel Ishikura, *Warlock*, said, pointing back at her without looking. "After she attacked the bases at *Sarmarsh*, and destroyed everything we had to fight her with, she added insult to injury by redirecting an asteroid into the planet. The entire base, and a significant chunk of the surface of the planet, was simply annihilated."

Jessica heard the surprised intakes and yelps around the room as people processed the chain of events.

"I was given the choice of living to fight another day, or dying in silence," he continued. "I chose to fight."

All of the attention, both from the king and his Court, shifted to her. It wasn't hostile, exactly. Or rather, it was hostile, but it was a hostility at her gender as much as her uniform. There were very few women in the crowd that weren't obviously bimbos on the arm of someone important.

"Is this truth?" the king rumbled at her.

Jessica took a moment to scowl back at him. "It is."

She could see a new light in the man's eyes. *Here was a very dangerous player,* he was thinking. Almost dangerous enough to play games with the King of the Pirates.

If only he knew the real truth.

"Very well, *Warlock*," the King announced. "You are home, and you are a free man."

He paused for a moment, looking to the people on his left. "*Hellhound*," he called out, "I will allow your challenge to *Warlock*, but do not insult *Aquitaine* in your haste for revenge or justice."

Jessica picked up the man as soon as he moved. Not as tall as *Warlock*. Possibly as broad. *Hellhound* had medium length hair, brown and greasy. He moved with solidity, almost the opposite of *Warlock*'s easy grace. The scar on his face made him look like something of a wild animal. The light in the green eyes accentuated it.

He stepped out from the group into a space that suddenly opened as people scurried back out of the way. Perhaps five meters separated him from *Warlock* when he stopped.

The two men stared at each other for several moments.

"Captain Daneel Ishikura," the man began, an unlikely tenor voice coming from such a large frame, "you and I have unfinished business before this Court. The blood feud is not forgotten. I challenge your right to stand here as a Captain and not a slave."

Ishikura had pivoted to face the man and his friends, a bear brought to heel by a pack of dogs. Jessica watched closely as the pack dynamics played out.

Warlock was silent for a few moments. He raised his chin and flipped his hair back with disdain.

"Captain Rory Agano," he replied, equally formal, "I recognize your feud and your challenge."

He appeared to smile, from what Jessica could see of the side of his face.

"How like you to wait in an alley to ambush a lone traveler, with only a dozen of your dogs for help. Will they be enough?"

Jessica nearly laughed as the captain known as *Hellhound* turned beet red. It almost felt like one of those children's cartoons where steam would come out of the villain's ears.

"You came here with her." *Hellhound* pointed at Jessica with a hiss. "She can stand Second as your Witness."

Jessica was pretty sure she actually heard a pin drop, somewhere over in a corner. Certainly nobody was breathing at that instant. Several of *Hellhound*'s mates suddenly looked nervous. Even the King of the Pirates stirred uncomfortably.

Warlock turned to face her with his own nervous look. She pasted a neutral, questioning look on her own face and stared back at the men, daring either of them. She might have only come up to their shoulders, but she was pretty sure she could take either of them in a pinch. Maybe both of them.

"Admiral Keller," *Warlock* began. The formal edges were gone from his voice, so this sounded much more like a conversation than a challenge. "It is customary to have an ally stand close by to witness the challenge and testify to the fairness later, if necessary."

She watched something appear in his eyes. Not pleading. This was not a man who pled, and certainly not with a woman.

Perhaps a simple request for help?

"I do not have such an ally close at hand," he continued. "Given the public nature of this challenge, nothing more would be asked of you than to bear witness today. You aided me once. May I ask a second favor?"

Jessica watched the flow of energy around the room.

Had he no friends in the room?

On the one hand, this had been planned to some degree, to put her in an awkward position. She couldn't back out now without losing face with these people. And she suddenly had to take sides in a situation utterly foreign to her.

Again, testing the Republic for weakness, and trying to back-foot her. It probably had less to do with being a woman, although she could see some of that in the looks strangers gave her. It was more the uniform she wore. These men saw themselves as Robin Hood, and her as the law.

Fine. Let's play rough, you assholes. I have an imperial admiral prisoner on my ship who could have taught you better. Maybe I should bring him down here, sometime.

Jessica stepped up to stand next to *Warlock*. She studied the stranger known as *Hellhound* for a few seconds, very obviously, the way a woman might inspect a man. Or, in this case, a side of slightly-spoiled beef.

She met his eyes for a moment and leered at him, followed by a snort of derision loud enough for many people to hear. Marcelle had taught her that one, one night when a too-full-of-himself senior flight centurion got a little too free with his hands in a bar.

The blush on *Hellhound*'s face took on a darker tinge, clear to the tips of his ears. Jessica heard snickers from deeper in the crowd, off to her left. They seemed to grow in intensity for a few seconds, rolling around her like a wave.

Hellhound's snarl was reward enough.

"Captain Ishikura," she said, loudly, her voice pitched in just the way First Lord had taught her to. "I will grant you this boon. See to it that my trust in you is not wasted."

Warlock grinned at her. From the set of his jaw, he was stifling a laugh at *Hellhound*'s expense. Much of the rest of the room wasn't trying.

He turned to the rest of the Court with his own grandiose flourish. "I have no blade to answer this challenge. I call on the Free Captains of *Corynthe* to aid me."

Jessica was amazed at the number of men who suddenly drew their belt-knives and presented them hilt-first for inspection. When she got home, all of this was going to make some ethnographer at the University of *Ladaux* quite happy to hear.

Warlock walked carefully around, hands behind his back until he stopped in front of an older captain, perhaps in his fifties when the average here was late thirties, and nodded. He silently took the blade and tested the balance.

He nodded again, this time to the man, almost a bow, and turned to smile at her.

From her vantage, the blade was interesting. In *Valse d'Glaive*, the saber was long and single-edged, with a slight reverse curve, while the *main-gauche* was a short, heavy, straight, two-edged weapon designed to block or stab, but not slash particularly well.

This borrowed weapon was almost a yataghan. It was single-edged with a slight bow forward at the midpoint, rather than being straight over the sixty-centimeter length. The tip was sharped on both sides, and the sharp edge trailed back perhaps ten centimeters before fading suddenly into the heavy spine. The addition of a crossguard indicated that it was intended to be used in close combat, rather than slashing from horseback, unlike the original design.

The quality of the workmanship was excellent, over and above the gold and silver worked into the hilt. It appeared to be made from very high-grade steel rather than something exotic. In *Valse d'Glaive*, that was traditional. Here, probably raw economics.

She watched Daneel flick the blade back and forth a few times to get the feel. The smile on his face said all she needed to know about the quality of the weapon, and the bearer.

She fixed him with a questioning look.

He nodded formally as he approached. “Admiral Keller,” he said carefully, pointing at a spot on the floor and very obviously not touching her. “If you would stand here, we will draw the circle from this point.”

Warlock turned to look across the space that had opened. “*Hellhound*, were you able to find someone willing to stand Second for you in public?”

He was rewarded by more snickers. Apparently, *Hellhound* was not universally loved in this room. He had the look of a bully.

Jessica disliked bullies.

“I will stand,” a man said. He was obviously one of *Hellhound*’s cronies. The rest took a few steps back.

By now, there was a clear space about ten meters across, roughly the shape of an egg, with what looked to be the more blood-thirsty captains closest.

Warlock stepped into the makeshift arena and faced his opponent. “Rory Agano,” he called loudly, “I repeat for the record that your brother was a coward and a thief. By continuing this feud, you show the world that you are also a liar and a fool.”

Jessica watched Daneel lower his weight into a fighting stance. It was not one she used often, but *Hellhound* only held one blade, and she doubted that either man could do a spring-over cartwheel if his life depended on it.

Pirates were two-dimensional fighters. Useful to remember.

“I invoke the blood-feud on you, Daneel Ishikura,” *Hellhound* responded. “Only death will settle this.”

“So be it,” *Warlock* said.

Daneel drew a deep breath and let the extra oxygen flow into his limbs. Things were about to get interesting. More interesting. The week was already off the charts.

It wasn’t as if he hadn’t expected something like this, but there had been really no way to get around it once that woman decided to drag him along with her to the palace.

Just his bad luck.

At least Rory was mad. Hopefully that would lead him to make mistakes. Otherwise, he was very, very good. Probably almost as good as his brother had been.

Nothing like a fight over a woman to keep getting you in trouble, even years later.

Warlock shifted to his right. He and *Hellhound* were both right-handed, so the man began to mirror him, swirling slowly around the observation bowl.

Hellhound's blade flicked out like a snake's tongue, tasting the air without committing. *Warlock* relaxed into stillness, primed to move without telegraphing. Around them, the air was still, but charged, like the sky right before an electrical storm.

Warlock moved, presuming that *Hellhound* was still working himself up to the courage of a duel to the death. It was not a thing to take lightly.

Daneel hopped forward and slashed quickly upwards from the hip. The other man was out of position to block it, but managed to skitter backwards out of range without bleeding.

Hellhound quickly found his balance, stepped to the side, and thrust forward.

Warlock blocked the strike with his stout crossguard and a ringing of steel. He jumped back, but not fast enough to evade a fist to the side of the head.

Apparently, Rory had learned a few tricks sometime recently. And was out for blood. Daneel felt a trickle of blood on his ear, probably from a knife-edge on the glove. Hopefully not a poisoned one.

Warlock took two steps back suddenly and put a hand up to feel his ear.

"Had enough already, coward?" Rory called. Daneel could hear the anger in his voice.

Time to play the gallery.

"Just making sure you didn't put venom on the blade in your left hand, *Hellhound*," *Warlock* replied.

Around them, the crowd had a sudden surge of angry grumbling. Duels were one thing. Cheating was a fast way to lose your crew and your place. And your life, if enough people decided to do something about it.

That was just one of the reasons *Hellhound* had never risen to the top ranks of captains. He skirted the edges of the few rules the pirates did honor.

Hellhound held his left hand up, open, to the room. "No knife," he yelled, even more angry.

Warlock countered by holding up his own hand, stained with fresh blood. He felt a few fresh drops land on his shoulder. He wiped his hand on the seat of his pants and stalked forward, blade pointed at the man's heart.

It was a trick his father had taught him when using blades. He let his own anger show.

Across the way, *Hellhound* took a half-step back and blanched.

Daneel could see the man's pupils shrink when he glanced up, before forcing his eyes back down.

Always study the center. Everything moves from there.

Daneel saw the feint before it even began. *Hellhound*'s hands moved outward, but not the hips. He faded to his left, towards the supposed strike, shifting his weight and ignoring the trick.

Hellhound's hips told the truth. He lunged forward suddenly, a slash intended to open *Warlock*'s stomach if he hadn't already been moving out of the way. Instead, he got kissed on the right hipbone. Cloth parted, but not skin.

Warlock's counter should have finished the affair. *Hellhound* was out of position, unable to block, and over-extended.

Daneel drove the tip of his blade forward.

And felt it bounce.

Hellhound was wearing some sort of armor under his jacket. Nothing heavy, but Daneel had just pricked him in the belly button instead of hammering the tip of his poniard through the man.

He danced backwards ahead of Rory's reverse slash. He would need half a dozen stitches on his right arm when this was done, but nothing worse. He was supposed to have been caught totally off-guard and killed by now, based on the set up.

This wasn't an honorable duel. It was an assassination.

And it was a trap. *Hellhound* was gambling that nobody would catch him cheating, or that he would be protected by someone important if he was caught.

Daneel skipped back two steps to catch his breath. He was always amazed at how much energy was burned in a few complex passes.

Hellhound smiled at him now, a predator playing with a mouse. One who had already drawn blood twice without losing any.

Daneel smiled back. He gestured at the man, a silent conversation between just the two of them, encompassing the little tricks and cheats Rory was counting on to win.

"And that," Daneel said quietly, "is why Matilda preferred me."

A bull will get that look in the eyes, when goaded sufficiently. A shark as well. Powerful, dangerous, mean.

But mindless.

For a moment, *Hellhound* went white, before all the blood surged back into his face like a tide of rage. *Warlock* thought the man's eyes had even turned red. He heard a growl, but wasn't sure which of them it came from.

Hellhound rushed forward, blade forward like a stinger. There was no feint, no subtlety. Just a wild stabbing.

Warlock shifted to his right, instead of the left as *Hellhound* expected, and punched upward with the hilt and crossguard of his borrowed blade.

He met *Hellhound*'s blade and thrust it upwards, not quite clear, as he felt the tip enter his shoulder, ripping flesh.

His own blade tip spun around and caught the man high in the belly. Daneel put all the anger of the last three weeks behind the blow.

Losing his base. Watching it be obliterated by *that woman*. Coming home in disgrace. Being subject to an assassination attempt.

He was angry.

And he held an exceptional blade.

Hellhound's own inertia drove him forward onto the point, even as Daneel drove it forward and up. It caught on something inside there, maybe a rib, maybe the back of the armor.

Daneel grabbed the man by his throat and pulled him further onto his death, crunching bone with a sawing motion.

He looked into the other man's eyes as death approached. "See you in hell, Rory," he whispered as the light slowly faded.

Two down.

Warlock held *Hellhound*'s corpse weight with one hand. He looked around the room with an angry scowl before tilting the weapon down and letting Rory Agano's body slide backwards and fall to the floor.

The room was silent for a moment.

Daneel kneeled down and ripped open *Hellhound*'s jacket. Sure enough, the man was wearing something like a girdle around his middle, heavy chain links sewn into the cloth. Good enough for most fights.

"What are you doing?" someone called.

Daneel ripped the armor loose and stood up, displaying it to the room. His left hand suddenly wouldn't work.

The mob got ugly at the realization. Duels were duels. Cheating was a death sentence, one way or the other.

Daneel stumbled a bit.

She was there suddenly, holding his weight up with an arm around his waist. *How strong was this woman?*

"Poison?" she whispered.

"Maybe," he replied. It was suddenly hard to concentrate.

He saw her point at Arnulf's herald with her other hand.

"You," she commanded, "I need a doctor. Now."

It was not a voice to be brooked. She sounded almost as angry as he had been.

Had been? Had?

He let the darkness overwhelm him.

CHAPTER XXV

Date of the Republic October 31, 393 City of Corynthe, Petron

Jessica looked up with a silent snarl when someone approached her. She softened it when she realized that it was Marcelle intruding.

Warlock was stretched out in a hospital bed before her, machines beeping quietly as the man slept. According to the court surgeon, he was only still alive because all of *Auberon's* marines were cross-trained as medics to some degree, and carried all sorts of interesting surprises in their packs. As did, apparently, Marcelle.

Good to know.

It had been a day of surprises. Obviously, *Warlock* hadn't expected an assassination attempt right after he landed. At least not one so public. From the anger of King Arnulf, she deduced he had been willing to accept an honest fight. That, or he was a much better actor than she would have given him credit for.

The room where she waited was a private clinic reserved for members of the Court, and the *King's Own* were guarding at the door, along with two of her marines who had refused to stand down.

Not that she blamed them. They were chewing-nails angry. Nobody liked assassins. Especially not after the effort her people had been through getting all these people home safely. They took that sort of insult personally.

"Yes?" Jessica asked, softening her voice, bringing her mind back to the present and forcing her anger at the situation back into a bottle.

Marcelle paused and licked her lips, mimicking the exact tone and intonation of the King's herald, an octave higher. "His Excellency, King Arnulf Rodriguez, requests a private audience with his staff to discuss recent diplomatic and political developments. He would appreciate your attendance."

Jessica drew a breath deep into her lungs. She glanced down at *Warlock*, heart rate beeping strong, unsure why she was reacting like this.

"He'll be safe," Marcelle said quietly. "*Necromancer* is sending over more marines, and I'm told Ishikura's people have been notified, so they'll be along."

"Now?" Jessica asked, harsher-sounding than she intended. Marcelle wouldn't take offence. Jessica could see the anger smoldering in the other woman's eyes as well.

"Aye, sir," Marcelle replied, coming to parade rest.

Jessica nodded. *Warlock* wasn't going anywhere, and nobody was getting in here without trouble.

And there were questions. She was not feeling especially polite about asking them.

"Very well," she said. "Let us go see what the King of the Pirates can do for us."

Jessica let herself be personally fawned over by Arnulf's herald and ushered into a private conference room.

It was a small-ish space, comfortable for perhaps a dozen people, rather than the hundreds who had danced attendance this afternoon. A giant oval of a table, polished from some local speckled orange stone, dominated the space, surrounded by a bevy of comfortable chairs and cloth-covered walls.

King Arnulf was there, dominating the space in his own way.

Up close, the man was still impressive, even seated, but she could see the stress of aging beginning to sap him. This was not a place with rules and organization. And he could not rely on any divine right of kings to hold his palace. It would be a daily battle to remain king until he finally lost, or chose to step down.

Jessica could not see this man voluntarily relinquishing power. Especially not if he truly wanted to found a dynasty that would reign after him.

Next to the King sat a man who had been hovering close by on the dais, but not prominent. He was tall and skinny, bald but for a ring of short gray hair around his skull. Obviously not a man desperately concerned enough about his physical appearance to be vain about it. Unlike most of the men in the room.

Jessica noted the appraising look in the stranger's eyes as she took her seat. It was not a man looking at an attractive woman, but a shark recognizing another one in a small area. She almost expected him to puff up like a cat, but he merely smiled.

"Jing Du," he said quietly by way of introduction, "Chancellor to the king."

Ah. Roughly the local equivalent of the Premier of the Republic Senate, back home. Probably almost as dangerous.

The other half dozen were largely faceless nobodies, flunkies here because they were important enough to be seen, but not particularly relevant to the discussion at hand. She memorized names and faces as they were introduced, but only because she wanted to be able to keep track of them later.

Only the last one stood out in her mind. He was a rangy man, with wiry muscles, but the sort of bulk an athletic man will attain after he gets into his forties and stops trying to out-run kids half his age. His red hair was medium length and he had what Jessica's mother would have called Irish freckles.

"Captain Ian Zhao," he said with a roguish smile. "We've actually met once, if only briefly."

Jessica let one eyebrow ask the question.

"At *Sarmarsh IV*," he continued.

"Ah," she said, "yours was the Mothership we did not pursue."

"Indeed," Zhao replied. "If I may inquire, what happened to the Imperial corvette after we left?"

"We boarded her for a customs inspection," Jessica danced lightly around the truth, almost vapidly. It had worked with Admiral Wachturm, to think her an over-rated airhead. Perhaps the pirates would make a similar mistake. They had even less to go on. "A few of the guests were detained for commercial irregularities, and the vessel was sent on its way."

If she hadn't been so closely studying the man as she spoke, she probably would have missed the look that passed between Zhao and the chancellor, seated across from him. She didn't know what it meant, but it did confirm at least some of her suspicions about the layers of subtlety and misdirection at work.

Arnulf appeared to miss it.

She would have put Denis Jež and *Auberon* on a higher level of alert, but there wasn't one. Anyone attempting to ambush Jež and his crew right now was in for a very rude surprise, for a very short, very terminal, period of time.

"I see," Chancellor Du said after a beat. "And will your guests be available to entertain? It would be remiss of us to ignore anyone important while you are here."

Jessica smiled back at him with just the same hint of cruelty. "Unfortunately, no. They are technically prisoners of *Lincolnshire* for the time being, until such time as the authorities at *Ramsey* can provide us better guidance as to their status."

The sour look on his face was reward enough to Jessica for playing the obnoxious little political power games being thrust upon her. She still preferred the clean movements of battle squadrons.

"How is *Warlock*?"

King Arnulf apparently had decided that the small talk had gone on long enough.

Jessica looked both ways down the table before responding, noting interest, hope, and disdain in equal parts, as one would expect from rivals and comrades.

"He will survive," she announced. Leave it at that. Nothing about luck and timing, plots and assassination attempts. Just a simple fake smile from an ignorant foreigner.

"Very good. Thank you, Keller," he said simply. "And thank your medical crew for being so fast. It would have been a great embarrassment to me, to have one of my own captains die of poison, having just survived a duel."

Jessica noted the way he seemed to speak out of the side of his mouth, glancing sidelong at the chancellor seated on his immediate right. Perhaps there was something there she could explore.

"Oh," she replied lightly, "those were just my line marines, not field medics. The actual medic is currently en route from the DropShip that delivered us to the surface."

It was rewarding to see that bit of information register. The blinks. The pupils cycling. That little hint of whiteness as the surprise drained blood from faces. The reminder that they were dealing with professionals now. Even if their commander was just a harmless, little girl surrounded by all these big, bad pirates. She still had marines.

She could have told them that her dragoon was a stickler for that sort of cross-training, and famous across the fleet for the quality of marine non-coms he promoted out to other vessels on a regular basis. But really, letting the other guy think your people were all three meters tall was useful. Never know when that sort of thing would be the edge you needed on the battlefield.

"I see," the man replied gravely. He did play the part of regality well. "There will be an investigation as to why Captain Agano was prepared as he was, with a poisoned spike on his ring and body armor hidden under his jacket."

Arnulf took a deep breath to lend gravity to his words. He was very, very good at that aspect of rule. "If he hadn't died, Rory Agano would have been exiled from the Court and stripped of his name for his behavior. As it is, I declare the feud with Daneel Ishikura over."

He turned to the chancellor with a deeply serious mien. "See to it that Garth Agano and the rest of the family are made aware that they have reached the limits of my patience."

Rather than speak, the man bowed his head. For a moment, Jessica saw the ghost of a smile pluck at his lips.

Arnulf turned to Jessica and studied her face for a moment before he continued. On one hand, it was a politician sizing up a potential rival. Commanders did it in bars and classrooms the galaxy over. There were also hints of a man studying a woman, although it felt as if he intended conquest rather than seduction for his part.

Because some men never learn.

"So, Keller," he began, "why are you here?"

Interesting.

Blunt, pointed, a-political. Not quite the opposite of what she had expected, but close enough. Beside him, the chancellor nearly cringed before he caught himself.

Jessica took a deep breath and held it. This was exactly what both Premier Horvat and First Lord Kasum had wanted her to learn, the intricacies and subtleties of good diplomacy with dangerous men.

And, instead, she was dancing with a bull in a china shop.

However, she thought that way normally. If she could have something of an honest conversation with this man, this King of the Pirates, maybe she could sort out this mess without having to get the Republic involved.

More involved.

She was here now, wasn't she?

And maybe pigs would fly.

"*Lincolnshire* had a problem with criminal elements," she said. *Past tense. Leave it at that.* Not quite as blunt. Not quite as direct. The man was a big-shot pirate, treat him like one. Play to his ego.

"They asked *Aquitaine* for help. I came." Jessica realized that she was tapping the table-top for emphasis as she spoke. At least she had learned that trick from the First Lord, one of many useful things he had taught her over the years.

Almost as a mirror, both Arnulf and his chancellor leaned forward to put their elbows on the table. She suppressed a smile as the two men flinched at each other.

"No," King Arnulf said forcefully. "Why are *you* here?"

Jessica leaned forward again. It created an element of intimacy in the conversation, rather than the sort of righteous grandstanding other Republic officers might employ. She could imagine some of them, right here, right now, doing just that. "That base is ended," she said flatly. "*Lincolnshire* is willing to consider a war over it. *Aquitaine* is willing to back them."

"And you?" he said. Not rude, but hard and short. This was a man used to command. Being in command. Pride in being tougher, better, meaner. Being the King of the Pirates.

She lowered her voice to a level almost better suited for pillow talk, not that she had had any experience in such a thing. But she had read enough books.

"I consider the matter closed," she said, barely above a whisper. "I would have annihilated *Warlock* and his people on the surface. If they come back, I will."

"*Corynthe* has no treaty with *Aquitaine*," the king murmured back. "No common border."

"No," she agreed, "but *Lincolnshire* does." She let the thought dangle. Diplomacy, as the Premier had said, was the art of the unsaid, as much as the said. Bluff and bluster were fine in combat. Here, she needed a touch of ambiguity.

Really, it was just like fighting her combat robot, right? She could do this.

"And you come here?" he said, leaning back and his voice starting to work itself back up to a good towering rage. That was probably a sign of success, rather than failure. "And you would threaten me in my own Court?"

The eyes gave him away. They were still too calculating for the anger in the voice. This man would have made an amazing senator, had he been born on *Ladaux* or *Anameleck Prime*. Jessica was glad she didn't have to deal with him on a regular basis. She could see how he became king.

"No," she said, voice even a shade quieter.

He had to lean in again to hear her.

"A threat suggests that I'm not serious, Arnulf, King of the Pirates," she continued. "Consider this a promise."

She leaned back and sized up the rest of the room. The looks she got back were surprise, disdain, and in a two cases, outright lust. Apparently, no woman talked to a man that way here. Something else she would have to consider changing if she had to come back.

The king's laughter was jarring, considering the situation.

The chancellor had just decided to do or say something when he was interrupted. He blinked in surprise and held his counsel.

"Are you sure you are not interested in a marriage contract, Keller?" the king boomed. "You are an amazingly-rare woman."

The men around her evinced shock, bordering on apoplexy at the thought. *Jessica Keller, Queen of the Pirates? Please.*

She cocked an eyebrow at him, but remained silent. Very definitely a moment to allow the unsaid to speak. Who knew how serious this crazy barbarian king might be? And he was most certainly not her type.

Still, she seemed to have found an opening in his bluster. She smiled at his continuing laughter, a joke among warriors, unshared by the common folk.

"Du," he said suddenly, clapping his chancellor hard on the shoulder and nearly knocking the smaller man out of the chair, "let us have a proper banquet to welcome our esteemed colleague, Admiral Keller. We can show her what *Corynthe* society is truly about."

Jessica imagined what she saw on the Jing Du's face as he looked down was the origin of the saying *Staring daggers at someone*, for just the briefest instant, so fast she might have imagined it.

When he looked back at his king, he was all smiles.

"Of course, Your Excellency," he said smoothly. "It shall be as you wish."

Jessica doubted that, but at least she had a better understanding of the undercurrents here. The sneaker waves. The rocks. Now she just had to figure out how to maneuver in them, and if there were any allies she could make in this place.

CHAPTER XXVI

Date of the Republic November 1, 393 City of Corynthe, Petron

Denis never worked in the command centurion's office, even after Keller had moved down to mostly work from the flag bridge and the previously unused Fleet Lord's office.

His own office was much more cozy. And it was his office. His space.

Right now, he was reviewing scanner logs in his office with his two scouting experts, Giroux and *da Vinci*. She had brought in a portable hologram projector and was running it on a sped-up loop.

"It's not obvious at first glance," *da Vinci* drawled, pointing at the emerging patterns. "Things like this never are. But when I speed it up, what do you see?"

She leaned back and kind of draped herself across the chair. Denis knew Ainsley well enough to realize that she wasn't trying to be sexy. This was just her normal default as a hot-shot pilot, looking down on everyone who didn't fly. They were all born that way.

"Crap," Denis replied. That pretty much summed it up.

"All of them?" Giroux continued, studying the image.

Denis watched the scene play out on the recording as *Auberon* and her consorts came into a high polar orbit. Up here, they were generally out of everybody's way, as far as transports and local vessels went. Plus, they could quickly get anywhere on the surface of the planet if they needed to.

Not that he was expecting to execute a combat run on ground targets. But that wasn't the same as being unprepared. Keller had trained them all to what she considered the proper level of paranoid preparedness. The locals would probably be aghast at the depth of tactical planning that had been done, or the number of targets that could be destroyed by calling out a single number.

At the speed of the recording playing back, he could see several of what the locals considered warships, the big Motherships that looked like geese in his eyes, all pull back, and then break orbit at different times and head off the same general direction. One by one, they leapt into Jumpspace and vanished.

"What's left?" Denis asked.

da Vinci leaned forward from her pose just enough to press a button. Her arms and fingers were longer than his. He would have pulled something, twisting like that.

On the screen, the image froze. Two dots lit up, one docked to the only big station in orbit, and one floating free in a relatively nearby orbit.

Denis looked close, gave up, and zoomed the image manually.

"Docked is the 3-ring *Sky Dancer*, according to traffic control," *da Vinci* continued. "The other one is a 4-ring named *Supernova*. That latter one appears to be their flagship."

"What's the count?" Denis asked.

"Three of the 4-rings left the area, plus five of the 3-rings," Giroux said. "In addition, more than a dozen vessels the local call Strippers, and nearly two dozen freighters, generally small but a couple of medium ones."

"Strippers?" Denis wasn't sure he had heard the man correctly.

"Portable chop shops, sir," Giroux replied. "Locusts that descend after the pirates have captured someone. They set up portable air seals around parts of the vessel so they can cut out the parts they want, from what I have been able to gather, sometimes in the field, and sometimes in orbit."

"How much firepower are we looking at?"

da Vinci shrugged. "If they were all top-of-the-line Imperials, maybe three full Fleet Carriers worth of fighters," she said. "A 4-ring can carry around twenty craft. The 3-rings have twelve to fifteen if they are full, but they rarely are. For comparison, there are also 2-ring craft with about eight to ten, and 1-ring Motherships that haul up to six."

"Bear in mind," Giroux interjected, "that the fighters we're looking at are extremely old, and not nearly as capable as even our older M-5 *Harpoon* fighters, although I did see an M-6 *Gungnir* on one of them."

"Really? How the hell did a first line Republic fighter get all the way out here? And in their hands?" Denis was amazed. Even *Auberon* had to make due with older craft, although he had high hopes that Keller's connections to the First Lord would eventually rate them better gear.

"Mystery for the ages, boss," da Vinci shrugged.

"So now what?" Giroux asked.

"You've done your part," Denis said. "Now I need to talk to Keller, brief her, and figure out her contingency plans. You'll know not long after I do."

The two nodded, packed up their stuff, and departed, leaving him to ponder options and corners.

There was an entire Battle Fleet worth of firepower out here.

Apparently, piracy was *far* more profitable than he had ever imagined.

Did anyone else back home know that?

CHAPTER XXVII

Date of the Republic November 2, 393 City of Corynthe, Petron

Jessica mentally reviewed the file that Denis had sent her from his watchful spot in high orbit.

The implications were…unsettling.

She hoped that the departing Motherships weren't immediately on their way back to *Sarmarsh IV* to try to reestablish the base. Of course, since it would take years for the moon to settle from all that energy, it might be worth watching them try. *How did you build a base on a suddenly earthquake-prone moon?*

Worse, they might have all decided to run off and attack somewhere else. That was the downside. She couldn't be anywhere near *Lincolnshire* to foil attacks if she was here. Hopefully, she could stop them permanently instead. *Nobody out here was dumb enough to provoke* Aquitaine, *were they?*

She looked around the room and reconsidered things.

Tonight, the wealthy and famous of *Petron* were here. In a way, it reminded her of her reception at *Ramsey*, except everyone here appeared to be dressed for what they thought a pirate ball would look like. Or maybe, what one should be.

She *was* in the land of the pirates.

Marcelle stayed close, a second shadow everywhere Jessica went. Not that she minded. Tonight, she was only drinking from bottles and eating food brought to the event and supervised by her own marines. Appearances be damned.

Still, she circulated politely. Many wanted nothing to do with her. That was fine. She was the barbaric foreigner in this gathering, dressed in her boringly simple dark-green dress uniform, without even a knife at her belt.

Marcelle had a knife. Several of them, as a matter of fact, hidden about her body, along with two pistols. And a handful of marines close by. And all the rest of the firepower she might need to bring to bear, if Jessica screwed up so royally that she managed to start a war instead of preventing one.

Small steps.

A woman approached. A very tall, rangy, *slinky* kind of woman. One who gave off the faintest hint of spring flowers.

Jessica guessed her to be a very-well preserved middle age. She was showing off less bronze-colored flesh than a twenty-year-old would have, but doing a much better job of it. Her face was beautiful, if artfully maintained. It was her hands that gave the decades away. Too many spots and wrinkles.

Jessica would have suggested gloves to a woman who was a friend.

"Command Centurion Keller?" the woman asked, as if there was any doubt to the question.

Jessica nodded and studied the woman closer. She had not been announced at that rank at any point on this planet, so this was someone who knew who she was, or knew *Aquitaine* naval uniforms well enough to understand.

This stranger had shoulder-length hair. Jessica had a few grays starting to appear, so she had done enough research on the topic to know this woman's head was probably completely gray by now, but it was dyed a rich black, and then tinted again with hints of violet that made her eyes stand out of her face.

They would have done that anyway, but the make-up made her unforgettable. Jessica had never met anyone with eyes that were such a dark shade of blue. Usually, blue meant lighter, tilting towards gray. These were the color of dark blue sapphires.

The rest of the face was equally well made up. And well maintained. She was utterly gorgeous, not just for her age, but for any age.

Jessica felt the weight of her stare, as if they were already enemies, having barely met. She was at a loss. Competition, perhaps?

"Desianna Indah-Rodriguez," she said, matter-of-factly.

Jessica bowed politely to her, no more the wiser.

"Arnulf's First Wife," she continued.

Oh.

Yes, she supposed the woman might consider her competition, given that Arnulf had already proposed to her twice.

Jessica cocked her head. "First wife?" she tried to ask politely. No deportment class had ever covered something like this. Perhaps she should give a lecture at the Academy when she got back. She suppressed an unprofessional giggle.

"He has had three," she replied, a touch frostily. "So far."

"And you honestly believe I would consider being number four?" Jessica fired back, herself a touch frosty. *How dare this woman... No, be polite. When in Rome, and all that... Maybe.*

"Having met you in the flesh," Desianna said, relaxing a trifle, "no. I don't see it. Not someone like you. Unless the Republic has radically changed the way they handle such affairs. Or wants to feed Arnulf to a black widow."

Jessica felt her eyes grow bigger unconsciously.

From the corner of her eye, she saw Marcelle step forward and to one side, able to watch the newcomer and anyone approaching from behind. Paranoia on her part, but it let Jessica know she could concentrate on the woman before her and not worry about her flanks.

The two of them made a very good team that way.

Desianna smiled tightly, her eyes twinkling. She saw it as well.

"I had not expected..." Jessica trailed off whatever she was going to say.

"To find someone who knew the Republic so well? Here? Personally?"

"We are a long ways from those worlds, madam," Jessica replied. "Perhaps, sometime soon, we could meet privately and discuss such things."

And pick your brain about these men, to see if you had any axes to grind that I might find useful.

Jessica tried to imagine herself as a dilettante spy from a movie. It didn't work.

But still, *Aquitaine* society was all about the small, intimate tea. These major events, these soirees, they always left her drained. Tonight, she would go back to her room and sit quietly in the darkness for at least an hour before she felt human again.

"That would be lovely, Command Centurion," Desianna replied. "I look forward to it."

"Indeed," Jessica replied. "Now, how may I be of service, First Wife? Or should I call you Queen of the Pirates?"

"They have no queens," Desianna said with a hint of storm cloud on her face. "Only a harem of wives, some of who may, occasionally, be allowed to have an opinion outside fashion, or sexual gymnastics."

Oh ho. Yes, very much an axe to grind. Possibly a potential ally. Perhaps an agent provocateur. Still, an avenue to explore.

"Lady Indah, perhaps?" Jessica continued delicately.

The taller woman studied her with an even greater intensity than before.

Jessica could see her leap of faith, even before the woman spoke. She felt the same way.

Two strangers, possibly met on the road to Damascus. It was like the sun deciding to rise.

"Desianna," she said simply.

"Desianna, please, call me Jessica. I will hope that you might be someone who can help me to better understand this world and the people."

"Are you really here to make war?"

Jessica felt her eyes narrow and her mouth purse a shade. *Leap of faith?*

"No," she said, just as simply. "I wouldn't have gone to the hassle of bringing *Warlock* and his people home if that was the case. *Sarmarsh IV* would have been their tomb."

Desianna nodded minutely to herself.

Jessica could see some conclusion reached, but the woman would say no more.

"It has been lovely to make your acquaintance, potential sister-wife Keller," she said suddenly. "I hope you will be able to call on me tomorrow afternoon for tea and we can get to know each other better."

Jessica felt like the ground had shifted under her feet. Again. Still, she rolled with it, nodded politely, and smiled. "I look forward to it, First Wife."

Desianna was gone in a swirl of fabric and lovely scent.

Marcelle suddenly shifted in that way she did when she was sizing someone up for a kick. Jessica glanced at her to make sure, and then turned to look the other way.

Jing Du, King Arnulf's chancellor, in all the resplendent glory of his official red robes, approached, obviously full of his own self-importance.

"I trust you are enjoying yourself, Admiral Keller?" he purred as he moved up beside her. It was like watching an iceberg ooze along. Or a glacier. Almost as warm and friendly, for all the smile on his face.

Jessica nodded. "Indeed, Chancellor. It has been a most illuminating evening already."

"Pity you could not partake of the food we have prepared."

Oh, please. Eat something here, out of a random buffet, after someone tried to assassinate Warlock *in broad daylight? Not bloody likely, pal.*

"Unfortunately," she replied with a sad smile. Ever the airhead. *Sell it well.* "Fleet regulations are very explicit about such things. Perhaps, with a bit of planning, I could entertain a small, intimate group of prominent locals such as yourself aboard *Auberon* sometime soon. Perhaps a dozen or so? Fly you all up for the evening? I have a truly fantastic head chef who lives to entertain lavishly and compose fantastically complex meals."

If I would ever let him. Unlike dinner last night, which was shrimp in curry over rice, with leafy greens on the side and a glass of fruit juice.

Best not to mention that part. Chef Aoiki really was magic when she let him turn it loose. She just had far simpler tastes than that. *Maybe I should reward him by letting him go crazy some night soon. I'm sure they don't deserve his best efforts, but I might. Especially after all these posturing fools.*

Jessica smiled vacuously at the man.

He muttered something that sounded like, "Perhaps, m'lady," as he nodded briefly to her and headed off.

Jessica smiled at his back as he left. She would consider this evening a double win. Frost the chancellor, and possibly meeting an ally.

That might make up for the noise.

Desianna moved through the large chamber at a healthy pace. Not awkward or hurried, but obviously *Headed Someplace Important.*

Here and there, she diverted her course long enough to chat as she made her way through the crowd, but paused only briefly until she came up to a young man, well-dressed in the latest pirate fashions.

On him, however, it worked. And looked good. She had made sure of that. Arnulf wasn't going to live forever, regardless of what he thought. David, her first child, Arnulf's oldest son, would be in line for the throne in any proper monarchy. Here, it also put an extra-large target on his back. One she had to work to protect.

And she did.

He leaned down to kiss her on the cheek as she stepped close. He had all of his father's height, if not the muscular bulk that had made the man King of the Pirates. But he had gotten brains from both sides of the family, as well as charisma.

In any other place, she could see him making a very good king.

The old hidebound captains who ruled here would never allow it.

Not for the first time, she considered talking him into fleeing. She had contacts and relatives in *Aquitaine*, her own dirty secret. They could start over.

He would never accept her logic. At least not until it was too late.

She looked backwards over her shoulder at the crowd, seeing them as a mother bear eying a pack of weasels. Hungry, but still vermin.

She smiled and turned back to her son.

"Whatever plans you had tomorrow," she whispered as she leaned close to kiss him on the ear, "you need to cancel and visit me immediately after lunch. No questions. Smile at all the people like I have just told you a particularly funny joke."

She felt his hands turn hard for a second, gripping her upper arms tightly before he relaxed. His laugh even sounded almost natural.

"Of course," he said as he kissed her on the forehead with a ready smile before he turned back to the group standing nearby.

Desianna smiled at them, kissed a few more young men, complimented a few wives' outfits, and then made her way to a side door.

She paused there, turning back to examine the room. Arnulf was on his platform with Mei Fan, Wife Number Three, close by, still looking utterly gorgeous. Arnulf really did have a knack for finding beautiful women who aged slowly, something she still teased him about on the few nights she had him to herself.

Across the room, Mei Fan met her eyes suddenly with a harsh glare. The woman could be territorial about such things, insecure about her own place in the palace. Pity they could never be friends.

Elsewhere, that worm of a chancellor seemed intent on Keller from the corner where he was currently conspiring with Captain Zhao. Several other men circled them. Nobody she trusted. Few she liked. Many she would happily poison, given the opportunity.

When she felt no eyes upon her, Desianna slipped through a side door.

Things were coming to a head. It felt like clouds suddenly rushing upwards as the lightning was about to begin. She didn't know what was next, but she trusted that she could ride it out. After all, she had successfully navigated the shoals of palace politics for more than a quarter of a century.

And now *Aquitaine* had arrived as well. Was that a beneficial outcome, or merely a respite before the storm?

CHAPTER XXVIII

Date of the Republic November 2, 393 City of Corynthe, Petron

Jessica walked down the clinic corridor past four of her own marines, plus two of the *King's Own*, currently in a very polite pissing match about precedence and who was the bigger bad-ass.

Boys being boys.

Marcelle waited outside, with the boys. Probably would make them all look like pikers in seconds. She was good at that.

Inside, *Warlock* was awake, his eyes bright on her as she entered and closed the door.

He looked sallow, almost yellow, eyes bloodshot and tired even after a night of sleep.

"Apparently," he said with a smile, "I'm not dead."

Jessica cocked an eyebrow at him. "Is this your vision of what hell looks like, *Warlock*?"

He shrugged, painfully from the wince on his face, and then smiled. "Heaven, maybe."

"Really?" Her voice dripped with utter sarcasm.

Warlock grinned at her and tried to leer. The yellow hue to his cheeks ruined the effect. And she was in no mood to play nurse.

"Feel like answering some useful questions for a change?" Jessica inquired, hoping she could play on his weakness and emotional debts.

"Depends, Keller," he replied, suddenly going all cagey on her. "What type of questions?"

She looked closely at him. Wounded on hip, forearm, and shoulder, plus the after-effect of the poison. Tired, weak, perhaps a touch angry, although at her for bothering him, or at himself for being bedridden, was a hard call. An active man like him couldn't enjoy that level of disability.

"I met Desianna Indah-Rodriguez last night," she began.

Warlock smiled. "She worried you'll supplant her as First Wife?"

"Not anymore," Jessica replied. "I hope. We're meeting later."

The man pursed his lips, but remained silent.

"What kind of woman is she, *Warlock*?"

He was silent for several moments.

"Driven," he said finally. "She's been with Arnulf for nearly thirty years, protecting him, protecting the kids." He thought for a moment. "Hard. Tough. Smart. Reminds me of someone."

Jessica's eyes threatened to roll back in her head. Flirtatious banter from a pirate was absolutely not on her menu this morning.

"She and Chancellor Du get along?"

"Nobody gets along with Jing Du," Warlock replied. "He is simply a fact of life. Not a force of nature like Arnulf, but a quiet little schemer who makes things run."

"He the one who tried to have you assassinated?"

"What do you mean, Keller?"

She had his interest now.

"*Hellhound* cleared it with Arnulf before he challenged you, Ishikura," she said simply. "I presume that he felt he had some level of protection. Arnulf was so angry he warned the family off you, under penalty of exile, so it had to be someone else who would have given him that protection, if the fight had gone the other way."

"Really?" *Warlock* got a thoughtful look on his face. "That would explain a lot."

He started to say something else, but stopped himself.

"What?" Jessica asked, leaning closer. Not quite in his face, but hovering over him.

"It would…" he trailed off.

"Talk, Daneel."

He looked up in surprise at her hard tone. She was tired of dancing with him. Either she got something useful, or she abandoned him, right here.

"One of the reasons I got sent to *Sarmarsh* originally was because of *Hellhound*'s brother."

"I knew that already," she sounded exasperated. She considered walking away right now.

"Willem was one of Du's people. So was Rory."

That stopped her.

Jessica's tactical mind locked in and began spinning out scenarios and testing them, at a speed that probably would have frightened *Warlock*. She could see lines and tides, patterns she had remembered from the first audience, the fight, the meeting, the reception.

She also began filing names into dangerous players and bystanders likely to be collateral damage. At least she had something to work with now.

Like a rock dropped into a still pond, her arrival here had probably upset a number of carefully laid plans. Now, she just had to figure out how she could press the course of that river into something useful to herself, *Lincolnshire*, and *Aquitaine*.

A voice intruded from behind. Marcelle.

"Sir?" was all she said. The tone was enough to bring Jessica's head around.

The door to the room was open. She could see Marcelle standing in the door, not quite barring someone else, but preventing them from coming further.

"What is it, Yeoman?" she said, careful to drop into the formal set of rules. Public behavior for the civilians. Someone was out there beyond the doctors they already knew. Someone interesting enough to make Marcelle get formal.

"Someone to see *Warlock*, sir," Marcelle replied carefully. Neutrally.

That in itself said something about Marcelle's opinion of the person.

"Show them in, please," Jessica replied. Marcelle would come along. The six boys with guns outside could probably hold the door without her help. Probably.

"Aye."

Marcelle escorted a tiny woman into the room.

She was well dressed by the local standards, and extremely attractive. Like people on all worlds, she represented an interesting mix of ethnographies. Brown hair framed a heart-shaped face and brown eyes. Her figure was verging on lush, for lack of a better term to describe it. She might have been any age between twenty-five and forty-five. It was hard to judge.

Jessica could see worry scribed on her features as she approached the hospital bed.

"Daneel?" she said, barely above a whisper.

"Hello, Teri," he said. Jessica rated his carefully neutral voice about the same level as Marcelle's.

Interesting.

Teri paused for a moment, obviously looking for the right words. "Are you okay?"

"You should see the other guy," he replied with a laugh.

Jessica stepped to her left so that she could see both of them at the same time, accidentally mirroring Marcelle, who was doing the same from the other side.

Jessica also felt like a giant next to this newcomer, which was rare, as short as she was compared to most women, to say nothing of men. However, they both probably massed about the same, given the shorter woman's curves and bosom.

The stranger turned suddenly to Jessica. "Keller, right?"

Jessica nodded.

"Thank you."

"For?" Jessica felt like she had come into the middle of a previous conversation.

"Bringing him home. Protecting him. Helping."

"You're welcome," Jessica replied. She felt the neutral tones of the room bleed into her conversation as well. *Time to fix that.* She forced a polite smile. "And you are?"

"Ekaterina Estes," the young woman replied. "Teri."

She paused, looking for the next words. She didn't find them quickly enough. The woman was an open book. Concern. Uncertainty. Something deeper?

"Teri," *Warlock* said quietly. "Why are you here?"

Teri took a deep breath, almost a sigh.

Jessica felt uncomfortable just listening and watching.

She didn't do emotional scenes. She didn't enjoy watching them, either.

"I wanted to make sure you were okay, Daneel," Teri said in a pleading voice. "Isn't that what friends do?"

"I'm good, Teri," he replied. "for nearly dying in a duel. In good hands now. And I'll be back to normal in no time. Does Jean-Michel know you're here?"

Teri reacted exactly as if *Warlock* had gotten out of bed and slapped her with an open palm. The look of pain and anguish that took over her face almost made Jessica want to punch the man, on general principle.

She refrained, barely.

Marcelle seemed to be thinking similar dark thoughts.

Instead of speaking, Teri turned to Jessica. Jessica felt her look up one side and down the other, with a wild, angry gleam in her eyes, even as Teri's face flushed.

Jessica almost stepped back from that look. She even considered a couple of blocks and strikes from close range, before she stopped herself.

This woman wouldn't be crazy enough to attack her. Right?

With a flash of insight, things crystalized around Jessica. The woman, the look, the language, the body language. The banter with *Warlock.*

Jealousy.

Teri saw her as a romantic rival for this man. *Really? Her? Him?*

Teri glanced back at *Warlock*, even angrier. "You're right, Daneel," she sneered suddenly. "I should be home with my husband instead of worrying about you. You're fine. You're always fine, aren't you?"

The woman gave Jessica another hard look, but she was speaking to *Warlock* anyway. "I can see that I'm not needed here. You'll be just fine. I'll take my leave, thank you."

In a flash, she was gone, with Marcelle trailing in her wake.

Jessica took a breath and tried to figure out what had just happened. She looked back at Daneel. He shrugged.

"It's complicated," he said, by way of explanation.

"Ex-girlfriend?" Jessica hazarded a guess.

"Close," he replied. "Ex-wife."

Jessica raised an eyebrow at him.

"Complicated."

"She thought I was the new one, apparently," Jessica said.

"Teri can be a drama queen," he said. "Besides, would that be so bad?"

"I beg your pardon?"

Jessica didn't bother trying to keep the anger out of her voice.

Maybe she should punch him. Knock some sense into the man.

She was tired of getting marriage proposals from pirates. It was getting old, and hadn't been funny to begin with.

He at least had the courtesy to look chagrined as she rounded on him. Both of his hands came up, although she couldn't tell if that was a defensive response or surrender.

Better be both, mister.

"Sorry, Keller," he said. "I spoke out of turn. It won't happen again."

"See that it doesn't, Daneel," she half-snarled back at him. "We do that sort of thing differently in *Aquitaine*. Perhaps you should learn that sometime."

Jessica didn't wait for a response. She stomped to the door, flung it open, and stomped out, surprising Marcelle and the boys guarding the room. Marcelle fell in immediately, letting her longer legs keep up with Jessica's agitated pace.

About thirty meters down the hallway, getting back into the main parts of Arnulf's palace, Jessica stopped so suddenly that Marcelle actually ran into her shoulder.

Had she really just told *Warlock* to learn *Aquitaine* customs if he wanted to court her? It had sounded like that coming out of her mouth, once she had time to consider her words.

Crap.

She certainly couldn't go back and explain what she really meant.

What had she really meant?

Jessica blinked up at Marcelle, almost in embarrassment, and then continued back down the hall without a word. Silence seemed the least possible evil right now.

But strange thoughts intruded, atop all the tactical and strategic politics that had been filling her morning.

She certainly couldn't tell Marcelle how the man smelled. There was a rightness to it that hadn't registered on her before now.

Marcelle would give her no end of grief. Besides, she was the one that chased after men, or women, as the mood struck, not Jessica.

That was not her style. He was not her type.

Did she have a type? Had any man turned her head, ever? Well, one, but he was happily married and didn't see her that way.

Crap.

Jessica growled under her breath and set out to locate Desianna's apartment. Hopefully, that would go over easier than this had.

She really needed another session with the fighting robot.

CHAPTER XXIX

Date of the Republic November 2, 393 City of Corynthe, Petron

Desianna waited.

She did that well.

Patience.

Water was soft, and yet would grind down mountains with time.

It was patient.

Fire was hot and fast and often painful.

Wind was a burst of energy and then nothing.

Kind of like a few of the men she had known.

This sitting room was as perfect as she could get it. Cozy. Discrete. Subdued.

Nobody was allowed in here except her. Locals would have found the space disconcerting, claustrophobic.

It was, for Desianna, a shrine to her mother. To the time before Father had taken them to the frontier to find his fortune. Before poverty and piracy and *Corynthe.*

Not that she would ever whisper a hint of that to anyone.

She had spent four decades fitting in, making do, overcoming obstacles, going from that little girl in pigtails to the First Wife of *Corynthe.*

Not that she entertained Arnulf very much anymore. Mei Fan was the favored consort now, since Charlotte had died. But still, Desianna kept his attention from time to time, with passions the younger woman hadn't learned or never discovered.

Her place in his palace was secure.

As long as it was *his* palace.

What did *Aquitaine* want? What did it mean, that they were here, now?

The riptides were building. She could feel them tug at her toes.

Fools would fall. Fortunes would be made.

And an *Aquitaine* fleet hovered overhead.

Desianna remembered to breathe.

She felt almost dowdy today, dressed in simple slate-gray pants and a maroon tunic, Arnulf's favorite colors. The ensemble made her hair glow softly and her eyes glow like fire.

Only the barest minimum of jewelry today, all gold: a ring from Arnulf, all those years ago; earrings from her son; a bracelet that had been her mother's.

She felt almost naked without half a pound of gold in bangles and chains and fripperies, to say nothing of pearls and gems and the sorts of jewelry an important, beautiful woman can acquire for a favor or a smile.

And the room was too subtle for someone from *Petron*, even a native of the capital city. The walls were done with a fabric dyed a very dark green, highlighted with gold and white.

Before Keller had arrived, very few people would have seen those colors and realized they were the colors of the Republic.

The space was a proper sitting room such as one might find on *Ladaux* or *Anameleck Prime*, comfortable for two, cozy for four. Small enough for tea. Or conspiracies.

A knock startled Desianna from her reveries.

The door opened partway and a woman peeked in.

"Yes, Intan?" Desianna asked, suddenly breathless with nerves.

"Your guest has arrived," the woman replied quietly.

"Please, show her in."

Desianna rose to her feet.

She wiped her suddenly damp hands on the backs of her pants and centered herself.

Calmness. Courtesy. Perfection.

Aquitaine was here.

Jessica entered the inner chamber with a touch of trepidation. The rooms she had passed through had had a very homey feel to them, but in a completely feminine way she found almost alien.

At that last door, as the maid knocked, Jessica flashed back to First Lord Kasum's door at Fleet HQ. Room 2304.

The Dragon's Den.

This was almost as far as you could get from that place, socially or politically.

And yet…

Inside, the surprises multiplied.

Her mother would have had a tea room like this, had she ever stopped crafting long enough to dedicate a whole room to formally entertaining visitors. Indira Chastain-Keller, however, would have never parted with the sort of money required to purchase the intricately crafted tea set on the table, nor the little statue of Ganesh, or the Kali-ma, the jade carved rose, or the matched set of antique measuring cups. Even after she could have afforded it.

Not even on a wild splurge. She was just too moderate and careful with her money.

Jessica had been in salons like this, though. When visiting Fleet Lords who represented the Fifty Families of the Republic. Money. Power.

Desianna, as far as she knew, wasn't one of them. But this room had not been assembled overnight. And it could have graced any number of mansions, back home.

Jessica took the offered chair and sat with all the care she would have, had she just discovered she had navigated into a minefield. A real one, and not just a social construct far beyond her experiences.

Hopefully, not beyond her preparations.

The maid left. The door closed with a heft similar to the primary airlock hatch to Engineering.

Solid.

They were alone. She could trust Desianna. She could trust the food.

She hoped.

The tea was amazing. The little cucumber and dill sandwiches could have been served by her mother, or one of her aunts. And they took those sorts of things extremely serious.

The small talk was carefully vague and obtuse. The weather, the room, the ball.

Idle chatter.

Jessica would have been willing to bet anyone good money that there was not another room like this in the palace, let alone on the planet. Meeting here was a message she hoped she could work with, from someone telling her, in her own way, that she understood *Aquitaine*.

Jessica set down her mostly empty tea mug. She dared hope.

Desianna eyed her warily.

"I don't know where to begin, Desianna," Jessica said carefully. Social maneuvering was an alien thing. She was still working on it.

Desianna's stress levels went down. It was there in the relaxation around the eyes, invisible if Jessica hadn't already been looking so closely at the woman to see it.

"What brings you to *Corynthe*, Jessica?"

Jessica considered herself again.

At the end of the day, nothing so much as raw Gunboat Diplomacy.

A reminder that *Aquitaine* was an ally of *Lincolnshire*, and *Corynthe* should mind its manners and abide by its treaties. A hope that maybe she could prevent a war that would draw *Aquitaine* in, at the very time when the *Fribourg Empire* was already feeling the weight of the fighting after all the damage she had done a year ago at places like *2218 Svati Prime* or *C'Xindo*.

Desianna waved a hand to forestall whatever words she thought Jessica was going to say.

"You destroyed the base at *Sarmarsh IV*, Jessica," she continued. "You could have easily killed them all. Why didn't you?"

Jessica took a breath, and a leap.

"*Aquitaine* doesn't want a war, Desianna," she said. "I have a reputation back home as a fighting commander. The hope was that *Corynthe* would recognize what I could do if turned loose. Instead, I'm trying to play nice. Will they?"

"I don't know, Jessica," the woman murmured back. "Arnulf has enemies. They would overthrow him in a heartbeat if they could. Every day is a challenge to keep the monsters at bay."

Jessica eyed her carefully.

"Desianna, I'm *Aquitaine*," Jessica said bluntly. The conversation suddenly seemed to demand it. "I'm not sure we aren't better off fostering that sort of civil strife here. A weak *Corynthe* is less trouble for the neighbors."

Her reward was a look of pain that quickly turned hard.

"Without Arnulf," Desianna replied, "the wolves will run wild. Study your history. What was it like fifty years ago? A hundred? He's trying to make *Petron* a place, and not just a bar and a brothel and a skid row."

Inside, Jessica shrugged. Should she tell this woman that all of *Corynthe* barely rated more that *Here there be dragons* in most history books of the galactic fringes, or the *Fleet's Gazette*? *Lincolnshire* might have been able to tell her more, but it had seemed more important to strike the pirates hard and fast, before they could prepare. At *Sarmarsh*, she had even caught an Imperial Admiral with his hand in the cookie jar.

Jessica's blood went cold. Several pieces of a puzzle clicked, all at once, into an entirely new configuration from what she had been seeing before.

Admiral Wachturm really *had* had his hand in the cookie jar. Doing just exactly the opposite of what she was trying to do, as was entirely appropriate from where he stood.

She had envisioned an Imperial plot to help *Corynthe* invade *Lincolnshire.* And that might still be the case.

But what if the plot was against Arnulf? Bring back the wolves, let them run wild over *Lincolnshire*, blooding *Ramsey* and other places. Draw *Aquitaine* farther out onto the frontier, since the *Fribourg Empire* ran closer to the fringes than *Aquitaine*, bordered directly by *Lincolnshire*, and then *Corynthe* beyond it. The Republic would have to respond.

"You begin to see?" Desianna said quietly, apparently noting the change in Jessica's eyes.

"At *Sarmarsh*, when Ian Zhao fled, we captured an Imperial Admiral, Emmerich Wachturm. He claimed diplomatic immunity, so I can't just throw him in the brig, but he was most certainly meeting with Zhao and Daneel Ishikura."

"The Red Admiral?"

Jessica was impressed, but the man's reputation was spectacular. It was possible he was known this far out.

"Zhao is Jing Du's man," Desianna breathed, leaning forward.

"And Daneel?"

Desianna was silent for a moment. "He was always loyal to Arnulf. After he killed Willem Agano, Arnulf sent him to *Sarmarsh*, partly as a punishment, and partly to keep him away from Rory and the rest of the clan."

"Did he know that?"

Desianna shrugged.

"Better, was he mad enough about it to listen to promises from Jing Du?" Jessica could see a thread binding all the bits together, like popcorn on a thread.

She blinked. This room really did remind her of home. She hadn't done something silly like make a popcorn necklace since she was a little girl.

"That I could believe," Desianna said. "But why assassinate him now?"

Jessica was far enough ahead in her logic to guess. It was not a pretty sight.

"They wanted him isolated out there, Desianna," she said. "Him here, with my fleet, suggests that he might have turned loyal again. Or it might be to keep him from revealing their plans to Arnulf in order to buy his life."

"Or," Desianna said, "they don't need him anymore, since you destroyed the base that was his reason for being involved in the first place. Du is a cut-throat son of a bitch."

Jessica considered the angles. They were all bad.

"Could we turn him loyal again?" Desianna asked.

Jessica felt her face harden. Her shoulders came up all by themselves. And she had suggested he learn how to court her? "Why would we care?"

Desianna blinked at her and leaned back. She started to speak, stopped herself, and looked closely at Jessica.

Jessica felt like grinding her teeth, but managed not to. Barely.

"He can be a very charismatic man," Desianna said obliquely, a vague smile painting her lips.

Jessica let both of her eyebrows rise, although she kept her sarcastic, caustic comment to herself.

"He owes you his life twice now," Desianna continued. "Contrary to what you might think, he can be an honorable man."

"He's a pirate," Jessica growled back.

"We're all pirates, Jessica. These are poor worlds on the fringe. And only eleven are loyal enough to Arnulf as king to pay their taxes regularly. There are dozens of others determined to go their own way."

"And what does Daneel have to do with that?"

Desianna smiled a private smile. "Let me talk to him, Jessica. He might confide in me. We have been friends for a long time."

"Lovers?" The world came out before Jessica could stop it. She clamped her jaws tight. Not grinding. Crushing, perhaps.

Desianna shook her head. "Never with Daneel. Contrary to palace rumor, I am not a wanton slut bedding every virile young man I see." She shrugged.

"If I have occasional needs, Arnulf knows of those affairs. Many have been political, tools of statecraft."

Jessica found herself silently mouthing the words. "Tools of statecraft." They didn't make any more sense the second time she heard them.

"But I have never taken Daneel into my bed, Jessica. He is a dear friend, and nothing more."

That seemed to help her relax.

Where did all this anger come from? Especially over a man? One she barely knew? A pirate?

Grrrrr.

Jessica drew in a breath, held it, let it escape. Some of the energy went with it. Fleet maneuvers in three dimensional gravity fields made more sense. And made her less angry.

"So *Lincolnshire*'s security relies on Arnulf's staying in power?" Jessica said.

Who knew interstellar politics would provide welcome conversational respite?

"I believe so," Desianna said, relief creeping into her voice as she relaxed as well.

"How do we convince him to bother other people?" Jessica said. The King of the Pirates wasn't about to just lie down with the lamb.

Desianna thought for a second, eyes darting back and forth, staring at an invisible horizon. For a moment, it was just like watching Moirrey at work. That made Jessica smile.

"Isolate the main players," Desianna said abruptly.

"Huh?" Jessica felt like she was back in Introductory Fleet Tactics class on the first day, trying to learn the vocabulary, the ships, and the vectors in real time, all while being graded.

That actually made it feel better.

She could learn this. Future First Lord Nils Kasum had been her instructor then. Perhaps she could learn what she needed from Desianna. The woman was obviously just as serious an expert in her chosen field.

"We need to get Arnulf, the chancellor, Ian Zhao, and Daneel Ishikura away from *Petron*. If the plot centers on them, we derail it by being elsewhere. Certainly, we can't leave the others here without adult supervision."

Jessica could follow that line of logic.

Just like maneuvering fleets.

She laughed to herself.

"What?" Desianna said.

"My aide, Marcelle, uses the phrase *adult supervision* occasionally, usually to describe my pilots on *Auberon*."

"Pilots are pilots." Desianna laughed back.

"So what would you suggest, Desianna? How do we isolate the key people and work on them?"

"A Promenade."

"A what?" Jessica felt the ground shift under her again.

"Would you be willing to take a tour of several *Corynthian* worlds, Jessica? Take your squadron and several Motherships and be seen by the locals?"

"Would that help solidify Arnulf's hold on power, by showing them that he has a new ally in *Aquitaine*?"

"Yes," Desianna said. "Meanwhile, we can work on the others and see if we can find out what they have planned. I'm sure whatever it is it will happen when we get back. Without Du and Zhao here, no coup could succeed."

"There is one thing you will have to do for me, Desianna Indah-Rodriguez."

The woman stared at her closely for a moment, her eyes suddenly serious, though she remained silent.

"You will also need to convince Arnulf and Jing Du to fly in state aboard my ship, aboard *Auberon*, while the others escort us."

"So, hostages?" Desianna concluded.

"Your lives will be in my hands, yes. Will Arnulf accept those conditions?"

Desianna smiled slyly. "I have known the man for three decades, Jessica. I can convince him."

Jessica nodded. It would be interesting to have Arnulf and the Red Admiral, together for dinner. She held out her hand to this woman who was apparently now her co-conspirator.

Desianna took it, held it.

Jessica tried to relax.

"Now," Desianna said, rising and pulling Jessica to her feet. "I have a young man I would like to introduce you to. You may not seduce him, Jessica Keller."

Jessica's confusion felt evident on her face.

Desianna opened the door to let the outside world in.

"I asked my son, David, Arnulf's oldest child, to join us this afternoon, but that will be nothing more than idle chatter."

Jessica smiled at the implied compliment and followed the woman out into the outer chamber. Hopefully, there would be no more marriage proposals from pirates.

At least today.

PART IV: PROMENADE

CHAPTER XXX

Date of the Republic November 21, 393 Walea System

Desianna waited as Intan closed the door to her salon and departed. Technically, it was verging on inappropriate to entertain a man privately, but this was a conversation she didn't wish to share even with her maid, a woman who had been with her for over a decade.

Back home, there were a few people she might invite, mostly to provide camouflage, but they were many light years away right now. So she would settle for whatever whispers might start.

It would all be moot soon, anyway, one way or another.

Daneel Ishikura sat nervously across from her, as though called to the principal's office and about to get in trouble with his parents. Desianna could only imagine what thoughts were going through his head, what guilt.

She poured tea and handed him a mug before pouring her own.

"Daneel," she began, quiet but firm, "how have you been faring?"

Best to put him at ease, especially considering what was coming next.

"Well enough," he replied neutrally. "The effects of the poison were flushed out of my system within a few days. There are still occasional moments of weakness, like phantom pain in a joint, and my dreams are a bit more vivid than before."

"Nightmares?"

"Sometimes," he shrugged. "Other times…"

She felt the uncertainty in his voice, this man she had known for better than a decade. But she also heard other tones. Deeper, for lack of a better term. From a man well known for his embrace of the pirate lifestyle.

As with Jessica Keller, it felt like time to take a gamble.

"Daneel," she said, "I need your help."

One eyebrow rose and spoke silent volumes about the man. Two years ago, he would have said something. Anything. Just to fill the silence.

Being exiled to *Sarmarsh* had changed him. Nearly dying twice had as well. Hopefully, for the better.

"What's Jing Du up to?" Desianna asked bluntly. Better to get it out into the open early, like tearing a bandage off. Quick pain, and then relief.

Daneel squinted at her carefully. Unlike with other men, there was nothing of an eye wandering about her bosom and curves.

This felt like a man measuring her for a blow. Which said a great deal all by itself. *Warlock* used to be about as shallow as a mud puddle.

"*We* know." She emphasized the parties unknown to make him understand that this was bigger than just the two of them, "We know that he has gone well beyond his usual posturing and triple-crossing. This isn't about him retaining his power in the palace, Daneel. He is becoming a threat to Arnulf."

"And?" Daneel asked her back, just as bluntly.

Desianna stared closely. She could barely discern the old *Warlock* in this new person sitting across the small salon from her. That man had been gruff and loud.

Now he was turning subtle.

"I would like to think," Desianna replied, "that they wouldn't have tried to assassinate you in open Court, if you were working with *them*. Arnulf tends to agree. Jessica Keller isn't so sure."

She watched his eyes growl and his nostrils flare. Interestingly, not at the mention of Arnulf, his king, but at Jessica.

"That woman…" he growled under his breath.

"Is deeper and more dangerous than you realize, Daneel Ishikura. She's had three opportunities to see you dead. So far. And yet, here you are."

"Three?"

She watched his anger morph into a vague confusion.

"At *Sarmarsh*, you should have been dead. She stood your Second when *Hellhound* tried to kill you. And you only survived because her marines are that good and she brow-beat the royal surgeon into putting you in Arnulf's personal clinic. Anywhere else and the poison would have done you in before you arrived."

His eyes were unfocused, his whole body language vague.

"Three," she heard him whisper.

"So, again," Desianna pressed, "whose side are you on, Daneel?"

She watched him come back to himself with a start. For a moment, he stared at her as if she had appeared out of thin air, before he blinked and centered.

"My side, Desi," he said. "Always my side. Ask anyone. Loyal to the throne. A good little minion, doing what he's told. What more could you ask?"

"Loyalty to Arnulf?"

"Ha," he cried. "That man sent me to *Sarmarsh* in the first place."

"Yes," Desianna agreed. "To keep you safe from the Agano clan and their allies trying to get revenge for Willem."

"Well then," he snarled at her quietly, "that certainly didn't work. It took Rory all of five minutes to try his luck when I got back."

"Arnulf thought that you were conspiring with Ian Zhao and the Red Admiral to overthrow him," she replied, trying to keep any emotion out of her voice.

"And now?"

She could see his anger running just below the surface, like a hungry leopard seal hunting.

"Arnulf told them that they risked his anger if they touched you. That he would protect you from them if they tried again. Does that count for anything?"

"I had heard that, from *her*," he said. "Did he mean it?"

For a moment, she could see the crack in his armor. Jessica. Apparently, she had gotten to him.

Desianna wondered if either of them realized how they reacted when the other's name came up. Or rather, if they understood why.

She kept a serious face, even as she smiled inside.

"He wasn't sure." Desianna pressed her point home, like a duelist against a suddenly-lame foe. "Jessica convinced him to bring you with us on this Promenade. Probably since you wouldn't be safe with Arnulf absent."

"Keller did that? Why?"

Desianna had once had a small lap-dog that would occasionally give her that same confused look, that odd cock to the head, when she spoke to it.

She fought down the laugh that threatened to erupt from her lips at the memory. This was most certainly not the moment for such levity.

"Apparently," Desianna said ambiguously, "she saw something in you worth salvaging at *Sarmarsh*, and again at *Petron*. Perhaps she thought you had it in you to grow up and become someone more interesting than just another pirate from *Corynthe*?"

For just a moment, Desianna thought she had gone too far. Certainly, with the old *Warlock*, that would have been too much. But this new person, this Daneel Ishikura, former governor of *Sarmarsh*, former conspirator, former Captain, had plumbed new depths.

At least, that's what she was counting on.

His next words confirmed it.

"So what would you like me to say here, Desianna?" he said simply. "Shall I dance to Arnulf's tune? Implicate Jing Du and Ian Zhao in such a way that I'm an innocent bystander? Spin tales of treachery and conspiracies to fill his need to settle old scores?"

"No," she replied. "Because you wouldn't even believe them yourself, Daneel."

He blinked, shock blanking his face.

Really? Were there any men out there with half a brain?

This was another one of those times when she wished that *Corynthe* was sophisticated enough that Arnulf could show off his brains, and that men like Daneel Ishikura could become educated, instead of being big, dumb warriors.

"Two things," she continued, letting her own anger bleed slowly into her voice. "First, you need to figure out whose side you plan to be on when the flag goes up. You don't have long. Second, you really need to decide what it is you want to be when you grow up. Or were you planning on being a man-child for the rest of your life?"

He just sat there, apparently an empty shell.

Desianna decided that she didn't want her tea after all. She rose, stepped around him, and opened the hatch.

"I still don't know what it is that Jessica sees in you, Daneel," Desianna said, looking back. "Hopefully, something good."

She stepped fully into the outer chamber and closed the door before he could see the tremendous grin on her face. He was almost as transparent as Jessica. If only one of them could be made to see it.

"Mistress?" Intan said, rising from a comfortable chair and setting a book down.

Desianna waved her off, letting her smile turn mischievous.

"Intan," she said, "I'm going to retire to my cabin, feeling unwell, if anyone asks. I suspect *Warlock* will emerge in a few minutes, probably somewhat bewildered. Make sure he's okay when he departs, please."

"Yes, madam," Intan smirked back. "Was the tea and the company too much for our poor pirate to handle?"

"Indeed, I suspect it was."

"Very good," her maid replied. "I will see him off."

Desianna crossed the chamber and entered her personal suite, normally apparently a place for visiting admirals, but currently hers.

Jessica had entrusted her to bring *Warlock* around. She just really didn't understand what Desianna planned for him. Or her.

CHAPTER XXXI

Date of the Republic December 3, 393 Hemera System

The comm chirped just as he was sitting down to dinner.

"Aeliaes. Go ahead," Robertson Aeliaes, *Brightoak's* command centurion, replied.

"We just got hailed, Skipper," his second in command said. "You'll want to be up on the bridge in about twenty minutes or so when they get close enough to talk real time."

"Who is it?"

"*CR-264* just dropped out of Jumpspace and transmitted a big packet of data for whoever was here to carry back to the fleet. When he realized it was us, he also requested a face to face."

"Jessica Keller and *Auberon* with him?"

"Negative, boss," she replied. "Just Tomas Kigali for now."

"Acknowledged," he said. "Wake up the flight deck and deploy a shuttle over to pick him up. And send a bottle of wine over when you do. Knowing Kigali, he just set another navigation record from wherever he was before this."

"Roger that."

Brightoak's primary conference room alone was larger than *CR-264*'s entire bridge. It was an odd thing to come to mind as Tomas Kigali walked into the room. It made him smile.

CR-264 was designed for long sails with a small crew, an old Revenue Cutter. She was compact, designed to maximize efficiency. A piloting room, where he practically lived, with his office opposite the head. Space for him, a pilot, and a comm yeoman.

The fighting deck was down a level, with sensors and tactical scrunched in tight together so they could fight as a team with a minimum of friction and distraction.

But *Brightoak* was a Destroyer Leader, bigger than even *Rajput.* Kigali felt like he could probably stuff his whole vessel inside her flight deck. He couldn't, not even on *Auberon*, but it felt that way.

So much open space because they had enough power to do anything they wanted.

He smiled to himself. Except sail halfway across the galaxy without stopping for potty breaks every thirty days.

Command Centurion Aeliaes, an old acquaintance he still called Robbie, was already present, along with members of his command staff. He stood as Kigali entered.

Physically, Robbie was an impressive officer. Tall and well-kept, the man had muscles like a swimmer, or a polo player. Chocolate-brown skin and darker hair, with eyes that appeared brown or golden, depending on the light.

Mentally, a brilliant man always on the edge of insubordination with Jessica's old nemesis, Fleet Lord Loncar, according to some of the stories Kigali had heard through the fleet grapevine.

Right now, just what he needed most in the world.

"Tom," he said, "good to see you again."

Tomas crossed the space and shook his hand. "Robbie. You have no idea how happy I am to find you guys. How the hell did you end up here?"

"We were attached to the fleet sent out to the *Cahllepp Frontier* after you guys left. But Jessica's old commander, Fleet Lord Loncar, just doesn't like us much," Aeliaes replied. "He sent us out here as a punishment detail. Keeps us out of his hair."

They sat and settled as a yeoman brought coffee and tea.

Robertson Aeliaes speared him with a hard look finally, his chocolate skin getting all wrinkly with the seriousness of his thoughts.

"Okay," he said, "out with it. I thought you were cruising the fringes with Jessica. What brings you to *Hemera*?"

Kigali nodded and smiled grimly. He quickly related the events at *Ramsey*, *Sarmarsh IV*, and *Petron* to a roomful of rapt listeners.

"So this, what did you call it, a Promenade?" Aeliaes asked.

"Correct. A Promenade," Kigali replied.

"Right," Aeliaes continued. "Promenade. So she's sailing the King of the Pirates world to world to show off that we're friends now? Are we?"

Kigali looked at the assembled officers with a serious face. "Between us, she's expecting all hell to break loose when she completes the circuit and gets back to *Petron*." He shrugged. "She sent me on the mail run before she knew more than that."

"And what do you want from us, Tom?" Aeliaes asked.

"I was just dropping into *Hemera* to leave a log packet and pick up news," Kigali smiled. "From here, a straight jump across to *Ramsey* to see if I can talk the governor into letting me borrow *CR-255* and *CR-219* long enough to scare the bad guys back at *Petron*. *CR-264*'s out of her league solo against that many Motherships, but an interlocked escort squadron is a whole other beast. Jessica figures that more guns to back her play might convince whoever is being dumb over there to walk away instead."

"Will it work?"

"Anybody but Jessica," Tomas shrugged, "and I'd say no. Loncar for sure. But this is Jessica Keller we're talking about. The woman always finds a way."

"That she does. Need help?" Robbie Aeliaes asked slyly.

Kigali watched *Brightoak*'s first officer tap the table, just loud enough to get everyone's attention.

"Devil's Advocate, Commander?" she said. "First Fleet Lord ordered us to *Hemera*, not off on adventures beyond the pale. Much fun as they might be."

Aeliaes smiled serenely. "Loncar ordered us to quote/unquote *Show the flag and remind the frontier worlds that the Republic still cares about them. Lincolnshire* would certainly welcome the morale boost that such a visit would entail."

"And *Petron*?" she asked, formal in voice, but with a mad twinkle in her eyes to match his.

"Them's pirates," Aeliaes smiled. "Who cares what they think?"

He turned to Tomas Kigali. "Want some company?"

Kigali sniffed at the assembled officers and did his best Loncar impression. "Can this poor bucket of rust even manage such a jump?"

The room howled with laughter.

"I'll have you know, Kigali," Robbie Aeliaes replied after things calmed down, his dignity all mock-serious, "I was trained by Jessica Keller."

"Well, then, *Brightoak*," Kigali smiled. "Let's see if you can keep up."

CHAPTER XXXII

Date of the Republic February 4, 394 Above Callumnia

There was a quiet little observation bubble, dimly lit and well aft, down on A Deck, tucked in under the engines. Not inaccessible, but nowhere near any crew quarters or rec facilities. That made it a nice place to sit and watch the stars. Or, in this case, the big tumbling marble of a planet below them as *Auberon* slowly orbited.

Callumnia. Third stop on the Grand Promenade with the King of the Pirates. Jessica snorted to herself at the grandiosity of the title. Still, it had been a success to hear Desianna give her all of the gossip during their weekly teas.

Certainly *Auberon* and *Rajput* looked fierce and intimidating when they dropped out of Jumpspace. All the more so when escorted by Arnulf's flagship, the 4-ring Mothership *Supernova*, plus Ian Zhao's 4-ring, *Kali-ma*, and David Rodriguez aboard his 3-ring, *Sky Dancer*.

Others also came and went. The 4-ring *Valhalla* had been with them for one stop. *Warduck*, a battered old 3-ring, had joined them here. The 2-ring *Black Prince* and a tiny little 1-ring named *Lithuania* called *Callumnia* home port.

Throw in a random collection of a dozen or so Strippers and a whole caravan of freighters, and it was something of a rolling party.

A very motley party.

Jessica smiled at that. They might talk about how civilized and proper they were, but every *Corynthian* merchant with an excuse had come along, happy to be protected from pirates. *Other* pirates.

Certainly, nobody would bother a war fleet like this. Jessica figured that with six weeks of training, she could probably take Loncar's whole fleet, both *Ajax* and *Archon*, with just the ships in hailing range right at this moment.

"Am I intruding?" a voice asked quietly.

Jessica blinked. Apparently, she had been lost deeper in concentration than she realized. She had been doing that a lot lately.

And Marcelle hadn't said anything about someone approaching.

"Hello, Daneel," she turned to face him. "Not at all. What can I do for you?"

He was dressed in a simple outfit, dark blue pants and matching tabard, with a gray tunic underneath. It was almost severe by the fashion standards of *Petron*. It wouldn't have turned heads on *Ladaux*.

She watched Marcelle and *Warlock*'s marine escort move a discreet distance, back into the hall and somewhat removed. Far enough away that they weren't obviously eavesdropping.

He moved to the rail next to her, staring out at the stars.

Jessica turned to watch his profile. For the first time that she could remember, he looked relaxed. Serene.

Desianna had said that she was making progress in bringing *Warlock* around, but Jessica hadn't really spent a lot of time around him recently to tell. Still, if Desianna was sure, she was willing to trust that.

"It's odd," he began, "not being in charge of anything. For the first time in many, many years, nobody's life is dependent on my actions, my decisions."

He turned to study her face, close enough to touch but pointedly separate.

"I wanted to say thank you," he continued.

She started to say something, but he overrode her gently.

"I know I've said it before," he said, "but I've had a lot of free time over the last month to just sit and think. To see where I was going with my life, where I wanted to go. To see that there might be more than just being a chief pirate in a kingdom of pirates. That was your gift to me, unintentional as it was. So, thank you."

Jessica smiled to hide her confusion. Certainly, she had not had time to have a conversation like that with this man. Her interactions were generally formal, save for regular, much more relaxed meals with Desianna and occasionally Arnulf. Or the more political ones that included the big players, such as the Red Admiral, Jing Du, and Ian Zhao.

Jessica didn't do personal, or emotional.

But Desianna had said to trust him.

And she wasn't sure what to say here. Or rather, what the textbooks said sounded all wrong. And the soap operas were far too gooey and false.

She retreated back into herself and turned to watch the stars as well.

Moments passed. Or minutes.

"So what does a big, bad pirate do after a mid-life crisis?" she finally said, teasingly. It was amazing how easy she could drop into that tone with this man. That manner of speech. That ease.

It probably would have frightened her, if anything actually did.

"Be liberated," he said.

"How so?"

"In *Corynthe*, only the captains have a vote in how things are run," Daneel said. "When I was the governor of *Sarmarsh*, I was a major player. Before that, I captained the 4-ring *Sunset.* My brother has her now, so I have technically no standing at all until I can challenge someone for command of a ship, or buy or build one of my own."

"And will you?" Jessica asked quietly. The gravplates in the room seemed to be off. She kept finding herself leaning to her left, closer to this man. And his smell.

"A month ago," he replied, "I had already lined up a number of candidates."

"I meant to ask," she said.

"Go on."

"If you challenged another captain and beat him, would his crew be loyal to you?"

"Absolutely," he said. "It is one of the iron-clad rules. Because to challenge a captain for command, it is a duel to the death, unless the man retires completely. That makes it very serious, and very rare. Occasionally, a captain will be promoted by acclaim, when an older captain retires or is promoted to a larger ship, and the remaining crew all agree on his replacement. But the pilots who will not abide will never fly again."

"I see," Jessica whispered. "And when you get home, will we see another challenge?"

"That had been my plan. Then."

"And now?" she asked quietly.

He turned to face her, his whole body, not just his head.

Jessica fought not to take a half step back. On *Ladaux*, she would have been violating this man's personal space to be this close to him in public. Here, she was almost breathing on him.

"Now," he said quietly, "I have found that the galaxy is larger than *Corynthe*."

He looked down at her from almost close enough to kiss.

Almost.

She considered it. Stopped herself from moving closer. Or further away.

Desianna had said to trust him.

Jessica had certainly gamed out the various scenarios, just as she did before any battle.

The stakes weren't as high here.

Probably.

She wasn't sure.

She did. And she didn't. Desire him. Want him. Distrust him.

And she could smell him.

He had obviously showered recently enough to be clean, but not so recently that he had no scent about him.

She placed her palm flat against the center of his chest. Not pushing, nor protecting.

Touching.

His heart pounded far louder that his face showed. She could see the adrenaline in his pupils, in the flare of his nostrils. It wasn't anger or lust.

It took her a moment to identify.

Fear.

Of her.

Of this.

Of change.

Anything else would have put her off. Angered her.

But this wasn't a man intent on conquest, nor seduction. There was no threat. No promise.

No naked, raw emotion to drive her off. No histrionics. Not the *Corynthian* way.

Quiet. Honest. Calm. The *Aquitanian* way.

Jessica closed her hand on the fabric. Not to pull him closer. Just to hold him.

She looked up and recognized her own fear, reflected down.

She remembered to breathe.

"Not tonight, Daneel," she whispered.

She could feel him start to slump in defeat.

"But soon," she continued quietly. "Very soon."

His heart rate surged even greater under her knuckles.

She held him there for a second longer, until she saw the beginnings of a smile on his face.

She smiled back. "Very soon."

Jessica let go of his cloth and flattened it carefully back down, enjoying the play of muscles under her hands as she did.

She gave him a look that encompassed a promise, both to him, and to herself. She smiled and turned to go.

He caught her hand in his and held it for a second.

She glanced back, but he smiled and let go, turning back to face the stars again.

Jessica smiled, smothered it, and then walked into the brighter hallway.

Maybe, just maybe, it was possible, after all.

CHAPTER XXXIII

Date of the Republic February 6, 394 Above Callumnia

Jouster looked out over his assembled flight wing with a face of serious Doom.

"You ready for this, kid?" He scowled at the pilot in the front row.

The kid smiled up at him. Flight Cornet Murali Ma. *Hànchén*. The rookie. Tall and skinny. Bright gray eyes under a mop of black hair. Off-the-chart smarts. Still wet behind the ears. Not even a year out of flight school.

Hànchén blinked serenely at him, and then cocked his head slightly to one side. "Pfft. Are they?"

Yeah, he belonged here.

Back a row and over two sat Flight Centurion Darya Lagunov, *Bitter Kitten*. *Jouster*'d never gone head to head with her to be sure, but she might be better than him. Certainly, it would be close. *Old age and treachery, young lady.*

Jouster smiled. He was all of seven years older than *Bitter Kitten*. This was a young person's game.

"Okay, folks," he announced. "Here are the rules of engagement. Every carrier puts up their two youngest pilots. *Auberon*, *Supernova*, *Kali-ma*, *Sky Dancer*, *Warduck*, and *Lithuania* are playing. *Black Prince* will be scoring and hosting."

A hand shot up in back, attached to a gorgeous, lush babe. One who would never give him the time of day. Or any of the men aboard.

"*Vienna*?" Jouster asked.

"*Lithuania*'s in on this?" she asked. "She's a 1-ring, *Jouster*."

"Home port honor, *Vienna*," he replied.

"Shit."

"Something like that. Instead of racing the clock, everyone starts from the same relative rest, like yacht racing."

He smiled and brought up a projection. "It's a slalom course in orbit. *Black Prince* will pick out three freighters at the last minute and transmit coordinates. You have to pass within two hundred meters of each flag on the way out, flip, and then do it again coming back in. If you miss you circle back and do it again. Best combined team time wins."

"Racing for pink slips?" *Bitter Kitten* asked with a gleam in her eyes.

"Air boss and dragon lady would never go for it," he shook his head ruefully. "But there is an M-6 *Gungnir* out there today, so it would be nice."

"Have we yet determined," *Hànchén* asked, "how such a craft came to be in their possession, *Jouster*? It is technically the legal property of the *Republic of Aquitaine*."

"Kid," Jouster said with a smile, "they're pirates. Any story they tell you will be a lie. And this ain't the movies, where we all get dressed up like ninjas and steal it in some complicated caper move."

Hànchén smiled coolly and looked sideways at his mates. "Maybe *you* don't."

The room laughed.

"And remember, we're being friendly with these people," *Jouster* continued when it quieted down. "But watch your ass around the two from *Kali-ma*. Dragon Lady does not like Ian Zhao one bit. Expect reciprocity."

Bitter Kitten wiggled her butt a touch to get it just right into the acceleration pad.

This wasn't going to be complicated computer flying today. No tactical runs through the combat planner to find the best approach angle. Just raw power, finesse, and nerves. ID the first target, light the fires, run like hell. Find the next target midway and plot a double slingshot with a bootlegger reverse at the end. Rinse. Repeat.

Child's play.

These boys didn't stand a chance. Well, boys and one girl. One seriously deranged chick off *Sky Dancer*. Had to be good to get a slot with all the male chauvinist pigs in this neighborhood. Probably somebody's daughter, or niece. Had done some crazy-ass flying over *Walea* to show off, though.

Or maybe it was a mating dance.

You never knew with pirates. Not that some of them might not clean up well. But really, dude? Pirates?

Hànchén, on the other hand, cleaned up pretty well. Little too book-nerdy, but at least better conversations than sports and girls.

They might have to celebrate when this was done.

Okay, over on the port side. Cayenne *playing rescue tug, just in case.* da Vinci *sitting in a high slot with her scanners on, broadcasting the entire racecourse to everyone so there were no surprises. Few surprises, anyway. Time to party.*

On her board, a light turned yellow, signaling the countdown was terminal. *Bitter Kitten* popped her knuckles with either hand without losing touch of the control yoke.

She dialed up the generator to max output and feathered the thruster valves wide open. Until she lit the engines proper, there was only auxiliary power reactor exhaust to vent. Barely enough to move a craft like this. Still, it was the difference between drifting in the right direction and being cold in orbit when the flag went up.

You had to be careful doing this. She just knew the other yahoos were going to slam their throttles to the stop and redline the engines when the signal came. Wouldn't necessarily blow the engines this time, but you were gonna, one of these days. *Difference between bad-ass pilot and bush-league pirates, punk.*

Green light.

Yup, someone on *Black Prince* was feeling rude today. First way-point was almost straight up, a freighter camped in high orbit.

She loosed the gyros with her control stick and let her craft slowly rotate backwards in place. Everyone else would move first and then maneuver. They would be fast, sure, and completely out of position as they gunned it before they had their first nav point plotted.

Amateurs.

And, sure enough, some ijit blew his engine apart overloading it from a cold start. Looked like the craft was still intact, so maybe *Cayenne* just needed to pull him back to his carrier for repairs, rather than scraping him up off the insides of his tin can. *This is why you take care of your machine, dumb-ass.*

Bitter Kitten brought her engines full in one smooth motion, rather than jamming the throttle all the way forward. Around her, her fighter, her chariot, shimmied just right as she dialed her thruster valves down to mouths spewing dragon's breath and broke out of orbit.

Hànchén was already moving, along with most of the others, as she brought her nose into the right vector and let the power rip. But, like the rest, he was headed the wrong way and fighting his nose around.

Enjoy the view of my pretty ass, boys. You'll be seeing it a lot today.

"How goes the racing, Denis?" Jessica said as she entered the bridge. She figured it would look better if she was actually present for part of it. Give it the imprimatur of respectability. Or something like that.

They were pilots. Respectability wasn't high on their list.

"There are a couple of really good pilots out there," he replied, glancing up at her from the screen he was watching. "*Bitter Kitten* is dangerously close to lapping the field. *Hànchén* is currently in fourth. *Lithuania* is apparently crewed much better than you would expect for a 1-ring. They have second and fifth."

"Who's third?"

"The only other female in the field today," Denis smiled. "*Furious* off *Sky Dancer*."

"Good," Jessica replied. "Makes sense out here. Any woman flying with these yahoos has to be twice as good as any boy she encounters."

Denis fixed her with a hard, thoughtful look. A sneaky, mischief-filled look. "Got a second?"

Jessica nodded slowly, carefully. You never knew what interesting thoughts would cross this man's mind.

He rose from the command chair and headed to the little day office he used occasionally for paperwork. She followed warily.

Inside, he waited until she closed the hatch and then smiled the most evil smile she had seen all week.

"Have you considered," he opened strong, "recruiting out here?"

Jessica blinked. "Pirates?"

"Pilots."

"Same thing," she replied. "Why?"

"Two birds," he smiled wickedly. "One stone."

"What?"

"If we were to do some recruiting out here, boss," he said carefully, "we would take only the best right?"

"Sure. Waste of time to do anything less."

"Right, so we take their best pilots and turn them into *Aquitaine*. And pull them out of the recruiting and training pool of pilots out here. Pirates get worse. We get better. And they already come trained, so all we have to do is socialize them properly. You know, salad fork and wine glass kinds of things."

"Okay, hotshot," she shot back. "Why would they be interested?"

"The War Zone," he said simply. "Give them the chance to go head-to-head with the best the *Fribourg Empire* has, in real combat, instead of weasels chasing chickens in the boonies."

"Oh, hell, that might work," she whispered. "Little miss *Furious* would probably jump at the chance to fly in a wing that was half or more female."

"So who do we ask? And when?" Denis asked.

"Normally, a lovely topic for dinner," Jessica replied, eyes tracking the horizon, "especially tomorrow when we have all the big shots for a formal state affair. But I think I'd rather not ask Arnulf for permission, in front of the Red Admiral. I think I'd like that to be a surprise. Let me talk to David first and see if he'll go for it."

"They do owe us," Denis smiled slyly.

"That they do," she said. "I just haven't figured out how to collect yet."

Bitter Kitten had a moment of utter panic as she watched the situation unfold.

Some fool of a pirate had seen her pull a bootlegger reverse and tried the same thing. And hadn't the slightest clue how to do it.

You have to shut the engines down completely, dumb-shit. Zero thrust, but keep everything warm. Tweak only two of the gyroscopes, manually, so they spin you end-for-end while momentum keeps you going forward. And you have to take that moment to make sure everything is lined up before you redline the engines at the other end.

Dipshit over there had dialed them back to almost nothing. *Almost nothing*. And then started his spin. And threw in a good deal of yaw as well.

That turned into a barrel-rolling corkscrew.

And then he had panicked. And red-lined the throttle. Without looking around.

From the rear scanner, it was going to be close. Like, paint-scraping-the-hull close, if he didn't just slam right into the side of the last way-point freighter at full power.

This was going to be messy.

At least it would be one of those Uglies: front half Imperial, back half Creator-only-knew. It would be a shame to street-pizza one of the nicer fighter craft.

And, cannonball.

There was no sound in space. That was good. Otherwise, that would have been a roomful of anvils thrown down a flight of stairs. Probably sounded exactly like that on the freighter.

Both craft seemed to have survived, although the Ugly was shedding parts and wobbling. The freighter was probably leaking at the seams in a few places, but it looked like it had been more of a bad parking job than a hit and run. Minimal debris.

The radio came alive on the private channel.

"*Cayenne*," *da Vinci* said from her high orbit overwatch, "you're on."

"Roger that," *Gaucho* replied. "EVA marines already suited up. Be there in seven minutes."

"Make it four, hotshot," *da Vinci* replied, her voice cool and almost bored. "Don't think his frame will stay together that long."

Bitter Kitten smiled.

Amateur.

Speaking of…

She recognized the craft, a late-model Imperial off of *Kali-ma.* Probably an *A-6*, although she hadn't really paid that much attention earlier. The pilot was running in last right now. What did he matter?

Except that he was lined up nose-to-nose with her.

Bitter Kitten grumbled at poor manners and blipped her nose up a notch. She could blast right over the top of him at full speed.

Too bad there wasn't an atmosphere to slipstream him when she did.

She watched the other craft shift up as well, again dead-on to a collision course.

You son of a…

There was no chance that was accidental. *Bitter Kitten* shifted her path a shade to her left.

Sure enough, he shifted as well.

Little punk wants to play chicken, does he?

She cursed the lack of guns right now. In the real world, he would be a puff of flaming wreckage slowly de-orbiting right about now.

Stupid lame-ass pirate.

Bitter Kitten red-lined her engines briefly. And then he did too.

She smiled. It was kinda like dancing, although she had never done a dance fight at this rate of closure. You did that stuff in a club, not orbit. Usually.

Or you did it with guns.

If I'd have known it was that kind of party, bucko, I'd have brought the little black dress...

She smiled wickedly. Targeting scanners didn't register a lock on her, so punk-boy over there was flying purely on visuals.

Time to go weasel.

Bitter Kitten rolled her craft ninety degrees to the right, standing it on one ear if the planet had been closer. Sure enough, dancer-boy did the same.

They would pass belly-to-belly if they didn't slam into each other.

No reverse cowgirl for me, bad-boy. Not that kind of girl. At least not on the first date with some lame pirate punk I barely know.

She eased the throttle slowly back. Not so fast he would notice, but enough to throw his timing off.

Now the fun part.

Slowly, she eased the primary gyroscope out of alignment. The nose of her little craft began to drift up, out of the line of flight.

And the engines went down.

It was like dropping her foot in the snow on a sled as a kid blasting down the street. Still going like hell, but now starting to wobble off that straight-line that was going to slam you into a mailbox.

And dumbshit over there wouldn't pick up on the drift until it was too late.

She could feel inertia driving her up instead of back. For fun, and to play with the kid over there, she rolled half over, so she would be looking up at him as they passed.

Again, assuming he wasn't trying to kill her.

These people weren't that crazy, were they? No terrible samurai bad-ass warrior code that requires suicide over failure? Right?

She took a deep breath.

There we are. Past the last check-point.

Bitter Kitten red-lined her engines and blipped her nose back up, like she was pointed at the boy and going to ram him. Except now there was an S in her flight path. She was aimed right at him, but still drifting up and away even as she closed the distance.

He panicked anyway and flinched his yoke away from her, diving straight down relative as fast as his engines could take him.

Too bad there was no atmosphere this high, bucko. Would have been nice to watch you start tumbling and then shatter.

Bitter Kitten looked around. Clear skies in every direction.

Hànchén and the girl-pilot were still a ways back, redlining engines and dancing their own dance fight. If she wasn't careful, they might even catch her.

I don't think so.

CHAPTER XXXIV

Date of the Republic February 7, 394 Above Callumnia

Jessica was there to greet David as he stepped down onto the deck from the ugly little gunship made of parts someone had stolen from the Imperials before she had even been born. She hoped he recognized the honor she did him, the trust, to let him land his own craft, his own armed shuttle, onto *Auberon*'s flight deck instead of relying on *Gaucho* and *Cayenne*.

Nobody else got that. Hell, Ian Zhao got transported with a small cadre of armed marines when he came aboard. At least until he started to act nicer.

David stepped onto the deck and smiled at her. "Permission to come aboard, Admiral?"

"That's Command Centurion, Captain Rodriguez," she said lightly.

"According to the King of the Pirates, m'lady" he said with a smile down at her and a slight bow, "you're Admiral Keller. Far be it for me to gainsay the man."

Jessica smiled back and shook his hand. "Welcome aboard."

She led him back to the hatch and suffered to be escorted on his arm, as if he were a proper *Aquitaine* gentleman, rather than a blood-thirsty pirate. She could see Desianna's touch in everything about the man.

Marcelle awaited them in her office, water boiled and beans just ground and ready for coffee.

David took the seat with a soft whistle.

"So," he said as Jessica sat, "to what do I own this honor? You didn't ask me to come early for a purely social visit."

Jessica smiled as Marcelle brewed and poured.

"I'm not sure," she began, "how much your mother has told you about the purpose of this grand Promenade."

He had an easy smile. In fact, there was a very relaxed manner about him that was so different from most of the pirates. Only Daneel…

Jessica could tell he would make a good king someday. He was already a good prince. Not that the Captains would ever allow it. Too much of a threat to their own power base, especially if they allowed Arnulf to change the laws of succession to something less bloody.

"Ian Zhao and Jing Du are up to no good," he replied after a beat. "Father thinks he can control them, rebuff them. You and my mother don't agree. She suggested this to throw off their timing, because the Imperials are probably involved as well and they have so far to come to get out here and cause mischief. Having the Red Admiral in your hands also throws things off. Close?"

Jessica blinked.

Apparently, Desianna had told him everything. Or she hadn't and he had done the math himself.

It was so rare to run into someone else capable of seeing so many moves ahead. If not for Daneel, and her promise to Desianna, she might find this young man extremely interesting.

Really? Her type were pirates? Who knew?

She took a breath as Marcelle served the coffee and departed.

"Close enough," she said. "*Aquitaine* has a vested interest in the stability of *Lincolnshire*. Desianna has convinced me that keeping Arnulf in power as long as possible serves those ends. And when his time comes, to have a peaceful transition of power to you as a dynast, hopefully turning *Corynthe* into a peace-abiding galactic citizen."

"And you want me to swear fealty in return for your support?" David asked with the barest hint of sarcasm.

"You wouldn't mean it," she shot back lightly. "No, I want to help."

She watched his eyebrows climb.

"And you don't think this convoy helps?" he asked.

"Not enough. I want to suggest something really radical and get your opinion, quietly. It serves both our ends."

He leaned forward now, sipping on the coffee. "Go on."

"Would *Corynthe* acquiesce to *Aquitaine* recruiting pilots out here for our fleet?"

David had that same trick to his eyes that Desianna had. Or Moirrey. He picked out a spot on the horizon and flickered his eyes back and forth, like an abacus calculating.

"Which ones?" he said a moment later. He had a smile like a great cat hunting.

"Good, but potentially-politically-unpalatable ones," she replied.

"Thereby removing trouble-makers from the pool, now and in the future," he concluded. "What would you offer them?"

"The war," she said simply. "Flying with the best *Aquitaine* has, against the best the *Fribourg Empire* can field. Pilots are pilots."

He leaned back with a laugh. "That they are," he said. "Five years ago, I would have leapt at the chance."

"Would it work here?"

"Let me ask Arnulf privately. Jing Du would never go for it, but he can be maneuvered out of position on this one," David said seriously. "Having never been a pilot himself, he won't understand the allure. And yes, I can see why you wouldn't want to discuss this over dinner with the Red Admiral."

"Exactly," Jessica replied. "That would be the war out here I'm trying to prevent."

CHAPTER XXXV

Date of the Republic February 7, 394 Above Callumnia

She had done this twice before. Hosted the major players in a formal dinner aboard *Auberon*. Let Chef Aoiki go completely over the top with several days planning, and a whole new planet below to gather ingredients.

It would be easy. Right?

The first had been a tactical success, using Jessica's elaborate personal scoring procedures. Total strangers, many of them mortal enemies and back-stabbing gunsels, forced to dress nicely, behave nicely, and eat a formal meal in nine courses with a dead minimum of wine to keep them sharp.

There had been no duels as a result. The Red Admiral had even complimented her afterwards for being such a pleasant and gracious host. Hopefully, he would continue to believe this mirage. Certainly, most of the *Corynthe* contingent seemed to.

And it wasn't as if *Aquitaine* had never promoted extremely well-connected incompetents to high command before. Her predecessor commanding *Auberon*, Augustine Kwok, one of Loncar's relatives, had probably fallen into that category. And her opinion of Fleet Lord Loncar wasn't much higher.

Jessica pushed those thoughts out of her head and projected this new image. She had worked very hard on the coquettish giggle she gave the Red Admiral, getting the tone just right and the little toss of the hair just so.

Probably not as well as Moirrey had trained her to do, certainly not as well as the little pixie could have done it, but Jessica seemed to have set the bar low with Admiral Wachturm early on. She could fake *bimbo* fairly well with these men, by now.

Jessica bit her lip to keep from giggling out loud at the memory. Until that moment, she really hadn't believed Desianna and Moirrey's intense belief that boobs and eyelashes could lead any man astray.

And now, they were going to go through it all again. She still wasn't sure if studying Desianna as closely as she had was a genius move, or a dangerous distraction.

She had always worked harder than anyone else to be better. It felt like cheating to wiggle her hips at a man to break his concentration.

And yet, it worked.

Deep breath. No giggles, young lady. Serious business. Dangerous men, at least in their own minds.

Jessica smiled and let her warmth fill the room.

Sure, dangerous men.

Jing Du arrived first. Part of his responsibilities as Chancellor of *Corynthe* was the diplomatic tasks. He was formal this evening, both in dress and bearing as he entered the room, nodding carefully to Jessica in her role as ambassador to the Court from the barbarians of the distant interior.

Probably still shocked that the barbarians had mastered internal plumbing.

In some ways, Jing Du was the most transparent player, so caught up within his own intellectual superiority that he was occasionally blinded to the motives of the people around him. But he was also deeper than the rest, by orders of magnitude. Still waters. Dangerous depths. Had Jessica been put in charge, he would be the first one up against the wall.

Admiral Wachturm was next. He was still technically her prisoner, but Jessica had tried to play to the man's ego by asking him to be her co-host in these affairs. The *Fribourg Empire* considered women too inferior to handle difficult, dangerous tasks, anyway. Jessica suspected that both his wife and two daughters were at least his equal in many things, to hear him talk them up, but it would be impolite to suggest that to the man's face.

Especially not when she wanted him to see the role she was playing, rather than the truth.

They were still enemies.

He had won at *Iger*, and at *Qui-Ping*. But that had been Loncar in command the first time, and her desperately out-gunned squadron running for their lives the second. There had never been a true test between them. Not yet.

It would be to the death, one of these days.

The Red Admiral took up a spot exactly diagonal from Jing Du, at Jessica's right hand, just as the chancellor would be at Arnulf's when everyone was seated.

Others arrived quickly after that, less bound by the formal rules around an event like this. *Bitter Kitten*, *Furious*, and a pilot of the 1-ring *Lithuania*, a young, blond man who went by the callsign *Sõdalane*, as the first three places in yesterday's fighter pilot race. Daneel Ishikura, Ian Zhao, and David Rodriguez, plus the captains of *Black Prince* and *Lithuania* as locals. Tomas Kigali and Alber' d'Maine for balance. The governor of *Callumnia*, a seedy little man who looked more like a crooked lawyer than anything else.

Everyone was seated and beginning to engage in small talk when Denis Jež entered and rapped on the bulkhead with a flat palm to get everyone's attention. He did that well.

"Ladies and gentlemen," he announced, quietly booming his voice across the entire assembly without actually shouting. He did that well, also. "I present to you His Majesty Arnulf, Admiral Rodriguez, Supreme Commander of the *Corynthe* Fleet, Governor of *Petron*, King of the Pirates."

Denis quickly stepped to one side as Arnulf entered, Desianna on his arm. She looked tiny by comparison to Arnulf, barely coming up to the bottom of his ear, even in her stiletto heels. It was only when she towered over Jing Du that Arnulf's absolute size became apparent.

Jessica smiled. She supposed that a society that embraced trial by personal combat with edged weapons as a primary legal tool would favor big men.

Arnulf, David, and Daneel were all more than head and neck taller than her. Even Ian Zhao made Marcelle and the Red Admiral look small.

She glanced at the walls surrounding her. *Auberon's* Dragoon had assigned only female marines as guards tonight. She doubted that anyone at the table not in green would recognize that fact.

Correction. Little miss *Furious*, the black-haired hotshot pilot off David's 3-ring, *Sky Dancer*, had noticed. Jessica watched her force her mouth closed and fix a questioning eye in her direction. Jessica just smiled serenely at her.

"Ladies and gentlemen, I bid you welcome," Jessica said. "As we prepare to depart for our final stop in the Grand Promenade, I hope that this will be another stone in a great bridge of eternal peace and understanding between our nations."

She fixed a smile on her face.

And the horse might learn to sing.

Desianna smiled.

Tonight was a night for gold.

Yellow gold. Rich and lustrous that set off her hair and was framed, in turn, by it.

Four different length necklaces, intricately bound together by a black pearl pendant that hung just the perfect depth into her cleavage. Matching teardrop earrings set in the most delicate gold lacing. A single gold bracer that covered all of her left forearm, like some barbaric shield. A welded-gold chain extravaganza on her right forearm that linked across the back of her hand to rings on her middle two fingers.

Tonight, she wore her little black dress. Not so short, as befit a woman of her stature, both political and physical, but plunging in front and in almost absent in back, strategically held together by fine gold chains that ran at exactly the line of her nipples, diaphragm, and navel. In addition, it had been slashed up the left to nearly her hip bone, showing an amazing flash of bronzed and toned thigh to the Red Admiral when Arnulf pulled out her chair and seated her himself.

She smiled at the man as he attempted to close his mouth.

Tonight was Jessica's night, but that meant Desianna's job was to distract these silly men and their chauvinistic upbringings, so Jessica could play them without them paying enough attention to consider how badly they were being out-maneuvered.

Besides, of all the men at the table, only Denis Jež had treated her like a proper gentleman, and not a conquest he had planned, or dreamed about.

Desianna wondered if she might could convince Jessica's first officer that Arnulf's statecraft would be advanced by a light seduction.

Her eyes twinkled as they met Jessica's.

Men.

Still, it was an extra bonus to be surrounded by so many women tonight.

That was rare, especially at formal dinners. Here, she had the two pilots, plus Jessica. All the girl soldiers around them were just icing on the cake, even if they were probably less girly than some of the men present, were push to come to shove.

And none of them could compete with her for the men, which was exactly how she and Jessica had planned it.

Briefly, Desianna considered emigrating back to *Aquitaine*, just because the men there would treat her the way she felt she should be treated. Spoiled. Utterly rotten with a side of fresh cream. Men were men. Maybe she should treat herself to the attentions and devotions of a gentleman.

Did *Corynthe* need an ambassador to *Aquitaine*? Maybe she should retire from being First Wife and travel.

Desianna felt her own smile expand to encompass the entirety of *Auberon* and all her crew. Oh, the delicious potential for trouble.

A smell distracted her before she began to purr.

Jessica's chef was standing at her left hand, holding a silver bowl for her to inspect.

Figs and arbequina olives brined in red wine vinegar. Desianna shot Jessica an inquiring look.

Someone had blabbed.

She smiled up at the man, aware that Jessica would probably kill her if she tried to seduce him away. He seemed to share their dirty little secret as he placed the bowl before her with a half bow.

The men could wait.

Desianna delicately speared a fig and nibbled, wondering what it would do to her reputation if she spiked the first hand that reached for the bowl. It was a close-wrought thing. That might be embarrassing, seated between Arnulf and David. But still.

The fig was perfect.

She speared two olives before she consented to share, and then only because a steward set down a cheese plate and a tray of pickled vegetables, half of which she couldn't hazard a guess at, even by color.

There was a very good reason she had skipped lunch today.

Daneel considered the evening's underplay and bi-currents swirling and eddying around the table as *Auberon*'s crew removed the main course and the head cook again appeared, to again personally attend Desianna and deliver…

Were those strawberries? In cream?

The capital region on *Callumnia* was in winter right now. And the governor was a hack, a tax farmer mostly kept in the palace by Jing Du and protected by Arnulf as long as the revenues flowed. That fool wasn't smart enough to bring something like this to the party.

That meant it had to come from Jessica.

Her little smile as he glanced over seemed to confirm his suspicions. Gods, that woman just kept getting more and more amazing.

How had any man let her get away? More likely, what man had ever kept up?

Ian Zhao was constantly at the edge of being insulted to be seated across from Daneel. He was a big-shot captain, after all, and *Warlock* was a has-been nothing who was only invited because that female bitch captain wanted to rub it in their faces.

Ian, you need to learn to play poker better. Or, better yet, don't, and let me take all your money some time.

Daneel smiled. Just the right level of carefree and innocence that seemed to drive burning splinters under Ian's fingernails. Not that he hadn't dreamt of doing exactly that sometime.

No, the most fun tonight seemed to be watching Jessica and Desianna play people like an orchestra.

Daneel wondered if he would have even noticed, back when he was someone else. Before *Sarmarsh*. Before resurrection. Before Jessica.

Was this what it meant to be civilized? Leave behind all that crazy pilot shit and actually look forward to living longer than the next raid, the next fight, the next romantic conquest? Worse, to dress so boringly?

Daneel grinned at his own dark gray and dark blue outfit, across from Ian Zhao in fuchsia and aquamarine like a half-drunk peacock. Come to think of it, he sounded about as useful as well.

Maybe get him fully drunk sometime, with all that anger, might let more details flow.

Jessica barely trusted him. He knew that. But Daneel didn't know the key details of the bigger plot, and at this point couldn't tell her anything she didn't already know.

Daneel gauged Ian's face and wondered just how much farther Ian could be safely pushed this evening.

A *thunk* on the table brought his eyes around. Along with everyone else.

Damn, Arnulf knew how to work a room.

Arnulf grinned back at everyone, slowly making eye contact, politely establishing his pack dominance with bulk and size and charisma. But, oh, such a deft touch.

It was a shame Arnulf would never survive what Daneel knew was coming. Daneel had developed a much greater understanding and appreciation of the man recently.

He sighed internally.

"Admiral Keller," Arnulf began slowly, deliberately, humorously, "we have talked in the past about the difference between *Aquitaine* as a nation and *Corynthe* as a collection of loosely aligned worlds."

He paused for effect, dangling everyone in the room as he seemed to choose the right next words.

"It seems to me," he continued, "that one of the differences is that *Aquitaine* was *founded*, while *Corynthe* simply grew into existence over time. *Corynthe* needs to be re-founded, so we can turn it into a nation. I have studied your history, but I am more interested in your founding myths."

"Myths, Admiral?" Jessica volleyed.

To Daneel it was like watching a sporting match, as heads swiveled back and forth.

"Yes," the big man smiled easily. "Three hundred and ninety-four years ago, the Republic was proclaimed, with *Ladaux* as its capital. But that was an ending to the story, not just a beginning. Tell me of the time before. Tell me of the time that ended."

Jessica smiled, a thoughtful look on her face as she sipped her coffee, eyes a thousand meters away.

"To do that," Jessica began, "I need to tell you about the Story Road."

Arnulf smiled expectantly. Daneel watched the king's left hand reach out and come to rest on the back of Desianna's, fingers twining together.

"Three millennia ago," she continued, "the *Homeworld* was destroyed in a war. Fools pounded it with giant rocks, small moons really, until it was a bed of lava. I haven't been there, but I have seen pictures taken in the modern era. The old maps are irrelevant, because the entire face was changed. Even the gravity has been altered, so much material had been cast down from the heavens."

Crew members brought out a fresh batch of coffee, apparently recognizing that the evening wasn't going to wind down nearly as soon as they had originally expected.

"A thousand years ago, from out of the Darkness, *Zanzibar* contacted *Ballard*, uplifting them from the steam to the stellar age in a single generation. Without a war. *Pohang* and *Saxon* followed soon after."

Jessica smiled to herself at some secret memory as she spoke. Daneel made a mental note to ask her what she had been thinking at that moment, later.

"Those four worlds quickly formed the nucleus of a trade network," she said after a moment, "with *Ballard* at one end. When the ancient library was lifted into orbit, technology took off, and lifted civilization with it. Because the four worlds were like pearls on a string, travel between them came to be known as the Story Road. Ancient wisdom from the library headed out, new ideas sailed in."

The Red Admiral muttered something quiet in a deep voice. It sounded angry. Daneel considered the weight and heft of his metal coffee mug before he looked over.

"Admiral Wachturm?" Jessica asked politely.

"The Abomination," he growled again, loud enough this time that everyone at the table could hear him clearly.

"How so?" Arnulf asked from the far end.

"So it is written: that no woman shall have authority over a man," Wachturm stated harshly. "It is the root of all evil."

Jessica nodded. "And thus was *Fribourg* founded, Admiral," she said. "But I am speaking of *Aquitaine*."

The Red Admiral fixed her with a sharp look

"Perhaps your founding legends would be a good corollary when she is done, Admiral Wachturm?" Desianna asked, breaking the spell that was taking hold on everyone.

The Red Admiral turned, relaxed his scowl into something neutral. "Just so, m'lady," he bowed his head to her. "I had nearly forgotten myself."

"Jessica?" Desianna prompted.

"One of the visitors to *Ballard*," Jessica continued, "was a young man from a backwater world, *Bayonne*, close enough to the Story Road to travel it in search of knowledge. He was a bard, a musician, a seeker of songs."

Jessica paused to sip her coffee, letting the energy bleed out of the room. It was obvious to Daneel that she was not a natural story teller, but it was also obvious that she was trying to become one.

Daneel wondered what she might turn herself into, given time. What he might turn himself into, given space.

"At *Ballard*, he studied the sciences instead," she said. "This man, Henri Baudin, invented the modern Jumpdrive as we understand it, opening up the galaxy to exploration in a way that had been lost. With his skills and vision, he was able to forge a new nation, well to the interior of the Story Road worlds, though they joined later of their own free will. Thus is *Aquitaine* a beacon of hope and learning in the galaxy, and not just another conqueror."

"Truly?" Arnulf inquired. "A bard invented the modern age?"

"Indeed, Your Majesty," Jessica smiled. "However, Admiral Wachturm also has his founding legends, for *Fribourg* is a very different place. Admiral?"

Daneel watched the Red Admiral compress himself like an angry bear woken in winter. His eyes bespoke the Apocalypse.

She hoped she hadn't overdone it. Jessica had watched Desianna's use of physicality to induce men into misdirection, and had tried to emulate it, but she had no idea if it worked. She didn't have Desianna's body to lead men astray, but she also wasn't trying to seduce the Red Admiral, merely convince the man that she was just a lucky, bubbly airhead.

The last thing she wanted was to lead him to wonder if she might be his equal. That would be all kinds of bad.

Still, that tilt of the head as she spoke was beginning to feel more comfortable. The little toss of the hair. Even the resting of her shoulders was different, more relaxed. Slinkier, to hear Desianna judge it.

She was just a silly little girl, easily out-maneuvered by the big, bad men around her.

Honest.

Anger practically radiated off of the top of the Red Admiral's skull, like the special effect speed lines from a children's cartoon. Where Arnulf had slowly drawn everyone into his web with a smile, Wachturm bound them with his fury.

"*Fribourg* remembers the distant past," he said slowly, gravely. "*Earth* was destroyed by robot starfleets. Electronic demons turned loose to wreak havoc and devastation on all worlds. Without any human oversight."

He paused to let the weight of his words settle. Jessica watched his hands squeeze the sides of his indestructible coffee mug, turning white with pressure that did not carry into his words. She had never imagined this level of emotions from the man. He was always the consummate commander. This was something special to know.

"During the Dark Times, the AIs, the Immortals, went mad, becoming unto themselves gods or destroyers. No man was safe in their grasp."

The Red Admiral slowly turned his head from right to left, spearing each of them with a look before coming to Jessica. She understood much better now what made this man tick, just gazing for once into the angry depths of his soul.

"When they destroyed the Homeworld, they nearly ended all humanity with it," he growled, speaking mostly to himself. "Because they did not stop with one planet. No, they also destroyed many, eventually their own lives. Starfleets need bases, factories, industrial civilization. When the fools unleashed Armageddon, those things were lost. And thus did the Creator spare us from the Pit. The armies of the Dark One could not sustain themselves, and they fell. Where we have found them, we have destroyed them without mercy."

Jessica watched him put down his coffee and begin to drink instead from a glass of water cut with lemon. Perhaps that was better than the bitter richness of the coffee, at this moment.

"So, aye," he continued, "*Ballard* re-ignited humanity, but they were aided by the AI who is the Librarian. They did so by opening Pandora's box and birthing a modern demon. As with Eve and her apple, so the Demon of Ballard seduced the *Explorer*, Iwakuma, and then the *Bard*, Baudin."

He turned now, focusing his entire being on Arnulf. Jessica could almost see the waves of energy connecting the men as unspoken messages passed back and forth.

Arnulf leaned forward, lightly resting his chin on a fist, but remaining silent lest he break the spell.

Jessica had never heard Admiral Wachturm be so emotional. Had never even thought that the man was capable of it.

"*Fribourg* will not suffer such things," he said, barely above a whisper. "The demon there portrays herself as a young woman, the better to seduce the people of the galaxy. My great-grandfather, Gunter Wiegand, the founding emperor of *Fribourg*, made it clear from the outset that such a woman would lead the many worlds down the path to darkness. *Aquitaine* is beholden to her ideas, and thus uplifts her as an ideal woman. *Fribourg* rejects her, and rejects her power over men."

"Is not all knowledge simply a tool?" Arnulf asked simply.

Jessica blinked a little, happy that nobody was looking her direction. She kept forgetting how sharp, how canny, the King of the Pirates really was, under that grand showman exterior.

She wondered what his smile held.

But she needed to play the airhead. Letting these people see the wheels turning in her head right now would spoil that artful charade

"*Knowledge tainted by evil furthers the course of evil,*" Wachturm intoned.

"And you do not believe that this creature, this Oracle, this woman who is the last of the immortals, has anything useful to teach us?"

"She is a black widow spider, Your Majesty," the Red Admiral bowed his head. "Mate with her at your own risk. If it were my decision, I would take a fleet to *Ballard* and destroy that creature tomorrow."

Jessica fought down her own laugh, or comment, or snort, lest she mar this wonderful *social* development.

Arnulf was looking for how to transform *Corynthe* into a place where his own dynasty might prevail. Certainly, *Fribourg* offered a more compelling case for dynastic hegemony, but this was a king who had to win over his rivals and transform them all into something they had never wanted, generally against their will.

Aquitaine offered exactly that solution, the possibility of co-opting these *Captains* into something like the Fifty Families, those disciples who had joined with Henri Baudin at the beginning.

She could see the same calculations, the same conclusions on other faces about the table as she watched.

Most of them were concentrating on Arnulf, or the Red Admiral, or their own avarice. They could see the present, not the possibilities the future might be shaped into.

Only Desianna smiled at her.

CHAPTER XXXVI

Date of the Republic February 8, 394 Above Callumnia

According to all the entertainment videos, there should be a thin fog of smoke from burning herbal products hanging in the air. And the room should be darker, more ominous to go with being smoke-filled. Possibly music to heighten the tension.

Captain Ian Zhao laughed at himself and his foolish notions. Let Arnulf and that silly bitch from *Aquitaine* paint him as a villain. They didn't have the balls to do anything about it, and nobody was going to be able to save Arnulf at this point, if *Warlock* hadn't already told his new little doxie everything.

Not that that would help, either. Without *Sarmarsh* or Daneel Ishikura, the major players had modified the plan enough that Ishikura was almost as much in the dark as the rest.

Still, Ian smiled. His office was bright and clean, as befit one of the senior-most captains of *Corynthe* in command of a 4-ring Mothership. It was only in the movies that such a space was squalid and vile.

A watercolor, done by his youngest daughter when she was eight hung framed across from him, where other captains might have kept a picture of their first command.

A rap on the door preceded Jing Du. Ian rose and shook his hand as he entered.

"Chancellor."

"Captain Zhao."

Jing Du seated himself and watched. He did that. No movement except the eyes.

It was a stillness you almost never found outside of a dead, orbiting hulk.

"The plan proceeds apace, Captain," Jing Du said finally.

"Without *Bunala*?" Ian asked.

"*Bunala* is as close as we will get to our neighbor *Salonnia,* Captain Zhao," Jing Du said with a solemn nod, "but there is too much risk. Arnulf will be weaker here, but someone could escape in the chaos, return to *Petron,* and rouse the rabble. Would you care to fight twice for the crown?"

"No," Ian said, "It is a good plan. But what of *Aquitaine*? *Auberon* is at least the match for a 4-ring, maybe two 3-rings, if you count her escort."

"Messages have been sent to our associates in *Salonnia,*" Jing Du replied dryly. "Assumedly, they have in turn notified their *friends*. It is another reason I expect nothing to happen until we return to *Petron*. Those people will need time to adjust their plans and forces accordingly."

Jing Du studied him carefully.

"And you, Captain Zhao?" he continued. "Will you be prepared to pay the price they ask?"

Ian felt a harsh smile cover his face. "Surely *Salonnia* does not believe they will be able to dictate terms to me when I am king? Those *merchants*?"

He laughed.

"Jing Du, what they want is to disturb the frontiers, because most of the chaos will spill over into *Lincolnshire*. *Salonnia* will be sheltered and believes themselves prepared. In addition, they can pile on, wresting worlds and trade routes away, so they can control all the trade in this sector. Certainly, that is *Fribourg*'s calculation."

"And Admiral Keller?" Jing Du asked pensively.

"A well-born *Aquitaine* fop," Ian replied. "Much more concerned with entertaining than command. If not for Jež, I imagine that ship would be a complete mess."

"Really?" Jing Du asked. "I was given to understand that she is a prominent commander, at home."

"The Red Admiral believes her to be an over-promoted woman who got lucky at the right times, not a competent field commander. Did you know that she once *rammed* an Imperial fighter craft in the middle of a battle? Intentionally?"

Jing Du leaned back with a look of mild surprise on his face. "Interesting."

"So if she does actually choose to fight, rather than simply withdraw when ordered to leave," Ian continued, "we will have more than enough forces to overwhelm her. Granted, she has excellent pilots, but they will not be able to overcome raw numbers, regardless of what they think, especially with that nasty little escort ship detached and sent home."

"Could the escort be getting help?" Jing Du leaned forward again, apprehensive.

"If it is, they would have to be the best sailors in the galaxy to arrive in time from *Aquitaine*. And *Lincolnshire* would never help *Corynthe*, especially not after we already invaded them once this year. No, dear Chancellor, I am not worried about taking power from Arnulf. What we should be concerned with is how to hold it when the other captains get restive. Someone will get the idea to do to me what I did to Arnulf, and *Lincolnshire* and *Salonnia* will not remain passive."

"The strong will rule," Jing Du intoned solemnly, "and the weak will fall. So has it always been."

CHAPTER XXXVII

Date of the Republic February 16, 394 Above Callumnia

"So, young lady," a voice snuck up on Moirrey as she carefully welded a line, "will it work?"

She flipped up her visor as she powered down the laser and carefully slid it home in its little carrier, the one decorated with sparklies and bangles. The chief engineer hovered close by.

Oz couldn't exactly lurk over her, being not much taller than she was, but he were twice her mass, and that counted f'r something.

"The wee beasties seemed to prove it, Oz," she replied carefully, turning her shoulders to look up at him.

And they had.

Fist-sized, remotely piloted, little toy fighter craft, plinking around engineering with the gravplates turned off, stalked by even smaller hunter-killers, with an elaborate scoring system to test theories, tactics, and blow off steam. The engineers certain didn't tell the pilots about their new hobby. Not safe, at least not until they had mastered it and could take all the flight-jocks' money.

Then, t'were open season.

"That they most indubitably did, Yeoman," he observed carefully with a serene smile, hands crossing behind his back as he rocked back and forth.

Oz had a gift fer pilotin' the craft, and the current high score. "However, the proof, as the ancients teach us, will be in the pudding. Will it work?"

"I plan on betting my life on it, Chief," Moirrey said tartly. "Yers, too."

She paused to look at the section of tubing in front of her, big enough for three of her fists to fit inside.

"Will she be needing them at the next stop?" Moirrey asked, all serious-like.

"It is my understanding, Moirrey, that the next stop is *Bunala*, just across the border from *Salonnia*." He paused to consider something. "I would rate the possibilities low, but greater than zero. How many of the weapons will be ready when we arrive?"

Moirrey did the math quickly. These were numbers that had haunted her sleep for weeks.

"Five of the Mark I, Oz," she said. "Ya knew that. Another five of the improved Mark II, after we figured out how to put in a fourth warhead. Past that, as fast as we can turn them out. I gots to sleep occasionally, ya know?"

"I am aware of that, Yeoman," he said crisply. "And I am aware that you taking the time off to train others in the intricate tasks may not be time well spent, at least until we know how soon we will require their usage in hostilities. Pray, continue."

"Rights," she said, flipping the visor back down and grabbing the welding laser on muscle memory.

More *Mischief* for the Lady. Would it work?

CHAPTER XXXVIII

Date of the Republic March 1, 394 Bunala System

Cayenne flew a slow pass, almost leisurely and polite. If she hadn't known any better, Jessica would have thought that *Gaucho* had been on the medical report and someone else was flying today. He did this so rarely. Fly like a sane person, that was.

Jessica smiled across the VIP transport room at Desianna, seated like a proper queen, fingers intertwined with Arnulf's. Apparently, that woman had charmed *Gaucho* into submission, something no Fleet Lord had managed in two decades of trying.

Today, Jessica wore her field utilities. Dark green, as appropriate, but with a subtle pattern to the fabric that made it hard to look at directly. Knee-high heavy boots, polished black leather with metal toes and metal soles. Damned near indestructible to anything short of a beam weapon.

Desianna wore a similar outfit, apparently issued from *Auberon*'s stores at some point, but then significantly modified. Tailored even, to a degree that would get a regular crew member in trouble for showing off the wrong amount of flesh in the wrong places.

Jessica smiled even broader. Only Desianna could make utilities sexy. Although she had probably had some significant assistance along the way from the ship's seamstress pixie down in engineering. Moirrey knew cloth. Desianna knew distraction.

Dangerous team.

Jessica wondered what she would look like, if she had Moirrey do the same thing for her.

She snorted under her breath at the thought. She really was getting too enamored of her image to the pirates, and especially to the Red Admiral, as an air-head fluff more worried about fashion than command.

At least she could take her occasional frustrations out on the fighting robot with nobody around.

Today, she didn't have to maintain the charade. Despite the open invitation to take a flying tour of the sights, all the supposed conspirators had passed. The Red Admiral was apparently working on his memoirs, a fancy term for a spy report. Jing Du was having a meeting with Ian Zhao and a few others aboard *Kali-ma*.

The friendly vessels: *Auberon*, *Rajput*, *Supernova*, and *Sky Dancer*; were all quietly at red alert, ready to unleash the Apocalypse if anything happened. Not that she expected it. And if it did, Denis Jež and David Rodriguez could handle themselves, at least long enough.

Instead, it was a cozy little sight-seeing outing. Arnulf and Desianna. Daneel Ishikura. Her. Jessica's brain suddenly clicked and she wondered if Desianna had set this up as a picnic, a double date of sorts, without bothering to tell her.

Desianna would do something like that.

The woman spoke now to get her attention. "Admiral Keller," she called over the low hum of the ship's engines, and gestured expansively with her free hand, "how big did you say this, what did you call it, was?"

"A breaker yard," Jessica said, loud enough to be heard. "And this is a large one. One of the largest I am aware of in colonized space. The estimate is roughly forty square kilometers."

"And it's all dead starships?" Desianna asked, turning to include Arnulf in her question.

"Well," Arnulf said, "it's not completely covered, but yes, there are huge piles of parts and equipment, plus a boneyard of decommissioned vessels that strippers have brought here over the centuries. Think of it as an open-faced mine, except we dig up starships here, instead of ore."

Jessica nodded. That was about as accurate as one could get. Most of the craft here were the size of fighters or freighters, designed to land on a planet.

Auberon couldn't do that. Well, it could, exactly once, but would never lift off again.

Below, she could see one vessel at least twice the size of *Auberon*, dominating an entire corner of the boneyard. She keyed the microphone to the cockpit.

"*Gaucho*, could you overfly that big ship on the starboard bow? And do we have an ID?"

For a moment, she expected him to stand the DropShip on one wing and make an assault pass. That was how he flew. But no, he gracefully banked and elevated a touch to bring a better view onto the big projection screen dominating the drop bay.

The screen abruptly transformed to a craft flying in orbit. It had that bright sharpness of a generated-animation, rather than scanner footage. The warship was gorgeous.

"Vessel is an ancient legend, and a local landmark, Commander," *Gaucho* said politely over the intercom. "The Concord Warship *Kinnison*. She was the last and biggest super-dreadnaught the Concord fielded before the Dark Times. Nearly two kilometers long. Crew of only two hundred."

"How was that possible?" Arnulf wondered aloud.

Jessica smiled. "This is one of those things that would have set Admiral Wachturm off, had he joined us today," she said. "The vessel would have had a master *Sentience* controlling most of the systems, with subsidiary *Entities* handling Engineering, Weapons, and Navigation. You have a lot of space left over for power and guns if you don't have to carry much in the way of consumables and crew."

"But how would it work?" Desianna asked.

"You have a command staff for the bridge," Jessica replied, "plus a maintenance crew to handle day-to-day repairs and such. If it was a carrier, you would also have an entire flight wing staff, but a super-dreadnaught would only have had a handful of shuttles, probably none of them a quarter as big as *Cayenne* here."

Jessica patted the bulkhead behind her.

"And when it all failed," Arnulf observed, "there were no people who knew how to fix things, because the machines had done it all before that."

"Correct, Admiral Rodriguez," Jessica nodded. "When *Aquitaine* was founded, the Provost at *Ballard*, the woman AI named Suvi, was allowed to teach, but not to do anything greater. Henri Baudin believed precisely that: the Dark Times had been caused because humans let the machines do their thinking. All the more so because he knew her and had learned technology from her. If you look at the bridge on *Auberon*, on your next visit, you will see that my pilot has a control board that looks like an old church organ, not because we could not fully automate many of those functions, but because humans need to be doing the work, not machines."

"Then why is *Fribourg* so different?" Arnulf asked.

Jessica shrugged. "Their founding was a result of adding a religious overtone to Baudin's proscriptions. The AI, Suvi, appears female, so all females must be inherently bad. Tainted. It goes back to elements of their religion that actually pre-date spaceflight."

"Are they right?" Arnulf asked seriously.

Jessica felt her face harden. "Are you seriously asking a female starship commander if she thinks women are weak, evil creatures that must be controlled by men in order to protect human civilization?"

Arnulf quickly bowed his head with a soft smile. "My apologies, Admiral Keller. Perhaps I could have phrased that more diplomatically," he said. "Were the AIs evil? Is she? Should she be allowed to live, or destroyed before she causes a second apocalypse?"

Jessica shrugged, softening her glare. "I have never met the woman, although I have been to *Ballard* once, fresh out of Academy. Human civilization is as large and robust as it is today because of her. Without her knowledge and memories, we might still be stacking rocks atop each other."

"That does not answer my question, Admiral Keller," he said across the aisle with a grin. "Are the AIs useful? Can they be reborn, but better controlled this time?"

Jessica paused to think. "It would make some things easier, certainly, Your Majesty," she continued, "but at what price? Humans are an inherently lazy species. If we could automate everything and let the machines handle it, most would leap at the opportunity, under the guise of labor-saving. But that would set us up again for failure."

Daneel tilted his head and looked at her. "But could one single point-source failure cause that much system instability? Haven't we progressed to a point where the loss of any one system would not cascade laterally across all civilization? The Homeworld was unique in that measure."

Jessica just blinked in surprise. She would have lost a good deal of money betting anyone that this man wasn't hiding that much intellect and knowledge under that blond hair.

Then she smiled. All that, and smart, too.

Jessica was really, really happy she hadn't had to kill him.

"Today?" She shrugged. "Who knows? I've heard legends of a system far towards the galactic core and spinward where one of the *Sentiences* survived and is worshipped as a God-Emperor, never having fallen into barbarism, with technology far in advance of our own, having had a two-thousand-year head start. If it exists, and gets aggressive, it might manage to bind us all back under its yoke."

"Would *Aquitaine* accept that?" Desianna asked.

"I don't know," Jessica replied. "I know *Fribourg* would fight something like that to the death. Would *Corynthe* welcome conquest, with all that the benevolent dictator might bring?"

"No," Arnulf said simply. "Or rather, the captains would never accept it. But if they were broken, destroyed, I suspect the general population would approve. It is a battle I fight daily."

"Which brings us to today's flight," Jessica said. She keyed the microphone to the cockpit again. "*Gaucho*, please find us a quiet corner near the super-dreadnaught to set down. I'd like to walk around and inspect the wreck."

She turned back to Arnulf and the rest with a wry smile. "To quote an ancient poet," Jessica said, gesturing to the horizon, "Look at my grand works and despair."

It was as if a long ridgeline had erupted out of the ground in some tremendous, seismic spasm, throwing up a boulder larger than most sports stadiums or prince's palaces.

Daneel had a hard time reconciling the gray-green wall of hull metal in front of him with the picture of the warship in orbit he had seen earlier. Somehow, someone had managed to bring the vessel down intact, under power, and land it here. Softly.

How?

But more importantly, why?

Bunala was a terribly dry world, as planets went. Perhaps it had been chosen for that reason. Certainly this entire area was as desiccated as old bone, downwind from a pair of massive coastal mountain ranges that would suck all the water out of the air. That weather pattern would protect a ship that was landed here from all elements except wind and sun, but anything built for the perils of deep space would probably just laugh at weather like that.

Daneel watched four of Jessica's marines disappear into an open garage door, passing from light into near darkness. Another dozen or so remained, armed to the teeth, just to protect the four of them. Apparently, Jessica's dragoon was not a man for half-measures.

When one emerged, she gave a hand gesture that caused the rest to relax, at least a little.

Jessica grabbed his elbow and dragged him forward. "Let's go, *Warlock*," she said.

He always forgot how strong the woman was. But the human contact was a good thing.

Daneel tucked her arm in around his elbow, just as he had learned, just as the book on *Aquitaine* culture said to do.

He was rewarded by her smile. It lit the morning more than the bright sun.

Inside, the bay was cavernous. Huge. Monumental. There was no easy term to cover it. But for the small size of the door, barely large enough for a modern fighter-craft, the DropShip *Cayenne* could have fit comfortably inside, with space to spare.

Now it was his turn to drag her along, as he walked to a series of strange holes cut into the deck.

Ah. Someone had stripped out a machine that sat here, once upon a time. He supposed that on a ship as automated as this one was supposed to have been, there would have been a fantastic number of machines to remove, as the darkness began to close in.

But *Bunala* hadn't survived as a civilized power. Had whoever done that taken the parts elsewhere? *Petron* wasn't all that far away, as things went, nor were several worlds in what was now *Salonnia*. Nor *Lincolnshire*, for that matter.

Truly, a mystery for the ages. The last, greatest ship built by a galaxy-spanning nation, reduced to a near-skeleton in a desert on the fringes of the galaxy. Just a skeleton of hull and ribs.

Thus could anything be brought down, like ants hunting mastodons.

Was that what she saw, here? Was that what Jessica was confronting? The end of civilization?

How could anyone stand thinking like that?

Of course, this was Jessica Keller. Her crew was in awe of her. The Red Admiral had apparently considered her a potentially dangerous foe as well. At least at the beginning, before. She and Desianna had taken Daneel into their confidence about the great game to confuse Wachturm and people like Jing Du and Ian Zhao. To try to stop this.

But how could one prevent something like this?

Daneel felt her stare boring into him.

"You see," she said. It was not a question.

"I think so," he replied quietly, unsure of his footing.

Things had just gotten large and dangerous. Or perhaps they always had been and he had been too wound up in trying to seduce this woman to truly appreciate her.

She signaled Desianna to bring Arnulf closer. The marines kept their distance, most inside, but a few on the outside, just in case. Professional paranoia meets professional killers. At least he was on their side.

Daneel blinked in realization. He was on their side. Her side. Committed.

No more games with Jing Du and Ian Zhao. No more playing all sides against a squishy middle, secure that he could out-maneuver anyone else when the blade dropped.

This had been the greatest starship ever built, once upon a time. Now they stood inside her corpse, forgotten on a lost world.

"Damn you," he whispered, mostly to himself, partly to her, at her, because of her.

She smiled with understanding, possibly empathy.

Her? Empathy?

Maybe.

Desianna pulled Arnulf close enough for an intimate conversation.

Daneel felt Jessica's hand wrap closer around his elbow, felt her heat against his side.

"Your Majesty, *Warlock*," Jessica began, quietly but with a great intensity, "you know parts of the truth, perhaps most of it. Now is time for the rest."

The King of the Pirates stared at the two women mutely, appraising them carefully on scales of kingship.

"Go on," he said simply, regally.

"Once upon a time, *Warlock* dabbled in treachery," Jessica stated flatly. "Treason, if you will, before Desianna and I saw a way to bring him back to loyalty."

Daneel felt those regal eyes boring into him, a nearly physical weight settling on his shoulders. Again, he was reminded how this man came to rule.

"Truth?" the King asked.

"Aye, Arnulf," Daneel nodded. "Before…"

Before. How to explain such a world-shaking transformation to this man in simple terms and not be here all day? Before *Sarmarsh*. Before planet-wracking devastation. Before *Hellhound*. Before Teri.

Before Jessica Keller.

Before.

Now, it was the present, verging on the future. Possibly eternity.

How do you convince a man like Arnulf?

"Yes," Arnulf replied simply, looking at the two women in turn. "Before."

Daneel learned another facet of rule.

Arnulf paused a moment before he continued, eyes focused on Daneel like a hungry cat. "So what is the state of the conspiracy?"

"I do not know, Arnulf," Daneel said simply, ready to finally embrace his future, whatever it was. "At one time, I was supposed to challenge you for your crown. You would have lost, due to a treachery that was not explained to me. I suspect something like *Hellhound* tried to do to me. I would have reigned in your palace. Jing Du would have continued on with another generation of bureaucrats. Ian Zhao would have become first among the Captains, and the world would have returned to the way it was before you started bending minds towards civilization. David would have fled or been destroyed."

Daneel felt a planetary weight lift off of his shoulders as he listened to his own words.

Up until now, he had been without responsibility.

Now he was free.

He felt Jessica squeeze his arm in support. That alone meant more than any smile on Arnulf's fierce face.

The king turned the weight of his terrible visage next to Jessica, the shortest person here, but far from the smallest. He put an arm around Desianna's hips to pull her close.

"And why," he continued, "does *Aquitaine* care?"

Jessica Keller looked up at the giant of a man, even bigger than Daneel by two fingers, and smiled.

"Because *Aquitaine* is civilized, Arnulf, King of the Pirates," she said simply. "If you survive, perhaps there is hope for *Corynthe* as well. I am not an ambassador. You wouldn't have listened to one. I am a warrior. You will hear me."

Arnulf turned to kiss Desianna on the forehead. "For thirty years, Admiral Keller, this woman has been my partner. My co-conspirator. My rock. My safe harbor. She tells me to trust you. Backs you. Helped you to convince *Warlock* to come clean."

He took a deep breath that Daneel felt himself mirroring. It was as though the whole weight of the world rested on the next words spoken.

"So I will trust the foundation of my throne on the words of an *Aquitaine* admiral, and my first love," he said heavily. "How do we defeat them? I am merely a king. I cannot order Ian Zhao arrested without a better reason, or better proof, or I will turn the rest of the captains firmly against me. And I certainly cannot eliminate Jing Du without plunging the whole kingdom into chaos."

"I have studied the patterns of ships coming and going, Your Majesty," Jessica said quietly. "There was a chance the ambush would have occurred here, or at *Callumnia*. We were prepared for that eventuality. When we return to *Petron*, I expect their conspiracy to come to fruition. How, I do not know."

"How prepared?" he said. "Who is involved?"

"David knows," Jessica replied. "He has been working very closely with my team."

"David knows? Why was I not informed?"

"An ancient philosopher once said that a secret known to three people," Jessica said seriously, "is only a secret if two of them are dead. David is the only other person Desianna and I felt we could trust. You had enough work, making everyone behave during this Promenade. We had to prepare for the rest."

"But prepared," he replied to her with a hot, savage smile, "is forearmed. We will walk into the lion's den one last time, my friends. Perhaps, I can even retire and make David the new king when this is all done. Certainly, I will have broken the captains to the bit."

"And if we fail, my love?" Desianna asked quietly.

"Then make sure," he looked at each of them in turn, "that you avenge me."

Daneel felt a savage chill race up his spine.

CHAPTER XXXIX

Date of the Republic February 27, 394 City of Lincoln, Ramsey

Ramsey Governor Wapasha had the look of a man who was going to be stubborn. Certainly he was an important personage in these parts. He had eventually let the two of them come to his office for this meeting, but this looked like the point where he was about to dig his heels in and start to buck.

Tomas Kigali smiled. It was an easy smile. Breezy, even. On a man who was tall, and lean, and rakish, and good looking. And not about to take any crap from some pissant bureaucrat in the back of beyond who thought he was the shit.

Tomas glanced over at his cohort on this adventure, Command Centurion Robertson Aeliaes. Robbie just grinned back and nodded, happy to back his play.

Tomas turned the searchlight of his smile back to the governor.

That man was a dandy, in every sense of the word.

"Look, *Aquitaine*," the governor began, "you can't just waltz in here and start making demands. *Lincolnshire* is independent and sovereign. I am not about to just give you two of my warships so you can go flitting off on some adventure in pirate country. You make a polite request through formal channels and we'll get to it in due course."

"We don't have time for bureaucratic niceties, governor," Tomas replied. "In about forty hours, we have to break orbit and run like hell to *Petron* so we can be there when Jessica Keller gets back. We need your help."

"Help *Corynthe*? Are you deranged, *Aquitaine*? They're pirates."

"Yes," Robbie leaned in and agreed, his dark skin and deep voice providing such a rich contrast to Kigali. "And Jessica is trying to negotiate a treaty with them to make them play nice, with the full backing of the *Republic of Aquitaine* behind it."

"And just what makes you think they'll listen to her? She's a woman in a land of chauvinistic men."

Kigali smiled. He pulled a small holo-projector from his pocket and set it on the desk between them.

"She already has their attention, Governor."

Tomas pressed play.

The projection was an amazingly-lifelike composite. You could do that when you had that many scanners and cameras orbiting a target and watching, plus all the power of a navigation computer to process the animation afterwards. And a wizard like Yeoman Kermode directing.

The scene came up with the pirate base on *Sarmarsh IV* approaching, taken from a gun camera on one of the M-5 *Harpoon* fighters in *Jouster*'s wing as they crested the abrupt horizon.

"The pirates," Moirrey's soothing radio voice intoned, "had established themselves on *Sarmarsh* like ticks, burrowed deep into a dog's fur and dangerous as trapped rats. *Lincolnshire* couldn't handle the task of clearing them out, so they asked for help. Jessica Keller and *Auberon* answered. We came, we saw, we conquered."

It was a lovely reconstruction of what the base looked like, the day before *Auberon* arrived. Well laid out, with a number of small gun emplacements protecting the launch bay. The monstrous Type-4 beam at the bottom of the valley. The twin Primary turrets watching the sky like hunting dogs.

"The pirates thought they were secure. Heavily armed. Untouchable. They had not reckoned with the *Republic of Aquitaine*."

An explosion blew out the flight deck as the stealth missile snuck home, followed by several more explosions as the stored missiles and fuel cells went up.

"They were pirates," Moirrey continued soothingly, "prepared to fight Johnny Law and hold him off until they could escape. They were not ready to fight a war. They had no idea what a real war would be like."

Rajput came into view now, flying backwards and bow down as the ground installations opened fire and missed. *Rajput* responded with her big guns, followed quickly by *Auberon* destroying one of the turrets.

"*Aquitaine* offered them terms, but were refused. So we brought war instead."

The gun turrets exploded, flames and rubble spewing in all directions as the flight wing immolated the last tower with guns and missiles. Truly, it was hell on Earth.

Cut to a view from above. Later. The fires were out, but the destruction was wide-spread. Evocative. Intoxicating.

"Again, Jessica Keller offered them terms for their lives. This time, they understood that she was not bluffing, and that their only choices at this point were the meekness of the lamb, or making their peace with the Creator."

The camera panned slowly back and withdrew from the scene as the giant asteroid came into view, tumbling like a lazy bullet. It plunged into the heart of the pirate base like a knife, cutting the heart out of a sacrificial victim.

To Tomas, it was like watching a soufflé swell gracefully, and then collapse in failure. Not that his ever did. But he had seen pictures, heard horror stories.

"The pirate base on *Sarmarsh IV* was annihilated," Moirrey's voice worked up to a proper intonation of *Doom* at this point. "It will not be rebuilt in your lifetime, because Jessica Keller and *Auberon* were not about half-measures to protect *Lincolnshire*. But right now, she is talking directly to the King of the Pirates, and she needs your help. The *Republic of Aquitaine* is here to protect you. But *Lincolnshire* must help as well. Call your representatives. Call your mayor. Call the governor. Tell them to bring peace by making sure the big guns are there when Jessica Keller needs them. Our future depends on it."

Tomas pressed the stop button and pocketed the projector. Yeoman Kermode was an amazing talent. And she understood the locals in a way that nobody not born here could.

The governor sat across from them and visibly ground his teeth in anger. "There is no way in hell, *Aquitaine*," he snarled, "that I will let you broadcast that over the planetary net."

Tomas smiled serenely. "You don't have to, Governor," he said. "We transmitted it to some friends over at the university's Journalism department when we first asked for this meeting."

He checked his mechanical wrist watch with a flourish.

"Had it not taken three hours for you to agree to meet with us," Tomas continued, "you probably would have had time to stop them. I suspect it's a little too late now."

As if on cue, an aide knocked at the door, opened it, and entered.

"Governor," she said, taking a moment to check the two strangers out, "the comm system has gone completely nuts. People are calling in from all over. From the sounds of it, we're talking pitchforks and torches angry."

Governor Wapasha nodded and waved her out of the room silently.

"I don't have a choice here, do I?" he asked.

"You have a number of options, Governor," Tomas smiled ruthlessly. "The one that probably leaves you in the best position would be to send the former *RAN* vessels *CR-255* and *CR-219* with us to *Petron*."

"And if you fail there, boy?" the man asked harshly. "You'll have cost me a significant amount of my defensive forces for *Lincolnshire*. *Winnipeg* and *Admiral Matsushita* are what keep *Ramsey* safe from those pirates."

"Governor," Robbie said, leaning forward to lend a quiet gravity to his words, "if something happens to those two vessels, it will be because they've already gone through me and *Brightoak* to get there. And I promise you I intend to make that a very expensive bargain for those fine folks at *Petron*."

"And if they overwhelm you, *Aquitaine*?"

"A great many of them will have to die trying first, *Lincolnshire*. The survivors won't be bothering anyone for a while."

CHAPTER XL

Date of the Republic March 1, 394 Bunala

Emmerich Wachturm looked down at his notebook with satisfaction as he closed it. He hadn't really expected it, but that didn't mean that he wouldn't take advantage of the situation. Although he supposed that the wyrm could still turn at any time.

And he wasn't about to trust his innermost thoughts to a computer controlled by *her*, but she had been happy to provide him with simply-made paper notebooks and a stylus. It was almost like being home.

In a nearby courier pouch, two other notebooks had already been filled, carefully encoded in such a way that only a handful of people, most of them blood relatives, could easily decipher them.

His papers were secure. He was generally allowed to tour this ship, if not one of the motherships, with one of Keller's officers as a minder and tour guide. The regular dinners with Keller, Arnulf, Jing Du, and others. Even the big state dinners at every tour stop.

Better still, Keller had recognized all the diplomatic niceties, treating him with all the honors and care of an Imperial ambassador, even if he was just a Neutral with a story that smelled like four-day-old herring.

He smiled at the thought. Once upon a time, he would have expected so much more from Command Centurion Jessica Keller. At least he could report home with authority on that front.

Obviously, the conspiracy had had to become more circumspect, of design. It had been a master stroke, the work of Arnulf's First Wife to grab all the chess pieces and hide the board.

The shame, the amateur mistake, lay in letting the main players continue to talk, even here in semi-exile, and to schedule the return to *Petron* with so much fanfare. But, what could one reasonably expect from females? Obviously, *Fribourg* was right, in that aspect. Wonderful Amazons, granted, but substandard spies.

Emmerich looked forward to returning home. He had always hoped that his youngest daughter, Heike, would grow up into a reasonable facsimile of Jessica Keller. Now he needed to tell her to aim higher and achieve true success.

His one great fear was dying out here, for no useful cause. Getting caught in the revolution, when Arnulf was deposed, and being trapped aboard *Auberon* at a point when Ian Zhao ordered the vessel to depart and she chose to fight instead.

Dying was one thing. Dying stupidly was something else.

That woman was a natural warrior, not a diplomat. She would fight. And be utterly destroyed by a wall of fighters descending on her like locusts. Hopefully, he could get Ian Zhao, in a first act as king, to demand his release. Certainly, *Fribourg* would have enough firepower close by to lend credence to such a thing.

Still, it had been a useful sojourn. Five months, so far, aboard Jessica Keller's flagship. Certainly, her crew held her in awe, but his star was even greater in that pantheon. *Auberon* was an absolute case study in the use of chance in campaigns. Perhaps he should write another book on tactics. What was it the ancient general had once said? "I would rather be lucky than good."

Jessica Keller had been lucky. Amazingly lucky.

That luck was just about to run out.

CHAPTER XLI

Date of the Republic March 1, 394 Bunala

A chime at the hatch interrupted Daneel's thoughts. Not that they had been anything useful, or focused, or whatever.

Thinking about her. The feel of her hand on his arm. The sound of her voice. Her smile.

Daneel sighed and set his mind to useful tasks. Whatever those might be.

He set the book on *Aquitaine* history back on his nightstand and rose from his rack. He could have opened the door by voice command, but this was a good excuse to stand and stretch. He had been doing too much reading lately.

Learning. Expanding.

Becoming.

He shook his head with a rueful smile and opened the door.

She stood there.

"Am I intruding?" she asked.

Apprehensive. Unsure.

Nervous.

Her?

"Not at all," Daneel replied, somewhat taken aback. "Please, come in."

He stepped back. The cabin was huge by the standards of his old 4-ring mothership, *Sunset.* Nearly twice as long, and three times as wide as his captain's cabin. And this was just for middling-importance guests.

It suddenly felt tiny.

She did that to a room.

There was one chair, so he sat on the edge of the bed.

"Sit, Commander," he said, gesturing to that chair, equally unsure himself.

She moved to the chair and poised on the edge of it.

Daneel realized that Jessica was out of uniform, possibly for the first time since he had met her. Tonight, she wore a dark blue tunic, long over dark gray slacks, rather than the forest-green uniform of the Republic. Her brown hair was just long enough to be pulled back into a tail. He could detect no makeup, but she didn't need it.

Something was wrong with the chair. Or perhaps, she just had the fidgets. He felt the same way.

They stared at each other for a long moment. Wordless.

"Commander?" he said quietly.

"Please, Daneel," she replied. "Call me Jessica."

"Jessica."

Daneel had finally read enough about *Aquitaine* culture to understand what that level of *personal* meant, at least between a man and a woman.

He felt hope flicker. Embers in the darkness.

"Daneel, I…"

Her words trailed off. Knowing her, there had probably been a speech prepared. Really knowing her, probably three.

He realized suddenly that she was no better at this sort of thing than he was.

The fear in her eyes made him nervous.

Daneel took a deep breath and leapt into space.

He mutely held out his hand to her.

She grasped it like an escape pod off a flaming wreck.

Her hands were warm, moist.

His were suddenly blocks of ice.

"Watching the stars over *Callumnia,*" she said finally, quietly shattering the silence that had engulfed them, "I thought about kissing you. Or slapping you."

Daneel held his breath, fidgets suddenly frozen solid in his chest.

"There had been too many casual proposals of marriage," she continued, "from a group of worthless men-children with no understanding of manners, or courtship. Or even style. Just words. And braggadocio."

She studied him for a moment. Apparently, she found what she sought.

"When I visited your hospital bed on *Petron*, you asked me if that would be so bad. You have no idea how angry that made me."

"You're right, Jessica," he said quietly. "I didn't. Then. That was before..."

Again. Before.

He had a feeling the entire rest of his life was going to be measured in Before and After.

"And I told you, in my anger," she picked up the narrative, "that if you were serious, you would do it the *Aquitaine* way."

He nodded, unwilling to speak. Her anger had been nearly solid that day.

He could still taste it.

Without looking down, Jessica put her other hand down on the cover of *The Modern History of the Republic*, by Voisson, sitting on his nightstand.

"And you did," she concluded, eyes locked with him.

Daneel nodded again.

"I have to know. Why?" she said.

Daneel took a deep breath. Like her, he had prepared speeches for this moment, hoping it would come, afraid it never would.

None of them worked. Not here. Not now. Not with this woman sitting here, as vulnerable as he ever imagined she might be. More.

Daneel felt his eyes wander to horizon, looking for that word, that perfect turn of phrase, that thing that would convey it to her.

To Jessica Keller.

"If I told you," he said finally, eyes coming back to hers, pain evident on both sides, "that every other woman I have ever known, including the two I had been married to, should be rendered in black and white, and you in color, that might begin to explain it. Perhaps."

Daneel fought for the words.

Him, the glib dancer never at a loss.

She did that to him.

"That no woman has ever made me want to become something better than I was," he continued. "That losing you, even if I never had you, would be the single greatest regret I could ever imagine having to live with."

Daneel squeezed her hand.

She squeezed back.

"That..."

He got no further with his thought before she stopped him.

"Shhh."

She tugged at his hand.

Daneel slid forward.

He started to rise as she did, but she pushed gently on his chest with both of her hands, holding him in place.

She stood before him.

Close enough to kiss. Almost.

Daneel found her face just a touch above his own.

She smiled down at him.

He could see a tear welling in one corner.

Nothing could have shocked him more. Absolutely nothing.

Her? Jessica Keller? Human?

He raised one hand to catch the tear before it fell.

Instead, she caught his hand and held it to her face as she closed her eyes.

She was warm to the touch. Soft. Feminine in ways you could not see. Only feel.

Cautiously, Daneel let his other hand find her side, her hip, her back.

Muscles. Hard and taut. Female, but not girly.

Powerful. Dominant. Commanding.

He felt her begin to relax under his touch.

How long they stood there, he didn't know. It didn't matter.

He had this. Now.

Even if he got nothing else, ever.

He had gotten this much.

Jessica opened her eyes after a bit.

Her eyes had turned to bright emeralds.

He felt a hand close on the cloth of his shirt, pulling him closer.

She was always so much stronger than he expected. But he always expected a woman of *Corynthe*. Not Jessica Keller. Not a force to be survived, rather than a woman to be overwhelmed.

She kissed him.

They had crossed into that place where *Aquitaine* demanded that he let her lead. So unlike *Corynthe*.

Her other hand came up around his neck, holding him close enough that he could feel her heart pounding, almost as fast as his. Almost as loud.

She broke the kiss finally.

Eternity might have passed. It was hard to tell.

Daneel didn't really care.

Jessica Keller had a twinkle in her eyes as she leaned back slightly, still within the circle of his arms. He within hers.

"Am I intruding, *Warlock*? I happen to be off-duty, tonight." she whispered with an evil grin.

"Well," he replied, catching the wild energy in her body and drawing into his hands, "Voisson had just gotten to an especially interesting bit on modern mating rituals. I really should probably finish it. You know, research. Just in case."

She did something like a hop and was suddenly straddling him, seated in his lap with her legs wrapped about his back, arms still where they had been.

Had he ever met a woman that strong? That coordinated? Hell, that capable?

"Yes," she whispered, suddenly leaning close and kissing him on the neck, "you probably should. Never know when that sort of thing might be life and death."

Daneel stood, holding her in place as he did so and kissing her back. He turned sideways to the bed, put an arm down, and laid her down on her back underneath him, never breaking contact, just as she never let go with her legs.

"As you command, Admiral," he whispered between kisses.

PART V: HOMECOMING

Chapter XLII

Date of the Republic March 14, 394 Jumpspace Approaching Petron

"What do we know?" Jessica asked.

It was a small group today gathered on the flag bridge. They were deep in Jumpspace now, and trying to coordinate a score of vessels to a mid-hop stopover for a conference would be nigh-impossible. Especially when several of them weren't exactly friendly. Certainly, she would have done it had it just been *Auberon*, *Rajput*, *Supernova*, and *Sky Dancer*. Those captains knew their jobs.

No, best to stick to the plan. There were too many moving pieces right now. Too many unknowns. To many maybes.

"The landing was advertised well in advance," Denis Jež said. "The only issue is the rough timing. We're moving at the best average speed of the rest of these laggards, so the window for arrival is about twelve hours wide. Figure we'll come in a little ahead of center."

She nodded and turned to the flag centurion. He had not had much to do that was interesting on the Promenade. Things that could have been handled by a signals yeoman, except for so many of the people at the other end of the line being potential enemies. Occasional polite diplomacy to prickly pirate-types, for the most part. Flirting with pretty girls, according to Marcelle.

"Are we ready for war, Enej?" she inquired.

"Secure channels have been established with *Supernova* and *Sky Dancer*, Commander," he grinned back at her. "I have also spent some time with their key officers, people the king and David Rodriguez identified as safe, teaching them our vocabulary and some tactics, so they have an idea which way to jump when the flag goes up."

Jessica felt a warm smile grow. "Gold star, Enej," she said. "Very good idea."

That might be the difference between life and death out there. She had been too busy with the Big Pictures Things. It was nice to know she had a crew like this to catch things she might drop. Creator knew she was going to drop something. Hopefully, not the *Big Thing*.

Jessica turned to the three women at the far end of the conference table: Tamara Strnad, Iskra Vlahovic, and Moirrey Kermode.

Moirrey first.

"How close did we get?" Jessica held her breath.

"Five of the Mark I, ma'am," Moirrey replied, her grin growing into a smile that threatened to engulf her whole face. "Eleven of the Mark II. *Mischief* made grand."

"You do realize," Jessica said with a tease to her voice, "that one of these days First Lord Kasum is going to take you away from me and stick you in a weapons design facility with a big budget and a staff, right?"

"You won't let him, will you, ma'am?" Moirrey seemed on the verge of despair suddenly.

"Never, Moirrey."

Jessica turned to the other two.

"We have committed *Mischief*, ladies," she said. "What's the load-out?"

Tamara spoke first. Not that Iskra would speak much, anyway.

"*Auberon* has four of the Mark I's, Commander," Tamara said calmly, professionally. "Gaming scenarios suggest Imperial carriers with flight wings, rather than main-line warships, so we'll have them loaded two and two, first in the missile racks. Just in case, I plan to have crews down in the bays with stealth missiles on sleds, ready to swap out with about four minutes warning, if you need sneaky first."

"Reasons?" Jessica asked. Again, top-notch crew, thinking ahead. She felt less like a commander and more like an Academy instructor, grading PhD candidates. These people were among the best.

"Defense Centurion suggested a scenario where an enemy carrier or mothership starts off with a lot of bluffing and talk, rather than going straight to launch. You might want a swift-kill opportunity. Probabilities were ranked pretty low, but above zero. This gives you the most flexibility to engage. We figure things might get to knife-fighting very quickly."

Jessica nodded. Lot of gold stars today for her crew. They might just pull this off. Creator knew it might be nearly as bad as when the Red Admiral ambushed them at *Qui-Ping* last year.

"Iskra?" Jessica asked last.

Jessica was rewarded by a smile she rarely got from her otherwise-dour and quiet flight deck commander.

"Standard fleet tactics call for something like the *Mischief* missiles," Iskra said, "what Moirrey calls Archerfish, to be put on the big hitters. *Necromancer*, *Damocles*, and *Starfall*. That's a dumb idea. They've already got lots of firepower. Twelve missiles. Twelve launch rails on *Jouster*'s group. Sending him out loaded for bear."

Jessica did the math. Certainly not the way she would have executed it, but she could see the advantages to surprise. And she could plan accordingly. *Jouster* would be the hammer that kicked in the front door, rather than *Necromancer*. Unpredictable. Good.

"Very good," Jessica said after a beat. She felt like she had said that a lot today, and would probably say it more. She simply couldn't have done all of this without these people, these utter professionals, working at the top of their game. It felt right.

"I have no idea if they'll try to jump us the moment we arrive, or wait." Jessica stopped long enough to sip her nearly-forgotten coffee. "The original plan called for an assassination attempt to succeed, by methods unknown, followed quickly by the arrival of an overwhelming force that is supposed to cow us into submission and withdrawal."

She took a breath to meet everyone's eyes.

"I have no intention of dying in *Le Beau Geste* out here. Grand gestures of futility are for idiots," she said. "That being said, this is the back end of beyond. We're better flyers and gunners than they are. Your people have proven that, especially at *Callumnia*. So if it's close, we just might fight. Nelson said it best, once upon a very long time ago. 'Aquitaine expects,' ladies and gentlemen. So do I."

CHAPTER XLIII

Date of the Republic March 14, 394 Petron System

Just like they had at each of the stops of the Promenade, Jessica had Denis Jež drop *Auberon* out of Jumpspace well out from the edge of *Petron*'s gravity well. This wasn't a combat assault, drop hard and fast, crash launch the wing, go immediately to close combat.

At least, it wasn't supposed to be.

They certainly didn't need to show off. Or show the bad guys just how good they were. That might have to come later.

Auberon came out high and wide, anyway. Well above the ecliptic, far enough out that nobody would be close.

The big projection on the flag bridge continued to light up with vessels as they arrived or were identified.

Sky Dancer was already there, and had apparently been early enough to launch half her wing, although they were flying around as escorts rather than strafing anyone. In David's case, that might just be paranoia. He had the most to prove with many of these people, and the most to lose if things went wrong. Reliable and competent.

For a moment, Jessica considered recruiting him for the *Republic of Aquitaine* Navy. He could probably give Tomas Kigali a run for accurate, long-distance navigation.

Maybe a race sometime? She smiled wickedly.

Supernova, with King Arnulf aboard for this last leg into home, had dropped dead-center into the target. Fortunately, nobody was waiting for them. If he wasn't the king, she might have considered saying something, but she doubted he would listen. Arnulf's style was brutal and straight-forward. As were most of the pirates around here.

They had made that clear with their flying, these last few months.

Two-dimensional killers, generally thinking of the ecliptic plane as *ground* and everything in terms of *up* and *down*. It was a bad habit to get into, when there was no gravity. If their prey had been any good, they might have had to up their game.

Jessica was reminded of that first duel, when she had just arrived on *Petron*. The one that almost killed *Warlock*. She looked over at him now, carefully quiet at a training console to one side, watching and absorbing, but not saying anything.

He smiled back at her. That made the day brighter. She wondered what he would do now, when he had the opportunity to return to the top of *Corynthe* society. Would he stay? Did she want him to?

Ian Zhao's 4-ring Mothership, *Kali-ma*, came in low. Not particularly close to anyone, but not that far away. *Auberon* still had every big gun aimed at her as soon as she dropped into realspace. Aleksander Afolayan, *Auberon*'s Gunner, knew what her priorities were. Denis hadn't said anything, either.

After several minutes of nobody doing anything, Jessica spoke into the general comm to the bridge.

"Sensors," she said in that formal voice she used to get everyone's attention. "Do we have a catalog of all the players handy?"

"Affirmative, Commander," Giroux replied immediately. "*Supernova*, *Kali-ma*, *Valhalla*, and *Siberia*, of *Corynthe*'s 4-rings, so nearly everyone we know of, lacking only *Warlock*'s old command, *Sunset*. The 3-rings in scan range are *Warduck* and *Sky Dancer*. I also have the 2-ring *Chevalier* and the 1-ring *Ares* in close orbit of the planet. The 3-ring *Andromache* and the 1-ring *Baba Yaga* are undergoing serious repair work at the lunar maintenance yard and are unlikely to be ready to be involved if anything happens."

"*Wei Chi*'s missing," Daneel said into the quiet.

"Who commands her?" Jessica asked.

"Garth Agano." Daneel grimaced. "Rory's father. And Willem's. If I were Ian Zhao and I was going to do something as big as we think he might, I'd want Garth involved."

"Could they be leaving him out?" she said.

"Maybe," Daneel replied, "but I think it's more likely he's out at the edge of the system right now, waiting. If *Salonnia* or the *Fribourg Empire* are involved, they might be out there with him, just waiting to jump down close."

"Food for thought," Jessica said.

She turned to the flag centurion, "Enej, compliments to the admiral. Let him know we're ready to escort him into the station. Break. Denis, maintain red alert, but let's have *Auberon* and *Sky Dancer* on the corners, just in case. Tuck *Rajput* in close for now."

"Roger that, commander," her first officer replied. "Want the flight wing out?"

"No," she said simply. "I don't know how quickly anything might break, and I'll want them ready to go quickly, but they don't need to be in their cockpits to quick launch yet, except *Jouster* and *da Vinci*."

How soon until they sprang their trap? Moments? Hours? Days? Would they wait until *Auberon* departed? Certainly, she couldn't stay more than a few more days without a reason.

Who would be in charge when she left?

CHAPTER XLIV

Date of the Republic March 14, 394 Orbital Palace Station, Above Petron

Arnulf's Orbital Palace, a night-sky jewel in geosynchronous orbit above the city of *Corynthe,* really brought home the absolute poverty of the kingdom, in ways that weren't easily masked. Rather than a sphere, it was just a disk, and not even a particularly large one.

Jessica knew there were two docking bays, opposite each other, but neither was big enough for *Cayenne* to fit, with the dozen or so smaller shuttles that needed to share the space, so she had entered via an airlock slightly around the ring. Now, she trooped her small army of marines and guests and crew through slightly curved hallways and airlocks that were a whole step down in quality from the poorest station *Aquitaine* might build, or the *Fribourg Empire*. Narrower. Shorter. Raw, painted metal in most places, rather than covered with hangings, or plants, or decorations.

Poverty. Even for a king. A proud one, who aspired to bring his nation up to the standards of the rest of the galaxy, if he could just get his people to understand the joys of indoor plumbing.

She snorted. That was a rude thought. Most of the people here were very nice and generally extremely civilized. Just poor cousins to the rest of the neighbors.

That, perhaps, she could help fix.

She glanced over at Desianna, who had chosen to ride the last leg home with her homeland rather than her husband, and smiled. Today, the woman looked like a queen, in an outfit she had apparently been saving for this occasion.

It fell somewhere between a dress and a gown, a shiny material in dark green that blended well with the *Aquitaine* uniforms around her. Her long, dark hair was contained in a mesh net created from large gold rings that made the black and the purple glow all the more. Her leather belt matched with decorated bracers on each forearm, lending her a fierce, nearly barbaric effect, without ever losing femininity.

And gold.

Rings. Bracelets. Earrings. Necklaces. Even a chain around her waist, outside her belt, that just made the whole outfit all the more impressive.

Jessica was happy in her best day uniform.

Partly, she didn't want to be constrained in formal robes, if things did turn to combat. But also, because this was Arnulf's *Triumph*. He was the King of the Pirates. And this lovely woman beside her would shortly be at his side.

As Senator Horvat had said, politics was the art of the perception, as well as the reality. If you looked like a king, acted like a king, people were more likely to accept you as a king. Here, she *was Aquitaine*, it was incumbent upon her to represent the Republic in its best light. To impress these people, barbarian pirates that they might be.

Especially if she was about to start a war with them.

It still felt like coming home. And it didn't.

Daneel breathed in the air. It had that sharp tang of ozone from an overworked air filtration system. Sharper and more noticeable than usual because he had just spent so long on a well-founded ship where the air was pure and smelled nice.

It reminded him of how much had changed since he had left *Petron* eighteen months ago for his ill-fated mission to *Sarmarsh IV*.

Perhaps not entirely ill-fated. He watched Jessica walk and appreciated the play of muscles in her back and bottom. The women of *Corynthe* went for long and slender when they could, like Desianna, or lush and overripe, like Teri. Very few did athletic. None of them as well as this marvel of a woman in front of him.

He smiled. Perhaps this wasn't home anymore. Perhaps there was more to the galaxy. Certainly, his brother didn't need him coming back and wanting to take command of *Sunset* again.

Did he even want a ship? Perhaps, but a sailing yacht, long-running and lean, so he could see the beauties of space, rather than looking down a barrel at victims about to lose everything to him and his boys. Maybe even a few museums and arboretums.

After all, what did a reformed pirate do with his life?

The reception hall was large, as befit the sort of space you needed to use to impress barbarians from the edges of civilization. Daneel looked him around with a grin. *Worse* barbarians from the *further* edges of civilization.

Ian Zhao was already there, with a small group of retainers and associates. David Rodriguez would remain aboard *Sky Dancer* as an insurance policy. Several other captains had arrived already as well. Some of them were friendly. Some of them were friendly with Ian Zhao or Jing Du. Things could be a rat's nest on *Petron*.

The chancellor was in his accustomed spot atop the platform, four steps above the crowd, where he could serve as a master of ceremonies. High enough to be able to see over the true giants in the group, like himself, or Arnulf.

Jing Du smiled warmly out over the crowd. At least that was how a complete stranger would have taken it.

Anyone who knew the man would be checking that his wallet was still intact.

For Daneel, it just confirmed that things were about to go heavily wrong.

He knew some of what had been planned, at least from Arnulf and Desianna. Jessica had been more tight-lipped. Not because she didn't trust him. Or perhaps not just. Reticence was in her blood.

Learning to be quiet enough for her had been his biggest challenge.

Arnulf would be last in, as befit the King of the Pirates. Mei Fan, Wife Number Three, mother of Sebastian and Karel, awaited him on the stage, not far from Jing Du. She hadn't gone on the Promenade with everyone else.

Daneel knew that Arnulf hoped to make it up to her now, letting her shine by hosting the welcome home party. She looked absolutely stunning up there, in a traditional gown that emphasized all the right parts about her, almost as long and slinky as Desianna, but with an air of fragile porcelain about her rather than the fire in Arnulf's First Wife.

Desianna, dressed absolutely to the nines, waited down in the crowd with the folks from *Aquitaine*. Daneel took a step forward, to stand next to her, and offered an elbow, which she took with a smile and quiet surprised laugh.

That earned him a sly, sideways glance and grin from the woman on his other side. Not that Jessica could say or do anything. They had decided to keep everything completely under wraps in public. Again, the *Aquitaine* way. Daneel wondered if he would be expected to travel to *Ladaux* and ask her father for her hand.

And they thought we were primitive?

He was distracted by one of Jessica's people, her male aide, suddenly stepping up on her other side and handing her a piece of paper. Apparently, a written message.

Written?

She wondered if Daneel was just being charming, or being a goof. Certainly, he was frequently both. And she knew she didn't have to worry about him and Desianna. Not after all this.

It felt strange to have friends. Real friends. Not just fellow command centurions and people you knew in school, once upon a time.

People you liked. People you trusted.

She sensed her flag centurion approach. He just had a sound to the way he walked, even when he was trying to be silent.

Enej handed her a small piece of paper, folded over. His grin could have lit the room, had anyone but her been paying any attention to this corner.

She felt an eyebrow go up, almost an automatic response to that level of wickedness from him. She read the note.

RSVP: Tomas Kigali + 3.

He had done it. Three? What the hell had he done to get that much help? For once, half a dozen enemy motherships didn't seem as tall of a challenge. Certainly, whoever Kigali brought to the ball wouldn't be up to his high standards, but she suddenly had a really nasty ace in the hole.

"How did this arrive?" she whispered to Enej.

The man leaned down to whisper into her ear. "Somehow," Enej said, "he dropped a probe on the edge of the gravity well without being noticed.

It sat there waiting until we tripped it when we dropped out of Jumpspace. Narrow-beam laser. Burst comm pulse. Science Officer Giroux confirms the message and the authenticity."

"How did you get the message here?" Jessica asked.

He leaned back and turned to point at one of the *Auberon*'s smallest marines, a dark-skinned woman wearing a large metal backpack instead of her normal field gear. Enej made a gesture and the woman turned slowly in place so Jessica could see the entire device.

"Portable flag bridge," he said proudly. "Secured, encrypted comm capable of seventeen light-seconds range from the surface of *Petron*. Deploys to stabilize a projector identical to the one you normally have."

"Where did this come from?" Jessica was stunned. She had expected to have to rely on David Rodriguez, an unknown, and Denis Jež, a warrior, if things went wrong.

"I had engineering build it for me," he said with a smile, "based on gaming out all the various political scenarios. Someone has taught me the importance of flexible planning."

"Moirrey?" Jessica asked. Her crew just kept surprising her in better and better ways.

"She was too busy with *Project Mischief*, Commander, so no rainbows or kittens. However, that is planned for version two."

It was all Jessica could do not to laugh out loud. The room was generally quiet, filled with only low conversations, but to laugh right now would draw unwanted attention to her group. Someone might notice that she had twice as many marines as normal with her, today. Heavily-armed ones.

Navin the Black was not fooling around.

Neither was she.

Daneel wondered if it would seem more barbaric or less to replace the three trumpeters by the door with recorded music. Certainly, the audio would probably improve, but you would absolutely lose something when they tilted their heads back and blasted their notes off the ceiling to announce that the King of the Pirates, with his own theme music, had returned to his home.

The crowd grew silent in anticipation.

Every time he did this, Daneel was reminded how powerfully charismatic the man was. He entered with a retinue today, mostly bodyguards, plus a couple of pilots off of *Supernova*. None of them came up to his eyes, although two were about as broad as he. It looked more like a rugby team getting ready to take the pitch than anything else.

The crowd cheered, as was expected. It was a raw, throaty sound, the kind made by a mass of aggressive men, or a pack of wild predators sighting prey.

Arnulf raised his hands as a lane parted through the mob. The noise continued as he ascended the platform, kissed Mei Fan, and turned to smile out over the group. He basked in it for a few moments before waving them to quiet things down. Mei Fan leaned close to say something into his ear.

"My friends," he bellowed as the sound finally ebbed, "my warriors, my comrades, it is good to be home. I am informed by my lovely wife, Mei Fan, that she has something special planned. First off, we will have a toast."

Daneel noticed palace staff circulating from several nearby hatches. Each carried a tray filled with mugs that appeared to have been made from metal, rather than glass. Daneel nodded to himself. That was far more practical. A group like this would probably end up destroying more than half, regardless of their intentions.

He started to reach for a mug as a waiter came close, only to have Jessica step between him and the tray.

She fixed him with a hard stare that would have melted steel. "No," was all she said, but it conveyed an amazing amount of determination. Even for her.

Daneel subsided. He wasn't sure what she was up to, but she was in charge, and he was willing to follow her lead.

He was? Huh. So be it.

Up on the platform, Mei Fan retrieved a small bottle that looked like champagne, and a delicately fluted glass, from a waiter that stood on the floor below. Not for anyone else to be seen in the Triumph today. Only Arnulf, Mei Fan, and Jing Du.

She carefully opened the bottle and expertly poured the honey-colored liquid into the glass, taking a small sip before handing it to Arnulf with a coy smile.

The King of the pirates leaned his great height down to delicately kiss her on the forehead and whisper something with a smile.

Arnulf turned to the room and raised his glass to the room proudly. "I give you the strength of the nation: the warriors of *Corynthe*."

The crowd cheered and then turned silent as everyone drank.

Daneel felt a cold spot appear in the pit of his stomach.

"And now," Arnulf continued, handing his empty glass back to Mei Fan. "I have returned from the Promenade to remind the many worlds that they are part of *Corynthe,* and therefore part of something greater. What say you?"

Before the crowd could roar their approval, a single voice called out.

"And I have come, Arnulf, King of the Pirates, to challenge you for your crown," Ian Zhao yelled, using the formal phrasing.

Only because he was watching her face did Daneel see the flash of glee on Mei Fan's face, before it flashed to anger, and then a simple, beatific smile.

Shit.

Daneel was torn. He could say something right now, and be branded a coward. No, he couldn't. Only captains could speak now. This was Challenge.

Shit.

It had been so long since he hadn't been one of them, that he sometimes forgot the rules of engagement.

Jessica seemed to sense something. She pulled his arm to drag an ear down to her level.

"What is it?" she demanded in a fierce whisper.

"It's a trap," he whispered back. "Mei Fan's in on it."

"What can we do?"

He felt the grip in her hand harden.

"Nothing," he said quietly. "This is *Challenge.* No one may interfere at this point. If we tried to, Arnulf would forfeit his throne, and probably his life."

"How did we miss her?"

"She's had lots of opportunity to kill him," Daneel breathed into her ear, "I'm guessing they promised to protect her when it was done."

Jessica paused for a moment. "Mei Fan has two sons," she said in a leap of logic. "Ian Zhao has daughters, doesn't he?"

Daneel felt all the pieces suddenly rotate ninety degrees and lock into place. "Dynastic marriage. Wrong dynasty. Sebastian instead of David."

"A story as old as monarchy," Jessica said. "What to do about second sons?"

A space had been cleared down in front of the platform, lined by a wall of expectant observers. It had been twenty-some years since Arnulf came to power. After a few early attempts, no one had challenged him like this in a long time.

Daneel felt ashes in his mouth. They were very likely to crown a new king today.

Jing Du acted as referee, standing over the pseudo-arena from the front of the platform. Mei Fan had retired to her chambers, claiming to be overcome by the emotions of the day.

Everything was formal now. One of those rituals that could be claimed as Founding Legends.

The fight between he and *Hellhound* had been much less prescribed. Duels like that were serious between the parties, but rarely had any long-term implications. It had allowed *Hellhound* to hide his armored girdle and the poison ring.

Things like that were not allowed here.

This was for a crown.

Arnulf and Ian Zhao had both stripped to the waist, showing off two lifetimes worth of scars and old wounds.

Daneel was happy to admit that Arnulf, in his thirties, in his prime, had been bigger and stronger than Daneel had been. Nobody else had come close, but Arnulf had a few fingers of height, and width, and had outweighed him by nearly five kilos. Now a man of fifty, he was still amazingly impressive. If the stomach had gone a little slack, he was still stronger that at least half the men present.

Ian Zhao was all wires and whipcord. Arnulf was taller and broader across the shoulders, but it was like comparing a bear to a panther. Both amazingly-dangerous creatures, but in entirely different ways. Where Arnulf had a body covered with curly, dark hair, Ian Zhao had little, but his freckles ran halfway down his torso.

Daneel had been allowed to stand in the front row as a witness, even though he wasn't a captain anymore. He stood next to Jessica on one side and Desianna on the other.

"Desianna Indah-Rodriguez," Jing Du called formally, "would you retire?"

Daneel could feel the pure rage boiling off of her.

"Nay, Chancellor," she called back, angrily, made of far sterner stuff, "if I am to be made widow today, I would rather carry the memory to my own grave, than rely on others to tell me."

Jing Do nodded, the last of the formal ceremony nearly done.

Arnulf smiled warmly at her as he readied. His blade today was almost a cutlass, three fingers wide and longer than Daneel's forearm, with a wide, flat spine and a straight edge for most of its length.

In contrast, Ian Zhao held a much lighter weapon, nearly fifty centimeters of blade, finely ground to edges on both sides and then painted black except for the very edges themselves. He held it in a thumb-and forefinger grip, blade parallel to the deck, like a dock-side fighter.

"Captain Ian Zhao," Jing Du called across the silent room, "you have challenged the King of the Pirates for his throne. Such a fight only ends in death. Are you prepared?"

"I am," Ian called back, flexing his back and arms to loosen them up.

"King Arnulf," the chancellor continued, "a challenger comes. Will you retire and withdraw for the betterment of society, one whose day has passed?"

"My day has not passed, chancellor," Arnulf answered formally. "If he would take it, it must be done in blood."

"Captain. King of the Pirates. Begin," Jing Du intoned before stepping back.

Daneel expected the men to circle and test each other. Certainly, neither knew how the other would fight, it had been so long since either had been in the arena.

Instead, Ian Zhao leapt suddenly forward and thrust the point of his knife at Arnulf's belly.

It was easily blocked with a ringing of steel on steel and a few sparks. Arnulf countered with a slash that found Ian Zhao bounding backwards just as quickly as he had closed.

The room roared with barbaric approval.

Daneel thought Ian Zhao looked like a kangaroo, bobbing his weight back and forth on each foot. It made no sense until he glanced at Arnulf, and saw how flushed the man had suddenly become. How frequently his eyes blinked.

Then Daneel knew.

It wasn't going to be an obvious poison. Arnulf couldn't die mysteriously like that, assassinated in the night. No, it had to be like this. Public. Aboveboard, as much as something like this could be. In a duel for kingship.

Daneel knew the truth when the two circled for another pass. Ian Zhao ended up facing him.

For a moment, eyes locked. Ian smiled at him.

Yes. They both knew.

And there was nothing he could do. Nothing at all.

Arnulf charged suddenly. Perhaps he knew as well, and was intent on killing this man before the poison did him in.

That heavy blade flickered out like a snake striking. Behind it, all of Arnulf's mass and strength.

The lighter blade could not block it. The smaller man could not repel it.

Arnulf kissed him once with steel.

It would not be enough, a shallow slash across the ribs and a small divot in the thigh. But it was blood.

First blood.

The mob went insane with noise.

Daneel could barely hear his own thoughts, so intense the sound had become.

Arnulf hacked again, but Ian was gone, a ghost spinning away with his own lethal edge slashing out.

Ian drew blood in the separation, a thin crimson line across Arnulf's shoulder. Again, not lethal, just bloody. Almost an aphrodisiac for the rowdy, dangerous men here.

The sound became nearly solid.

The smell was that of fifty men on a surge of adrenaline, musky and at the same time rank and sour.

Ugly.

Barbaric.

Daneel ground his teeth in utter frustration, locked on this combat that would forever determine the future of *Corynthe.*

Such a stupid way to live. Had he really been like that? All the worse.

The dancers spun again after another noisy pass.

Arnulf ended up facing Daneel, but Daneel didn't think he was seeing anything at this point. His eyes were all pupil, no color. He was covered in sweat in a way that the regular room temperature did not explain. It looked as though he was burning up from in inside.

Perhaps he was.

Perhaps he was using every bit of his kingship right now, as fuel for a bright flame.

Better to die gloriously than live in shame.

And then it was over.

They came together, passed, parted.

Daneel watched Ian Zhao come to rest almost exactly across from him, empty-handed.

He looked back, saw the blade quivering in Arnulf's chest, slid expertly between two ribs and trapped there.

Arnulf collapsed to his knees as his eyes glazed over.

He opened his mouth to say something, but there was only blood.

And he fell.

Beside him, Daneel felt a sudden weight fall into his side.

He caught Desianna before she collapsed as well.

As if cut as well, the sound ended.

It was over.

And he had failed.

Ian Zhao leapt lightly onto the platform and turned to smile out over the crowd.

"King Arnulf is dead," Jing Du said. It sounded like a yell in the utter silence that had fallen. "Long live King Ian."

The cheers were more subdued. Almost polite. Perfunctory, if one could say that about such a monumental event.

Jing Du stepped forward to stand next to the new king with a pleased smile on his face.

"Captains," the Chancellor intoned, "a new king is proclaimed. Would any of you dispute his right to rule?"

Daneel let go of Desianna and braced her upright until he felt her strength take hold.

He stepped forward once, appearing out of the crowd and entering into that bare area.

Before he could speak, Ian Zhao pointed a finger at him.

"You have no standing in this Court. Daneel Ishikura," he sneered. "You are no longer a captain."

Daneel cursed inside. Of course they no longer cared about him.

"In fact," King Ian continued, "you are nothing at all. I look forward to destroying you next, *Warlock*."

He was nothing. And David Rodriguez wasn't here. They were doomed.

And then she spoke. The *Angel of Retribution*.

"I have a ship."

CHAPTER XLV

Date of the Republic March 14, 394 Orbital Palace Station, Above Petron

They did not get to win.

Simple as that.

All this work. All this planning. All this *everything*, and the bad guys would not walk away laughing.

Every eye in the room was locked on her. As they should be.

She was angry.

It was a room like she would find anywhere in the *Fribourg Empire*.

Men. Accustomed to cultural superiority. Unused to hearing a woman speak. Unwilling to listen.

They would listen to her. They would listen now.

Jessica stepped out into the clearing, past Daneel Ishikura. *Warlock* couldn't do anything at this point.

They had taken him into account, their former conspirator. There were rules that even pirates would obey, marking them at least vaguely civilized.

Fine. Because she wasn't feeling benevolent right now. Or civilized.

Destructive.

She had been sent to *Lincolnshire* to make it safe from people like this. She had come to *Corynthe* to do just that. Not to try. To succeed. If it had to be over the body of two kings, so be it.

"You aren't one of us," Ian Zhao sneered down at her.

He wasn't a big man. There weren't many people he could look down on, without the benefit of the platform.

"The rules don't say *one of you*, assassin," she snarled back. "They say only a captain may challenge a king. Besides, before you murdered him, Arnulf Rodriguez made me an admiral. So that does make me one of you."

"And you would fight me for the crown, *Aquitaine*?"

She had his attention now. There were murmurs behind her that sounded ugly. Words like *assassin* and *murder* had gotten people's attention.

"If that's what it takes to see justice, Ian Zhao," she replied, not angry now, but hard enough, loud enough, clear enough that every person in the room would hear her.

Command voice. Taught to her, once upon a time, by the man who would become First Lord of the Fleet, Nils Kasum.

The best.

"What is justice, woman?" he snarled back, anger coming to the fore.

"I say you poisoned King Arnulf," Jessica called, "because you could not face him in a fair fight. I'm sure you won't trust an *Aquitaine* doctor to test for the poison. I'm sure we can find a local who is neutral. Will you stand for such a thing?"

Ian Zhao stepped forward and dropped off the platform with a resounding crunch, aimed directly at her.

For a moment, she considered that she had goaded him too far, and that he was about to charge her. Jessica shifted her weight subtly and prepared to receive him.

Valse d'Glaive did not *require* blades. It just made effective use of them.

But he stopped after a long stride into the clearing.

"I cannot have your ship if I win, can I?" he said conversationally.

She could see the wheels turning in his head, plans and angles. In any other circumstance, she might have found him to be an adequate king.

But not here. Not now.

"No," she replied simply. "But my squadron will leave, and leave you alone to rot on your barbaric throne forever, King of the Pirates."

She turned and nodded at her flag centurion.

"Aye, sir," Enej nodded back.

"And if I chose not to accept this Challenge, *Aquitaine*?"

She could see something in his eyes. Perhaps nervousness? Even a touch of fear? *Come so close to victory to have it all fall apart at the last moment? Welcome to my world, you bastard.*

"Explain to your captains, *Corynthe*," she replied sweetly, gesturing at the crowd behind her, "that you were afraid to face a woman in the ring."

Yes. There. That particular flash of anger. Like a splinter under a fingernail, wasn't it? Like a wolf with a paw in a trap. *Willing to gnaw it off to escape me, pirate?*

"And if I am weak from my wounds, *Captain*?" he sneered.

"Oh?" Jessica observed tartly. "Your wounds did that?"

She prepared to pivot, pretty sure she had taken Ian Zhao right up to that line where rational thought stopped and he lost his temper. It was just as useful in single combat as it was in fleet actions.

She could see the anger boiling off of him.

It warmed her from the sudden cold that Arnulf's death had draped her in. She drew a breath deep, held it, released it.

Cold, flat eyes stared at Ian Zhao and dared him.

"But if you require ministrations before we dance," she waved a hand negligently, "by all means. I will in turn make it fair and only fight you with one hand."

That was almost a bridge too far. She watched him draw a breath to charge her before he came to his senses.

Instead, he moved to the edge of the platform and seated himself. A medic materialized and began to dress his wounds. Most of them were superficial, clean slices with razor-sharp edges that could be glued back together until they healed. Only the one in the thigh required work, and that not much.

Jessica watched him drink something while he waited. She presumed a regular energy drink of some sort. They couldn't have planned well enough to buff him up with some near-magical concoction that would make him super-human.

Not that it would matter. Not now.

Jessica considered the room, and all these men. A pit viper might have smiled like that.

She began undoing buttons on her outer tunic, stripped out of it, and handed it to her flag centurion. She was still wearing the heavy-duty boots she had worn to the surface of *Bunala*. They had felt more appropriate this morning than the ship's slippers she normally wore. Perhaps she had known the day would end thus.

The under-tunic went next, leaving her in just close-fitting pants and a sports bra.

The men fought naked to the waist as proof they weren't wearing any armor. No tricks.

Men.

Jessica peeled the sports bra off next and handed it to Enej as part of the bundle he held.

His jaw hit the floor first, followed closely by every other man in the room. The cold air bit at her nipples. That what she told herself.

Morons.

What was it her mother had used to say? A man loses fifty percent of his IQ when he sees a boob?

Here, have two.

Let her be the object of their lust. If she won, she would be their queen.

Jessica smiled suddenly.

If she won, she would be their Queen.

Jessica Keller, Queen of the Pirates.

It was a shot of pure adrenaline to the base of the skull that was better than an orgasm. She turned and smiled at him, wondering if she could just strike Ian Zhao down with a Zeus-like bolt of lightning from here.

It had that kind of mad power to it.

She turned back to the men around her, the captains that upheld this throne, and smiled even broader.

"Gentlemen, I have no blade to fight this Challenge. I call on the Free Captains of *Corynthe* to aid me."

A forest of steel erupted around her. Men pushed and shoved at each other to try to get closer. All for a pair of boobs. And, perhaps, men who didn't particularly like Ian Zhao, or wondered what had been put in that wine glass, or if they might be next.

Someone had taken the time to remove Arnulf's body, treating it like a holy relic as they did, and then to wipe down the floor in preparation for the second round.

A king had died here. A second might follow.

Valse d'Glaive used a saber and a *main-gauche*. Long and slashing, heavy and blocking.

Ian Zhao was about of a size with the fighting robot she danced with regularly. It hadn't been a fair fight, so she couldn't rate him against it for ability, not with Arnulf poisoned and probably already dying.

Still, the man would have height and reach comparable. His stiletto was fifty centimeters of double-edged blade, more of a short sword than anything else. Cut on both the pass and the exit.

Jessica drifted right to left, letting these men get a really good view of her body as she inspected weapons.

Only one of you gets to touch, she smiled to herself.

In the end, she took a short, heavier blade, almost a cleaver, from a smaller captain, himself almost a dwarf compared to the giants around them. It was thicker than her training *main-gauche*, and ground down to only a basic edge, a tool for dismantling chickens.

She looked over her shoulder as Ian Zhao rose and stepped forward.

Chickens, and kings.

Jing Du seemed content in his spot again, overlooking the mob below with a warm smile.

Jessica had no intention of being his second victim today.

She held the blade in her right hand. Most of these people were right-handed, so it would seem normal to them. It even felt like her *main-gauche*, literally the *left-hand*, that she normally parried with, so being in her off-hand was natural.

While Ian Zhao stood prepared in a fighter's crouch across the way, she stood upright and held the blade loosely at her side.

"Ian Zhao," she drawled loudly enough to be heard by everyone, "you are a coward and an assassin. You are unfit to lead and should take up the nun's robes and retire to a life of introspective prayer to whatever God might accept a worthless loser like you as a follower."

A little bit thick, but these people weren't exactly known for subtlety.

The room had grown warm. Or she had. She could feel sweat dripping down her neck and back, running between her small breasts.

Always watch the center of a man's chest when knife-fighting, her ground combat instructor had taught her on day one. Ian Zhao seemed to be looking in the right place, but she doubted that his eyes were focused on her sternum, from the way that they flickered back and forth.

"And you, *Aquitaine*," he called back, anger slurring his words, "are an abomination in this Court. A woman pretending to be equal to a man. I will not have it."

"Oh, no, *Corynthe*," she said. "I am Civilization. You are a mongrel only fit for the servant's entrance."

That gibe hit home.

Jessica watched Ian come nearly out of his crouch with rage, before he sank back down and edged forward crabwise, blade leading.

She relaxed from sudden tension.

It wouldn't be the sudden bull rush that had initiated the duel with Arnulf. But then, she hadn't drunk anything that was going to dull her senses and her reflexes, and needed to be spurred into the bloodstream.

She settled down into the Fifth Form, blade flat against her thigh, standing almost upright, but with her toes poised to go up, left, or backwards.

It was an odd stance, so unlike any of the traditions that *Valse d'Glaive* had inherited from all its ancestor-forms. But then, humans had had eleven thousand years in space to experiment with movement. They were bound to find interesting variations.

This one, so her first instructor had told her, had been the best at inducing a mugger to actually attack, instead of letting you pass and preying on an easier victim later.

Ian Zhao rocked as he moved. It was like watching a crab eke its way up the surf, back and forth, blade and free hand.

He didn't seem to be sweating now. Or rather, an aide had toweled him off and then a chill had settled over him.

Perhaps Arnulf's ghost.

Jessica, on the other hand, was warm. Calm. Poised.

Again, perhaps Arnulf's smile.

She stood perfectly still as the man closed for his first strike, blade held loosely for a flat slash. At least he acted like a professional, gripping the killing blade in a way that did justice to the setting.

She wasn't above bad killing. Not here. Not now. But she could appreciate good form.

It also made the man more predictable.

For Jessica, the world slowed down.

Ian Zhao slashed with his right hand, a flat arc parallel to the deck. It wasn't close enough to be very dangerous, just annoying.

Unlike Arnulf, the man had no idea how she would react, so he wanted to probe her.

And as with any physical task and a new partner, you had to find the corners, whether it was dancing, or sex.

Or death.

Jessica let her anger erupt out of her soul. This man was expecting her to flinch backwards, possibly forgetting how close she was to the edge of the circle and a wall of men who would shove her forward again, possibly onto a waiting blade.

It was a good opening gambit. Low risk, possibly high reward. Like kissing a girl on the back of the neck.

She wasn't that kind of girl.

Jessica surged straight at Ian Zhao, twisting crossways like a tornado to slam her *main-gauche* into contact with his poniard, blocking him just like in a musketeer video.

If she had had a second blade, it would have been over right then. Right there.

Pinwheel withershins around him to continue the spin, anchored to his blade by the impact. Ride it around the maelstrom and slash neck high as she came out the far side of the pass.

With her saber, she could have possibly decapitated the man on this first pass. Certainly killed him.

Jessica settled for back-handing him with her left as she exited. It was probably not something many women had ever done to Ian Zhao.

The blow echoed off the walls and ceiling like a crack of thunder.

For a moment, the crowd fell utterly silent. She hadn't realized the roar, the volume of sound that had erupted at the combat, so lost in herself.

Ian Zhao almost stood upright in surprise, but Jessica was too far away to take advantage of him.

She had ended up clear across the space. Looking back, Ian Zhao was framed where he stood by two people behind him. Her two favorite people right now. Daneel Ishikura and Desianna Indah-Rodriguez.

Beyond, a flicker of movement. Her flag centurion. Enej was talking to someone now on the comm, standing next to the marine with the big tactical backpack, one that apparently had a two meter tall whip-pole with a flag atop it.

Auberon's flag. She had missed that earlier.

Her flag.

She felt another pulse of power flicker all the way down to her toes as she moved to First Form and closed.

She wasn't evading Ian Zhao now. She was hunting him.

Something of that seemed to get through to the man. He started to back away, caught himself, and slid to his left, back to the crab walk.

She could see a bright red mark on the side of his face. Not quite the color of fresh blood. She would have to fix that soon.

Ian Zhao shifted to his left as she closed, backing crablike around the arena, butt-first, blade staying centered on her as she closed.

Jessica decided to return the favor. She flared her left hand, open at his eyes, to make him blink, and slashed wide and overhand with her right. She had the heavier blade, the stronger. If he moved to block square, she just might shear it off into a stump.

Very few people understood the physics of sword-fighting anymore.

Ian Zhao wasn't an expert, but he was a knife-fighter, and she seemed to have spooked him. Rather than stand, he skittered back another half step as her slapping hand came up, and let her blade pass rather than try to resist.

It was a good defense. Hang back, let the enemy over-commit, strike at an opening. A useful strategy when fighting in two dimensions, or a simple foe.

Jessica was already three movements ahead of him in her tactical planning.

She was a lunge and a thrust away from the man now. She smelled rather than saw it as his weight shifted forward and he prepared, turning slightly sideways to present his blade and less of his body.

Someone else who watched old musketeer videos.

She smiled to herself. His stiletto would be nimbler. Her blade heavier.

He would lunge. It was there in the set of the hips, the drawing of the back leg under instead of keeping it out as a pivot, ready to crab-step again. It was there in the wrist, suddenly rigid instead of flowing.

Jessica flowed to her right to create movement.

There.

Ian Zhao was good. She was going to bleed. There was just no way to avoid his speed.

Jessica didn't have to. She had watched him fly *Kali-ma*. He thought in two-dimensions like the rest of the pirates. Brawlers with a single blade.

She pushed off and up as she flowed, turning an aerial cartwheel over the lunging sword.

The surprise on his face was priceless.

Jessica felt the kiss on her hip. It might have missed a man, or a woman with no curves. Cost of doing business, especially as a woman in this place.

She landed square and rotated, pivoting her right foot back first to open the bleeding hip. Her center turned, rotating her stomach, her breasts, her shoulders. The arms came along for the ride, long lines moving like whips, hands at the end like bolos.

A lighter blade would have left a vicious slash. Messy. Unprofessional.

Bad killing.

But that nasty little cleaver, barely sharp enough to bone a chicken, impacted with a dull, hollow thump. That rich, crunching sound a carcass makes just before it goes into the stew pot.

Bones separating.

Death.

Jessica flashed out with her open hand and caught Ian Zhao's wrist as he sought to gut her with his own blade. They stood like dancers, like lovers.

She was stronger than she looked. And angrier.

There are sensitive bones in the hand and wrist. She felt every kilo of Arnulf's betrayal, every moment of Daneel's love making, every secret giggle with Desianna.

She transformed the rage into fuel and let it all flow down into her left hand, crushing those little bones in Ian Zhao's hand and preventing him from killing her.

She sawed the cleaver in her right hand, but it was wedged deep, high into his chest, through the thorax and into lungs.

Blood leaked around it, but not much.

More came out of his mouth.

In the videos, the hero was always supposed to say something pithy, something memorable, right about now.

She didn't have it in her. Instead, she held him close, like a lover, like a dancer, and watched the life flow out of his eyes.

Death was sudden. One moment a flicker. The next, nothing.

Jessica stepped back as Ian Zhao's body fell limply forward. She let his weight pull the cleaver from his ribs, even as she caught his sword and held it.

Not quite *Valse d'Glaive*, but with these two blades, she could kill any man here.

She turned and gave every single one of these captains a look that conveyed that utter, calm conviction.

The room fell silent again. The noise had apparently been solid, obvious only by the sudden absence.

Jessica Keller came back to the present.

"Does anyone else demand to die this day?" she called.

From any of the men, that would have been a challenge. A *machismo* thing. *Braggadocio*.

From her, it was a promise. Simple as that.

And they knew it.

And accepted it.

And they accepted her.

Jessica Keller, Queen of the Pirates.

Movement caught her eye. Jing Du was making a break for it, fleeing towards a hatch behind the stage, no doubt to escape her and rally his allies.

"Someone stop him," she pointed, using the bloody cleaver for emphasis.

Heads turned. Some men took a step to try to do something, but it was obvious they were just going to get in each other's way.

Jing Du made it to the open hatch and stopped.

If she hadn't seen it, with her own eyes, she would have called the storyteller a liar to his face.

Jing Du stopped moving. And began to levitate off the deck in a slow, elegant motion.

And then he drifted backwards into the room, followed by a shadow of utter darkness that looked at first like Arnulf's ghost made flesh, made *Vengeance*. It had that size, that mass, that solidity. It resolved itself into *Auberon*'s dragoon, her two-meter-tall ground combat master.

Navin the Black.

The man had caught Jing Du by the neck. Jessica had studied enough anatomy to know it usually took minutes to strangle the average man with your bare hands, with the victim normally fighting you all the while.

The dragoon wasn't crushing Jing Du's throat. He had picked the man up by wrapping one giant hand delicately around the chancellor's neck and lifting on the underside of his jawbone, perhaps pinching those two sensitive nerve clusters behind the ears as he did so.

Jing Du hung perfectly still as this terrible ogre transported him back into the chamber. Perhaps he swayed a little, as one might when all rational thought has fled and only gravity was active.

The dragoon strode to the platform and mounted it in one stride, truly a dark angel, a demon, an ogre. He looked down upon the room from his great elevation and smiled, head shaved bald and carefully-trimmed Vandyke white with vast maturity.

"Your Majesty commands," he rumbled.

Dragons have that smile when dwarves stumble into their lairs.

The silence was just as intense as the sound had been.

And then the room erupted in cheers.

Her flag centurion brought her back to earth.

"We have a problem," Enej said as he stepped forward and handed her back her sports bra. Daneel and Desianna also surged forward, but kept a step back.

The fighting circle evaporated like a soap bubble.

Arnulf's staff, no damn it, her staff, took charge, under the watchful eye of *Auberon*'s marines. The pirate captains might have blades as a mark of their manhood and authority. Her marines had guns and attitude. Everyone else was going to be exceedingly polite.

Jessica handed the blades to Daneel and took a towel from an unseen hand to wipe herself dry.

The men here had seen enough of her chest today, so she quickly climbed back into the sports bra and undertunic. The rest could wait.

"An Imperial squadron has dropped out of Jumpspace," Enej continued as she dressed. "*Auberon* and David Rodriguez aboard *Sky Dancer* have both launched everything and challenged them, but they continue to come in. They appear to be led by that missing 4-ring, *Wei Chi* and Garth Agano."

"What are we facing?" Jessica asked, oblivious to the rest of the mob standing around them listening.

"From *da Vinci's* scans," Enej said, "three of the big 4-ring motherships, *Wei Chi*, *Valhalla*, and *Siberia*, plus a 3-ring, a 2-ring, and a 1-ring. The Imperials have an Escort Carrier, two Carrier Tugs, and a trio of escort corvettes."

A laugh got her attention. It was harsh and mirthful. Inappropriate.

She turned to Jing Du, standing now, with her dragoon's paw holding him by the scruff of the neck.

"You have failed, *Aquitaine*," he sneered. "Your reign will be barely longer than Ian Zhao's. By nightfall, another king will be crowned."

Jessica felt the growl start deep in her stomach. *Was it going to be necessary to destroy* Corynthe *in order to make it a better place?* She thought of her uncle's farm, how he burned the fields in the fall, after the harvest, to fertilize them for the spring.

Very well. If it took that level of destruction to get their attention, it would have to do.

This would be the diplomacy of the blade. The only kind these people apparently understood.

"Put me on the general push, Enej," she said sharply.

"Go ahead."

"Pilots and captains of *Corynthe*, this is Jessica Keller," she said, intoning her words carefully, formally, to deep space, just as she had done when she read aloud her orders to take command of *Auberon,* once upon an eternity ago. "By right of combat, I am your queen. I will have your oaths, or I will have your heads."

She paused to let the words sink in.

Queen of the Pirates. Yes, it would be the diplomacy of the blade.

"The enemy squadron is *Wei Chi* and her allies," she continued. "If they will not surrender or retreat, they must be destroyed. Otherwise, you will become just another world suffering under the Imperial yoke. I will not allow that."

She paused again, looking around the mob until she found Ian Zhao's second in command, a man named Yan Bedrov. He looked nothing like the former king, so she hoped that he was not a brother, or a cousin.

Or a fool.

Jessica fixed him with a look that commanded.

The man blinked for a moment, deer in the headlights, before he understood and dropped to one knee before her, head bowed in duty.

As if on cue, the rest of the room did the same. Including Daneel and Desianna. Within moments, only Jessica and her people and Jing Du remained standing.

Now, time to rattle cages.

"Cho Ayaka Nakamura, callsign *Furious*," Jessica continued, naming the hotshot girl pilot from *Sky Dancer*, "you will take command of the *Corynthe* flight wing."

"But I'm not senior, ma'am," the young woman gasped into the radio.

"Did I stutter, *Furious*?"

"No, Your Majesty."

"Is this too much for you to handle?" she asked, well aware that every pilot was marked by their ego.

"Negative." *Furious* sounded like her namesake now.

"Then *take command*."

"Roger that," Furious replied. "Hey, Enej-baby, can everyone hear me, flag-boy?"

Jessica watched her flag centurion turn beet red.

Obviously, he and the pilot had apparently gone beyond a purely formal working relationship somewhere along the way. She would have to ask him at some point, but not today.

"Affirmative, Cho," Enej said, apparently grinding his teeth in embarrassment as the men around him smiled.

"Right," *Furious* called. "You heard the boss. All friendly fliers identify yourselves with a radio beacon of *Monarch*."

"*Monarch*?" a man's voice called, one of the other pilots out there. "What's up with that, Nakamura?"

"Jessica Keller, Queen of the Pirates, *Wolfhound*," *Furious* replied. "We are now *The Queen's Own*."

Jessica smiled regally at the men around her.

The Queen's Own.

Jessica took three strides to stand before the man who had been Ian Zhao's right hand.

He looked up as her boots appeared in his line of sight.

It was the look of a man who expected to be next on the chopping block.

"I will take command of *Kali-ma*," she said, loud enough to be heard by everyone, but speaking only to him. "We will go out to meet these Imperial interlopers and convince them to go home."

She waited for him to nod, and start breathing again as she nodded regally down at him.

Jessica turned to the rest of the room and sized them all up, her face turning more serious, more ominous.

"*Warlock*," she said to the man, "you will take charge of *Supernova*. Other warship captains will join us, or resign their commands, right now."

Heads looked up at her and nodded. She gestured them to stand. Her anger at this moment probably could have soured milk.

"If you command a freighter or stripper, you will remain here with my palace staff and my marines, until I get back."

Jessica softened her scowl to smile at these men. It was the same smile she remembered on Nils Kasum's face more than once.

Her life depended on the captains around her now.

"Gentlemen, Garth Agano wants a war. Let us not keep him waiting."

CHAPTER XLVI

Date of the Republic March 14, 394 Above Petron

The bridge of the 4-ring Mothership *Kali-ma* was cramped. Not as tight and claustrophobic as *CR-264* or *Rajput*, but nowhere near as open as *Auberon*, or even *Brightoak*. Still, Jessica found it homey.

She sat where Ian Zhao had most recently been resident. Before her, on her right, her flag centurion sat, with his comm-marine and the radio close by. Enej's shadow, Yeoman Orly, was the smallest marine *Auberon* carried, both by side and weight, and, according to *Navin the Black*, probably the meanest. She smiled at the pirates like a woman getting ready to beat up an entire dock-side bar by herself.

On the opposite side was the man who had been Ian Zhao's second in command. Yan Bedrov was tall and skinny, and still very nervous. He also had a marine escort, but this one was not a radio tech. Instead, Navin had sent First-Rate Spacer Arlo.

The two marines could not have looked less alike, but they watched the bridge like hawks, conveying the certainty that they could take on the pirate vessel's entire crew alone and win.

Just like she was about to do.

"Gentlemen," she announced as everyone settled. "I don't know your ship that well, and I don't know you. I will assume you are as good as my crew on *Auberon* until you show me otherwise. And *Auberon*'s people are very good."

She turned to size up Bedrov, her new first officer. "Yan," she said simply, "I will command the Flag, that is, all vessels. You will handle general orders and translate them into commands for this crew."

She waited until he nodded and then pointed at Enej.

"This man is my flag centurion," she continued. "He will transmit orders to the rest of the friendly forces. You command the flagship, so everything *Corynthe* forces do will be based on our movements. Questions?"

Yan Bedrov bit his lip in thought. "What do you know about Motherships, Captain?" he asked, falling back into some level of what passed for normalcy, at least for him. Professionalism. It was a good start.

"Good defensive armaments and shields," Jessica replied. "Nothing in the way of big guns, since you rely on the flight wing for your hitting power. *Auberon* or *Rajput* could slaughter a mothership or one of the Imperial vessels if we get close. We have to stay back because we can't take on that many fighters."

"Right," he agreed. "And the sensors are kinda crap, because who needs good scanners, except to send the rings off. Permission to set an initial course for the squadron?"

"What do you have in mind, Bedrov?"

"Bring her around to zero-five-zero, come to max speed, plus ten degrees," he called to the pilot.

She watched him plot his movement on a flat screen until Enej and the comm-marine brought their projector on line and put the sphere where he could reach.

"Oh, that's nice," Bedrov said as he moved the image around. "Here, Cap'n. Puts us in line with the sun on their approach vector. Probably not worth much, but he were an ijit for coming in where he did."

"They were sitting out there waiting for the coup," Jessica retorted, careful not to invoke their dead captain right now. "I like this course. Initiate it and have the *Corynthe* forces form on us."

"That reminds me." She turned to Enej. "Open a channel and hail *CR-264*. I really need him right now."

The flag centurion nodded and spoke into a sound-deadening microphone, one hand absently holding on to an earpiece.

Enej turned to her with a wicked smile. He flipped a switch on the comm to fill the bridge with Robbie Aeliaes' voice.

"Flag, this is *Brightoak* and an escort squadron from *Lincolnshire*. Requesting orders."

Brightoak? Here? This was suddenly, at worst, a fair fight.

Jessica smiled wickedly herself.

Yan Bedrov began to look nervous. "Captain?"

Jessica reassured him with a smile as she reached for the mic.

"*Brightoak*, this is the Flag, aboard *Kali-ma*," she said, quickly doing the math in her head. "Attach your two local escorts to *Auberon* while you bring *CR-264* to join up with my squadron soonest."

"On the way, Fleet Lord Keller," Robbie said with the same sarcastic smile in his voice she remembered from when she had commanded the destroyer squadron from *Brightoak* and he had had *Vigilant*.

Wheels began to turn in her head.

"Enej, what's the balance of forces?"

The projection zoomed back to a much larger area.

"Enemy forces include nine carriers of various sizes and three escort corvettes."

Nine. Jessica was briefly in awe, even considering that they were second-tier vessels and pirates.

Nine carriers.

"Incoming forces appear to be right about one hundred melee fighters and roughly twenty-five heavier craft, comparable to our S-11 Bombers, *Damocles* and *Starfall*."

He spun the projection again, adding four new dots for the *Aquitaine* Destroyer Leader named *Brightoak* and three Fleet Escorts/Cutters to the two groups of friendly vessels.

"We have *Auberon*, plus three carriers, *Kali-ma*, *Supernova*, and *Sky Dancer*. And apparently three fighters from the 1-ring mothership *Baba Yaga*. Captain Larionov sent the only three that could fly, while his ship and the rest are undergoing long-term repairs out on the lunar platform."

"Larionov?"

"You borrowed his blade today," the flag centurion said diplomatically.

Oh.

"We have fifty to fifty-five melee fighters, fifteen strike fighters, plus *Necromancer* and *Cayenne*. There is nothing on the other side comparable to the DropShip, let alone the GunShip."

"They have double our flight wing. We have firepower," Jessica smiled. "And Moirrey."

She considered the projection. It was messy.

Auberon sat at one point of a triangle, with *Rajput* and the two *Lincolnshire* vessels close by and the whole Wing airborne. *Cayenne* was probably asking for permission to fly with whatever strike she ordered. He was like that.

Her three Motherships were breaking out of close proximity to the orbital station and climbing up out of the gravity well as *Brightoak* and *CR-264* raced down and around to join them.

The enemy force sat much closer to the edge of the gravity well. Still inside, where they couldn't quickly escape to Jumpspace, but far enough away that they could probably flee if they felt they needed to.

Jessica considered *Sarmarsh IV* again. This very vessel meeting with the Red Admiral and planning the sort of show of force that would convince people to keep Ian Zhao as their new king. She had given the conspirators ample warning to time this little escapade, but they didn't have the Red Admiral in charge over there. That was probably her single greatest saving grace right now.

Still, there were a tremendous lot of them out there.

She studied the projection. *Wei Chi* and the Imperial Carrier *Admiral Schmitz* sat at the center of their little knot, surrounded by a ring of other ships, and then a hornet's nest of little signals.

It was like watching flies on a carcass on a hot day.

"Open a channel," she said while Bedrov busied himself with trim, speed, and weapons. Maybe this was a good enough crew.

"Go ahead, commander."

"Imperial vessels," she called. "This is Jessica Keller, Queen of the Pirates. You are not welcome here. Load up and return to Imperial space immediately, or I will destroy you."

She stopped to wait. They were far enough away that the signal would take several seconds to reach them.

Their answer did not require the radio. The carrier launched a single missile in the direction of *Auberon*.

Apparently, someone over there had associated her name and the *RAN* carrier, and assumed she was in command. It was a good assumption, if you wanted to raise a middle finger. And it would give her defense centurion, Nina Vanek, something to do to baseline the two *Lincolnshire* crews as escorts, if things got messy.

"Oh, that were a dumb thing to do," Bedrov opined calmly under his breath.

Jessica nodded. They were about to get very serious.

"*Jouster*, this is the Flag. What is your status?"

"We are prepared for *Mischief*, Your Majesty," *Jouster* replied.

She wondered if that exact tone of bored, laconic superiority was something he was born with, or had worked extra hard to make sound natural.

"*Furious*," Jessica continued, "form your team up around *Jouster*'s as a single spearhead and prepare to attack the Imperial forces. Let *Jouster* take point."

"Acknowledged," *Furious* called. "*Queen's Own*, you heard the lady, boys. Slashers on the wings, hammers in the back. And *Warduck* is out there, so we'll get a little payback, too."

On the projection, it looked like two armies of ants, forming up to attack a hornet's nest.

Hopefully the ants were better.

CHAPTER XLVII

Date of the Republic March 14, 394 Above Petron

Jouster smiled. It was a lovely, evil smile. This was about to become a lovely, evil day.

Over there, a hundred and twenty-odd bad guys. And a crap-ton of defensive guns.

And almost no missile launchers. He hated Imperial missiles.

Sure, there were a pair on the Escort Carrier, and probably single tubes on the Tugs. And that was it.

Twenty-four first-line Imperial melee fighters. The nasty A-8a model. Not as good as the Republic's *M-6 Gungnir*, better than the *M-5 Harpoons* his two teams had. Forty-eight launch rails. Comparable guns.

And behind them, a half-dozen of the A-3f strike fighters. Six rails each.

Then there were seventy-something pirates.

Big, tough guys. Even scary looking.

Right until he looked over his shoulder at the ugly caravan of junkyard castoffs he was leading.

And he had shields. And a whopping crap-ton of missile rails pointed down-range, not just his wing, but *Auberon*, and *Rajput*, and *Brightoak*, as well as *Necromancer*, and the two bombers, *Damocles* and *Starfall.*

You didn't kill ships with guns. Well, not unless you were a battleship, or some other big, dumb, lumbering armadillo. You went full Agincourt on them. Or let them fight in the shade.

"*Jouster*, this is *Auberon*," Denis Jež said into the calm as the fighter wings began to close. "Barn owl."

"Acknowledged," *Jouster* grinned.

How to explain to the friendlies that there was a stealth missile about ten seconds from impact over there? That the fox that was about to get into the hen house? *Auberon's* wing could use the encrypted signal, and they already understood what Jež had just said, but he had to transmit in the clear to talk to the *Monarch* element. People were listening. Hell, the two sides had even settled pretty quickly on different comm channels so they weren't constantly yelling over each other to transmit orders back and forth.

War was weird, some days.

"*Furious*, this is *Jouster*," he said, that grin growing into a smile. "I'm about to redline my engines. You folks keep up?"

"Dunno, *Jouster*," he heard her sarcastic reply. "*Bitter Kitten* is the only one of yours that's managed to outrun me so far."

Yup, she would do. *Jouster* could see why the dragon lady put her in charge.

"*Aquitaine* and *Monarch* elements," Jouster said, "go for max speed now."

If he had timed it right with Jež, the stealth missile *Auberon* had fired would be close to impacting in a few more seconds.

Jouster slammed the throttle to the stops and let the thrusters go into overdrive. Around him, his team did the same on cue, momentarily opening a small lead on most of the friendlies.

Most.

Sky Dancer's lead pilot had that stolen *M-6* that could keep up, and did.

And there was something truly ugly over on the right flank. It appeared to be two huge engines welded to a gun, with a cockpit slung underneath, almost as an afterthought. *Furious* called him *Eel*, but whether that was the pilot or the craft was open to interpretation. But he was fast. And started to get ahead of everyone.

His loss if he got too far out front when this happened.

The scanner lit up with a flash as the engines got to their peak. The skies in front of him lit as well.

"Barn owl," *da Vinci* called merrily. She was tucked deep in the back of the formation, all sensors and one little popgun, and worth a squadron of the pirates by herself.

"Gimme a read," *Jouster* called back.

"Stand by," she said coolly. "Total surprise. Looks like we just blew the shit out of the 4-ring Mothership named *Siberia*. One sensor tag just turned into three signals. She's coming apart."

"Roger that," Jouster's evil grin was back. "All elements, prepare for *Mischief*."

"Bedrov," Jessica said, "turn the squadron and prepare to close at flank speed. Enej, get *Brightoak* and *CR-264* out front, just like we do with *Rajput*."

The flag centurion nodded.

Her first officer was aghast.

"Close with them, Captain?" Bedrov asked in a tiny voice.

"That's right. We have many more guns and missiles than they do. We need to get close enough to drive off the fighters so we can kill the carriers."

"But that's not how it's done," he almost cried, eyes as big as saucers.

Jessica fixed him with a hard stare. "It is now, mister. Do you want to win, or die? If we sit back here, they will eat us alive, piecemeal. We have to take the war down their throats."

The projection suddenly lit up as *Siberia* died.

"What was that?" Bedrov asked plaintively, still coming to grips with real war after a career of piracy.

"That is what happens when pirates take on the *Republic of Aquitaine*, Bedrov."

Jessica turned to the *Kali-ma's* pilot, himself watching the interplay expectantly. The man was young, perhaps not yet set in his ways.

"Turn to three-five-zero, down eight, roll to ninety, and come to max speed. Now, mister."

The pilot nodded and put his head down over his controls, fingers dancing. It was like the piano concertos *Auberon's* pilot, Nada Zupan, played for her.

Kali-ma was more graceful though, more responsive than *Auberon*. Massing half as much helped.

Perhaps going to battle aboard a ship named for the Goddess of War would help, as well. Certainly, *Kali-ma* kept up with *Brightoak* as the Destroyer Leader began her charge.

"Nina," Denis said, louder than he intended. Too much adrenaline. And no Flag aboard listening, and possibly overriding him. "Where do you want the two Escorts?"

The defense centurion actually looked back at him over her shoulder with a nervous glance. "Normally," she replied, "I would say down front, where they get their hands bloody to the elbows, but I'm not sure these folks are up for that. Plus, we have more *Mischief* coming. Can we go dorsal/ventral and keep them on our beam?"

"Affirmative," Denis said. "Gunner, let *Rajput* know they're on point alone. We'll cover their flanks."

Someone acknowledged. The message would make it. The crew knew what they were doing.

Auberon was going to war.

It was a shame he couldn't consult the Red Admiral at a time like this. If they were just facing pirates, he might have invited the man to the bridge to take overall command, just so the crew could watch the legend in action.

It would have been utterly epic, a story for the grandkids. This might still be. Assuming they survived.

But that might not be polite today. Especially if the Red Admiral was as deeply involved in everything as the sudden appearance of an Imperial Carrier task force suggested.

At least *Auberon* didn't have to run home with her tail tucked between her legs, like they otherwise would have. They had enough guns today to make other guy run. Maybe.

Definitely an improvement over *Qui-Ping*.

"Gunner, *Rajput*," he said, keying the comm open. "You are authorized to take long-range pot shots with the Primaries as we close. Anything to make them twitchy."

Rajput responded by firing a shot from so far outside range as to be laughable. But it looked really intimidating on the sensors. That would help.

"Why are we doing this?" Bedrov asked.

His tone was calmer now. Polite inquiry tinged with a bit of awe, suggesting that he had begun to appreciate that he was in the hands of a master.

Jessica gave him the sort of smile she would give a bright cadet just learning Fleet Maneuver Basics in First Year.

"There are more of them than us, Yan," she said, softening the verbal blow she would have otherwise landed. Instead, she held up her hands at shoulder height, closing them into fists as she did.

"Right hand, left hand," she continued. "The fighters open a path to the carriers so we can get in and kill them. At that point, their fighters are doomed."

"But we barely have enough guns to damage another mothership, Captain," Bedrov replied.

"We're the escort here," she smiled grimly. "*Brightoak* and *Rajput* have enough firepower to slaughter the Imperial ships, if we can get them into range safely. We have to keep them alive long enough to do just that."

"But we're the flagships," he continued, confused. "*Kali-ma*, *Supernova*, the other 4-rings. We lead."

"Today, we're the shield, Yan. The destroyers hold the blades."

It was no better on the sensors, so *Jouster* focused on the sky around him. Two hundred signals made a mess as the sides closed, even with the chasm that still remained between the two forces. But in the empty darkness of deep space, they were isolated little flashes of light.

At least the Imperials were feeling traditional today.

Instead of taking point to engage him, like they should have, they were letting their allies handle the task, standing back behind a wave of uglies and stolen fighter craft.

Jouster smiled. *Mischief* wouldn't work worth a damn on First-Line Imperials like those. It was, however, medicine for the pirates.

He probably should just settle for buying Moirrey Kermode drinks forever. At this rate, she was going to keep him alive way longer than he had ever expected.

The Imperials ought to be launching missiles soon, although that might be difficult to do in the mess that was about to come ashore like a tide.

Time to beat them to the punch.

"*Auberon* element, unleash *Mischief* now. Repeat, launch *Mischief*."

Jouster smiled that evil smile.

Yup. Gonna owe Moirrey drinks.

He watched a hail of missiles, the things Moirrey called Archerfish, erupted around him. It wasn't Agincourt, or Crecy, but it would do. Out there, it was about to get silly.

"All elements, maintain full speed and prepare to blast through the center and circle back to melee."

Let the pirates make of that what they will. Probably expecting a bull rush. That's almost what they were going to get. With a little icing.

Jouster owed Moirrey more than drinks.

Maybe he should just marry her, instead.

Twelve Archerfish missiles went downrange, along with several of the shot missiles. The Shot versions quickly separated into their four smaller missiles that fanned outward instead continuing forward, just as they had been programmed.

What the remaining missiles did was just all levels of rude. Moirrey Kermode rude.

Jouster watched the casings peel back, just like the Shot missiles did. Instead of smaller missiles, however, these had charged warheads. Each one contained four single-shot Type-1 beam generators and just enough thrusters and brains to aim the dangerous end at the nearest target and shoot it.

One shot from a Type-1 wasn't going to kill a fighter with shields. It might not even penetrate.

Very few of the pirates had any shields to begin with. And the Archerfish wasn't smart enough to identify individual targets to prevent overlap.

Instead, two or three might all line up on the same poor bastard and shatter him.

And they did.

Regular missiles might have had more physical impact on the enemy formation. This was like hitting a piece of glass with a BB gun. One little star in the center that spider-webbed outwards.

Jouster could watch the psychological impact of the Archerfish as that hole opened in the enemy force like a tear, or a whirlpool. The survivors closest flinched away, chased or killed by the little Shot sub-missiles hunting them in the aftermath.

For a long moment, *Jouster* considered blasting the combined wing straight through the gap at max speed and going after the carriers. He had the firepower behind him to take on those three escort corvettes. But his orders had been clear: dog-fight the skies clear and keep enemy craft off the big hitters. Let *Rajput* have the kills. And *Brightoak*. If he was feeling generous.

Command Centurion d'Maine would certainly wield that hammer ruthlessly enough.

"*Auberon* and *Monarch* elements," he said calmly, even as the adrenaline hit a new high in his brain, "go to melee now. All units, break into teams and start hunting. Good luck."

He glanced over to make sure his wingmates, *Uller* and *Vienna,* were handy, and stood his fighter on an ear.

Time to go kill things.

"Helm," Denis heard Tamara Strnad call as he watched the scene unfold on his own little projector, "hard left. Three-four-five, down fifteen, roll three-fifty. Now, damn it. Signals, bring the escorts down with us. Defense, prepare to engage left to right. Guns, stay on support for targets of opportunity."

He had one of the best tactical officers he had ever known. Tamara was simply an artist when they got into this kind of a situation, almost psychic in her ability to predict an enemy.

They needed it right now.

Rajput was, as they used to say back home, all guns and no butter.

She could stand toe-to-toe with a cruiser in single combat for a little while, but could still be mugged by a pair of six-year-olds in a park.

And she was about to be.

Denis watched a group of mismatched fighter craft and a team of Imperials come at the Heavy Destroyer from a low corner. They were moving laterally, too fast for the big guns to track for a kill shot.

That's what he was for. Sure, *Winnipeg* and *Admiral Matsushita* were better equipped, and even trained to a reasonable level, but they were county militia.

Auberon was the warrior.

"Defense," Tamara's calm voice continued, "prepare and launch Moirrey's first ace in the hole."

Denis always forgot about that nasty little surprise. Moirrey and Nina Vanek had removed the observatory telescope and mounted a missile launcher with a pair of Shot missiles in its place.

One of them leapt into the fray now, one dot on the sensor turning into four and racing downrange.

Denis watched one of the uglies get spiked like a butterfly. The first Imperial fighter took enough of a hit that his shields evaporated, sending him and his wing-mate racing off for cover.

Auberon's Type-1's and Type-2's went to work.

"Vishnu," the man said in awe.

Jessica glanced over at the look of slack shock on Bedrov's face and had to agree. The Imperials had finally gotten their act together.

The six heavy strike-fighters on the Imperial side had stayed well back up until now, satisfied to hide under the cover of the escorts.

They had just launched a wall of missiles. And absolute wall. Something like *Jouster* had done to them, earlier.

Jessica turned to the man handling the guns. *Kali-ma* didn't have a tactical officer. The pirates followed the Imperial model of expecting a captain to fight her own ship.

That was so inefficient as to be stupid. She was too busy flying this bitch to shoot at the same time. Instead, she had promoted the man who was second officer to tactical and let him loose.

It has been a good choice, so far.

"Tactical," she said sharply, waiting for him to register and look at her. "Stop engaging fighters and put every gun on those missiles. Immediately."

She looked over at her flag centurion. Enej nodded and continued talking into his microphone, having anticipated the command.

"Captain?" the tactical officer asked.

"The fighters might be painful." she pointed at the screen. "That is death. If we don't stop them, we get the same messy demise *Siberia* did. Move."

He nodded with understanding and went to work.

They just might survive.

"Sensors," Tomas Kigali asked, "any of those targeted at us?"

The screen looked like an avalanching mass of army ants, or killer bees. Certainly likely to ruin someone's day.

"Negative," the woman called back.

Someone else's day.

"Ladies and gentlemen of the gun deck," Kigali called into the comm with a lazy drawl. "About time you earned your keep."

He grinned at the navigation crew in close range. The gunners were down a level. He could see their faces on one edge of his screen.

"Engines to flank. Someone tell *Brightoak* to drop back and let us handle this," he smiled. "Helm to three-five-five, up twelve, begin a slow corkscrew spin left to bring every gun to arc sequentially."

The sky was going to look like a Founding Day fireworks celebration in a bit. If he had either of the other two escorts, this would be a cakewalk. But *Rajput* needed the cover. Here, he at least had *Sky Dancer* sitting out on an aft wing taking potshots. David Rodriguez and his crew were pretty good.

On the screen, the wall of missiles began to diverge into two separate elements. Kigali checked the projections and cursed under his breath.

"*Kali-ma*," he said into the secured comm. "You are the primary target of half that group. Go defensive immediately."

He could keep enough of them off of *Brightoak* to keep her going, but the other half was going to pass too far on his starboard flank to engage, even if he abandoned *Brightoak* right now.

Good luck, boss.

"Helm," Jessica called. "Hard right turn, right now. Redline the engines once we come about and spin two-seventy to keep the guns bearing."

The pilot looked at her with huge eyes and kept typing furiously on his console.

Jessica felt the grav-plates blur with the stress as every available erg of energy went into the engines and gyros.

Auberon could never have made this turn, but *Kali-ma* was the Goddess of War. She understood.

"Guns, forget safe firing rates," she continued. "Override the interlocks and burn out the barrels and generators if you have to. The next twenty seconds are life or death, people."

"Right, Captain," someone called. *Kali-ma* began to spray fire sideways and aft.

It was like something from the Vedas back there, as if *She* walked the field of battle again.

"*Supernova*," the flag centurion yelled, accidentally leaning back from his microphone. "Shear off. You are blocking our field of fire."

Jessica watched the icon that was *Supernova* cross *Kali-ma*'s stern, making a similar turn, but wider and slower.

Only Enej heard the response, but he uttered a word that would have normally made him blush. Here, he slammed a fist into the counter hard enough to make hardened pirates next to him flinch.

Kali-ma came out of her turn and raced away, a warhorse turned thoroughbred smelling the home stretch.

Jessica's heart stopped as she realized what was happening behind them.

The Imperial missiles were set to go after *Kali-ma*, but that was by size, not an active sensor signal. They were passively watching the sky in front of them as they closed.

And *Supernova* looked just like *Kali-ma* when the two signals blurred together.

Jessica understood why Enej had probably just broken his hand on the desk.

Those missiles had stopped following Jessica, because they had another target. A closer target.

"Engines, all stop now. Shut it down. Guns continue to engage."

Sky Dancer, *Supernova*, and *Kali-ma* poured their fire into the valley of death.

It was almost enough.

Two missiles got through.

One went off with a glancing blow, catching a corner of *Supernova's* shields and shredding them. The other went home into her engine well like a saber to the heart.

Jessica's heart.

Supernova went up like her namesake, a shockwave vaporizing her aft section and continuing forward until the bow shattered to pieces.

No one survived that fire.

For a moment, the entire bridge was silent.

In a corner, someone muttered the Mariner's Prayer for Lost Souls.

Jessica went cold. Completely numb.

It lasted for a second before the fire lit, deep in her chest.

It was as though the Goddess Of War whispered death in her ear.

She looked at the screen. The Imperial fighters out there had been more than decimated. Slaughtered, perhaps.

Annihilated.

The two-to-one Imperial ratio at the beginning had reversed in her favor. One of the *Lincolnshire* escorts had been mauled, but still held her station. *Auberon* looked a little rough. *Sky Dancer* had a gimpy leg.

The Imperial side was beginning a turn that would take them to the edge of the gravity well and safety. They had shot their bolt and failed. Now, they would escape.

The rage caught fire in Jessica's chest, flowing hot and mad to her fingertips. She took hold of the microphone and locked her eyes on the projection icon for *Wei Chi.*

"Squadron, this is the Flag," she said. "Raise the red flag."

"Please confirm, Admiral," *Furious* replied nervously.

"No quarter, *Furious*," Jessica said flatly.

She could taste copper.

They would taste death.

"Flag, this is *Auberon*," Denis said. "Negative on that last command. *Aquitaine* will not carry out that order."

She wanted to hit someone, something. She wanted to destroy everything, burn it down, sacrifice it in Daneel's name. *Abandon hope, all ye who enter.* That would be an acceptable memorial.

If *Aquitaine* would not help her vengeance, she was still Queen of the Pirates.

"*Furious*?" she said.

"Acknowledged, Your Majesty," the only female fighter pilot left said calmly. "*Queen's Own*, prepare to unleash hell."

The sound on the comm could have been mistaken for an earthquake, a dull rumbling slowly building in intensity. It was only after a second that she recognized the sound.

Forty hard men, growling with their own anger.

The *Fribourg Empire* was not welcome here. *Wei Chi* had signed her own death warrant by bringing them. These men, and woman, were about to make that point in the most destructive manner possible.

Brightoak and *CR-264* turned away as *Kali-ma* and *Sky Dancer* came out of their turns and began to charge. Interestingly, the one undamaged *Lincolnshire* escort, *Winnipeg,* accelerated to come to her side and engage as well. They had just as much dislike of the *Fribourg Empire*, and were making it known.

Enej waved a hand to get her attention. She had been a thousand kilometers away.

"The Escort Carrier, *Admiral Schmitz*, and the two Carrier Tugs are asking for surrender terms, Commander," he said forcefully.

"Immolation," she said simply.

She went back to where she had been.

"Jessica," a voice intruded on a private channel.

That was her name. Or had been. Before.

Now she was simply *Kali-ma*. Goddess of War.

Avatar of Destruction.

"Jessica, this is Desianna," the intrusion continued. "Please respond to me, Jessica."

Desianna. Arnulf's widow.

Her friend.

"This is Keller," Jessica finally growled into the microphone.

"Jessica, don't do this. Please. I'm asking you to let them surrender. There is a better way."

"They killed *Warlock*," Jessica raged.

"I know that," Desianna said soothingly. "But this shouldn't be your legacy."

"They killed Daneel," she repeated, shock and sorrow finally creeping into the rage, tinging the red to a more maroon hue.

"And they killed Arnulf. Jessica, you aren't the only one to lose someone you loved today." She paused for a breath. "You have already made many more than enough widows, Jessica. You need to stop the battle. This isn't how we're going to change *Corynthe*. There is a better way."

"How?"

"Your wrath has broken them, Jessica Keller, Queen of the Pirates," Desianna poured cool water into the hollow fire of her soul. "We can mold the survivors. Please, Jessica, let it go."

In her mind, she could still see the flash of fire as *Supernova* came apart, Daneel sacrificing himself to protect her.

She had lost him, the only man to ever touch her, ever hold her.

And he was gone.

Was it enough?

The Goddess of War nodded.

EPILOGUE: PETRON

Date of the Republic March 16, 394 City of Corynthe, Petron

She still thought of it as Arnulf's throne, regardless of the fact that it was hers now. Being so tall that her feet did not touch the ground hadn't helped. At least until she had exercised royal prerogative and added a small footstool so she could sit comfortably.

Queen Jessica surveyed her Court. Jessica Keller, Queen of the Pirates. Admiral of the *Corynthe* fleet. Mourning widow.

On her right, Enej Zivkovic, continuing his role as her flag centurion, regardless of where the fates took them. He stared down at the crowd from his height on the platform like a breakwater across a harbor mouth.

On her left, Desianna Indah-Rodriguez, Chancellor to the Court of *Corynthe,* widow of King Arnulf, Dowager Queen. Jessica hadn't asked what had happened to Jing Du. She suspected she was better off not knowing that answer. He was simply marked on the reports as having committed suicide in his cell during the battle.

Before her, her Court. Three mobs, carefully sorted into groups, separated by a meter of open space and facing her like pie slices. Unlike her first visit to this Court, where she had barely rated an interruption to side conversations, the room was nearly silent, every eye facing forward, every soul on pins and needles.

To her left, in the first row, David Rodriguez, representing the combined Captains of *Corynthe*, and beside him, Cho Ayaka Nakamura, *Furious*, representing the pilots of *The Queen's Own*. Uly Larionov, the captain of the little 1-ring Mothership *Baba Yaga*, had been granted precedence as well, having sent the only three fighters he had ready into the *Battle of Petron* when he could have simply watched.

Plus, his blade had killed a king.

On Jessica's right, senior centurion Denis Jež and Command Centurion Robertson Aeliaes were in the front row, along with senior flight centurion Milos Pavlovic, *Jouster*. The other flight commander, Marta Eka, *Southbound*, had been killed in the battle, along with the tower gunner from the *S-11* bomber *Starfall*, Ebbe Lanik. Considering the scope of the confrontation, *Vedic* in scale, *Aquitaine* casualties had been amazingly light.

It had been a slaughter among the pirate fliers, on both sides of the equation, as well as the Imperial pilots. Forty percent of the men who had gone into this battle had not returned, and all of the Imperials and all but one of the pirates were male.

In the center slice, the six captains of the Imperial Squadron stood in the front row, politely escorted by a team of heavily armed marines from *Auberon* and her own palace guards. Garth Agano and the captains of *Valhalla*, *Warduck*, *Chevalier*, and *Ares* stood close by, shackled with heavy iron chains, mostly as a public humiliation, but not part of the Imperial group.

Jessica looked at the group standing behind the Imperials. A few officers, many of the surviving pilots, all in a state of shock. She considered how she looked from their point of view, remembering that *Navin the Black*, all two plus meters and one-hundred-twenty kilos of him, stood behind her, looming over her like Arnulf's shadow brought to life.

Today, the man had actually brought a marine boarding axe to go with his field utilities. He probably looked like *Doom*.

Certainly, she felt that way.

One other face. Where was he? There.

Imperial Admiral of the Red Emmerich Wachturm, Duke of Eklionstic, cousin of *His* Imperial *Highness, Karl VII*. Dressed today in his most formal uniform and looking like the Imperial gentleman he was.

At the moment, he was part of the *Aquitaine* contingent, rather than in with his countrymen. That was important, considering what was going to happen next.

Jessica took a deep breath and rose from the throne.

Her throne.

The nervous energy would not let her do this seated. She nodded at Desianna's glance and stepped next to her.

Even breathing stopped.

"It is the will of this Court," Jessica began, her voice pitched to be clear to the marines at the back of the hall, as well as the people down front, "that mercy be shown."

After several hours of vicious arguments in her new private chambers, with the key elements of her new administration, primarily Desianna and David. Still, they had prevailed over her mad desire for vengeance at odds with all civilized custom. It was probably for the best.

Jessica gestured with one hand to indicate the group of Imperials in the center, carefully not including the Red Admiral.

"Your vessels are forfeit as reparations for damages done," she pronounced flatly. "As a condition of your surrender, you will additionally pledge on behalf of your government that you will return to the *Fribourg Empire* and never again operate in *Corynthe*. Anyone who does will be treated as common criminals, rather than organized members of a foreign military governed by the laws of war. Who speaks for you?"

The captain of the Escort Carrier stepped forward and bowed politely. Perhaps a touch more than necessary, but he had heard the comm traffic during the battle. He knew how close to death he had come.

"I speak for the *Empire*, Your Majesty," he said carefully, never once looking over at the Red Admiral. "It shall be as you say."

Jessica nodded curtly and the man stepped back.

She paused, looking over the group again, before turning to the Red Admiral.

"Admiral Wachturm," she said, much more politely, two colleagues discussing lunch plans, "it is my intent to hire a vessel to transport these men back to an Imperial world safely. Given the broader situation, I believe it would be appropriate to forego my earlier plans to review your circumstances at *Ramsey*, in *Lincolnshire*. I can offer you a place on this vessel, such that you will arrive home when they do. You are not subject to their sentence. Would you find that an acceptable outcome?"

It was diplomacy. Publicly. The art of the said and the unsaid. Treat him with care and dignity. They would face each other again, someday.

"Command Centurion Keller, Admiral Keller, Your Majesty, I thank you for your hospitality and hope that I can return the favor someday."

Jessica gestured him to move to the center. "If you would join them, then, Admiral?"

She watched the man move with great dignity.

He had not been mousetrapped and defeated by a lucky woman. He was still the victor at *Qui-Ping*, even on a technicality. He was still *The Red Admiral.* The Imperial officers crystalized around him like rock candy in cooling water as he entered their realm.

Jessica looked around until she found the two men she wanted next, the captains of the *Lincolnshire* escorts, *Admiral Matsushita* and *Winnipeg*. They were a few rows behind Denis, standing on either side of Tomas Kigali and trying not to look nervous, here in the lion's den. She smiled to reassure them, and then turned to David Rodriguez on her left.

"When the interlopers depart," she said calmly, as if the Imperials were already gone, "the Navy of *Corynthe* will impress the two Carrier Tugs. *T-87* will henceforth be known as *King Arnulf.* T-104 will enter the fleet," she took a deep breath to hold her voice, and her nerves steady, "as the Mothership *Warlock*."

The least she could do to keep his memory alive here. Both of their memories.

"What about the Escort Carrier?" somebody in the middle of the Captains spoke.

Jessica only saw who because Uly Larionov turned to a captain a row back and punched him in the stomach hard enough to double the man over. The rest of the captains stepped back, as though someone had left dog shit on the sidewalk.

Jessica held her snarl in check. This had to be done correctly, the first time. Everything else rode on this moment.

"That vessel, *Admiral Schmitz*, along with the escorts *Bremmen* and *Schlachtross*, will be transferred to the navy of *Lincolnshire*," Jessica replied, a queen doling out rewards to her faithful knights. "The third escort, *Porcupine*, will remain with *Corynthe*."

"May I inquire as to why, Your Majesty?" David stepped forward and spoke clearly. This had all been worked out well in advance, but the observers did not need to know that.

Diplomacy.

"Because," Jessica said, "when *Corynthe* asked for help in her time of need, *Lincolnshire* came to her assistance. That, ladies and gentlemen of the Court, is the basis of the relationship we will cultivate with our neighbor, going forward. We do this, in part, to thank them. But also to make sure that *Corynthe* does not grow so strong that we are tempted to prey on a weaker neighbor."

That seemed to satisfy the captains.

Jessica stepped back to Arnulf's throne and sat.

"Is there any other business to come before this Court?" Desianna called from her spot. After a moment of silence, she continued. "Ladies and gentlemen of the Court, you are dismissed. Good day."

Jessica watched the room slowly empty, Imperials being escorted to a nearby hotel rented to keep them safe while transport was worked out, captains returning to their crews, the *Aquitaine* squadron returning to their role as Protectors of the Throne, for now.

Desianna stepped close enough to whisper, just the two of them.

"I know you don't believe me now, Jessica," she said quietly, "but you will survive."

Jessica held back a fresh torrent of tears that wanted to erupt. She still had to shepherd *Corynthe* to a new place, ready to stand on its own.

And in the back of her mind, the Goddess of War still occasionally demanded blood.

EPILOGUE: RAMSEY

Date of the Republic April 30, 394 City of Lincoln, Ramsey

The governor of *Ramsey* hadn't gotten any better with time and familiarity. Or maybe Jessica had just been through too much.

The office certainly hadn't changed one bit, all dark wood and thick carpet, indicative of a man intent on his pleasures.

He still looked like a politician was supposed to, according to all the popular videos. Tall and reasonably good looking, with a full head of hair and perfect teeth. He had a ready smile, a good tan, and a firm handshake.

At least today, he was keeping the innuendo out of his conversation. Hopefully, someone had briefed him. Jessica wasn't in the mood to slap him if he propositioned her. She would probably just knock him down and start kicking.

The man was apparently perceptive enough to grasp that fundamental point.

"So what should I call you?" he said, apparently at an honest impasse. He was a good operator as a politician, but still struck her as being as dumb as a box of rocks.

Jessica took a breath and considered *diplomacy*.

"I am still the Queen of the Pirates, Governor Wapasha," she said quietly. "At present, I have declared a regency and appointed David Rodriguez to rule in my place until I return to *Petron* permanently."

Hopefully, after so long that everyone accepted David as their rightful king. Maybe she should retire there in a few decades and learn to knit. Or teach the youngsters *Valse d'Glaive*.

That got a smile out of her soul.

"In that capacity, I have delivered the Escort Carrier, *Admiral Schmitz*, and the corvettes *Bremmen* and *Schlachtross*, as a thank you from *Corynthe* for your assistance against the Imperial forces."

"You mean, after Tomas Kigali blackmailed me?"

"Governor," she leaned forward, sizing him up for a blow to the throat, "*Corynthe* lost two 4-ring Motherships and about seventy pilots, along with two kings and a half dozen of her top Captains. They will not be a threat. I could, however, keep those vessels with me and take them to *Aquitaine*. I'm sure the border forces facing *Fribourg* would appreciate the aid."

"Oh, no," he raised his hands defensively. "It was a masterful stroke on your part, all the way across the board. I wanted to compliment you. I haven't been played like that in a long time. And I still get to keep my job here."

"You're welcome," Jessica said carefully.

What had Kigali and Aeliaes forgotten to mention about that last meeting?

"And we would like to rename the vessel in your honor, Queen Jessica."

"No."

"But..."

"I said no," Jessica leaned in closer, quieter. Harder. "If you want to go down that path, I have a better suggestion. Name her *Auberon*."

The governor of *Ramsey* leaned back in his chair, wheels turning in his eyes as he considered the angles.

"Yes," he agreed, "that would do nicely. Will you stay for the commissioning?"

"I'm afraid not, Governor," she said. "I'm overdue at Fleet Headquarters at *Ladaux* as it is."

"One other question," the governor asked after a moment, in a sideways manner. "When you left, you took a local criminal with you, a young man named Tanis Bedrosian. What became of him?"

Jessica stared at the man.

"In light of circumstances, I decided to send him home with the Imperials. Perhaps he can make something useful of his life there. Leaving him on *Petron* or bringing him back here was just a slower way to execute him."

"I see." He rose to shake her hand across the desk.

"Thank you again, Command Centurion," he said quietly, sincerely. "I asked *Aquitaine* for help with a pirate problem. I could never have imagined what you would accomplish."

"See that you don't screw it up, Governor," she replied. "I would hate to have to come back here at the head of a hostile fleet."

A *Corynthian* fleet. Her fleet.

The governor nodded. He saw the same thing.

Jessica took her leave quickly.

Outside, she found Marcelle and two marines waiting for her. Moirrey Kermode leaned against the armored ground vehicle, waiting, and lit up with a smile when Jessica emerged.

"Did it go well, ma'am?" Moirrey asked, bubbly from her own trip to the family farm.

"Well enough, Moirrey," Jessica said as they all climbed into the vehicle, Marcelle driving up front with the marines. "I'm ready to go home now."

EPILOGUE: LADAUX

Date of the Republic May 26, 394 Fleet HQ, Ladaux System

It was the same cozy spot, deep in the bowels of the Officer's Club at Fleet Headquarters.

The Marquette Room.

So little had changed. And so much.

Jessica focused on just maintaining her equilibrium tonight. It had gotten easier over the last two months. That wasn't the same as easy.

She put on the face she had inherited from the Goddess of War and entered the room.

Joshua greeted her by name at the door and fawned over her as he escorted her to that same table, back in the corner. Premier Tadej Horvat was already there, along with First Lord Nils Kasum and a mostly empty bottle of red wine.

As before, Jessica sat on the outside next to Nils.

"Nils," she said lightly with a nod as she sat. "Tadej."

She could see the suddenly appraising looks on their faces as they nodded, somewhat taken aback.

Jessica felt about a hundred years old.

Joshua poured her a glass of wine and departed.

They drank in companionable silence for a bit.

The men obviously were expecting her to say something. That was an effort doomed to failure.

Jessica felt so tightly wrapped up that she might implode. Not that she would ever show it.

"I'm not familiar with that uniform." Tadej had cracked first, indicating her choice of clothing this evening with a hand.

Jessica glanced down, mostly for show.

It was not what they had been expecting her to wear to this place.

Desianna and Moirrey had been mostly responsible for the outfit. Arnulf had almost always preferred dark grays, so they had started there and worked outward.

Grays. Diplomacy. The art of the unsaid, as well as the said.

Charcoal gray pants, so tight as to be stretched on, in case she needed to move into combat suddenly, as a Queen of the Pirates might. Those same knee-high black leather armored combat boots from *Bunala*. Over her sports bra, a light gray pullover with a mock turtleneck collar. Atop that, a slate-gray jacket, in a shade midway between the shirt and the pants. It was longer than a bolero, but not much, just to the top of her hips. Functional for shipboard, with pockets inside, and a useful waterproof shell she could wear on the ground on any sort of moderately unpleasant day.

And it fit perfectly, as one would expect with Desianna and Moirrey so intently focused on the task.

On each wrist, a single band of color as wide as her fingers. It was a deep maroon, almost the color of the wine she drank.

On her left breast, over her heart, a stylized logo of a beautiful woman with blue skin and four arms, holding a saber, a *main-gauche*, a severed head, and a planet, specifically Ian Zhao and *Petron* respectively, in this instance, although these two men wouldn't recognize that.

At each side of her collar, a single hexagon, solid and the size of a Lev coin, forged with gold taken from one of Arnulf's favorite bracers.

Jessica's hair had gotten halfway down her back. She had it pulled back tonight into a simple tail to stay out of her way, although she tied it more forcefully in place when dancing with the fighting robot.

She was going to need a new robot soon. Settings Five and Six were no longer the challenge they had been when she went to *Corynthe*. Now, she kept beating this one nine-falls-in-fifteen at setting Nine.

She wondered what that said about her.

Still, she looked like a queen. If you looked the part, people had said, others were likely to accept you in it.

Jessica took a breath and fixed her gaze on the Premier of the Republic Senate.

He stubbornly refused to turn to stone.

"It is the uniform of the *Corynthe Navy*, Tadej," she said finally. "Specifically, the Admiral of the *Corynthe* Fleet. It is one of my many new titles, along with being Queen of the Pirates."

"I see." He nodded carefully. "And you are still technically the head of state?"

"I am," she said firmly. "David Rodriguez is the local regent in my stead. But I am still their monarch until I retire, or die. If I resigned now, it would have been almost as bad as if I had never tried. David would never be able to hold the throne, and one of the other captains would fight him for it. David rules, but he does so in my name, and they will be much more careful. They know I can always return. It is my duty as their queen."

What did she have to live for at this point, save her duty?

"And will you remain on active service?" Nils asked quietly.

And that was the crux of it, wasn't it?

She could resign her commission and return to *Corynthe* to rule in barbaric splendor, the rest of her life dedicated to bringing that nation up to the standards of the Coreward stars.

But that wasn't her place.

They had sent her out to learn diplomacy with a friendly power, and maybe chase off some pirates.

Nobody could have envisioned *this*.

Jessica saw Daneel's easy smile in her mind. Everything still reminded her of him, but being back at *Petron* would make it much, much worse, at least until she had had enough time to grieve.

She wondered if there was enough time left in her life for that.

"I plan to, Nils," she said. "My place is here. At least today. I cannot foretell the future."

"And the logo?" Tadej said, vaguely gesturing at her breast without actually doing so.

"That is my other flagship, gentlemen. The 4-ring Mothership *Kali-ma*. The Goddess of War. An interesting Consort to the King of the Fairies."

Tadej took a drink of wine, obviously to order his thoughts.

He had apparently been expecting a command centurion tonight, not a queen.

His loss.

"Until last week," Tadej continued, somewhat obliquely, "*Aquitaine* had never had formal diplomatic relations with *Corynthe*. Too far away, on the far side of *Lincolnshire*. Not that important. You can imagine my surprise when an ambassador arrived to present her credentials."

"Arianne Rodriguez," Jessica replied flatly. "David's half-sister. Charlotte's daughter."

"Yes," Tadej said. "And she brought with her two teenage boys she thought would be better served being educated at Ladaux…?"

"Sebastian and Karel. Mei Fan's sons. Also half-brothers of David, and the children of the woman who poisoned Arnulf, their father."

Jessica smiled hard at the two men.

"You should consider them young foreign noblemen, to be re-educated in proper decorum and behavior, but not David's hostages, nor mine," she said fiercely. "He would have put them to death, as happened to their mother. I expect David's mother's hand, Desianna's, in their survival."

Tadej nodded knowingly and shared a glance with Nils. Politics.

The three drank in silence.

So far, she could handle this. The two men were obviously at a loss as to how to deal with this exotic creature in their midst. Jessica had to agree. She had had a two-month head start, and was not doing much better.

"Jessica," Nils finally began slowly, carefully, "when we sent you to *Lincolnshire*, I'll be honest, this was not what we had intended."

"No," she replied from the distant place, a thousand light-years away, where she had often been finding herself recently. "You sent me there to learn, to become a better officer, and to maybe deal with a small trade issue. I had not intended things to end up as they did. Nor had you. In many ways, in many places, I felt I had no choice but to move forward, trusting my instincts and the advice of my advisors. To rely on the training provided by the two of you, although mostly from Nils. I believe I was successful, on balance."

Tadej laughed sharply, obviously in relief. "Jessica, you have been more successful than either of us dreamed…"

He paused, a sudden look of confusion and consternation on his face.

Nils Kasum's personal aide had entered the lounge and made a beeline towards them

In one hand, Kamil held a thick folder, actual printed pages, and a serious look on his face.

"Kamil?" Nils said, obviously concerned.

The newcomer approached and handed his boss the folder and then glanced at everyone in the room to confirm their identity before he spoke.

"This package arrived in-system sixty-three minutes ago, transmitted via fast courier and marked *First Lord, Eyes Only*. I took the liberty of bringing it here, because I did not believe it could wait until morning."

He paused while Nils opened it and read the cover page.

Nils quickly handed the cover document to Tadej without a word as he dug deeper into the details.

"Who do we have that can stop him?" Tadej asked after he scanned it quickly and handed the cover letter in turn to Jessica.

It was an executive summary of an Intelligence Report, normally reserved for a much higher security clearance than she rated. The name at the top caught her attention.

Fribourg Empire Admiral of the Red, Emmerich Wachturm.

The Red Admiral.

She scanned the rest.

"Is this credible?" she asked simply.

Not *True*. Not *Accurate*.

Credible.

The language of diplomacy and espionage. Grays and fog. Probabilities and options.

"Yes," Nils replied tightly. "Our spies report that, as of four weeks ago, *IFV Amsel* and her squadron consorts were preparing for a long-run jump to launch a surprise attack on the Republic world of *Ballard*."

He looked up at Tadej. "As for what we have to stop him, nothing. I don't have any vessels big enough that can be retasked and make it to *Ballard* before he arrives. Why *Ballard*?"

Jessica flashed back to the conversation this night above *Callumnia*.

"*Auberon* can get there," Jessica said into the heavy silence. "And this is partly my fault."

"How? What have you done?" Tadej had an angry look now.

She remembered again how angry the Red Admiral had been that night. The two men were of an ilk, right now.

"During the Promenade with Arnulf and Desianna, we talked as a group at length about *Ballard*," Jessica replied, letting her tone calm these two men. "Specifically we discussed the AI who is the provost of the university there. The woman named Suvi. The Red Admiral was quite angry that the Republic allowed her to even exist."

"And your part in this?" Nils asked.

"Arnulf had asked me about Founding Legends, Nils, looking for how he could turn *Corynthe* from a land of pirates into a nation. I told him about Henri Baudin and the Story Road. The Red Admiral did not respond positively."

"I see," Nils said with a nod, a light of understanding coming into his eyes.

Founding Legends. Powerful magic.

Jessica waited as these two powerful men thought, and considered the part she would have to play.

Again, history was demanding her presence.

Nils stared blankly into space for several seconds as he gamed out a number of scenarios in his mind. This was the man who had taught her how it was done, although she probably had passed him now.

A look passed silently between Nils and Tadej. Question. Counter-question. Assent.

"This is not what I had planned next for you, Jessica," he said finally. "Understand that. Pomp and celebration will have to wait for another day. How quickly can you get underway?"

Jessica had already done the math. "I'll need most of a day to round up my crew and take on supplies. If you can send along a Fleet Replenishment Freighter, we can travel fast and light. I'll need *Rajput*, *CR-264*, and *Brightoak*, plus whoever else is handy when we go to break orbit."

She tried to remember her last trip to *Ballard*, so many years ago.

That had been a happy visit, a newly-minted cornet with two days of shore leave and as much trouble as she could out-run.

This would be very different.

"The *Ballard* militia will have a squadron of local fighter craft stationed, and maybe a couple of Light Cutters?"

"Something like that," Nils replied absently as he flipped the folder open again and began scanning pages.

"Page one hundred six, First Lord," Kamil said quietly.

Nils found the page.

"Yes. Eleven fighters, one removed from duty and never replaced. Two small, older-model patrol cutters, mostly for revenue enforcement and search-and-rescue."

"I will need two weapons packs when I go," Jessica said, warming to the destiny playing out in her mind.

"Two?" Nils asked, his eyebrows rising.

"One will do to replenish the squadron's usage at *Petron*. The second is for Moirrey."

"You're going to give your weapon's tech an entire arms pack to play with, Jessica?"

"This is the Great White Whale, First Lord. *Imperial Fighting Vessel Amsel.* Moirrey nearly killed the *Blackbird*, once. At *Qui-Ping*. This time we'll have to finish the job."

In her heart, Jessica felt the Goddess of War smile.

ABOUT THE AUTHOR

Blaze Ward writes science fiction in the *Alexandria Station* universe as well as *The Collective*. He also write fantasy stories with several characters and series, from an alternate Rome to epic high fantasy in the desert. You can find out more at his website www.blazeward.com, as well as Facebook, Goodreads, and other places.

Blaze's works are available as ebooks, paper, and audio, and can be found at a variety of online vendors (Kobo, Amazon, and others). His newsletter comes out quarterly, and you can also follow his blog on his website. He really enjoys interacting with fans, and looks forward to any and all questions—even ones about his books!

Never miss a release!

If you'd like to be notified of new releases, sign up for my newsletter.

I only send out newsletters once a quarter, will never spam you, or use your email for nefarious purposes. You can also unsubscribe at any time.
http://www.blazeward.com/newsletter/

ABOUT KNOTTED ROAD PRESS

Knotted Road Press fiction specializes in dynamic writing set in mysterious, exotic locations.

Knotted Road Press non-fiction publishes autobiographies, business books, cookbooks, and how-to books with unique voices.

Knotted Road Press creates DRM-free ebooks as well as high-quality print books for readers around the world.

With authors in a variety of genres including literary, poetry, mystery, fantasy, and science fiction, Knotted Road Press has something for everyone.

Knotted Road Press
www.KnottedRoadPress.com

Don't miss *Last of the Immoratls*: Volume Three of the Jessica Keller Chronicles

The Red Admiral intends to kill Suvi, but he must get past Jessica first.

Jessica Keller has stopped the Red Admiral more than once.

Now he intends to go to Ballard and kill Suvi, the last genie in the last bottle, unless Jessica can get there first. Then she must stop an Imperial Battleship with her out-gunned squadron.

It will take everything Jessica has. It will take everything Moirrey has. It will take everything Suvi has.

And even then, it might not be enough.

Ebook, paper, and audio versions available from your favorite retailers.

Javier sometimes enjoys being a pirate, but he never forgets they made him a slave.

Join him in his adventures with the pirate ship *Storm Gauntlet.*

Part of the *Alexandria Station* universe.

Ebook, paper, and audio versions available from your favorite retailers.

Nobody expects a Bard to invent the future.

Henri sets out across space to find the perfect wood for his violins. However, star travel takes time, as humanity still digs itself out of the Great Darkness.

On his quest, he gets help both from his shipmates and his muse, the unreachable lady of his dreams. Until his visions lead him to Suvi, the last genie in the last bottle, and they forever alter the course of human civilization.

Part of the *Alexandria Station* universe, and the founding of the *Republic of Aquitaine.*

Ebook, paper, and audio versions available from your favorite retailers.

www.ingramcontent.com/pod-product-compliance
Lightning Source LLC
Chambersburg PA
CBHW070433170726
48291CB00002B/483

* 9 7 8 1 9 4 3 6 6 3 0 2 6 *